C.E. MURPHY

HANDS OF FLAME

LUNA™
www.LUNA-Books.com

LUNA™

Recycling programs
for this product may
not exist in your area.

HANDS OF FLAME

ISBN-13: 978-0-373-80312-5

www.LUNA-Books.com

Printed in U.S.A.

Author's Note

Leaving a world is hard to do. Three books in, and as a writer you've really gotten into its depths and people've begun to ask interesting questions that make you think of things you never thought of before. There are backstories to fill in and futures to consider, and they rarely settle back to sleep without putting up a bit of a fight.

This is the second time I've finished a trilogy, and the second time that I've been left thinking, "There are still a lot of books I could write for this world...." E-mail has suggested that people might be glad if I did—and someday I very probably will.

But now it's back to the Walker Papers for me! I've written a lot of books since *Coyote Dreams*, and I miss Jo and the gang, so I hope I'll see all of you there in a few months' time.

Catie

For Sarah
who was the first to want
an Alban of her own

ACKNOWLEDGMENTS

Thanks are, as usual, due to both my agent,
Jennifer Jackson, and my editor,
Mary-Theresa Hussey, for their insights.
It turns out Matrice really *did* read the
acknowledgments in the last two books,
and it was with great relief that I discovered she
thought I'd gotten it almost entirely right this time.

I'll never be able to say thank you enough to cover
artist Chris McGrath, or the art department, who
have worked together to give me gorgeous books
to show off.

Ted (and my parents, and my agent, but mostly
Ted, since he's the one who has to live with me)
did a remarkable job of keeping me more or less
functional during the writing of this book, and that
was no easy task. I love you, hon, and I couldn't do
this without you.

NIGH+ΠARES DRΘVE HER out of bed to run.

She'd become accustomed to another sort of dream over the last weeks: erotic, exotic, filled with impossible beings and endless possibility. But these were different, burning images of a man's death in flames. Not *by* flame, but in it: the color of her dreams was ever-changing crimson licked with saffron, as though varying the light might result in a happier ending.

It never did.

The scent of salt water rose up, more potent in recollection than it had been in reality. It tangled brutally with the smell of copper before the latter won out, blood flavor tangy at the back of her throat. She couldn't remember if she'd actually smelled it, but her dreams tasted of it.

Small kindness: fire burned those odors away, whether they were real or not. But that left her with flame again, and for all that she was proud of her running speed, she couldn't outpace the blaze.

There was a dragon in the fire, red and sinuous and deadly. It battled a pale creature of immense strength; of unbreaking stone. A gargoyle, so far removed from human imagination that there were no legends of them, as there were of so many of their otherworldly brethren.

Between them was another creature: a djinn, one of mankind's imaginings, but not of the sort to grant wishes. It drifted in its element of air, clearly forgotten by dragon and gargoyle alike, though it was the thing they fought over. It faded in and out of solidity, impossible to strike when it didn't attack. But there were moments of vulnerability, times when to do damage it must become part of the world. It became real with a weapon lifted to strike the dragon a deathblow.

And she, who had been nothing more than an unremembered observer, struck back. She fired a weapon of absurd proportions: a child's watergun, filled with salt water.

The djinn died, not from the streams of water, but from their result. The gargoyle pounced, moving as she had: to save the dragon. But salt water bound the djinn to solidity, and heavy stone crushed the slighter creature's fragile form.

The silence that followed was marked by the snapping of fire.

Margrit ground her teeth together and ran harder, trying to escape her nightmares.

She struggled not to look up as she ran. It had been almost two weeks since she'd sent Alban from her side, and every night since then she'd been driven to the park in the small hours of the morning. Not even her housemates knew she was running: she was careful to slip in and out of the apartment as quietly as she could, avoiding Cole as he got up for his early shift, leaving his fiancée asleep. It was best to avoid him, especially. Nothing had been the same since he'd glimpsed Alban in his broad-shouldered gargoyle form.

Margrit could no longer name the emotion that ran through her when she thought of Alban. It had ranged from fear to fascination to desire, and some of all of that remained in her, complicated and uncertain. Hope, too, but laced with bitter despair. Too many things to name, too complex to label in the aftermath of Malik al-Massrī's death.

Not that the inability to catalog emotion stopped her from trying. Only the slap of her feet against the pavement, the jarring pressure in her knees and hips, and the sharp, cold air of an April night, helped to drive away the exhausting attempts to come to terms with—

With what her life had become. With what she'd done to survive; what she'd done to help Alban survive. To help Janx survive. Her friends—ordinary humans, people whose lives hadn't been star-crossed by the Old Races—seemed to barely know her any longer. Margrit felt she hardly knew herself.

She'd asked for time, and that, of all things, was a gargoyle's to give: the Old Races lived forever, or near enough that to her perspective it made no difference. They could die violently; that, she'd seen. But left alone to age, they carried on for centuries. Alban could afford a little time.

Margrit could not.

She made fists, nails biting into her palms. Tension threw her pace off and she wove on the path, feet coming down with a surety her mind couldn't find. The same thoughts haunted her every night. How much time Alban had; how little she had. How the life she'd planned had, in a few brief weeks, become not only unrecognizable, but unappealing.

Sweat stung her eyes, a welcome distraction. Her hair stuck to her cheeks, itching: physical solace for an unquiet mind. She didn't think of herself as someone who ran away, but she couldn't in good conscience claim she ran *toward* anything except the obliteration of memory in the way her lungs burned, her thighs burned.

The House of Cards burned.

"Dammit!" Margrit stumbled and came to a stop. Her chest heaved, testimony to the effort she'd expended. She found a park bench to plant her hands against, head dropped as she caught her breath in quiet gasps that let her listen for danger. She'd asked Alban for time, and couldn't trust he glided in the sky above, watching out for her, especially at this hour of the morning. Typically, she ran in the early evenings, not hours after nightfall. There was no reason to imagine he'd wait on her all night. Safety in the park was her own concern, not his.

Which was why she couldn't allow herself to look up.

If she would only bend so far as to glance skyward, he would have an excuse to join her.

Alban winged loose circles above Central Park, watching the lonely woman make her way through pathways below. She was fierce in her solitude, long strides eating the distance as though she owned the park. It was that ferocity that had drawn him to watch her in the first place, the reckless abandon of her own safety in favor of something the park could give her in exchange. He thought of it as freedom, pursued in the face of good sense. It encompassed what little he'd known about her when he began to watch her: that she would risk every-thing for running at night.

That was what had given him the courage to speak to her, for all that he'd never meant it to go further than one brief greeting. It had been a moment of light in a world he'd allowed to grow grim with isolation, though he hadn't recognized its darkness until Margrit breathed life back into it.

And now he hungered for that brightness again, a desire for life and love awakened in him when he'd thought it lost forever. He supposed himself steadfast, as slow and reluctant to change as stone, but in the heat of Margrit's embrace, he changed more quickly and more completely than he might have once imagined. He had learned love again; he had learned fear and hope and, most vividly of all, he had learned pain.

He thought it was pain that sent Margrit running in these small hours. She'd asked him to stay away while she came to grips with it, but she hadn't said how far away, and he was, after all, a gargoyle. He watched over her every night from dusk until dawn, even when that meant sitting across the street on an apartment-building roof, patiently watching lights turn off in her home as she and her housemates retired to bed. He ignored the others who had demands on his time: Janx, the charming drag-onlord who'd lost his territory in the fight that had ended Malik al-Massrī's life; who had, in fact, nearly lost his own life and who was still healing from the wounds Malik had dealt him. Alban had helped him escape, had brought him below the streets, into the vigilante Grace O'Malley's world. Janx was safe there, but Grace and the children she helped were not, not so long as Janx remained. And yet Alban took to the skies each night, watching Margrit instead of resolving the conflicts that grew in the tunnels beneath the city.

If it were not entirely against a gargoyle's nature, Alban might say he was hiding from those responsibilities by insisting on another. But then, he'd lost his sense of what was, in truth, a gargoyle's nature, and what was not. A few months earlier he would have answered with confidence that a gargoyle was meant to keep to a well-known path, to be a rock against the changes forced by time. Now, though, now he had lost his way, or found it so reshaped before him that he had to gather himself before he could move forward. He hadn't wanted to leave Margrit when she said she needed time, but suddenly he understood. Distress might be eased when shared, but the need to understand herself—or himself, now that he saw it—could be as necessary a step toward recovery. To edge back and rediscover the core of what he thought he was, without outside influence, might be critical.

And the secluded nights did give him time to think. No: time to remember. Remembering was a gargoyle's purpose in existing, and for the past two weeks he would have given anything to be unburdened by that particular gift borne by his people.

Margrit sprinted away from a park bench without looking up, and Alban felt a twist of sorrow. Not anything: there was, it seemed, at least one thing he would not give up under any circumstances. He had killed to protect Margrit Knight, not once, but twice.

It might have meant nothing—at least to the other Old Races—had he taken human lives. But he'd destroyed a gargoyle woman with full deliberation, and a djinn thanks to devastating mistiming. Those were exiling offenses, actions for which he could—would, should—be shunned by his people. For all that he'd exiled himself centuries earlier on behalf of men not of his race, knowing he now inexorably stood outside the community he'd been born to cut more deeply than he'd thought it could. And for all of that, what disturbed him the most was the unshakable certainty that, given another chance, given identical circumstances, he would make the same choice. If he could alter the paces of the play, he would, yes; of course. But if not, if the same beats should come to pass, he would choose Margrit and the brief, shocking impulses of life she brought into his world.

He was no longer certain if he'd stopped knowing himself a long time ago and was only coming back to his core now, or if Margrit Knight had pulled him so far from his course that he had nothing but new territory to explore. He would have to ask Janx or Daisani someday; they had known him in his youth.

Startling clarity shot through him, the disgusted voice of another who'd known him when he was young: *You were a warrior once. You could have led us.* Biali hadn't meant it as a compliment, his shattered visage testimony to the battle skills Alban had once had. Maybe, then, the impulse to make war had always been in him, buried during the centuries of self-imposed exile. Maybe the ability to kill had waited until it was needed, or wanted: a vicious streak through a heart of stone.

Too many thoughts circling near the same ideas that had haunted him through Margrit's sleepless nights. Alban shook himself, leaping from the treetops to follow her, certain of this, if nothing else: he would not let the human woman come to harm, not after the changes she'd wrought in himself and his world. To lose her now would undo the meaning of everything, and that was a price too dear to be paid.

An impact caught her in the spine and knocked her forward. Margrit shouted with outraged surprise, hands outspread in preparation for breaking a fall she couldn't stop. But thick arms encircled her waist, and the ground fell away with a sudden lurch. A body pressed against hers, muscle shifting and flexing in a pattern that might have been erotic, had Margrit's incredulous anger not drowned out any other emotion, even fear. She struggled ineffectively, swearing as her captor soared above the treetops. "Alban?"

"Sorry, lawyer." The words spoken into her hair were gargoyle-deep, but not Alban's reassuring rough-on-rough accent. There was no sincerity in the apology, only a snarled mockery made of its form. "Hate to use you as bait, but I can't do this out in the open."

"Biali?" Margrit's voice broke into a rarely used register as she twisted, trying to get a look at the gargoyle who'd swept her up. Her hair tangled in her face, blinding her. "What the hell are you doing?"

An edged chuckle scraped over her skin. "Getting Korund's attention."

"You couldn't use a telephone like a normal person?" Margrit twisted harder and looped an arm around Biali's shoulders, so she was no longer wholly reliant on his grip around her waist. He grunted, adjusting his hold, and gave her a baleful look that she returned with full force. "This was your idea."

Exasperation crossed Biali's face so sharply that for a moment it diluted Margrit's anger. That was just as well: they were passing rooftops now, and pique might get her dropped from the killing height. With anger fading, she realized she had precious moments that could be better spent in investigation than in argument. "What do you want from Alban?"

"Justice." Biali backwinged above an apartment building, landing on messy blacktop. He released Margrit easily, as though he hadn't abducted her. She bolted for the rooftop door, though seeing its rusty lock stopped her before she reached it. She spun around, running again before she'd located the fire escapes, but Biali leapt into the air and cruised over her head, landing between her and the ladders. "Don't make me have to hit you, lawyer."

Margrit reared back, staying out of the gargoyle's reach, though she doubted she could move fast enough to avoid him if he wanted to catch her again. For the moment, though, he simply crouched where he was, wings half spread in anticipation, broken face watching Margrit consider her options. He wore chain links around his waist, a new addition to the white jeans she'd seen him in before. Wrapped too many times to be a belt, the metal made a peculiarly appropriate accessory for the brawny gargoyle, enhancing his thickness and the sense of danger he could convey. Margrit found it disquieting, the dark iron twinging as a wrongness, but that, too, added to the effect.

Any real expectation of escape blocked, she resorted to words for the second time. "Justice for what?"

"Ausra."

Dismay plummeted Margrit's belly. The name conjured as many demons as flame-haunted dreams did. Ausra

Korund had styled herself Alban's daughter, though in truth she was the child of his lifemate, Hajnal, and the human who had captured her. Driven mad by her own heritage, Ausra had lain in wait for literally centuries, stalking Alban, waiting for a chance to destroy him. She had been Biali's lover, and very nearly Margrit's death. The Old Races were meant to think Ausra's fate lay in Margrit's hands. Only she and Alban knew the truth: that Alban had taken Ausra's life to save Margrit's.

Only they, and, it seemed, Biali. Margrit felt all her years of courtroom training betray her as her mouth tightened in recognition. Dark humor slid through Biali's expression. "Everything make sense now, lawyer?"

Margrit drew in breath to respond and let it out again in a shriek as a flash of white darted over her head. Biali launched himself skyward to meet Alban, all attention for Margrit lost.

They crashed together with none of the grace she was accustomed to seeing from the Old Races. Too close to the rooftop to keep their battle aerial, momentum and their own weight slammed them to the blacktop. Margrit staggered with the impact and ran for shelter, putting herself against the rooftop access door. It seemed impossible that no one would come to see what the sound had been, and each roll and thud the combatants shared made it that much more likely. She didn't dare shout for the same reason, but she pitched her voice to carry, fresh fear and anger in it: "Are you crazy? Somebody's going to come!"

Neither gargoyle heeded her, too caught up in their private conflict to respond to sense. Biali lifted a fist and drove it down like the rock of ages. Alban flinched just far enough to the side that the blow missed. The rooftop shook again and Margrit skittered forward a few feet, sure that interfering would be useless, but driven to try. "Alban, stop! He grabbed me to make you come after him! Just get out of here!"

For a moment it seemed he'd heard her, an instant's hesitation coming into his antagonism. Biali took advantage with a backhand swing so hard the air whistled with it, his fist a white blur against the graying sky. Alban spun, dizziness swaying his steps. An appalled fragment of Margrit's attention wondered how hard a hit that was, to stagger a gargoyle. A human jaw would have been pulverized.

Her gaze locked on the shattered left half of Biali's face; the ruined eye socket that in gargoyle form was all rough planes worn smooth by time. Alban had done that centuries earlier, and if the blow he'd just taken hadn't conveyed similar damage to his own face, Margrit couldn't imagine what strength had been necessary to destroy Biali's features.

As Alban reeled and regained his footing, Biali backed away, unwinding the length of chain from around his waist. Unwanted understanding churned Margrit's stomach as the stumpy gargoyle knotted one end and began to swing it. It wasn't an adornment of any sort. It was a weapon, and more, a prison.

Of all the Old Races, only gargoyles had ever been enslaved.

Margrit let go a wordless shout of warning that forgot the need for silence. Alban responded, flinching toward her as if he would protect her from whatever she feared, but too late: Biali released the chain, sending it clattering toward Alban. Margrit sprinted toward them, her only thought to break the chain's trajectory, regardless of the cost to herself. She would heal from most injuries: that was the gift another of the Old Races had given her, and for Alban's freedom she would risk her fragile human form against the dangerous weight of metal.

But she'd taken herself too far from the fight, her safe haven now a detriment. Crystal-precise clarity played the seconds out, letting her see how the chain left Biali's hands entirely, flying free. Alban recognized the threat an instant too late, wings flared and eyes wide with comprehension and furious alarm. Metal wound around his neck and his hands clawed against it, desperate to snap the chain and shake himself free.

Dawn broke, binding iron to stone.

MARGRIT'S HEARTBEATS COUNTED out an eternity, incomprehension making a statue of her as if she, too, was one of the gargoyles, frozen in time. Then the need to act paralyzed her, useless choices rendering her as still as astonishment had.

Her impulse was to dart forward, to claw the chains away from Alban's throat just as he'd tried to do. To pound on his chest and demand he wake up, for all that she knew sunlight held him captive and only darkness would release him from stone. Failing that, she wanted to somehow scoop him up and carry him to safety, far away from Biali and his plots. All were physically impossible, laughable in their naiveté. Even if she could somehow remove him from the rooftops, Margrit wasn't certain she could loosen the chains that bound him.

Memory surged with the thought, twisted and half-shadowed and not her own. The half-breed Ausra's memories of Hajnal, her mother, bound by iron, pain driving her mad. Iron became part of stone when transformation took a gargoyle at dawn or dusk, and could only be released by the one who'd set the chains in place. Hajnal had never been free again, and her death had poured memories into Ausra's unprotected infant mind. It was more agony than Margrit had ever wanted to know.

She shuddered, pushing the alien memories away. What little she knew about enslaved gargoyles had suggested manacles, not iron chain wound around a stony neck. Maybe, if she could get Alban away from Biali, she might free him by simply unwinding the chains.

It would have been an elegant solution, had it not relied on moving a seven-foot-tall statue off a twentieth-story rooftop. Margrit had no idea how much he weighed in stone form; easily a ton or two. She flattened her hands against her hips, searching for a cell phone she should have been carrying and wasn't. Cole and Cameron would rail at her for that, if she admitted it to them. Even if she had the phone—and she should; running in the park at night was dangerous enough without at least carrying some form of communication—there was no one to call. The only obvious answer was her soon-to-be employer, and the prospect of offering Alban, frozen in stone and chains, to Eliseo Daisani, sent a cold shudder through her.

The door behind her banged open and Margrit swallowed a yelp of surprise as she turned to face an irate man, whose ring of keys suggested he was the building manager. "What the hell is goin— What the *hell* are those?" His attention snapped back and forth between the gargoyles and Margrit so swiftly it looked headache inducing.

She offered a lame smile. "Somebody's sculpture project?"

"Somebody like you?" The man was big enough to be physically threatening, but he kept his distance, as though the gargoyles behind Margrit might come to life and protect her. She wanted to assure him, blithely, that he was safe until nightfall, but instead swallowed a hysterical laugh and shook her head.

"I came up to see what all the noise was."

The building manager squinted. "From where? You're not a tenant."

Margrit couldn't imagine how Biali had managed to choose a building where the building manager knew his tenants, but she had the urge to turn around and scold him for it. "I'm visiting. I got up early to go for a run and heard the noise. My friend called you."

The manager's eyebrows unbeetled a little. "She didn't mention a guest. 'Course, she usually doesn't. How were you planning on getting back downstairs?" He jangled his keys, still looking sour, but no longer as if he suspected Margrit was to blame for the gargoyles.

She clapped her hands over her mouth, eyes wide with dismay. "Oh, God, I didn't even think of that. Wow, I'm such an idiot. Thank goodness you came up here or I'd be stuck all day. Thank you! You totally saved my life!" She felt her IQ dropping with the breathless exclamations, but the manager looked increasingly less dour.

"You should think things through more carefully." Chiding done, he looked beyond her at the gargoyles and sighed explosively. "Well, shit. I'm going to have to get demolition guys in here to get rid of those things."

Horror clenched a fist around Margrit's heart. "But they're so cool. I bet you could make a buck or two letting people up here to see them for a while before you got rid of them. Besides, somebody in the building must've done them, right? I mean, unless helicopters swept through in the middle of the night and dropped them off."

The manager twisted his mouth. "Or they flew here."

Margrit laughed, high thin sound of nerves. "Yeah, which would be totally freaky." A law-school education, she thought with despair, and she was relegated to *totally freaky*. "So if somebody got them up here, he must have a way to get them back out, right?"

"Do you know how many tenants I've got? I don't want to knock on every door asking who the damned fool who put a couple monsters on the roof is."

Margrit bounced on her toes, putting on her best helpful smile. "Look, I could do it for you. I'll wait a little while to be sure people are getting up so I don't disturb them, and you've got to have a million things to do in a building this size, and I don't mind lending a hand. Makes me feel useful as a visitor, you know? I'm Maggie, by the way." She stepped forward to offer a hand, wincing at the nickname she never used. *Margrit* had a plethora of short names, and she used one no one else did: *Grit*. But *Maggie* was close enough to her name that she'd remember to respond to it, and since she was on the roof under false pretenses, it seemed wiser not to offer her real name.

The building manager shook her hand automatically. "Hank. You're not Rosita's usual type, Maggie."

Margrit knotted her fingers in front of her stomach, hoping she looked winsome instead of nervous. She hadn't known she was potentially Rosita's type when she'd pinned her presence on a "friend," but she was unexpectedly interested in the answer to, "Better or worse?"

"Better. She's usually into— Well, look, it doesn't

matter. You seem like a nice girl, and I could use the help. Jesus, what kind of idiots…"

"I'll totally take care of it," Margrit promised. "Just don't call any demolition guys until I've talked to every-body, okay? They're too cool to smash up. Somebody'll want them."

"Yeah, all right. Come on." Hank turned away, open-ing the door. Margrit's shoulders slumped with relief be-fore she put Maggie's perky smile back on and followed him into the building.

The other time—the *only* other time—she had visited Eliseo Daisani's penthouse home had been an impetu-ous 4:00 a.m. arrival on the rooftop a few weeks earlier. Now, arms hugged around herself, Margrit stared hun-dreds of feet into the air at Daisani's mirror-glassed apex apartment, wishing she could enter the way she had then.

Wished it for a host of reasons, not the least of which was that Alban had carried her in his arms then, ignoring human convention and soaring across the sky in his haste to make certain of Margrit's safety. Malik had teased Alban with the threat to move against her during the day, when Alban was helpless to protect her.

Alban had turned to Daisani for help. That in itself might be reason enough for Margrit to do the same now, but standing outside his building in the small hours of the morning, she doubted herself.

Not so small anymore. Margrit shook herself. It was nearly seven, and Daisani would be on his way to work. Alban and Biali had to be rescued before *she* went to work; before Hank decided to take a sledgehammer to the statues on his rooftop. Daisani might not be a good choice, but he was the only one she had. Janx, even if she could get to him, no longer had the resources necessary to rescue a pair of wayward gargoyles.

She remembered too clearly that the first time she'd met Eliseo Daisani, he'd had two sealskins pinned to his office wall. One had been adult-sized, the other pup-sized. She'd thought then that he was a ruthless hunter, willing to take mother and child. It had proven that the furs were selkie skins, their presence in his office trapping a young woman and her daughter in their human forms. That he'd given them to Margrit as part of a bargain did nothing to reassure her: the fact that he'd had them at all said he was more than happy to take advantage of any powerful hand he might have over another. Turning Alban—and to a lesser degree, Biali—over to him while they were vulnerable was a last resort, something to be avoided if at all possible.

Margrit frowned toward the rooftop, knowing she was stalling, but not quite able to push herself forward yet. She wanted another answer to the problem at hand, but her heartbeats counted out passing moments in which Alban's danger grew.

She wasn't certain which held her back: a reluctance to owe one of the Old Races yet another favor, or Eliseo Daisani's endless distressing failure to fit into any of the legends she knew. The other races were easier to deal with: lesser known, they also fell into old mythologies more readily, with the djinn ability to dissipate or the thin blue smoke that always followed Janx fitting what they really were.

But it was the gargoyles who were bound to night, not vampires. Daisani had been standing in an office full of sunlight the first time she met him, all swarthy smiles and a charisma that made his middling looks handsome. His teeth were unnervingly flat, no hint of too-long canines or a mouthful of razor-sharp ivory weapons. The *dragon* had pointy teeth, but the vampire, no. Neither garlic nor silver crosses held him off, nor did he require an invitation to pass a threshold. Alban had pointed out, prosaically, that Daisani would certainly die if someone thrust a wooden stake into his heart, but then again, so would anything else.

If she'd not seen the impossible speed Daisani could move with, if she'd not been given a gift of his blood to help her heal, she would never have believed he was anything other than what he appeared: a slight man with a great deal of personal wealth and business acumen. That, more than anything, made her not want to bargain with him.

Margrit tightened her hug, then let herself go forcefully, driving herself forward with the motion. As if she'd summoned him with the action, a security guard approached her. "Sorry, miss, but there's no loitering here. You'll have to move along."

Genuine astonishment rose up as laughter. "Are you serious? This is a sightseeing stop. 'Oh, yeah, that's where Eliseo Daisani lives. He's supposed to be worth forty billion now, you know?' How do you get tourists to stop loitering?"

The guard gave her a tight smile and gestured her away. "Like this."

Margrit held her ground as the guard stepped into her personal space. "Eliseo's my boss. I need to see him." She tried sidestepping the guard and found herself caught in a dance with him.

Visibly exasperated, he stepped back, language turning formal, as though he repeated a well-rehearsed line. "I'm sure if Mr. Daisani is your employer, you'll find a more appropriate opportunity to speak with him."

It struck Margrit that using Daisani's first name—though she'd been invited to—probably put her in league with starstruck stalkers, not a properly subordinate employee. She grimaced, then stepped back with her hands lifted in acquiescence. The guard stood his ground until she'd headed well down the block, only returning to his rounds after Margrit disappeared around a corner and peeked back. She counted to thirty, then, grateful he hadn't waited to see if she'd return, put on a burst of speed and bolted back to face the doorman.

"Wait," she said as he reached for his radio. "I know I sound like a stalker, and I don't have an appointment, but my name is Margrit Knight. I'm Mr. Daisani's new personal assistant, and this really is an emergency. Could you please ring up to his apartment and at least tell him I'm here?"

"Miss," the doorman said more patiently than the guard had, "it's a quarter to seven in the morning. Even if—"

"Is it that late?" Margrit shot a look toward the horizon, cursing her lack of cell phone and therefore lack of timepiece. "Never mind. I'll try to catch him at the office."

"That won't be necessary, Miss Knight." Eliseo Daisani opened one of the lobby's glass doors himself, putting a stricken look on the doorman's face. "You may join me in the Town Car, if you wish." He gestured to the street, then fastidiously brushed a speck of lint off his overcoat. The coat, like everything Margrit had seen Daisani in, looked unbelievably expensive, the wool appearing so soft she had to stop herself from reaching out to touch it. Its cut added to his height; Daisani was taller than Margrit, but only just.

She shook off her fascination with his coat and glanced toward the car. "Does it have privacy glass?"

Daisani's eyebrows, then his voice, rose. "Edward, could you have the limousine brought around, please?" The driver, who'd stood at attention beside the car, actually clicked his heels together in response before climbing in and driving away. Daisani smiled, then turned to the still-stricken doorman. "Miss Knight is to be admitted at any time she desires. Don't look so pale, Diego. I hadn't left instructions. You weren't to know. Margrit, will you require a ride home? I trust you're not going to work in that attire."

"A ride home would be great." Margrit thinned her lips, staring between Daisani and the street. "I think. I don't know if I'm going to work."

"For reasons pertaining to your arrival here this morning, I trust." Daisani nodded as a limousine pulled up, a different driver leaping out to hold the door. Bemused, Margrit preceded Daisani into the car, waiting until the doors and glass partition were closed before slumping in the leather seats. Daisani opened a miniature refrigerator and withdrew a bottle of water, eyebrows lifted in question.

"Yes, please." Margrit sat up to accept and Daisani deftly poured two crystal glasses full, handing one to her and keeping the other for himself. The car pulled into traffic with a soft jolt of acceleration, then slowed again immediately. "Good thing we're not in a hurry. It'd be faster to walk."

"One of the tribulations of city living. Now, tell me what brings you to my doorstep so early in the morning, Margrit."

"I have a problem, and—"

Daisani chortled, then waved off her look of surprise. "Forgive me. It's just that it was only a few weeks ago I said something very similar to you."

"You said *I* had a prob—" Margrit broke off again, recognizing his point, and Daisani's smile broadened.

"And you assured me it was I who had a problem, not you."

Margrit muttered, "A lot's changed since then," earning another delighted chuckle. She glowered out the tinted window, trying once more to think of someone else with the necessary resources to rescue two day-frozen gargoyles, and came up, again, with no other solution. "I need help," she said to the windows, then transferred her gaze back to Daisani. "But I'm reluctant to tell you why until I've already established I'll maintain control over the situation."

"As opposed to?"

"You deciding you can get mileage out of it and using it to your own advantage."

Daisani's eyes half lidded in curiosity. "Suggesting it's a scenario from which I could benefit."

"Maybe. Probably," Margrit amended. "On the other hand, if it's not dealt with immediately, it's got the potential to be very bad for all of you. It behooves you to give me control."

"And in exchange you will give me what, Margrit? Your employment with me begins Monday, so that's no longer an enticement you can bargain with. I doubt very much you intend to offer up the delectable Miss Dugan— Ah." The last sound was one of smug laughter as Margrit's heartbeat accelerated. She clamped down on the reaction, doing her best to inhale both deeply and discreetly. Daisani had admired Margrit's housemate too many times already, and his choice of words reminded her that the man she sat with was not a man at all. Humanity lay as a veneer over a true form she'd never seen. In the one rendering she'd seen, vampires had been depicted as manlike, but Margrit doubted Daisani's other form was so familiar and reassuring.

"My friends aren't any part of this, Eliseo." The coldness in her own voice surprised her, its strength sounding as though she might somehow be able to prevent Daisani from dragging Cameron into the world Margrit had become a part of. Daisani's mouth quirked, recognition of and interest in Margrit's implacability. "I'll leave it an open-ended favor if I have to, but no way are you involving Cameron or Cole in any of this."

"Who is responsible for Malik al-Massrī's death?" Daisani spoke so abruptly Margrit sat back, fingers tightening around her water glass. "I swore an oath, Margrit, that I would exact vengeance against anyone foolish enough to cross me when I had extended my protection to him, and I will fulfill that oath. Don't deny you were there. I have enough friends in the police department to know better. Tell me, Margrit. Tell me, and you will have your favor."

The water she'd drunk turned to an icy leaden weight inside her belly. Sick with adrenaline, Margrit set her glass aside, fitting it carefully into a cup holder before folding her hands and leaning toward Daisani. Too aware she wrote her own fate with the words, she said, "Help me rescue the gargoyles, and when they're safe, I'll tell you what you want to know."

THREE

"YOU NEVER FAIL to astound."

Margrit was uncertain if Daisani meant humans in general or herself in particular, though as he raised a palm and added, "I know. You're a lawyer. Everything is a negotiation," she suspected the comment was meant for her alone. "Rescue the gargoyles. Margrit, do you deliberately set up dramatic deliveries or is it just fortune and happenstance? Never mind. I don't want to know. You have my undivided attention, Miss Knight. Do go on."

"Do we have a deal?"

"Oh, we most certainly do, as I wouldn't miss the rest of this for the world. One rescue for one piece of priceless information." Daisani finished his water and steepled his fingers in front of his mouth as Margrit explained the fight that had led to Alban and Biali's capture by sunlight. "I do think you're getting the better end of this deal, Margrit."

"Which has happened exactly never in me dealing with the Old Races, so how about you let me have this one? Besides, your honor's at stake here, right?"

"It is, but perhaps Alban would be so grateful for the rescue he would offer me what I want to know in exchange."

"No." Margrit's certainty earned another questioning look from the vampire. "You can't risk Alban being exposed. Being killed. His memories would go to the gestalt, and you don't want that to happen. I've watched enough of your interactions to know he's keeping secrets for you and Janx both."

She knew considerably more than that, but Alban had cautioned her more than once about letting either vampire or dragon know she could sometimes access the remarkable gargoyle memories. Psychically shared, the repository held aeons of history, not just of the gargoyles themselves, but of all the Old Races, ensuring none of them would be forgotten to time. Alban Korund had set himself apart from his brethren to protect the secrets of two men not of his race, refusing to share any memories at all in order to protect one that might have changed their world.

Centuries earlier Janx and Daisani had loved the same human woman, and she had—perhaps—borne a child to one of them. Only literally within the last few weeks had the Old Races lifted their exiling law against those who bred with humans. Margrit was confident that neither Daisani nor Janx was sure their transgressions, hundreds of years in the past, would be given carte blanche now. Even if they were, she was equally sure they wouldn't want their old secrets made public unless they controlled how and when. Alban's premature death would simply send his memories back into the gestalt via the nearest gargoyle, and then everything dragon and vampire had worked to hide would be exposed to all the Old Races.

"You've learned to drive a hard bargain, Miss Knight."

Admiration and warning weighed Daisani's words in equal part. Margrit allowed herself a nod, the same kind of understated motion she was coming to expect from the Old Races. A smile flickered across Daisani's face as he recognized their influence on her. "How do you propose we retrieve our wayward friends?"

"I was thinking helicopters, speaking of dramatic." Margrit pulled a face, then shrugged. "They won't fit in elevators. The only other thing I can really think of is just getting security in there so nobody's around at sunset. Anything else is going to draw a lot of attention to you."

"To me." Amusement lit Daisani's voice, reminding Margrit of Janx. "Are you so concerned about my profile?"

"Only insofar as it seems probable that Eliseo Daisani taking an interest in a couple of statues on a rooftop would make the media interested in them, too. I'm going to kill them," Margrit added under her breath.

"The media?" Daisani asked, polite with humor.

Margrit gave him a sour look. "Alban and Biali. Why they had to have a fight in human territory…"

"There is no other choice." Daisani traced a fingertip over his glass's edge, humor fled. "We're obliged to live in your world, Margrit, either on its edges or in its midst. Our other choice is to retreat, and retreat and retreat again, until we're mere animals hiding in caves and snapping at our brothers. It's no way to live, and so if we're to fight, to breathe, to sup, to speak, it must be done in your world. You may have stemmed the tide of our destruction, but I fear there will still come a day when we cannot hide, and so must die."

"You fear," Margrit echoed softly. "I didn't know you could."

"All thinking things fear. Sentience, perhaps, is facing that fear and conquering it rather than succumbing. A tiger will drown in a tar pit, but a man who can clear his thoughts may survive." Silence held for a few long moments, disturbed but not destroyed by the sounds of traffic around them. Then Daisani shook it off, bringing his hands together with a clap. "If common sense prevails over dramatics, then security is the best option. Either way, I'm afraid my name may come into it. Your building manager will want an explanation for security."

"Do you have a better idea?"

"Sadly, no. Vampires are quick, not strong, and even Janx would be hard-pressed to rescue a sleeping gargoyle." Daisani's expression brightened and Margrit found herself grinning, too, at the idea of Janx's sinuous dragon form struggling to haul a gargoyle through the sky.

"Good thing humans don't look up," she said to the idea. "Alban says we don't," she added to Daisani's quirked eyebrow. "Still, a news chopper would probably notice your company helicopters flying in a gargoyle statue."

A smile leapt across Daisani's face. "What if we give them something else to look at?"

"This afternoon, from atop the Statue of Liberty, legendary businessman Eliseo Daisani has called an impromptu press conference to announce the latest development from Daisani Incorporated's charitable arm. We have news cameras in the air and a reporter on the ground—or as close as it gets when it comes to the high-flying philanthropist. Sandra, to you—"

Margrit, smiling, thumbed the radio function on her MP3 player off and dropped it into her purse. She'd spent the morning at her soon-to-be former office, filing papers and reviewing arguments with coworkers who were taking over her caseload. After four years at Legal Aid, being down to her last three days was in equal parts alarming and exciting. Her coworkers were merrily marking off the hours with a notepad affixed to the side of her cubicle. Every hour someone stopped by and ripped a page off. When Daisani called at a quarter to twelve, bright red numbers on the notepad told her she had twenty-one hours left in which to wrap up a career she'd imagined, not that long ago, would see her through another decade.

She tore off the twenty-one herself as she left the building. By noon Daisani had captured every news center in the city with his ostentatious announcement. "The Liberty Education Fund Trust," he'd said deprecatingly, first that morning to her in the car, and then again to the newscasters. "So I can show people how far to the LEFT we're leaning here at Daisani Incorporated." It would be a hundred-million-dollar grant pool, available to any student seeking higher education whose family income was less than fifty thousand dollars a year.

The project, he'd assured Margrit, had been under development for months, and while it wasn't yet ready to roll out, it was close enough to finished that an announcement could be staged. The program's title combined with his own power got him hasty permission to make the presentation at the Statue of Liberty, and just as surely, that combination drew the attention of all the newshounds in the city.

Margrit, cynically, thought that the timing was convenient for the tax year, too, with April fifteenth on the horizon. But given that Daisani was helping her with an otherwise impossible situation—and, she reminded herself with a shiver, the price that would be exacted—she wasn't in a position to cast stones. Suddenly grim, she hurried into Hank's building, knocked on the manager's door and opened it in response to his grunted reply. "Hey. Good news, I got some guys who'll help me move the statues, and… What's wrong?"

Hank's glower was darker than it had been earlier. "Ran into Rosita awhile ago."

Blank confusion hissed through Margrit's mind, the morning's details rushing over her in a jumble as she tried to sort out who Rosita was, and why it mattered that the building manager had seen her. Then dismay knotted her hand around the doorknob. Long, telltale seconds passed before Margrit mumbled, "You said I was with Rosita, not me."

"Well, I've been all over the building now and nobody had a friend named Maggie staying over from out of town last night. And funny, nobody mentioned you knocking on their doors this morning, either." Hank clambered to his feet, expression grim. "So you wanna start again with the whole story? Who are you, and how'd you get those things up there?"

"Are they still there?" Even whispered, Margrit's question broke and cracked. "You haven't destroyed them, have you?"

"Not yet." Dangerous emphasis lay on the second word, but Margrit sagged with relief. "But if I don't get an explanation, I'm calling the cops and then smashing those things to pieces."

"Don't do that." Margrit cleared her throat, trying to

strengthen her voice. "I've got a collector on the way to remove them. Are you the building owner?"

"Am I—what? No, I manage the prop—"

"Too bad. I've been authorized by the collector to offer a substantial cash payment for the statues. Perhaps you'd like to give him a call." Margrit lifted her eyebrows and nodded toward the phone, trying to give the impression she was happy to wait all day. Hank couldn't feel the coldness of her hands, or, she hoped, see the way they shook. There was nothing illegal about offering the man a bribe to look the other way, not when the gargoyles on the rooftop were their own possessions, not stolen or lost property. Her erratic heartbeat, though, didn't believe her, and it took an effort to keep her expression steady as she watched the building manager.

He turned gray, then flushed with interest. "How substantial? I'm, uh, I make the decisions regarding the property, so you can just tell me…."

"Ah. I'm prepared to make an offer of twenty thousand dollars. Cash." Margrit slipped her purse off her shoulder and withdrew an envelope, holding it with her fingertips.

Hank turned redder, flesh around his collar seeming to swell. "For a couple damned statues?"

"The collector has some familiarity with works of this size and feels it's a fair offer." Like Hank, Margrit had turned pale when Daisani casually unwrapped a billfold and began peeling off hundred-dollar bills. "Cash," he'd said as he handed over considerably more than the amount Margrit had just offered, "tends to distract attention from most offenses. If your building manager proves at all recalcitrant, don't bother negotiating." Then he'd dropped a wink, adding, "Even if that is your specialty."

"Sure," Hank said hoarsely. "My boss'd be happy to let your guy take 'em."

"Great. Should we call him to—"

"No! No, that's okay, I'll, uh, I'll take care of it all, don't worry. How, uh, how're you getting them out of here?"

"Well, if you're sure the arrangements will be to your boss's satisfaction, I can have them picked up in…" Margrit turned her wrist up, looking at the watch she hadn't been wearing earlier. "In about five minutes. I'll need to go up to the roof, of course." She tilted the envelope toward Hank.

His hands twitched. "Sure, yeah, whatever you need." Margrit set the envelope on his desk under his avaricious gaze, and she heard paper rustle as she turned away. "Hey. Maggie. How *did* you get up on the roof?"

Margrit looked back with a sigh. "I flew."

She took the elevator to the roof, not wanting to lose time to twenty flights of stairs. Even so, she had too much chance to consider the ethics of what she'd just done. Margrit nudged her purse open, looking at the second envelope she'd put the rest of the money in. Daisani'd handed over nearly seventy thousand dollars without blinking, and she'd accepted it as readily. There was nothing illegal to the transaction, but it made her spine itch between the shoulder blades, as if she'd begun the slow process of setting herself up for a fall.

And if that was the price for Alban's safety, then she would spread her arms and plummet. It was an axiom that everyone could be bought, though her naive and self-righteous self would have said only a few months earlier that she couldn't. The mighty had fallen, and for all the nightmares and regrets, Margrit wouldn't change that if she could. There was too much heretofore unknown magic in the world, and learning of its existence was worth very nearly any cost. The moral high ground she'd stood on had far less appeal than living in Alban's society, outside and above the rules of the life she'd known.

That was the road to hell, jaggedly paved with good intentions. Margrit pressed her lips together, wondering if Vanessa Gray had found herself traveling a similar path a hundred and thirty years earlier. She would have to ask Janx; Daisani would never answer. The doors chimed open and Margrit scurried to the roof, searching her purse for her cell phone so she could call the helicopter pilots and supervise the pickup.

She pushed the rooftop door open, drawing breath to give the go-order, but silence caught her by the throat and held her.

The gargoyles were gone.

FOUR

MARGRIT SHOT A compulsive look toward the west, as if the sun might have gone down and brought night to the city hours early. It hadn't, of course: it was white and hard in the sky above. She looked back to the empty rooftop, aware that a double take wouldn't prove that she'd somehow missed two massive, stony gargoyles frozen in battle, but simply unable to comprehend what she saw.

Her body, less numbed than her mind, dialed the number Daisani'd given her and lifted the phone to her ear. Silence preceded a burst of static, and then a connection went through, a man's cheerful voice saying, "This is Bird One. We're coming in from the south. Turn around and you'll be able to see us."

Margrit said, "Abort," mechanically, intellect still not caught up with what she saw. "The statues we were going to collect have already been removed. No sense in drawing attention here. Thanks for your time, guys."

"Bird One aborting," the pilot said just as cheerfully. "Maybe another time, ma'am." Margrit folded the phone closed, straining to hear the helicopters as they retreated, uncertain if she did, or if it was simply the roaring of her blood and too-hard beat of her heart. She wanted to burst into speed, as though a mad dash across the rooftop would somehow retrieve a pair of missing gargoyles.

Hank had been too angry at her reappearance and not guilty enough at taking the money to be responsible, she thought. She would confront him, but gut instinct said the building manager hadn't broken the gargoyles to pieces and dumped them. Gut instinct and a lack of dust or rubble, though those could be taken care of with a broom. But unless Daisani had double-crossed her, Margrit had no other explanation. Color rushed to her cheeks at the idea, her vision tunneling and expanding again. There was nothing she could *do* to the vampire if he had, but there were things he wanted she could withdraw from the table. It was better than nothing.

The rooftop door's knob nudged her hip, making her realize she'd backed up without noticing. Margrit folded a hand around it, still staring blankly at the empty roof, then shook herself with deliberate violence and turned away. Whatever answers there were, they wouldn't be found by helpless inaction.

The building manager blanched so white Margrit had every confidence he hadn't been responsible for the gargoyles' disappearance. She left him with his wad of cash and found a subway station, unwilling to wait on a taxi making its tedious way through traffic.

Her slow burn had lit to genuine, body-flushing anger by the time she reached Daisani's building. She didn't bother checking in, using her key card for the elevators with impunity, and stalked through what had been

Vanessa Gray's reception area to throw Daisani's private office's door open.

He wasn't there. A dry crack of laughter hurt Margrit's throat as indignation deflated under the heavy weight of reality. Once in a while the world allowed itself to be set up for dramatic confrontations, but arbitrary disappointment was the more likely scenario at any given moment. She paused at Daisani's oversized desk to leave the envelope of cash on it, then stepped forward to lean against the plate-glass windows that overlooked the city. It looked serene from so far above, no hint that the lives taking place within it were chaotic and unpredictable.

The elevator in the front office dinged. Margrit straightened from the window, turning to find Daisani, looking as disheveled as she'd ever seen him, at her side. Genuine concern wrinkled his forehead, and he offered a comforting hand. "I came as quickly as I could."

Margrit's eyebrows arched and a faint crease of humor warped the vampire's mouth. "I came as quickly as humanly possible," he amended. "The pilot informed me they'd already been picked up. Who—?"

"I don't know. I didn't know what else to tell him. They were just gone. I don't think it was the building manager." Margrit thinned her lips, eyeing Daisani. He caught the weight of accusation and rolled back onto his heels, giving her a brief, unexpected height advantage.

"And now you suspect me. You promised me something I wanted in return for their safe rescue, Margrit. I rarely renege on scenarios which provide me with things I desire."

"You know that bargain's moot now. You didn't rescue them. I'm not spilling secrets for noble attempts."

Pleasantry trickled out of Daisani's expression, leaving his dark eyes full of warning. "That's a dangerous choice. Are you sure you want to make it?"

"This is twice you've failed to come through, Eliseo. Hell, right now I'm wondering why exactly it is I should come work for you. I promised I would in exchange for you keeping Malik alive. He's dead." An image of flames burned Margrit's eyes and she blinked it away as Daisani's countenance darkened. Sharp awareness that she should be afraid brightened Margrit's focus, but no alarm triggered. Whether the vampire's too-fast, alien nature had ceased to be a source of alarm, or if fatalism simply outweighed nerves, seemed irrelevant.

"You've become dangerously bold, Miss Knight."

"I always have been. I've just gotten to where I'm not afraid of laying it out with your people, as well as mine. Oh, don't give me that look." She snapped away Daisani's expression of faint dismay. "I wouldn't be any use to you if I was terrified. Vanessa couldn't have been."

"Vanessa and I," Daisani said after a measured moment, "had a very different relationship than you and I do. And terror has its uses."

"So does boldness. If you didn't take them, who did?" Margrit put the argument aside firmly, confident she'd won.

Daisani gave her a long, hard look, speaking volumes about the game she played before he, too, set it aside. "Even if he knew about their predicament, Janx no longer has the resources to move two gargoyles. Besides, he hasn't been seen in days. It's possible he's left the city."

"Do you really think he'd give up his territory that easily?" The House of Cards had burned, selkies and djinn moving into the vacuum left by its fall. Janx had retreated underground to lick wounds both literal and figurative, but Margrit doubted he'd readily walk away from the criminal empire he'd created. "There's still a lot of upheaval going on at the docks. Cops have been down there nonstop since the raid and they're still not keeping all the violence in check. The opportunity to take it all back is there for a strong enough leader."

"Ah, yes, the docks. Speaking of which, how's your friend Detective Pulcella? I've seen him on the news several nights a week since the House was raided. He's a good-looking young man, isn't he?"

Margrit's hands curled into fists. "Yes, he is. I haven't really talked to him since the raid." Tony Pulcella was a homicide detective, though the bust that had given prosecutors Janx's financial books had put Tony on a fast track to promotion and a wider range of responsibilities. The clincher was Janx's arrest, and he'd been working long hours toward that end, as evidenced by innumerable news-camera glimpses of him day and night. He was well outside his jurisdiction, but homicides linked to Janx cropped up all over the city, and Tony had long since been part of the team trying to bring the crimelord in. His determination to do so had helped tear apart his relationship with Margrit, and ironically, she was now far more deeply entangled in Janx's world than her ex-lover could ever have imagined.

"Quite the proper hero," Daisani went on blithely. "A pity for him that he can't see what's really going on."

"How could he?" Bitterness laced Margrit's question. "You'd kill him if he found out about you."

Newscasts didn't show the way the Old Races moved, too fluid and graceful, marking them as creatures unfet-

tered by the bounds that held humanity in check. Margrit
had learned, though, to look for other signs on the news:
djinn with their jewel-bright gazes, selkies with their tre-
mendously dark eyes, all pupil and blackness. The two
races had forged a treaty to support each other, making
natural enemies into one tremendous force, their numbers
vastly greater than any others of the Old Races. The
selkies had long since bred with humans to replenish
their failing numbers, breaking one of the few dearly
held laws that all five remaining races had in common.
The insular, desert-bound djinn had supported the selkie
petition to return to full standing amongst the Old Races
in exchange for selkie help in taking over and running
Janx's underworld empire.

Neither party appeared to be happy with the arrange-
ment now that it was met. Clashes on the street had the
feel and damage of gang warfare, leaving police bewildered when weapons were found abandoned at the
water's edge, blood on the ground and no sign of embattled people in sight. One journalist was dead, his camera
destroyed. Margrit had little doubt he'd captured a selkie
or djinn transforming, and paid the price for it.

Janx had run the House of Cards with an iron hand,
unapologetic in his activities but keeping a sort of peace
with his tactics. That was lost, leaving opportunistic
humans with knowledge of how to control a troublesome
empire to face two Old Races with ambition and a
slippery pact just strong enough to unite them against outsiders. Even hyperbolic newscasters, always eager for a
bad-news story, were becoming reluctant to dwell on the
troubles at the docks and warehouses, as if ignoring them
would make them disappear. But the city was suffering,

and that *was* news, not sensationalized or dramatized. Goods were coming in and shipping out more slowly than they should; dockworkers were striking for fear of their lives and police were under verbal attack for failing to protect citizens and materials alike. That they were up against an enemy they literally couldn't comprehend didn't matter.

It was the worst scenario Margrit could have imagined springing from her attempt to make the Old Races reconsider their archaic laws and move into humanity's modern world, the consequence of her arrogant belief that her way was the right one. "I wonder if talking to them would help," she said aloud, thoughts too far from the conversation she'd been holding to follow through on it.

Daisani canted his head in curiosity. "The police?"

"The selkies. The djinn. Somebody's got to do something to stop their fight, and Tony's not going to be able to do it. I set this ball rolling. Maybe I can—"

"Negotiate a cease-fire?"

"Yeah, something like that." Margrit lifted a hand to her hair, ready to pull her ponytail out so she could scruff her fingers through it, and discovered she wore cork-screw curls in a tightly twisted knot. Stymied, she dropped her hand again and caught Daisani's amused smirk. "I know," she muttered. "It's a tell. Remind me not to play poker with you."

"I very much doubt you'd allow yourself such obvious divulgences in a poker game, Margrit. No more than you would in court. We're all allowed our little slipups in day-to-day life, however."

"Even you?"

Daisani's eyes lidded. "Rarely, but once in a while even I have a lapse in judgment."

"Yeah." Amusement quirked Margrit's mouth. "I'll tell my mother hello next time I talk to her."

Surprise shot over Daisani's face, ending in a rare laugh. "Oh, well done. You see? I do have my tells. Do say hello, and I gather from that remark you're dismissing yourself. What will you do?"

Margrit spread her hands. "Find the gargoyles."

Her cell phone rang so promptly on Margrit's departure that she turned back to eye Daisani's building suspiciously, as though the vampire might have waited until she was out the door to politely ask just how she expected to accomplish that. The building gave no sign of whether it was Daisani calling, and the phone, when she pulled it free of her purse, came up with a Legal Aid number. Wrist twisted up to check the time, she imagined another hour had been stripped from the notepad by her desk as she answered.

"Margrit, this is Sam. The opening statements for the Davison trial have been moved up to this afternoon."

"They were supposed to be Friday!" Margrit overrode the receptionist's apologies with her own. "Sorry, it's not your fault they moved it. Look, Jim's prepared to take the case on alone. I'll come in as cocounselor, but this is his as of Monday anyway." She glanced at her watch again, promising she'd be at the courthouse as soon as possible, then closed the phone with a snap and shot a second glare at the Daisani building.

The single best reason to work for the business mogul was that when Old Races complications cropped up in her life, she could at least explain the situation without causing impossible difficulties. Biting back a curse, she hailed a taxi and returned, with a growing degree of reluctance, to what she still thought of as her real life.

FIVE

SUNSET CAME WITH a blinding burst of pain.

Alban flung himself away from agony, a howl ripping from his throat. He heard stone tear, deep wrenching sound, and a woman's startled curse, but neither stopped him from snarling and savaging his way forward. Taloned feet dug into the floor, muscle straining with fury. Iron squealed, tearing without breaking. He howled again, reverberating sound so deep plaster crumbled. There was no escape: iron bound him hand and throat and ankle, making walls distant and red with pain. He couldn't move his hands more than a few inches from his head, chains limiting his range of motion.

Panicked instinct drove him to try transforming, anything to escape the bone-deep fire of iron. Fresh pain spasmed through him, denying him the human form he'd become so accustomed to wearing. Tenterhooks curled into his muscles, ripping with an eye to deliberate, debilitating anguish. Every time, it shattered through him, and yet he could not stop trying.

Somehow he had never imagined it would hurt so

badly, not even with Hajnal's memories of captivity fresh in his mind. Perhaps he'd mistaken the pain of iron bound to flesh and stone for the pain of her injuries, or perhaps the passage of time had muted the outrage. It was possible that the filtering of so many minds experiencing the barbaric sting of slavery had, over the millennia, dulled its edge. If that was so, the gargoyles had lost something even more precious than Alban's freedom. They were losing the history of their people, of all the Old Races, to the inexorable wear of time. It could be their diminishing numbers as their own range of experience became so limited that they couldn't fully appreciate, and therefore fully recall, the passions and pains of history.

Three and a half centuries had passed since Alban had last joined in the overmind and shared his experiences with the rest of his people. It happened from time to time; a promise was made to remember, but not to make the memory open to all. They were made for finite periods, until some crux had passed.

Alban, friends with two men of other races, had made a promise to stand a lifetime alone to protect their secrets, and in the thirty and more decades since then he had never seriously considered breaking his word. His people called him the Breach, for selfishly holding back the memories of the last of his family, the Korund line, from the whole; he compounded it now with Hajnal's family memories buried within him.

Now, bound in chains, his blood recoiling and sending shards of pain through him at each encounter with the metal, it seemed he had something worth breaking his promise for. He could feel the metal's weight inside him, demanding obedience, and doubted he would be able to stand against any command Biali might give. That, too, was a warning his intellect spoke of: the distant recollection that gargoyles bound by iron could be made an army unable to refuse orders. It wasn't a worry that had ever haunted him, but now Alban feared blunted memory did his people and all the Old Races no good. If agony shared could sear open the depths of history his people could recall, it might yet be worth betraying onetime friends.

And perhaps the secret he carried for them could alter the status quo the Old Races had lived with for so long. Perhaps that alternation could awaken the Old Races to the possibilities of the future, as a fresh introduction of pained captivity might awaken the gargoyles to their neglected histories.

For shame, Korund. Such brief captivity, leading so easily to thoughts of betrayal. Margrit would say a little forced perspective was good for him.

Margrit. She had been in danger.

Pain surged through him again, inadvertent attempt at transformation, as though wearing a human form might somehow free him from his bonds.

Humanoid. A gargoyle's natural form was humanoid, unlike the other surviving Old Races. Dragons were sinuous reptiles; selkies, seals in their first-born form; the djinn barely held shape at all, their thoughts made of whirling winds and sand, and the vampires, well: no one saw a vampire's natural form and lived to speak of it. But gargoyles walked on two legs, stood upright, saw with binocular vision, as much like a man as a member of the Old Races could be.

Gargoyles did not leap and snarl like a dog in chains. Alban ground taloned toes into the stone floor and surged forward. Rattling chain scraped again, pulling him up short and choking his breath away. He roared fury, words lost to him.

"Sorry, love."

A woman's voice again, so unexpected it brought Alban up as short as the chains had, distracting him from pain and rage. Focus swam over him, the words giving him something other than himself to think about. "...Grace?"

"Ah, and so now he comes to his senses." In the blur of his anger he hadn't scented her, hadn't seen her, though a whisper of memory now told him he'd heard her alarmed squeak as he'd awakened so violently. She stood across the room from him, one foot propped against the wall, her arms folded under her breasts. This was her territory, the tunnels beneath the city; she ran a halfway house for teens down here, and had for some months provided sanctuary for Alban himself. His mind was still too muddled to make sense of his awakening there, and she gave him no chance to ask questions. "Sorry for the accommodations, Stoneheart. Biali won't release you, and I'll not be risking you tearing down the walls in a fit of temper. I can unfasten the locks that hold you to the floor, but only if you'll control yourself."

Alban lowered his head, panting, and even to him, the minutes seemed long before he lifted his gaze again. "I am controlled."

"Sure and you are," Grace muttered. "Like a tempest in a teacup. All right, it's only my own neck then, isn't it?" She came forward with a key, crouching as Alban relaxed and let slack into his chains.

"I wouldn't harm you, Grace." He spoke the promise in measured tones, reminding himself of that truth as much as reassuring her. Grace opened the chains at his ankles, letting them drop to the floor. He came to his feet, hands fisted around the chain at his throat; he was entirely helpless like this, arms folded close to his chest. Eating would be awkward, but he could spare himself that humiliation: stone had no need for regular meals. "We're in the tunnels. But Biali and I—"

"Were making fools of yourselves on the rooftops," Grace supplied. "I couldn't leave you there to fight it out at sunset, now, could I? What were you thinking, Alban?" she added irritably. "You're bright enough to stay away from that one."

"He'd taken Margrit. Where is he? Where is *she?*" Alarm spiked through Alban's chest and pain rippled over him again as he tried, fruitlessly, to transform. Grace slapped his shoulder, still annoyed.

"Stop that. It looks horrible, as if all the snakes driven from Ireland have taken up under your skin and can't get free. *He* is chained up in another sealed-off room, throwing more of a tantrum than you, and I've no idea where your lawyer friend is. Better off without you, I'd say," Grace said sourly. "Not that either you or she will listen to the likes of me."

Breathless confusion pounded through Alban, counterpart to the pain the chains brought. Speaking helped: being spoken to helped. Even Grace's clear pique helped push away the bleak, mindless rage. "I do not understand." He kept the words measured, trusting deliberation over the higher emotions that heated his blood. "How did we come here? What are you doing? What did Biali want?"

"Grace has her tricks, and a few friends to call on when she needs to. I'm trying to stop a fight before it schisms your people," Grace added more acerbically. "As for what Biali wants, you tell me."

Alban breathed, "Tricks," incredulously, then, distracted from the thought, said, "Revenge," the word heavy and grim and requiring no need of consideration. "Revenge for Ausra."

Grace stepped back with an air of sudden understanding, speaking under her breath. "So it wasn't Margrit who saved herself after all. And Biali found it out." She paced away, then stopped, hands on her hips, chin tilted up, gaze distant on a wall. "Then I've done what's best, haven't I?"

"What have you done?"

Grace turned, all leonine curves in black leather. "I've sent for a gargoyle jury."

The countdown calendar was at sixteen hours, failing to take into account the after-court work Margrit returned to the office to do. She waved goodbye as coworkers slipped out, and gave the calendar a rueful glance. If she was lucky it wasn't off by more than three or four hours.

She was alone at sunset, bent over paperwork that gave her a cramp between her shoulder blades, but it redoubled, then racked her with breath-taking shocks of pain. Semifamiliar images crashed through her mind in spasms, too brief and disconcerting for her to hold. They had the feeling of being seen through someone else's eyes, as though she once more rode memory with Alban. Minutes after the sky went dark with twilight, concrete chambers finally came into resolution, body-wracking shudders fading away. Fingers clawed against her desk, breathing short with astonishment and dismay, Margrit struggled to recognize the rooms. Finally, sweat beaded on her forehead and hands trembling from holding her desk too hard, her own memory clarified where she'd seen them before.

Belowground, in Grace O'Malley's complex network of tunnels under the city.

There were innumerable ways to enter those tunnels, but only one Margrit felt certain of. She stopped long enough to change shoes, then, still wearing the skirt suit she'd worn to court, left the office at a run.

Minutes later she scrambled over the fence to Trinity Church's graveyard, all too aware that she had no good explanation if she was caught. She dropped to the ground easily, suddenly surrounded by headstones, some worn beyond readability, others as sharply etched as if they were new. Wilted flowers lay on a handful of graves, though an April breeze caught lingering scent from one bunch and carried it to her. The church itself was a dozen yards away, glowing under nighttime lights, lonely without its tourists and parishioners.

Paths brought her to an inset corner of the church near its front entrance. She glanced over her shoulder, nervous action, and mumbled an apology to the dead as she stepped over a grave and placed her palm against one of the church's pinkish brown stones, pressing hard.

The scrape of stone against stone sounded hideously loud in the churchyard's silence. Margrit held her breath, as if that would somehow quiet the opening door, and for a moment heard the city as it actually was, rather than simply the background noise of day-to-day life. Engines rumbled in the near distance, ubiquitous horns honking. The wind carried a voice or two, but most of the sound came from mechanical things.

The door ceased its scrape and she stepped inside it, looking guiltily around the churchyard again. If she'd designed a hidden door, she would have put it at the *back* of the church, not the front. She saw no one, though, and pressed the door closed again as she used her phone for a flashlight.

The light bounced off pale walls. Margrit blinked at the steep stairs that led downward, never having seen them so clearly before. The walls had been scrubbed, an inch of soot washed away, and the stairway was much brighter for it. She trotted down, curious to see what other changes had been made.

The room at the foot of the stairs was almost as she remembered it, though cleaner. Walls reaching twenty feet on a side had been washed free of their sooty blanket, and the cot settled in one corner no longer touched those walls. A small wooden table was also pulled a few inches away from the wall, its single chair pushed beneath it. Bookcases lined the walls, candles and candleholders set on them. Electric lights had been added, wires looping above the shelves. There was nowhere to cook in the room, nor any obvious ventilation. Only Alban's books were missing, safe in his chamber in Grace's domain.

She switched on the lights and tucked her phone back in her pocket before moving Alban's cot to reveal the flagstone they'd escaped through. It was two feet on a side. Margrit sat down on the cot, dismay rising anew. She'd forgotten its size, and the incredible strength necessary to move it. Even in his human form, Alban was disproportionately strong. Margrit could barely conceive of his gargoyle-form's strength limitations. Certainly her own weight was inconsequential to him. Half-welcome recollection flooded and warmed her, the memory of his hands, strong and gentle, holding her, guiding her, seeking out her pleasure. In flight, in love, that strength had been sensual.

And in battle it had been terrifying. Margrit made fists and opened them again deliberately, trying to push away the remembrances, and stood to examine the stone. She had no other way to get into Grace's tunnels, so she would have to lever the stone out somehow. Grooves marked two sides of its sides and she slid her fingers into them, then laughed with frustration at the uselessness of her attempt.

Stone grated against stone again, sound rolling down the stairs. Margrit froze, eyes wide, then spun around in a circle, searching for somewhere to hide. There was nowhere, save under the cot, and for some reason the idea struck her as absurd to the point of embarrassment.

"Pardon me." A terribly polite voice came from the direction of the stairwell. Margrit, for all she knew someone was coming down the stairs, shrieked in surprise and whipped around again.

An Episcopalian priest with an erratic white beard peered around the corner. "Pardon me," he repeated drolly. "I hate to interrupt, but I saw you come down, and I feel rather obliged to tell you that— Er, Ms. Knight?"

"Father." Margrit squeaked the honorific, utterly at a loss to explain herself. "I'm, um. Oh, God. Uh."

"Merely a representative," the priest said cheerfully. "Ms. Knight, what an unexpected pleasure. What are you doing here? I haven't seen you in a while. Either of you," he added more calculatingly. "How is Alban?"

"In trouble," Margrit replied in a burst. "That's what I'm— I needed to get into the tunnels. I didn't even think to come ask if I could come here. I would have, if I had." The old man's kindness and his awareness of both Alban's presence beneath the church and Alban's secret had been evident the time or two Margrit had spoken with him.

"I'm sure you would have. I told you I grew up in this parish," the priest said after a moment's thought. Margrit nodded, but he went on without heeding her, and gestured toward the stairs, clearly expecting her to follow him. "I used to get in trouble exploring the church grounds. The tower in the corner of the graveyard held endless fascination for me. Have you seen it?" He led her back to the graveyard, striding across it with confidence, so familiar with the paths that their ruts and joinings had no fear for him, not even in the dark. Margrit scurried to keep up, unaccustomed to walking at his clip and unwilling to start running to match his pace.

"Sure. I always wanted to climb it."

The priest threw a delighted smile over his shoulder. "Exactly. So I did."

Margrit stumbled over a corner, more from surprise than treacherous footing. "Didn't you get in trouble?"

"Well, of course, but not until I got caught. I was nine the first time I climbed it and fourteen when I got caught. But by then I'd found all its secrets. I should write a history," he said wistfully. "The secret history of Trinity Church. There are so many stories to tell."

"Not all of them are yours to tell," Margrit said softly. He gave her a sharp look that softened into agreeability.

"True, true, that's true. Still, wouldn't it be wonderful to read? Now," he said, stopping at the base of the bell tower. "I'm far too old to go climbing this thing, especially at this hour of the night, but you're young and healthy. You should be fine. Be careful on the drop down. It's a doozy."

"What?" Margrit stared from the bell tower to the priest.

The priest smiled. "I told you I imagined dragons, Ms. Knight. This is where I fought them. Beneath the tombs, where God's power bound them. Evil could stain Trinity's walls and make them black, but it protected the faithful and I imagined myself helping it. There are tunnels under the bell tower, just as there are from Alban's room. After his room was discovered, I risked my old neck and went into the tower one more time to see if I could find a back door into his room from it. Didn't manage, nor could I find it from inside his room, but if I were he, I'd have had more than one way out."

"Or in," Margrit murmured. The priest nodded.

"There's a clever mechanism in the floor of the tower. The stone to trigger it is part of the floor, third from the right if you're facing north, two down from the wall. Press down hard. It takes more than body weight standing on it to set it in motion."

"What does it do?"

He gave her another sunny smile. "I wouldn't want to spoil all your fun, Ms. Knight. Good luck. Be careful down there. And take care of Alban." He nodded, making the admonishment a command, and stepped back.

Margrit blinked, then handed over her phone, letting him provide light for her to climb with. At the top of the tower she turned back and the priest tossed up the light to her. "North is to your left."

He saluted and strode off through the graveyard, leaving Margrit to drop into the tower's hollow center.

She gnawed her lower lip, watching him hurry away, then turned her attention to the tower bottom. It looked slippery, grown over with moss or algae, and her quiet laugh was hoarse. At least if she injured herself jumping down, Daisani's gift of healing blood would make certain she'd recover quickly.

She jumped before she had more time to think, landing with as much ease as she had in scaling the churchyard gates. Breathless, she found the stone the priest had describe and pressed hard.

The bone-rattling scrape that she'd expected didn't sound. Instead the entire floor lurched, sending her stumbling. Margrit dropped to her knees, fingers spread on the floor for steadiness as a mechanism clicked, clockwork sound of chain rattling through gears. The floor lowered, smooth after the initial jolt. She tipped her chin up, watching the walls roll away. Chains came into view, links thicker than her thumb and tarnished, but not debilitated with age, and she wondered if someone kept them in working order.

As if being lowered into the unknown wasn't bad enough. She had to wonder if the chains would break and *drop* her into the unknown. Margrit pulled a face and glanced at the floor beneath her knees. The priest had seemed confident. Of course, Margrit wasn't certain he weighed as much as she did, which sent a chortle of discomfort through her. Of all the times to suddenly be concerned about her weight. It seemed typically female.

The stone elevator banged to a stop before she could tease herself further. Margrit pushed to her feet and stepped forward, flashlight picking out a black-edged tunnel.

"I'd fight dragons down here, too," she murmured to the absent priest. "Looks perfect for it."

"Oh, good," a woman's voice said dryly. "That'll be what we're asking of you, then."

SIX

ᛗARGRI+ YELPED AGAIN, then slumped in exasperation. She'd never thought of herself as a good scream queen, but that opinion was fast formulating. "Grace. God. How'd you get here so fast? How'd you know I was here?"

"Grace has her ways." The blond woman came out of the darkness, bleached hair all but glowing in contrast to the black leather she wore. "Looking for Korund, are you?"

"I— What?" Margrit straightened, hope searing hot enough to take her breath. "Do you know where he is? Is he all right?"

"Depends on how you define *'all right.'* I know where he is, sure enough." Grace's accent swam across the Atlantic, burrowing into what sounded like North London to Margrit's ear, but she'd never been able to pin the vigilante woman's origin. Transatlantic, but beyond that, her rash mix of dropped letters and sentence structures came from all over the British Isles. Margrit doubted she'd answer if asked directly. "But he says you were there this morning."

"Biali chained him." Strain made Margrit's answer rough. "So I guess he's not all right, but he's safe? You got him off the roof? How? How'd you even know he was in trouble?"

"Oh," Grace said airily, "dead things talk to Grace, and stone's got no life in it. All I had to do was hold that cold form close and wish us somewhere else, love."

Margrit stared at her, uncertain whether to give in to laughter or exasperation. "Of course. God. I can't even remember the last time I got a straight answer from somebody."

"When was the last time you gave one?"

Margrit rocked back on her heels, breath suddenly short, and looked away. "Yeah, well, I guess it's a better answer than 'Grace has her ways,' but you're insane, you know that?"

"Says the girl with the gargoyle lover." Grace sniffed. "You'll be wanting to see him, then."

"And I need to see Janx," Margrit said uncomfortably, too aware of the tension between dragonlord and vigilante.

Grace's eyebrows—light brown, not matching her hair or especially disagreeing with it—rose in fine arches that preceded a laugh. "Do you, now. Calling in your favor now, are you? And for who? I wonder. Not for me and mine, for all you promised you'd keep him out of my territory. Do you know how fast I'm losing them to him? I've got no flash, not next to the likes of him."

"You've got heart. The smart ones'll stick with you."

"Smart goes a long way in an organization like Janx's. Smart means picking choices, not acting out of loyalty."

Afraid Grace was right, Margrit hesitated, then shook her head and bulled forward. "I don't want Janx screwing up your kids any more than you do, but there's a hell of a mess building, and I need his help. As for getting him out of here, if you show me where he is, I'll—" Margrit drew breath through her teeth, not liking what she was about to suggest, but abruptly willing to make the bargain. "I'll turn his location over to the cops. They're still looking for him, so all you need to do is get everybody clear when they come down."

"*All.* That's a big word, for not many letters, love. You broke a promise to me once."

"Come on, Grace. I promised I'd do my best, not that I'd keep him away from you. Everything ballooned out of control, with Malik dying and the House going up in flames and… I'm sorry, okay? I didn't mean for you to get involved, and I'm sorry. I'll call Tony the first chance I get and give him Janx's location, if you'll just show me where he is." Whether she'd warn the dragonlord she was going to do that, Margrit didn't yet know. She'd deliberately saved him from arrest once, and as uncomfortable as that was, she still couldn't imagine forcing one of the Old Races through a human court of law.

Grace studied her a long time before giving a short nod. "All right, then. Into Grace's kingdom, love, but you'll owe me for this, Margrit. You'll owe me large."

"I know." Margrit curled her hands into fists as she fell into step behind the other woman. "I know."

Tumblers fell, ricocheting sounds that warned of visitors. Alban lifted his head heavily, no longer raging and no longer constrained, but understanding why Grace had locked the door so thoroughly. It wasn't to keep him in, but to keep others out. He'd given up trying to transform, though all that prevented him was constant, angry awareness that each attempt would bring fresh agony.

Caught in his stony gargoyle form, it was safer by far to keep him locked away where none of Grace's street children could accidentally come upon him and have the scare of their young lives.

Weariness lowered his head again, a sudden dull lack of interest in the world beyond his prison door. Not in two hundred years of solitude, since Hajnal's death, had he felt so alone. All of that time his isolation had been of his own choice. Finding it impressed upon him chafed more than he'd imagined, and it was only a harbinger of what his future would hold. No gargoyle jury would forgive him for taking Ausra's life, nor Malik's. Moving to protect another and accidents were no excuse under Old Races law. The exile he'd chosen for himself would be ratified by a council of elders, and the idea, coupled with the throb of iron bound to his stony skin, exhausted him.

The best he could do was meet his fate with dignity. It was very early for Grace to return with the jury—gargoyles couldn't travel during the day, and the only two in New York were reluctant guests in Grace's tunnels—but surely she would come with news of when and where the trial would be convened. Alban pushed himself upward, wings folded at his back in a soft, stony cloak, and waited on his guest.

"Alban." Margrit flung herself through the door with the abandon of a child, relief stealing her breath. He grunted as she crashed into him and held on hard, hoping she could impart some kind of comfort and protection with her own touch.

His scent was almost familiar, more tanged with metal than she remembered, but the chaos of the day faded as she held on to the gargoyle with all her strength. It was irrational to believe that being with him would make everything all right, no matter what crossed their paths, but she floated on that comfortable deception as long as she could. "You're all right." Her words were muffled against his chest, barely audible to her own ears. "I could *kill* Biali. *Are* you all right?" She pulled back without releasing her hold, eyebrows pinching with concern.

The chains Biali had flung around him had become a part of him. Bumpy, ugly links were sealed into his throat and held his hands against his chest like broken wings. Margrit cried a protest and tried to touch the mass as Alban shook his head.

"Margrit, what are you doing here?" His voice was distorted, gravel scraping iron, but the gentle astonishment and relief in it made Margrit bite her lip against tears.

"I spent half the damned day trying to rescue you," she whispered, almost as hoarse as Alban himself. "Alban, this is horrible, can't I—"

"You can do nothing, Margrit. Only Biali can unwind these." Uncertainty colored his voice. "At least, I hope he can."

"Why couldn't he? He bound you—"

"But legends of our captivity tell stories of locks and keys, not iron coming to life under a touch to free us."

"So go into them and find out more! We have to be able to get you free!"

Alban hesitated, then lowered his head in agreement. Margrit bit her lip, watching him as his eyes closed. She knew she asked for too much: Alban wasn't welcome in the gargoyle memories in the best of circumstances, but maybe he'd be allowed in the worst.

Instead he flinched back with a gasp, hands spasming so that the iron lumped under his skin rippled. "It prevents me." His voice came more hoarsely than before, shock and pain in it. "The memories are cut off by the iron."

Margrit knotted her hands over Alban's, anger burning horror away. "I'm going to take a sledgehammer to Biali at high noon, I swear to God. How could he do this to you?"

"He loved Ausra." The simplicity of the answer silenced her. "As he loved Hajnal. I suspect he intended an eye for an eye in the matters of their deaths." Humor ghosted over his expression and he lifted his hands as far as he could, gesturing at his own face and reminding Margrit of Biali's scars. "I suppose that seems fair."

Sick, laughter-filled disbelief crashed through her. "How can you be making jokes? Even bad ones?"

"You've come." Alban sounded surprised at himself. "It seems that your presence eases even the worst of my fears. Margrit, forgive me for not stopping his abduction of you—"

Margrit opened a palm and threatened Alban's shoulder with it. "Forgive you? There's nothing to forgive. It's not your fault Biali's stone-cold crazy." She choked on her last words, hysteria swilling just below the surface. "Stone-cold crazy," she mumbled again. "Guess he'd have to be, wouldn't he?"

Alban sighed, dispelling her amusement. "I'm not certain he's mad. He's lost a great deal."

"You can give him the benefit of the doubt if you want," Margrit growled. "I'm looking at you standing here in unbreakable chains, and I think he's batshit nuts and dangerous. Maybe not like Ausra was, because he probably doesn't want to expose every single one of you to the human race, but he encouraged her to go after you, and now he's come after you himself. You said gargoyles don't go crazy, but you're wrong, Alban. Whether it's mad with grief or just plain bonkers, it doesn't matter. This is insanity."

"I agree." Grace's voice came from behind them, startling Margrit out of her passion. She'd forgotten the other woman had walked her to Alban's cell, and now turned to see Grace leaning in the doorway. "Which is why I called for a jury."

"The conclusion is foregone, Grace." Alban sounded calm, but Grace snorted.

"You think I've called them here to hang you. It's the both of you I'll see up on trial, Korund. You'll stand the test of ages, and we'll see who's in the wrong and who's in the right."

"The test of ages." Alban shook his head, echoed words spoken softly. "How do you know the things you know, Grace O'Malley? That test belongs to my people, not humanity."

"As if you're the first or last to judge a man by a trial of hand, heart and head. Grace trades in information, Stoneheart. You should know that by now. I know a lot I'm not supposed to."

"Grace, I have broken laws we hold dear. I am guilty. I will not stand the test."

"God save me from puritanical heroes," Grace muttered. "I'll ask for it anyway, and you'll stand it or you'll stand a fool." She thinned her mouth, glowering at the gargoyle. "I'd like to say I think you're not one, but I'd also not like to make a liar of myself."

"Excuse me." Margrit broke in, voice high. "Would

either of you like to tell me what the hell you're talking about?"

Grace waited on Alban, but when Margrit turned to him, his expression was impassive as he stared at the vigilante. Margrit made a sound of exasperation and turned back to Grace, who spread her hands.

"He's to prove himself worthy in a three-stage battle. Strength, wit, compassion. The one who wins is honest or innocent in—" Grace made a throwaway gesture, as if knowing she spoke inaccurately, but choosing the simplest phrasing to convey her thoughts. "In God's eyes."

"A witch trial?" Margrit's voice shot up again, incredulous. "This isn't the fourteenth century, Grace!"

"It's gargoyle tradition. Ask him." Grace cut a nod at Alban, who shifted enough that Margrit recognized an uncomfortable admission in the movement.

"I don't care if it's tradition, it's stupid. Nobody in their right mind would settle—"

"You're the one who thinks Biali's lost his mind," Grace said, suddenly chipper.

Margrit curled a lip and tried again. "No one in this era—"

"My people are not from this era, Margrit." Alban broke in, voice a low rumble. "But it makes no difference. I will not participate in the test."

"Then you lose by default, Korund, and you're condemned."

Alban lowered his gaze. "So be it."

"Alban—" Margrit broke off, struggling for composure. "I don't understand you," she finally said, low-voiced. "You couldn't have always been so willing to let things roll over you. You fought for Hajnal. You protected—" She cast a glance toward Grace, then chose her words carefully. "You chose to stay outside the gargoyle memories to protect someone else's secrets. Why won't you fight now? I mean, it's a stupid, stupid way to settle a rivalry, but you're the one who's been so hung up on tradition all this time. If this is traditional, why turn your back on it?"

"Because I'm in the wrong, Margrit." Alban lifted his eyes to her, pale gaze steady. "Because two of the Old Races have died at my hands—"

Margrit made a strangled sound, hands curving to a throttling shape. "Because of me, both times!"

"You should know by now that motive doesn't matter. We act on results, not intentions. Margrit, I know this is difficult for you, but I don't see accepting our ancient laws as correct as being passive." Alban exhaled quietly. "And an exile placed on me by my people might ease my…"

"Guilt?" Margrit demanded. "Mea culpa, thank God, somebody else is blaming me, so now I don't have to lay it all on myself? Alban, you're going to carry this with you forever. *I'm* going to carry it forever. I can't sleep from the nightmares. I've been a criminal defense lawyer long enough to know that other people might determine your sentence, but you're the one who determines your guilt." Her anger lessened and she sat down on the cold floor, clutching the sides of her head.

"Maybe I shouldn't have pulled back," she said more softly. "I thought I needed the time to deal with it myself. Maybe I was doing my share of running away, or not facing it, myself. But not taking advantage of this trial, Alban, not using it to see if your people will accept you as innocent,

I can't understand that." She lifted her gaze, feeling tired. "The guilt's not going to be eased either way."

Alban sighed. "Margrit, if you had knowingly taken a life, would you stand against your laws to try to free yourself?"

"If it was an accident or self-defense, yes!"

"But Ausra's death was not an act of self-defense," Alban murmured. "I was defending you, not myself."

"So what am I, a second-class citizen? Not worth saving because I'm human?" Bitterness filled Margrit's tone and Alban's broad shoulders slumped.

"I clearly felt your life was worth preserving over Ausra's. But my people are not human, Margrit, and would not see my choice as the correct one. What if we lived in a world where the Old Races were known, and the positions were reversed? Would humans regard my life as more or less important than the human life I'd taken?"

Margrit folded her head down to drawn-up knees. "You know the answer to that," she replied dully. "You don't even have to be not human to be less important. You just have to be different in some way."

"So allow me this acceptance. It changes nothing for us. My position amongst my people will be as it always has been since you've known me." Rue colored Alban's voice. "And yours, I imagine, will also be as it has been since you've known me. Instigator, negotiator, troublemaker."

Margrit looked up with a quiet snort, then rolled forward to crawl toward Alban, tucking herself against his chest. Despite frustration, she felt her shoulders relax, his nearness almost as much salve to her frayed emotions as his arms would be. "I'm not a troublemaker. It just comes my way naturally when I hang out with you. I don't like this, Alban."

"I haven't asked you to like it, only to abide by my wishes."

Grace chuckled, startling Margrit into remembering a second time that the vigilante was there. "Good luck with that, Korund. Will you be staying, then?" She arched an eyebrow at Margrit, then chuckled again as Margrit shot a hopeful look toward Alban. "That's what Grace thought. I'll come back for you at sunbreak, lawyer. Sleep well." She slipped away, leaving the sound of tumblers falling into place behind her.

Margrit turned her face against Alban's chest another long moment before dragging a rough breath. "I feel like I should make a joke. Locked in a room together, the whole night before us…there must be something clever to say."

"Margrit…" Alban shifted and iron scraped, as if to remind her of his handicaps.

"No, I know. It sounds silly, but I just want to be here, Alban. I want to be the one who watches over you tonight. To be the protector. You must be exhausted."

Alban's silence said as much as his eventual admission of, "I am. The iron is far more wearying than I imagined, and I can't transform and escape it."

Margrit pressed her cheek against his chest. "Then rest. I'll be here." She heard her own silence draw out a long time, too, and only broke it with a whisper when the gargoyle's breathing suggested he might have found respite in slumber. "I'll always be here."

SEVEN

SHE HAD DOZED, if not slept, too aware of Alban's frailty and her own fears for the coming days. Half-waking thoughts had skittered all night, replaying Alban's capture, replaying his impossible remove to Grace's chambers below the streets. The vigilante woman had never shown any resources of the nature Margrit imagined necessary to steal two gargoyles from a rooftop in broad daylight, but when Grace came to fetch her in the morning, she shrugged off Margrit's questions again, ending the conversation with a sharp, "Does it matter, lawyer? He's safe enough now, isn't he, and you don't owe anyone for his safety. Count your blessings and let it go."

Chastened, Margrit did so, and emerged into the city morning to the realization that dawn came much too late in April, at least if she wanted to shower, change clothes and get to work on time. Barely beyond the tunnel entrance, her cell phone sang a tune to tell her she had voice mail. Expecting the trial time to have been moved—probably up, making it unlikely she'd get to the

office at all—she hit the call-back button and hurried
down the street with the phone pressed to her ear.

The recorded mailbox voice told her the sole message
had been left at 4:45 a.m. on Thursday, just a few hours
earlier. Margrit resisted the urge to shake the phone; it
wasn't its fault she'd been hidden beneath the city, well
out of reception range. At least the mailbox had picked
up the crisp-voiced woman who said, "Ms. Knight, this
is Dr. Jones at Harlem Hospital. A client of yours, Cara
Delaney, has been injured and she asked that we contact
you. We'd appreciate it if you came over." The doctor left
a number that flew through Margrit's mind and disappeared under a range of concerns.

Foremost was the horrifying idea that a hospital would
probably do blood work on the young selkie woman.
Margrit had never considered how the Old Races dealt with
injuries in the modern world, especially severe ones. Even
with selkies numbering in the tens of thousands, it was
unlikely they could litter enough hospitals around the world
to keep their own secrets safe. For all that they'd interbred
with humans, there *had* to be anomalies in a selkie's blood,
very likely curious enough to pique a physician's interest.

It was only as she ran to the subway that worry for
Cara's injuries surfaced, both their severity and how
they'd happened. The latter was too easy to guess: Cara
was likely to have been down on the docks, part of the
struggle between selkie and djinn. Gargoyles, Margrit remembered uncomfortably, calcified at dawn when they
died in their human form. She had no idea if selkies might
have some inexplicable conversion, too.

Her thoughts spun down the same lines no matter how
many times she pulled them back. She was relieved to

leave the subway and hail a cab, though staring out the window at passing traffic did no more to distract her than looking at her reflection in black stretches of subway tunnel had.

A matronly woman at the hospital gave the visiting-hours sign a significant glance when Margrit asked about Cara. Margrit said, "I'm her lawyer," as though the words were a magic pass, and with another sour look at the sign, the woman directed her toward the emergency department. Margrit nodded her thanks and hurried there to catch the first unharried-looking nurse she saw and asked, "Dr. Jones?"

The nurse gave her a pitying look, and spoke clearly, as though Margrit wasn't expected to understand. "I'm a nurse. Dr. Jones went home at seven. Dr. Davis took over her patients."

Color heated Margrit's cheeks. "No, I know you're a—" She drew a breath and held it, then made herself let both it and the explanation go, instead putting on an unintentionally tight smile. "Dr. Davis, then, please? Where would I find her?"

"He," the nurse said in much the same tone of pity, and pointed, "is down the hall. The good-looking one."

"Thank you." Margrit, fully expecting to have to find someone who would be more specific than *the good-looking one,* turned to look where the nurse had pointed. Halfway down the hall stood a tall man in a doctor's coat, surrounded by half a dozen clearly doting interns. Margrit shot a sideways glance around the ward, looking for a television camera. The man had a perfect profile, so flawless it seemed unlikely he could be equally handsome face-on.

He was, with dark eyes and a broad, white smile.

Margrit edged her way through the interns, hoping her voice didn't squeak as she asked, "Dr. Davis? I'm Margrit Knight, Cara Delaney's lawyer. She asked for me."

Davis dismissed all but one of the interns as he offered Margrit a hand. "Dr. Jones hoped you might be coming. Miss Delaney's going to be all right, but she's concerned about her daughter. We can check to see if she's awake. This way, please." He led her down the hall, Margrit swallowing a giggle of pure high-school giddiness. He wore a wedding band, and she hoped, for the good of the species, that he and his wife were planning on having a significant number of beautiful children. The wish felt startlingly ordinary and very human. A shiver of regret slipped through Margrit at recognizing it as such, as though she'd become something new and different herself.

A moment later, Davis pushed a room door open and ushered Margrit in. Young women lay in beds down the room's narrow length, Cara in the one farthest away. She opened her eyes as Margrit entered, then gave a pained gasp of relief and pushed up on an elbow. "Margrit. You came."

"Of course I did." Margrit hurried down the room to pull a stool up beside Cara. Davis remained at the door, murmuring, "Not too long, please, Ms. Knight. My patient needs her rest."

"Of course." Margrit smiled over her shoulder at him, found herself gazing too long, and, blushing, looked back at Cara as the door closed again. "There can't be anything people wouldn't agree to do for him. Oh, my God. I think I could be paralyzed from the eyes down and if he said get up and do a salsa I would."

Cara smiled faintly. "I guess he's not my type. He said, 'Feel better,' but I don't yet."

"Damn." Margrit took Cara's hand cautiously. "What happened, Cara? Are you all right?" She wrinkled her nose as she asked the question; *all right* depended on how it was defined. Cara was alive, but the delicate lines of her face were swollen and bruised, making dark blots of her eyes. Her right arm was in a cast, and the stiffness of her body suggested more restraining bandages in other places.

"I got shot." The flat statement struck Margrit as badly out of place, coming from a selkie. Mundane humans got shot, not mystical Old Races. Cara freed her hand from Margrit's and drifted her fingers to below the ribs on her left side. "In the back, above the kidney."

"Who…? Not a…?" Margrit didn't want to voice the word *djinn* aloud, but Cara, understanding, shook her head with a faint smile.

"No, we haven't been trying to kill each other. We have a common enemy."

"Humanity." Margrit ground her teeth. "So it was one of us who shot you."

"I didn't see who it was. But I was too far from the water to escape, so an ambulance came and picked me up. I have to get out of here, Margrit. I have to…" Passion left the slight woman and she sank back into the bed, even her bruises graying with exhaustion. "I would heal faster if I could transform. It helps put things to right."

"Cara, the only way I can think of to get you out of here is to ask Daisani to have you transferred to a private hospital."

"I don't want to owe him anything."

"I know, but you also don't want anybody looking at

your blood work too closely. Do you even know what they'd find?"

"We do our best to tend to our own sicknesses," Cara replied, answer enough. "But I didn't ask for you to help me get out of here. There's something else."

"Deirdre?" Margrit's stomach tightened in concern.

"She's safe. I sent her away when the fighting started."

"Why didn't *you* go when the fighting started?"

"Kaimana asked me to be here." Admiration bordering on reverence colored Cara's voice, reminding Margrit of how the interns had looked at Dr. Davis. Kaimana Kaaiai hadn't struck her as the sort of man to inspire such loyalty, but on the other hand, he'd engineered the selkies' acceptance back into the Old Races. That he'd done so in part by ruthlessly manipulating humans had soured Margrit against him. Cara, though, had no reason to feel that same disappointment. "I know you see me as young and weak, but Kaimana acted on my advice when he brought the quorum together. I'm stronger than you think."

Margrit began a protest, then bit it down. "You're right. It's hard not too think of you as a girl in too deep. Maybe because that's how I feel a lot of the time, and you're younger than me. So what are you, his lieutenant?"

"I'm the one holding this treaty together, here in New York. Without me to remind them who our enemy is, I'm afraid they'll start tearing each other apart, laws or no laws."

"Cara, no offense, but how are you managing that?"

Cara's gaze shifted away, then back again. "I have help. An adviser. But there's something else, too. This treaty is causing another problem."

"Worse than open fighting on the streets?"

"Much worse. Margrit, I need to know if you're our ally." Whatever Cara had hidden when she looked away now faded beneath resolution that turned her bruises into streetwise makeup and attitude. "I'd thought you were. You helped us shake up the world, and then you disappeared."

"Disappeared?" Margrit echoed, startled and stung. "Everything kind of went to hell. I'm just trying to get my head on straight. It's not like I left the city."

Something scathing darted through Cara's expression, hardening her beyond anything Margrit had seen in the past. For an instant she no longer looked like a battered young woman on a sickbed, but rather an embattled warrior, too marked with scars to have pity for anyone else's. "When a human walks away from the Old Races, she's gone whether she's in the next room or a thousand miles away. I thought you were on our side."

"On your side." The sting blossomed, as much an alpha-female reaction to Cara's change as an honest and justified anger. Margrit dropped her voice, not wanting to chance being overheard, but unwilling to let the challenge go unanswered. "I did what you wanted. I got the quorum together and they voted to accept the selkies back into the Old Races as full brethren. Yeah, that was on your side, but it was because I thought it was the right thing to do. You bred with humans because there was no other way to survive, and I think it's stupid to deny a people's heritage the way the rest of the Old Races did to you. But let's talk about *on your side,* Cara. Let's talk about the peace treaty you developed with the djinn outside of the quorum, to make sure your natural enemies would support you. Let's talk about how that treaty said you'd help destroy Janx and his House so the selkies and djinn could take over his underworld contacts and businesses. Let's talk about how that power play created a situation that led to Malik's death. Just what part of any of that did you mention to *me?* You *used* me. So forgive me if I don't quite know what *on your side* is supposed to mean anymore."

Cara lifted her chin, undaunted by Margrit's accusations and gaining strength from her own convictions. "You're right. We used you. We got what we wanted through you. From you. We have recognition amongst the Old Races. We have money and power, if we can hold on to Janx's territory." She took a breath and held it, then ended with grim finality: "We also have a treaty with a people who wish to decimate the remaining Old Races in retaliation for the death of one of their own."

Margrit stared, then laughed, a sharp sound of incredulity that bit into her anger and tore some of it away. "Tell them no. Are they nuts?"

"They're djinn." Cara's bruises lent depth to her short reply. "Read your mythology, Margrit. Djinn aren't known for their sanity."

"Then break the alliance. *You'd* have to be insane to agree."

"We need them." Despite lying on a bed, Cara squared her slender shoulders as if she was repeating another skirmish in an endless battle. "Without their acknowledgment of our people—"

"The quorum's already been met. What are they going to do, say *never mind, we didn't mean it?* I'd think if it worked that way, Janx would've repudiated you by now, since he's the one whose territory you took over. And you've got numbers. There are tens of thousands of you.

None of the other—" Margrit broke off, modulating her voice before she dared go on. "None of the other Old Races have that. You don't need to go to war over a stupid mistake."

Cara smiled, thin humorless expression. "That's what allies do, Margrit Knight. Mistake," she added clearly.

Margrit shook her head, uncomfortable realization clicking into place. Cara had never before used her name with such impunity. She'd called her Miss Knight, and Margrit had called her Cara, the relationship unequal. Cara's new confidence leveled it. Coarse embarrassment heated Margrit's cheeks as she realized she'd preferred having the upper hand, and how petty that was. She measured her response cautiously. "No money for nothing here, Cara. I'm finally starting to learn that you people all deal in information as a commodity. I've overplayed my hand too many times already."

"What do you want from me in exchange for information about Malik's death?" All the girl's former shyness had vanished, leaving behind a young matriarch of considerable power and confidence. Margrit dropped her gaze to the floor, hoping to hide regret at the change. Not that competence or self-assuredness were in any way bad, but she missed the soft, young woman she'd barely known.

"I'd have to think about that," she answered quietly. *Lied* quietly: she wanted to know how long Cara had known that Kaimana intended to use Margrit to manipulate the Old Races into the position they were now in. Her own delight and relief at finding Cara again, at being able to return her selkie skin, had been so real that Margrit hated to think Cara had known then that Kaimana intended to use her. But Cara had almost certainly known;

it was she who'd brought Margrit's point about strength in numbers to the selkie lord.

It was a question that could be brought up later. Margrit wanted to hoard the knowledge she had, in case there was a better way to spend it. Then, incongruous, the image of the countdown calendar her coworkers had made flashed in her mind, sixteen hours left on it. Margrit flattened her mouth at its reminder. "I've got to go to work, Cara. Is there anything I can do for you before I go?"

"Yes." Cara pushed herself up, cheeks paling beneath the bruises. "The reason I asked you to come in the first place. Not to get me out of here. There's a meeting this morning between—" She, too, broke off before lowering her voice to continue. "Between the djinn leaders and my people. Me. It's in part to discuss how to deal with the humans trying to gain ground in our territory—"

"Janx's territory," Margrit said sourly.

Cara went on with no notice. "And in part, a last chance for me to try to talk them out of avenging Malik al-Massrî. I need you to go in my place."

"Cara, I have to go to work!"

"This is more important. If you don't go, we may end up embroiled in race war. You're the only one who can prevent it."

"Me and Smokey the Bear. There must be somebody else. You've got to have a hierarchy of some kind, a second in command you can send. Nobody would listen to me even if I could go."

"You have to go get Chelsea Huo," Cara said implacably. "She's been helping me. If you arrive with her at your side, they'll listen to you. They'll have to."

"Or what, Chelsea will brew them a nice cup of tea? Cara, you aren't listening. I have a trial in less than two hours. I have a *job*."

"*This* is your job. Are you really going to risk us going to war for the sake of a single case in the human justice system?"

Margrit jolted to her feet, taking a few quick, sharp steps to let off steam, then swung back around to scowl at Cara. It came to her again that this situation, or any like it, was why she hadn't slithered out of the agreement to work for Eliseo Daisani. The Old Races were a tremendous disruption to her life, and only working for someone intimately involved with them would give her the leeway she needed to deal with the impossible circumstances they threw her way. None of her other reasons, legitimate as they might be, held a candle to that one. She had no intention of walking away from their wondrous, complicated world, and becoming Daisani's assistant meant she could remain a part of it without disappointing anyone else. "Shit. *Shit.* God*damm*it!"

Cara dropped back into the pillows, delicacy once more visible in her strained features, though a smile curved her lips. "That's what I thought. That's why you're the Negotiator."

"The what?" Margrit laughed, harsh sound. "I've got a title now? How very…*you* of you."

"It's a sign of respect, Margrit. We don't often honor your kind with titles. The meeting's at ten. Please, go see Chelsea. She has to go with you, or even the place you've earned might not carry enough weight."

Margrit rolled her jaw, irate and trying not to let it bloom into fresh anger. "You're going to owe me for this one, Cara. I'm about to make myself look bad in my last trial for you and yours. There's going to be a price."

"There always is." Cara nodded toward the door. "Now go."

EIGHT

"YOU'LL BE FINE, Jim. It's your case anyway, and I'm just standing as cocounsel." Margrit got dressed as she reassured her coworker. Halfway back from Harlem she'd decided there was no way she could face the morning without a shower and fresh clothes and had detoured home. Neither of her housemates were there, leaving the house quiet enough to make an apologetic call. "I know this is a long way from ideal, but I've had something unavoidable come up. Personal business. I'm sorry."

"It's okay." The resentment in Jim's voice betrayed him.

Margrit clenched her jaw, then deliberately loosened it. "I'll do my best to come by this afternoon if you want any advice, but you're as prepared for the case as I am. I've got to go." She repeated her apologies and hung up, then turned to glower at herself in the mirror.

If her expression could be ignored, the woman reflected back at her looked professional and cool, well collected in a skirt suit with a dark, subtly red blouse beneath it. Her gaze, though, was angry with frustration and resignation, and even loose corkscrew curls did little to soften its edges. Margrit sighed and twisted her hair back, jamming an ebony stick through it. It finished off the look, making her hard and unassailable.

Too hard for her own tastes. Margrit found a pair of gold filigree earrings and slipped them into place, feeling herself relax a little as she did so. If the clothes made the man, they could also remind her of what she *wanted* to be. The gold looked well against cafe-latte skin, bringing out warm depths. It was better to not be so cold. Feeling less grim, Margrit slipped low heels on and picked up her purse, and, armed for the day, left her bedroom.

The front door swung open and Cameron, wearing loose gym sweats and a snug T-shirt, bounded in and let go a shout of surprise as she nearly ran Margrit down. Margrit laughed and clutched her heart, staggering back. "Good morning."

"You didn't come home last night." Cam gave her a cheerful fish eye. "Did you have a hot date?"

"I did, as a matter of fact." Margrit tried dodging around the tall blonde, but Cameron swayed back and forth in the hall, deliberately blocking her. Half a foot taller than Margrit even when Margrit wore two-inch heels, Cam's long limbs ensured she could keep her smaller housemate stuck in place.

"With who? Alban? You haven't seen him in a couple weeks, right? C'mon, talk. And those are fighting duds, Grit. Don't tell me you've got a court case after being up all night."

"Okay. I won't tell you." Margrit ducked through an opening in Cameron's waving arms. Now that her housemate had mentioned it, she realized how tired she should be, but the long previous day didn't seem to be dragging her down. Daisani's gift in action, maybe, though she thought he'd said health didn't negate a need for sleep.

Cam reached over her head to bang the door shut. "Have you had breakfast, young lady?"

"I swear, you and Cole are like my parents. No," Margrit admitted reluctantly. Her stomach rumbled on cue and Cameron barked triumph.

"Is your court date at nine?"

"…no…"

"Then you have time to eat and gossip. Shoo. Go. Go." Cameron herded her down the hall toward the kitchen, making Margrit laugh again.

"When'd you get so pushy?"

"Right about when you started sneaking around and not talking to us anymore. Couple weeks ago now. What's going on, Margrit?" Cameron's jovial tone dropped away, leaving concern. "I know you and Cole are on the outs, but neither of you will tell me why, and you've been getting up to run in the middle of the night for the last ten days."

Guilty surprise sizzled through Margrit. She went to the fridge, an orange behemoth from the fifties, and stared inside it as a way of avoiding Cameron's worried gaze. "Did Cole make any bagels?"

"He did, and I'll prepare you the perfect peanut-butter bagel in exchange for some kind of actual information about your life. Otherwise I'm holding them hostage."

Margrit took jam out of the fridge and turned to face her friend, whose calculating expression turned satisfied as she put bagels in the toaster. "Talk. What's going on?"

"Honestly? Everything's completely out of control and I feel as if I'm coming apart at the seams. You ever get yourself into something so deep it looks like there's no way out?"

"Yeah. I've told you about how I got the scar on my leg." Cam edged Margrit out of the way to get to the peanut butter.

Margrit's gaze fell to her friend's shin, where she knew a long silver scar marked the tan skin beneath Cam's sweats. "A car wreck," she said, knowing she skimmed the truth.

Cameron turned, a jar of peanut butter in hand, and gave her a hard look. "A drunk-driving car wreck. The only thing about it in my favor was I wasn't the one driving. And I remember thinking if I could undo it, if I could get out of it somehow, if I could make it have not happened, I would never be that stupid again in my life. I wouldn't drink, I wouldn't drive, I wouldn't get in a car with somebody who had been, I'd do anything to make it unhappen." The bagels popped and she lathered butter, peanut butter and jelly on them with abandon. "So, yeah, I know what it's like to feel out of control and with no way out. What's going on, Margrit?" She handed one of the bagels over and sank her teeth into her own.

Margrit took hers and inhaled its warm, rich scent, trying to loosen the tightness in her chest. "It's work stuff, kind of." It was true, insofar as she was going to work for one of the Old Races in a handful of days, but it was also inaccurate enough to be a blatant lie. "I'll tell you about it as soon as I can." She'd promised Cole that much after he'd seen Alban's true form. He'd wanted to tell Cameron, but Margrit had put him off and he'd agreed, aware that without seeing Alban's transformation herself, Cameron would never believe them.

"Well, you know I'll be here to listen." Cam picked up

her bagel and stuffed a full quarter in her mouth all at once. "Eee yrr baghl," she ordered, then swallowed hard enough to grimace. "Eat your bagel before you go to work."

Margrit picked up the cooling bread and toasted Cameron with it. "Aye, aye, ma'am." She got as far as the kitchen door, then turned back. "Hey, Cam? Thanks."

Cameron smiled. "It's what friends are for."

The phrase lingered in Margrit's mind as she made her way downtown. Humans used it lightly. Margrit wasn't certain she counted any of the Old Races as her *friend,* and yet she was pursuing Cara's agenda with greater dedication than she typically offered any of her mortal friends.

Then again, humans had never asked so many impossible things of her. The Luka Johnson case she'd worked on for years had required by far the most devotion of any single project she'd ever been involved with, but it hadn't begun as a gesture of friendship. It had been part of the job. If Cara was right—and Margrit couldn't conclusively argue she wasn't—then mediating Old Races relationships *was* her job now, one she felt as strongly about as she had Luka's case.

And the reality was that Margrit had thrust herself into that position. Alban's plea for help had been the start of it, but her decision to act on behalf of the selkies was a conscious, deliberate decision on her part. She'd even taken a step further than they'd asked, pushing to overturn the remaining laws the five Old Races held in common. The anger she'd felt over Cara's demand was born from guilt at abandoning the mortal life she'd worked so hard to build. She would have to let that go somehow, though it would become easier once she'd stepped out of the legal world and began working for Eliseo Daisani.

It would become easier once she and Alban could put his trial behind them and take a chance on something new and extraordinary for both of them. Head tipped against the subway-car window, Margrit let her eyes slip shut and a smile inch into place. She could all but feel the strength of his arms around her, surprisingly warm for a creature bound to stone. Encompassed in that circle, she felt safe and adventuresome all at once, trusting in the comfort she found there, certain of a chance to search and explore things she'd never known existed. Human lovers paled by comparison through no fault of their own; Alban brought magic simply by being, and that was something she hadn't realized she'd craved until she found it. Her life had been built of deliberate goals and the steps necessary to achieve them. Finding those ambitions shattered by a single granite-strong touch was more exhilarating than alarming; that was the aspect of herself she'd never been able to explain to friends or family. Alban understood her in a way she'd thought no one could, and she hoped she offered him the same.

Her own quiet laughter made her eyes open. She *did* understand the honor-bound gargoyle. She thought he was frequently thickheaded and wrong, but the strictures he'd placed on himself made a certain sense to her. He lived in a world constrained by particulars, as she had always done. Now that she'd broken free of them, Margrit was eager to see Alban do the same. Maybe if she explained herself in those words, he would be willing to take the risks that she was herself investigating. Challenging the laws of his people was a drastic way to start, but then, it was how she'd begun.

And it seemed it was how she would continue. Margrit left the subway, brushing through crowds to make her way to the corner bookstore owned by Chelsea Huo. Clear glass with etched lettering proclaimed Huo's On First, and in smaller letters beneath it, *an eclectic bookstore.* Margrit had never examined the shelves closely enough to determine whether the selection was actually eclectic, but it was certainly chaotic. She edged the front door open cautiously, never sure a newly delivered stack of books wouldn't be balanced in its path, and made her way into the crowded shop.

The foyer—defined by being the only area in the store without books piled everywhere—was tidier than usual, an extra square foot or two available around the till. Margrit grinned and let the door close to the sound of chimes, echoed an instant later by a rattle of beads from behind the stacks. "Cara?"

"Hi, Chelsea." Margrit lifted her voice unnecessarily as the shop's tiny proprietor appeared from between the shelves. Surprise darted across her apple-round face as she peered at Margrit, then at the door leading to the street. "Cara sent me," Margrit said, then winced. "I'm doing it again. Every time I come in here, I start sounding like a noir film."

Chelsea put fingertips on a stack of books to keep it from toppling as she passed, then stopped before Margrit with her arms folded under her breasts. Margrit, looking at the top of her head, counted a handful of silver hairs among the black, and wondered how old the woman was. Something about her tea-colored eyes made her seem both wizened and ageless, but nothing in the way she moved suggested she was at all old. "Why didn't Cara come herself?"

"She's in the hospital. She's hurt. Fighting down on the docks got out of hand. She'll be all right," Margrit added hastily. "Assuming nothing weird comes up in her blood work, anyway. She called me. I'm supposed to go… Oh, you know." She sighed, suddenly feeling the weariness that had been absent earlier. "I'm supposed to go make sure their treaty holds, so they'll keep fighting us instead of turning on each other. And you're supposed to come along to shore me up, I guess."

Surprise snapped through Chelsea's eyes again. "Are you, now? You've come a long way in a little time, Margrit Knight. From novice to negotiator. I may be impressed."

"Oh, good. I hope they are." Margrit stuck her tongue out, feeling not at all impressive. "Are they going to listen to me?"

"They're there to negotiate, Margrit. They might be expecting Cara, but I've been helping her and they'll recognize you as her proxy if I'm there to back it up. Even in the worst scenarios, none of the Old Races want to expose themselves to humanity. They'll listen, if you're ready for this."

But I'm not *ready for it!* The protest rang through Margrit's mind as it had for the past hour, thoroughly clenched down. She knew too little about the situation, but at the same time she thought she understood the basic scenario. Most complications rose from one or two fundamental difficulties: she only had to address those, and with luck the remainder would come unraveled. She reminded herself of that as she climbed grate stairs in a dockside warehouse. Chelsea, a step ahead of her, looked calm and utterly collected, completely at odds with the butterflies in Margrit's stomach.

She was uncomfortably aware of the plummet just to her right. Workmen were visible below, forklifts beeping and crashes announcing the periodic drop of materials. Several moved with the characteristic ease of the Old Races, though more still were only human. She stopped to watch them, trying to find her equilibrium, and Chelsea glanced back with an arched eyebrow as she reached the door leading into the warehouse office. Margrit's shoulders slumped, and, more determined than prepared, she nodded her readiness. Chelsea pushed the door open.

The office was as far from Janx's alcove as she could imagine, with ordinary plate-glass windows and cheap furniture, none of it saying anything about the people who'd put it there. Functional, not personal: she supposed that did say something about them, after all.

Those people stood segregated, selkies on one side with their arms folded across broad chests so they made a living, glowering wall. Across from them, restless, slender djinn shifted and glanced around, their movements no more worried than the wind might be. All of them turned their attention to the door as it opened. Margrit caught one djinn begin a bow of respect, clearly meant for Chelsea, and then watched him arrest the gesture midmotion as he saw Margrit step up behind her.

A rustle of not-sound whispered around the office, uniting djinn and selkie in consternation, surprise, offense. The impulse to simply walk away rushed up and Margrit pushed it down again. Chelsea stepped aside, giving Margrit the floor. To her astonishment, none of the Old Races spoke, leaving her a heavy silence to break.

She had their attention with her presence; with any luck she could hold it with confidence and calm. "Cara Delaney's been badly injured and is in a human hospital. She asked me to mediate the discussion she'd intended to head this morning. As I understand it—"

"A *human?*" An unexpectedly familiar voice came from the group of djinn, and the man who stepped forward brought a shock of anger and fear that drowned Margrit's dismay at being challenged. Details she hadn't known she remembered stood out about the man: a rash of pocked skin beneath his cheekbones, keeping well-defined features from prettiness; the amber-clear color of his eyes; elegance bordering on arrogance. What she actively remembered was still there, maybe even stronger than before: disdain and anger mixed cold enough to be hatred. It was too easy to understand the rage that drove some of the Old Races; too easy to imagine what it was like to belong to a once-rich culture now forced into shadows. Margrit didn't want to feel sympathy for a creature who had literally held her mother's heart in his hand, but for a moment, caught up in his insulted, insulting gaze, she did.

"A human," she said as neutrally as she could, then reached for the name Janx had used when he'd mentioned this djinn: "And you're Tariq."

The djinn curled his lip, then offered a bow of such grace it managed to be insolent. "At your service," he added, then smiled. "Or your mother's."

She was too well trained to rise to the bait, the blatant attempt releasing a string of tension within her. Tariq, at least, was as strained as she felt. The camaraderie, regardless of how unwelcome he would find it, made her feel as though the ground was more level. "A human has no reason to favor one of your factions over another. I'm a more neutral moderator than Cara could ever be. It wouldn't have been a bad idea to invite me here even if she hadn't been injured."

Chelsea, at her side, didn't shift so much as to nod, but something in her stance relaxed, connoting approval or new confidence. Tariq stepped forward, full of airy belligerence. Margrit held up a hand, motion so sharp he actually stopped, then looked infuriated at having been put off by a mere human. This time Chelsea smiled, barely visible expression, and to Margrit's surprise, spoke.

"Margrit Knight has stood against her own kind to protect the Old Races. She has sat amongst a quorum of dignitaries as one of them, an honored and voting member. She has shown mercy where none was warranted. I declare her fit to stand among you as a mediator. Dare any of you dispute me?"

The djinn exchanged sullen, resentful glances. Even the selkies shifted, as if hoping someone on the opposite side might be foolish enough to argue. Curiosity sang through Margrit, making her heart beat loudly enough she was sure it could be heard by each and every being in the room.

Serene confidence radiated from the tiny woman as she met the gaze of each member of the Old Races. It reminded Margrit of Daisani's brief pause during the quorum, when he'd waited to see if anyone would challenge him as he declared himself. Chelsea shared that absolute certainty, as though the idea someone might stand up to her was both inconceivable and slightly amusing.

Almost as one, the selkies and djinn dropped their eyes, acquiescing for reasons that confounded and fascinated Margrit. Cara had wanted Chelsea there; this inexplicable iron hand was clearly the reason. Chelsea elevated feather-fine eyebrows and tipped her head toward Margrit, once more relinquishing the floor. Breathless with questions, Margrit reined in the impulse to give over to them and instead began again where she'd been interrupted. "As I understand it, there are two matters on the table. One is how to retain the territory you've taken. The other is an inquest into Malik al-Massrı's death. Am I correct?"

Her voice betrayed only professional calm, none of her curiosity in evidence. Eventually dealing with the enigmatic Old Races would cause all her control and calm to erupt in a barrage of wanting to *know*. She felt dangerously close to that breaking point now. Exercising the focus to deal with the problems at hand felt like a triumph of overblown proportions.

"Inquest," Tariq growled. Margrit angled herself toward him, now certain that he spoke for all his people, and that the selkies would abide by Cara's wishes, and let her speak for them. "An *inquest* is not what we desire."

"We'll get to that. You have a bigger problem on hand with this territory war."

"Bigger than the death of one of our own?" Incredulous anger snarled through the question.

Margrit set her teeth together. "Yes, in fact. You can't afford for your own people—any of you, no matter which race you're from—to end up in human hospitals like Cara. God help me for saying it, but you need to either eliminate your competition immediately or create enough of a united front between the selkies and the djinn to take ambitious humans in hand and use them. Nobody's happy about the mess you've created down here, and more bodies aren't going to get the cops off your backs. The problem is you people aren't criminals." She heard herself and laughed, more frustrated than amused. "You're temperamental and violent, but you're not criminals. You needed Malik, didn't you? Because he's the only one who knew anything about running drugs and prostitutes and gambling rings and protection rackets."

Muscle played in Tariq's jaw, answer enough. Margrit dropped her chin to her chest, muttering, "Kaimana's a billionaire. He should be better prepared for taking over any kind of empire than this. Or is that why he dropped it in your laps?" She glanced from djinn to selkie and back again. "I knew he wanted to keep his hands clean, but it didn't occur to me that he barely knew how to get them dirty. Hell, I could probably run this mess better than you can." Too late, she wondered if that was why Cara had insisted Margrit take her place at the meeting. She said, "No," out loud, afraid *she* needed the reprimand more than anyone else in the room.

Admonishment still echoing in her ears, she looked back to Tariq. "Cara's in charge of this, isn't she. You agreed to support the selkies in their petition to rejoin the Old Races in exchange for a position of human economic strength. But you're under Cara's thumb, and therefore Kaimana's, and they can control you by dint of numbers, if it comes down to it. But Cara's not a bad guy. She's gotten tougher, but she really doesn't have the stomach for dealing with this part of the world. So you're constrained by what she's willing to do. What Kaimana's willing to do. Am I right?"

Tariq nodded this time, movement sharp and angry.

Margrit muttered exasperation and scowled from one faction to the other. Dark selkie gazes remained neutral, though a growing sense of unfriendliness emanated from them. Margrit, irritated, said, "Not being a bad guy isn't a bad thing, people," then returned her attention to Tariq. "Given the circumstances under which we previously met, I'm sure you won't take offense if I characterize you as a complete bastard."

The djinn went still, then thinned a smile and nodded.

"All right. This is how you're going to deal with the infighting and the human encroachment, then." Tension rose sharply, minute shifting amongst all the Old Races bringing them closer to her. Margrit counted out a long breath, afraid she would come to badly regret the decision she was making. "I'm willing to offer Tariq the reins of this business."

The selkies spoke for the first time, sudden burst of incoherent sound that Margrit waved down. "If you're going to stop getting your asses kicked, you need a big bad, and Cara's not the right person for the role. Furthermore, this whole setup's a lousy one for the djinn. All the dirty work and none of the benefits. So maybe we can do a deal here." The term came easily, as if she stood outside a courtroom arguing over a client's sentencing, though the gathered djinn were an even more unlikely client than Alban had been.

A smile crawled across Tariq's face. "What are your terms?"

"Don't pursue vengeance for Malik. The Old Races can't afford a race war. There aren't enough of any of you. That's the major term."

Tariq's amber eyes darkened until Margrit had no sense of what he thought. "And the minor ones?"

"I recommend that your human competition not suddenly start waking up dead. I recommend you find a way to deliver them alive and in one piece, maybe neck-deep in prosecutable crimes, to the NYPD. I also recommend that you not expand on what you took from Janx in any meaningful fashion until you are damned good and certain of your grounding. The docks are a hairsbreadth from a war zone right now. I want to see them stabilized, not destroyed."

"And if I—we—choose not to accept your terms?"

"Then the NYPD and the FDNY will come down here with trucks filled with salt water and handcuffs lined with vampire blood and they will take you *down,* Tariq." His face tightened with astonished anger and Margrit shook her head, speaking more softly. "Don't underestimate me. Letting the Old Races continue to run Janx's empire creates a danger for my *own* race, and I'm the gasoline being poured on the flames. This is a good deal for you. Do not piss me off."

"For *them,*" one of the selkies spat. "It's a good deal for the djinn, not us."

Margrit swung to face him, reveling in the oversized action. Adrenaline burned through her, focusing her words. "The selkies wanted legitimacy amongst the Old Races. The djinn, who, as I understand it, have until now remained in their desert homelands and let time pass them by, wanted a piece of the modern world. You've both gotten what you were after. What you have right now is an opportunity to walk away from this mess and let somebody more ruthless put it back together. I'd take it if I were you."

"An abrogation of responsibility?" Chelsea asked quietly.

"Think of it more as me taking it on." Tension lanced

through Margrit's shoulders. Whether or not Kaimana had intended the selkies to help keep the djinn in check, she fully planned to do that herself.

Somehow.

Chelsea pursed her lips, but nodded, and despite looking far from convinced, the young selkie who'd spoken subsided. Margrit wondered briefly if their society was heavily matriarchal, though Kaimana's position as a powerful leader amongst them suggested otherwise. Regardless, she was relieved at the lack of argument.

"We will have to discuss this," Tariq said. "Malik al-Massrī's death is not something we take lightly."

Margrit inclined her head, the motion coming close to a bow. She hoped it hid the shiver of nerves that ran under her skin, lifting goose bumps. She could—and would—make good on her threat if the djinn didn't comply with her terms, but any investigation of Malik's death would end badly for her. If the Old Races accepted accident as a forgivable circumstance surrounding a death, she would confess to the part she'd played, but they weren't inclined to show clemency to their own kind, much less a human. Voice steady, she replied, "Nor should it be. Is a day long enough for deliberations?"

"We'll send a messenger when we've decided."

"Fine. Not more than forty-eight hours, though. This needs to be settled." Margrit nodded again, and trusting there was no ceremony for departures, took the opportunity to escape.

Chelsea exited a step ahead of her, blocking her on the grate landing as the door banged shut behind them. Accompanied by the rattle of windows, Chelsea asked, "Are you sure you know what you're doing?"

"Of course not, but never let them see you sweat, right?" Margrit wrapped a hand around the stairway's cold, metal railing. "I couldn't think of another way out of it. They *can't* go to war amongst themselves. If they're lucky, they'll just half wipe each other out. If they're not lucky, we'll learn about them."

"So the sacrifice you chose was your own people." Chelsea sounded more interested than condemning, as though Margrit had proven thought-provoking.

Margrit dropped her head, weight leaned into the railing. "The needs of the many over the good of the few. In one way, it doesn't matter. Nobody's going to come in and clean up Janx's empire. Whether the djinn run it or a human does…" She shrugged. "Either way, it's still going to be criminal. People are going to die in the long term. Maybe this will keep some of them alive in the short term. Do you have a better answer?"

"If I did, I would have suggested it earlier." Chelsea let silence hang for a judicious moment, then conceded, "The caveats were well done. I don't know if the djinn will agree, but your threat was a good one. Can you back it up?"

"I think so. I hope so. It depends on if Tony's willing to believe me." She motioned at the warehouse, evoking another one with the gesture. "He's still angry, but he thinks all my weird behavior was trying to help set a trap for Janx. If I told him fire trucks full of salt water were the only way to quell the violence down here, he might listen to me."

"I was more thinking of the vampire's blood."

"Oh." Margrit straightened away from the railing. "Actually, that part I'm more certain of. Daisani was pretty annoyed with me for making him let Tariq go. I think he'd like a chance to snag another djinn. Or thirty."

"Slippery ground you stand on there."

Margrit shot the smaller woman a sharp look. "I think I'm bending over backward here to give the djinn a fair chance. Especially since Tariq was the one who nearly pulled my mother's heart out. So if they don't hold up their end of what I've set out, I don't have many qualms about knocking this game board over. I'd like to have the moral high ground, but it's hard to find, much less stay on. I'm doing my best, Chelsea. It might not be good enough, but I'm doing my best."

A smile passed over Chelsea's face. "Good. The fire's still there. I just wanted to make sure."

"Oh, now you're manipulating me, too? Thanks." Margrit pulled a face at Chelsea's cheerful nod. "So how did you do it?"

"Mmm?" Chelsea's eyebrows rose in modest curiosity.

"You gave me legitimacy in there. Why didn't they fight you? No offense, but you're just a bookshop owner."

"Oh, that." Chelsea shrugged it off. "Even the Old Races can be taught to behave if you're firm enough with them. I think you may be learning that yourself."

"That's your story and you're sticking to it?"

"I am." Chelsea gestured. "Shall we?"

"Yeah." Margrit took the lead, trotting down the stairs. White-hot noise met her at the bottom.

NINE

SHE COULD TELL she screamed because the tang of copper tainted her throat, and with it came the raw, red feeling of too much force. Her ears, though, rang with a profundity that outweighed any hope of hearing her own voice. She knew her eyes were open because she touched them, felt the lashes parted and the sting of salt and minute dirt from her fingertips against their orbs. Fingertip pressure, as light as it was, sent bloody waves through the snow-blinding whiteness that had become her vision. She closed her eyes, instinct whispering that the comfort of expected darkness was better than the wide-eyed blindness. Red overwhelmed white, but reassuring black lay out of her reach.

Her chest heaved, telling her she still breathed as the brackish black taste of smoke began to overwhelm the flavor of blood at the back of her throat. Margrit coughed, then doubled over with her arms wrapped around her ribs. Didn't double over: curled on her side fetally, the scrape of concrete against her cheek advising her more about her position than intellect could. That made no sense, but she couldn't rewind her thoughts far enough to understand what was happening. A wall rose up every time she did, concussive force of light slamming into her and ripping coherency away. She opened her eyes again, as if doing so would force comprehension. Stars spun in her vision, then began to clear away in orange whorls of dust and grit. Daisani's gift, she thought, rather than human adaptability kicking in.

She pushed to her feet awkwardly, aches fading from her bones, but dizziness still swept her as the song in her ears rang louder. A clear thought cut through the sound: she had been in the city when the towers fell. The noise had been overwhelming, and then entirely gone, eerie silence broken only by crying voices and the wail of emergency vehicles struggling through the broken city. She could not remember head-pounding tinnitus accompanying, or following, the attacks.

Attacks.

Only then did the chaos around her resolve into something that made sense, insofar as an all-out fight in a warehouse could make sense. Smoke and dust billowed around her, making ghostly shapes in sunlight that shouldn't spill through the warehouse the way it did. The better part of a wall was missing, light filtering gold and blue through the grime in the air.

Those welcoming colors fought a losing skirmish against the more dangerous shades of red and yellow as flames began to eat the warehouse's sides and reach toward its roof. People rushed to escape, bumping past Margrit. She jolted with each contact, stumbling, but never moving far from where she stood.

They were all human, the ones who ran. To see that so clearly tore a sound from her chest, so deep it bordered on a sob. They were human, sharing Margrit's earthbound, compact grace, and within seconds they were gone, abandoning the warehouse for the safety of the streets.

But innumerable people remained, a whole line of men and women, a line of selkies, advancing on the smoking, swirling chaos. Margrit lifted her eyes, looking past the line of warriors to the blown-out wall.

A man walked through its remains, preacher-collared shirt and Chinese-cut silk pants making the line of him tall and slim. He pulled sunshine with him, its glint playing in auburn hair and its shadow darkening his eyes past jade into blackness. He laced his hands together in front of him, looking about the chaos of Cara's warehouse with a mild, curious smile.

"Janx." Margrit whispered his name out of compulsion, as though voicing it was the only way she could keep herself from stepping toward him. He could not possibly hear her, not over the distance, not through the sound she imagined must be roaring through the ruined warehouse. Could not possibly, and yet an eyebrow lifted sharply and he turned his gaze from examining the warehouse to unerringly find Margrit.

For the briefest moment, she thought she saw surprise, and then regret, cross the dragonlord's face.

Then for the second time in a matter of seconds, an impossible concussive force slammed through the warehouse, taking all the air with it as Janx transformed.

Margrit kept her feet by dint of distance, not willpower, but lost her breath as much through awe as the massive implosion of air as Janx's mass shifted from a man to a monster, vastly larger than he'd been an instant before. She hadn't *seen* him transform before: when he and Alban and Malik had fought, she'd been literally knocked aside by the process, too close to observe. Only close enough to be empirically affected, and terrified witless. Her heart hammered now, and her breath came quick, but the raw mindless fear she'd felt when she'd watched Alban and Janx fight seemed weaker. Watching Janx now was less shocking, though no less impressive.

As a vampire, Daisani moved impossibly quickly. Janx, too, was terribly fast, but his movements had the sense of a vast attention being moved from one place to another, rather than Daisani's blurring speed. His transformation was like that, too: it seemed to Margrit that she'd simply been unable to see him properly before, and that his shift from man to dragon threw off the illusion that she'd been tricked by. It was as though he always carried his weight with him, and the blast force of transformation was the dropping of a cloak. Alban's change to and from his gargoyle form was so modest in comparison as to be a different process entirely.

Janx had filled the office he kept in the House of Cards, seeming to take the very air from the room even in his human shape. But as a dragon he'd wound and twisted through it, nearly an oroborus out of necessity. In the unconstrained open floor of Cara's warehouse, he stretched sinuously, making himself long and dangerous. He was the color of burnished flame in the sunlight, deep red and glittering with silvery whiskers that floated about his face with the capricity of Einstein's hair. Short, powerful legs that ended in gold-tipped talons scraped gouges into the floor as he wriggled himself and leapt forward, crashing into the line of advancing selkies with catlike glee.

The selkies scattered, moving with the beautiful,

flowing poise of creatures born to water. Janx whipped
his head around, long muzzle turning to a gaping maw,
and spit fire after them. The roar of heat and sound came
up from below the ringing in Margrit's ears and reintro-
duced hearing, something she wasn't certain she was
grateful for. Hands clutched against her head, she stared
wide-eyed as Janx lifted his wings. They were long and
slender and spiny, and buffeted flame into swirls, sending
it after the selkies. As quick as the flame itself, Janx
twitched around for a second attack, exhaling fire at the
walls. Destructive heat made girders squeal in protest
and turned sheeted metal into puddles of silver.

The selkie army came back together, making a target
of themselves without faltering in their advance. Janx, to
Margrit's startlement, fell back a step, swinging his head
to bowl the nearest handful of warriors over. Flame
rumbled after them, but its bulk was concentrated on the
pallets and boxes that made up the warehouse's contents.

Astonishment pulled a crackling sound of disbelief
from Margrit's lungs. When she'd put the question to a
quorum of Old Races elders, only Janx had sided with her
in supporting the idea that killing another of the Old
Races no longer be an exiling offense. She didn't believe
that a fear of exile stayed the dragon's hand now, but
despite his visible advantages over the selkie fighters, he
shied away from killing.

Honor among thieves. Margrit had argued extensively
with Alban over the dragonlord's code, but now, watching him, knew she was right. Janx had his own honor, and
it stretched so far as to bow to the laws laid down by the
Old Races.

A fresh gout of flame blossomed, heat sizzling across

the warehouse. Margrit finally shook herself into movement, backing away and stepping through rubble. A thought caught up with her and she turned, squinting through the smoke and heat in search of Chelsea. She, like the other humans, had to have run: there was no sign of her in the chaos. As there should be no sign of Margrit, she realized, and took a breath of overheated air that she hoped would hold her to the street's comparative safety.

Cool, ash-free air splashed across her face, making her inhale again, sharply, her relief at finding a source of clean air stronger than the confusion as to its source. It whipped around her, gaining speed and direction, then plunged forward to attack Janx as he wound across the warehouse floor between burning pallets and unmanned forklifts.

The wind ripped the next breath of flame away from him, increasing its size for the merest moment, then tearing it apart and sending it into nothingness. Margrit gaped and started forward, but the gales pushed her back again. Selkies slid across the floor, as well, shoved away from Janx by the ferocity of an element with its own mind. Smoke and grit, caught by the wind, formed a vortex, shrieking with speed and tearing fragments of material free around the warehouse. Janx clamped his wings against his sides, hissing as he backed away from the attacking wind. Rubble snapped and broke beneath his weight, the pieces snatched up by the tornado as it pressed toward him.

A wall stopped his retreat and the wind's assault screamed victory. It tilted on its axis as if it were a living thing with intent, an impossible whir of debris and air angling itself to encompass the dragon entirely.

It *was* a living thing, Margrit realized abruptly. Janx

seemed to realize it at the same moment, letting go a bellow of fear-tainted rage. The wind sucked the sound away, whipping around Janx's head with deadly aim. He slithered farther back, rising onto his hind legs like a cat trapped in a corner, and the shrieking wind followed him. It was too late to transform: the tornado would only snatch up his human form and tear it apart. Margrit vibrated with indecision, too fragile herself to charge into the vortex and rescue the dragon.

The selkies gathered together again, picking their way around torn-up flooring and overturned heavy equipment. The youth who'd spoken upstairs stood at their head, watching without expression as the wind tore and ripped at Janx. He staggered under its onslaught, breathlessness beginning to take its toll. Margrit ran forward, putting herself amidst the selkies, and caught the youth's shoulder. "You have to do something!"

He looked disdainful. "Janx attacked us. This is the cost."

"You condone *murder* to protect your work?" Margrit flung the accusation, but turned away before it hit home, recognizing implacability in his eyes. She couldn't disrupt the whirlwind on her own, even with Daisani's gift of healing in her blood. She was too small, too delicate, but there had to be something that wasn't, something she could move.

Her shrill laugh sounded as though it belonged to someone else as she found what she sought, intellect finally catching up to her panicked thoughts.

A handful of seconds later she rode a forklift across the devastated warehouse floor, waving frantically at Janx and bellowing, "Down! Down! Get down!" at the backed-up dragon. Whether he heard her or whether the wind stealing his air had done its job well enough, he slithered down the wall as Margrit crashed the machine into the wall, literally around him. She had enough time to be startled that his sinuous form was slim enough to fit between the lift's teeth. Then the screaming vortex lost its strength, disrupted by the forklift in its midst and unable to lift its weight.

Like rain pattering around her, bruised and angry djinn fell from their howling whirlwind, and gathered around Margrit in a cloud of fury.

There were more than had been gathered upstairs, all men. Most of them wore human clothing, but two were dressed as Malik had been at Daisani's ball: flowing robes in the colors of sky and desert and blood, Middle Eastern in flavor but somehow distinctly not human in style. A touch more wing to the shoulders or a flow to the line of sleeve; it drew the eye and made it slide away again, as if the edges of cloth were woven with wind, not silk or linen.

Tariq wasn't among them. Margrit couldn't lift her gaze to search the warehouse for him, fear holding her in place. Her hands were knotted around the forklift's controls so tightly her fingers cramped. She hadn't thought through what to do *next:* keeping Janx alive had been an endgame, not just one more move on the board.

The need to act further disappeared beneath a peculiarly familiar rasp, and for a distant, bewildered moment it occurred to Margrit that a woman of the twenty-first century shouldn't so clearly recognize the sound of a sword clearing its scabbard. Maybe enough movies had ground the soft scrape of metal against leather into her mind; whatever it was, she had no doubt of it, and jerked her eyes to find a scimitar drawn and held by a pinch-faced man who looked as though he not only knew how to use the blade, but was eager to do so. She hadn't even seen that any of them were carrying weapons, and now stared down a curved length of metal with the vivid awareness that it was probably the last thing she'd ever do.

"I would not, if I were you." Janx's voice cut through the sound of air imploding around him as he shifted back into his human form. The djinn nearest him turned away from Margrit, baring teeth. Janx ignored him with aplomb, addressing the group at large. "Enough of you may defeat me," he went on blithely. "But Margrit Knight belongs to Eliseo Daisani, and a vampire has no natural enemies among the living Old Races. I would not, if I were you."

The irrational, absurd urge to protest at the phrase *belongs to Daisani* bubbled up in Margrit. She did not *belong* to Daisani. She'd thrown Janx's possessive touch off and challenged him on that very front more than once, unexpectedly earning his respect by doing so. The idea was offensive on a fundamental level.

Being dead would be much worse. Margrit bit her tongue and fought off hysterical laughter. She still couldn't uncramp her fingers from the forklift's controls.

"You took Daisani's woman from him only a few months ago, yet you live." The sword-bearing djinn threw the words in Janx's face. Janx smiled, genuine merriment in his jade eyes.

"Yes, but Eliseo likes me." Margrit couldn't tell which of the last two words he put more emphasis on: they were both spoken with precise, delightful clarity that rolled over into unmistakable warning. The sword carrier's jaw tightened, but his sword wavered, and Margrit found herself suddenly able to open her fingers again.

"I hear sirens." Her tongue loosened with her hands and Janx turned a cat-eyed look of slow amusement on her.

"Implying that we all must run and hide all evidence connecting us to the scene of the crime. My dear Margrit Knight, how the mighty have fallen." He offered his hand. "Will you join me? I think we have things to discuss."

Margrit turned her neck stiffly, looking at the ring of angry djinn and the selkies standing beyond them. Tariq was a shadow at the head of the staircase on the other end of the building, watching with an expression unreadable from that distance.

"Yeah." Margrit shivered and put her hand in Janx's, relieved to have an escape from the warehouse's tense, smoky atmosphere. "Yeah, I will. What about Chelsea?"

Surprise filtered through Janx's gaze for a second time. "If Chelsea Huo was here, rest assured she has the resources to care for herself and stay out of trouble. We, however, are growing short on time. If you will come?" Pressure on her fingers increased slightly, as if the dragonlord would lift her. Margrit came to her feet clumsily, stepping out of the forklift with Janx's hand to support her. She still felt thick with fear and the aftermath of disaster, but Janx's strength was steady and calm.

He led her through flame and smoke, and she couldn't tell if the flame bent away from him or if heat made it appear to do so. Illusion or not, gratitude rose in her. She wasn't sure she could have made herself walk through the fire without it. "This way, my dear." Janx gestured at the ruined, burnt-out wall through which he'd made his entrance. Margrit stumbled once, looking back as she made her way over rubble.

The desert-costumed djinn were gone, leaving only ordinarily dressed men in their place, all of them Old Races, smeared and marked with soot. Police burst into the warehouse, their voices adding to the general clamor of destruction. Even through smoke and fire, one of the cops had a familiar shape. Margrit let go a soft-voice curse and scrambled over debris.

But not before Tony Pulcella saw her go.

TEN

JANX'S NEW QUARTERS were posher by far than the ones destroyed when the House of Cards had fallen. Margrit stopped in the doorway of his chambers, fingers resting on a stack of aged stone that had gone unused in the tunnels' construction.

Soft carpets, thick and rich red with gold trim, sprawled over the stonework floors. A chaise lounge covered in leather and velvet languished empty beside a teak-and-redwood table; oversized chairs of the same make were drawn up opposite the table. The table itself sported a chess set, pieces carved of obsidian and ivory. Margrit walked forward to pick up the white knight, fingers curling-around it as she examined the room.

Warm air blew in from somewhere, stirring tapestries that had been hung over the walls. There were three of them, one dominating the back curve of the room and the others to either side. Abstract patterns of jewel-toned reds and greens seemed to leap from them, muted by unexpectedly subtle dune colors and grays. Electric lights covered with gold glass gave the room a comforting air, utterly at odds with the modern steel and hard edges of Janx's former lair. There was no hint of attendants, no suggestion that anyone other than himself used the room. Margrit ignored prickles rising on her skin and worked to keep her tone conversational. "Did you go steal all this furniture from the speakeasy? This room looks—"

"Just like it. The windows were copied from these tapestries." Janx crossed the room stiffly and took up a cane that leaned against the chess table. Stylistically, the cane suited the narrow black lines of the priest-collared shirt and flowing pants he wore, but he made use of it, moving awkwardly where she was accustomed to seeing grace.

Her gaze lingered on the cane's fist-sized head, daring to study it more than Janx. To her eyes it was glass, but Alban had told her it was clear, unblemished corundum, the same stone as sapphires were made of. Jewel-cut, it would catch light and glitter almost as brilliantly as a diamond, but it was only a smooth ball, twisting light no more dramatically than any sphere. It had belonged to Malik, and its presence in Janx's hand spoke volumes about his injury and the fate of the djinn who had been his second.

"Alban said transformation heals." She rushed the words. Janx paused and turned to her, fluidity lacking in the motion.

"Stone heals," he corrected after a moment. "The gargoyles have an advantage in their sleeping hours that we others don't share. They're encased in stillness, and that accelerates their healing. Transformation helps to put things as they were, but you may have noticed I require significant space and no little assurance of discretion to change. So I must go about the day as anyone would, rarely resting as much as I should, and even if I did, a knife to the kidney isn't quickly recovered from."

"You're on your feet. That's pretty remarkable in itself."

"There have to be some advantages to being a fairy tale." Janx's customary lightness was gone from his voice. Margrit's heart ached with the lack of it; when it had gone missing in the past, it had done so because he'd been angry with her, rather than the near despondence she heard now. Trying to push sentiment away, she crossed to the tapestries, the ivory knight still clutched in her hand.

"How old are they?" Margrit stopped short of brushing her fingers against the weavings. They looked soft and delicate, and she was afraid touch would prove them as rough as broken glass.

"Old enough that their makers are no longer among us." Janx joined her, tapestries lending vibrancy to his un-usually sallow skin. "Young enough that we could see which of us would linger past our time, but that has been evident for many centuries." As if challenging Margrit's reservations, he brushed his knuckles over the closest tapestry, then said, with surprising care, "I didn't think to see you again, Margrit Knight."

"Didn't you?" Genuine sorrow deepened the ache in Margrit's chest. "I still owe you a favor. I guess I figured there was no escaping it."

"You ran from our battle at the House of Cards. It was, I think, the one wise thing you've done since meeting Alban Korund. I might have even let you go."

"That's the knife wound talking," Margrit said with as much dry humor as she dared. "You'd get over it if some way to use me came along. What happened? You looked fine when you walked into the warehouse."

Janx's mouth thinned. "I overestimated my strength."

"You must really feel like crap to admit that." Margrit caught her breath to speak again and bit down on it, curiosity drawing her eyebrows together as she studied the dragonlord. He turned to her, expectation written in his gaze. Humor and warmth tangled inside her, pulling a crooked smile to her lips. "Nothing. Nothing important."

Or, if it was, she had no way at the moment of making use of its importance. Janx's admission spoke of more than simple weariness. For him to confess to overestimating himself—for him to allow her to see him at such a low ebb, rather than putting on the carefree performance she so often saw from him—he had to *trust* her, and that was nearly beyond Margrit's scope of comprehension.

"You're a very bad liar, my dear." Janx deliberately lightened his voice, using the endearment to return their relationship to grounds she knew. He reached out to pluck the chess piece from her hand and held it aloft. "Now, don't tell me I've rescued you from a difficult explanation only to have you steal my ivory knight."

"You haven't. At least, I don't think so. You said we had things to discuss." Margrit left the tapestries to drop into one of the lush chairs. Her examination of the chess table lasted barely a handful of seconds before the soft cushions reminded her she'd had no sleep recently. She let her head fall back with a groan and sank deeper into the chair.

"Margrit," Janx said with some dismay. "You're all sooty."

"Oh, crap!" Margrit jolted halfway to her feet, then relaxed again, muttering, "It's dirty now anyway. Sorry."

"I expect it can be cleaned." Janx folded himself down onto the chaise lounge on the other side of the chess table, looking for all the world as though he had been made to do such things. Unlike Margrit, his own clothes weren't stained with black, though their color would help to hide it if they were. "Unexpected company you keep."

"I've been keeping strange company for months. Believe me, if I'd known you were planning on raiding the place, I'd have…tried to talk you out of it." Her honesty, if not her skill with words, got a chuckle out of Janx as she continued, "I was trying to talk them out of similar idiocy."

"Did it work?"

Margrit passed a hand over her forehead and came away wondering if she'd just left herself streakier with soot. "I think it might have if you hadn't made your dramatic entrance. Now?" She shrugged, palms up. "They're angry over Malik, and they know we were there."

"And you, Margrit?" A thump of silence passed before Janx clarified, "How are you over Malik al-Massrī's death?"

"Not sleeping," Margrit replied, more candid than she expected herself to be with the dragonlord. "You?"

"It was my life he was trying to end. Despite our long years of association, I find it difficult to regret that he, and not I, failed to survive the encounter." Janx tilted his head in a semblance of a shrug. "On the other hand, it's a new and particular sin for me, being involved in the death of one of our people. In all our centuries of rivalry, Eliseo and I have never had such dark encounters. I find I do not care for it."

"If you were outside of it, a judge instead of a partici-pant, would it matter to you that it was an accident? That it happened because he *was* trying to kill you?"

Janx leaned forward, replacing the knight on the board and idly pushing a pawn forward, letting the action make him look thoughtful. The corner of Margrit's mouth curled, Janx's theatrics never failing to amuse her. "No," he finally said. "That it was an accident? No, it wouldn't matter. That he was trying to kill me, and paid for that error with his life?" He looked up from the board. "If I were a judge, Margrit, I simply don't think I'd believe it. Not even if three people said it was so. Not even if one of them was a gargoyle, who are not well known for telling lies. You remember Kaimana's response at the quorum."

"That Old Races would simply never turn on each other. Yeah. I can't decide if it'd be nice or alarming to be that naive." Since the game was met, Margrit moved a pawn forward, too, glad of something to do with her hands.

"There are stories that the djinn have different laws amongst themselves. That their rivalries are significant enough to cost lives, once in a while and their numbers high enough to tolerate the losses. Malik limped." Janx nodded at the corundum cane and advanced another pawn.

"I know. I always wondered how you hurt somebody who could dematerialize. I mean." Margrit set her teeth together in a wince. "Assuming they don't carry around toy pistols full of salt water."

"That was ingenious, by the by. It came to a rather horrific end, but I have to applaud your means." Janx actually did, sitting back to bring his hands together in staccato claps as she, cringing again, kept her eyes on the chess game. "They're saved, as I understand it, from materializing inside things by two objects inherently not desiring to share the same space. A safety buffer of sorts. But there's an infinitesimal window in which it's too late, and if you can slip into that window—" He lifted the cane and brandished it like the sword it held. "I wasn't Malik's first rite-of-passage challenge. He lost the other one, too, and his rival destroyed his knee and his place in the tribes."

"So he came to work for you," Margrit said, fairly certain of her guess. Janx nodded and she sighed. "How long ago was that?"

"Longer ago than Vanessa joined Eliseo," he said after a few seconds. "Unlike Vanessa, he wasn't always at my side. He didn't like cold climates. But, yes, it was…some decades longer than Eliseo's association with poor Vanessa Gray. There are moments when I miss his sour face. And then I remember he tried to kill me."

Margrit moved her knight forward and let her focus drift, watching ivory pieces swim with a life of their own. "If they don't accept the offer I made them, they're planning on retaliating for his death. I think that's part of what was happening at the warehouse today. Although you were a bit excessive, Janx."

"Excessive?" His eyebrows rose and he folded his hand above a chess piece, more interested in conversation than playing. "My dear young lady, they took everything from me. I intend to have it back or leave them with nothing. Is that excessive?"

"Listen to yourself. It's Wagnerian. There's a certain panache to it, but it's completely over the top. Do you really want to have a hand in starting a race war?"

"If such a war is to be had, I fear I've already done my part. As have you."

"Maybe, but I'm trying to mitigate it, not compound it. Look, how long can you and Daisani keep this up, anyway? He's been in New York thirty years. People gossip about who his plastic surgeon is. This is the modern world. You can't stay in one place much longer than this. Why not take this one on the chin and move on?"

"And what of you, Margrit, if we do? What of your lust for us—" Janx broke off with a laugh as a horrified noise burst from her throat, then finally moved a chess piece as he went on. "Perhaps not for me personally, to my everlasting chagrin, I assure you, but for what we are? A piece of magic brought into your world. Would you send Alban away, as well? Would you come away with us yourself, Thomas the Rhymer caught in our schemes?"

"Alban hasn't lived the kind of public life you have." The sly glance Janx gave her warned that he knew she hadn't answered the question, but Margrit continued regardless. "You'd still be out there. Even if you weren't charging in and blowing up my life, I'd know you were still out there. Alive, undiscovered, more or less safe."

"Caged by our comparative safety. You, of all people, should understand what it is to resent that."

Margrit moved another chess piece, looking for an opening to let her rook move freely, as if sending it on a run through the park. "Is that why you go to the dark side? Because playing with the underworld feels less constrained? I understand, but me getting caught on one of my adventures wouldn't end up with me on a dissecting table. I'd rather see all of you, even Alban, gone from New York if it meant you'd all stepped back from the edge of a genocidal war. I don't think it matters if you don't manage to wipe each other out. I'm afraid that kind of activity will get you noticed, and you know how dangerous that is."

"Would you come with us?" The air turned heavier with warmth as Janx transferred all his attention to Margrit, making her remember his true form.

She looked away. "I don't know. My whole life is here."

"As are all of ours, and yet you have no compunction against advising us to move on."

"No." Margrit's gaze sharpened as she returned it to the dragonlord. "This epoch in your life is here, not your whole life. I don't have any idea how old you are, but no matter what you do, there's only a limited window you can stay in any one human population if you're in any kind of visible position. You have to change your skin every once in a while. Your whole life isn't here. Just this go-around."

"So you would have us retreat."

"I would have you *live,* dragonlord. Grow stronger. Fight another day." Margrit closed her eyes, muttering, "I really am starting to sound like you," before refocusing on Janx. "Whatever it takes. You must've done it before. Why object now?"

"You're assuming I went gently into that good night in previous years, my dear. Does anything about me suggest that I might have done so?"

Margrit opened her mouth and shut it over an escaping bubble of laughter. "No." Then, seriousness overtaking her, she added, "But when *was* the last time, Janx? This century?" She flicked her fingers, trusting Janx to understand what she meant even if her words weren't literally accurate. "The world's population has doubled in the last hundred years, and I don't even have words to describe the difference in media from even fifty years ago to today. If you let this play out, you're no better than Aus—" Chagrin bit the word off too late.

Interest lit Janx's eyes. "Ausra?"

Margrit sighed. "She was so determined that Alban should pay for Hajnal's death that she couldn't see what her actions were doing. She was willing to expose all of you to the modern world in her quest for vengeance. Your survival as a whole is much more important than any individual grievance. You've got to be able to see that."

"And you will fight passionately to make certain we do, without quite being able to commit yourself completely to our world. Margrit, I do not mean this for a threat, but this is not a line upon which you will forever be permitted to balance. There are no half measures, something Alban has come to be reminded of, of late. In the end, you will choose your own world or ours. Don't," he added to her indrawn breath. "You're about to tell me you have, but you haven't. You believe you've chosen us because you've lied and sacrificed and put our needs above your own, but there's a martyr in that, and it is not a choice. You're still bedazzled, though not as badly as you were before you watched three of us fight and one of us die. There will be a moment, Margrit Knight, when you will make your choice, and that moment will be unmistakable. Don't cheapen it by thinking you've already made it."

Margrit's hands had curled into fists as he spoke, nails cutting into her palms. Color burned her cheeks until her eyes were hot with tears and her breath felt harsh and cold in her throat. "You think the last three months have been a *game* for me? Russell, my *boss,* my boss for the last three years at Legal Aid, is *dead,* Janx. My boyfriend dumped me. I've been nearly killed more than once and today I went to try to stop your people from getting into a war instead of doing my own job. You think I'm kidding around?"

"No," Janx said, unexpectedly sympathetic. "I think you underestimate the point at which you can walk away. You still can, and until that threshold is crossed, you should remember that you have a way out. I didn't mean to anger you or belittle what you've done for us. Or to us," he added more wryly. "But the truth is that if you had chosen our world, you would without hesitation join us if we left this city. Not without regrets, perhaps, but without hesitation. It's the cost of our friendships. It always has been."

Insult still heated her face, but curiosity leapt to throttle it. Margrit bit down on asking about a woman she shouldn't know anything of. Sarah Hopkins, who had been pregnant with Janx's child, or Daisani's, and had turned to Alban to escape the seventeenth-century fire that had burned London. She wondered if Sarah had been unwilling to pay the cost, and had been able to walk away far, far later than Margrit imagined possible.

"Is that what happened to Chelsea Huo?" The words came hard, tight voice putting Chelsea in Sarah Hopkins's place. "Did she choose the Old Races? She's this nice, ordinary woman, but she was able to stand there today and give me legitimacy. Because she chose you?"

Laughter glittered in Janx's eyes, and he unwound himself from the couch, leggy and comfortable in his own skin. "A nice woman," he echoed, clearly delighted by the sentiment. "How charming. I shall have to tell her. Would you call me a nice man, Margrit?"

"You're a bad man, Janx." Margrit deliberately unknotted her hands, shoulders slumping as she recognized that he had no intention of answering her question. *That,* more than anything, seemed to be the legacy of dealing with the Old Races. She could only learn enough to realize how little she knew, and how unlikely it was she would be told more. "You're a bad man, and you know it."

Janx spread his hands, an expansive cheerful gesture. "I know. Evil shouldn't look this good."

A jarring memory seared Margrit's vision, showing her the sneering, angry face of a man she'd once defended. He'd raped three women, murdering one of them, and had watched Margrit with open, domineering scorn. Watched her as if she were a victim, waiting for him; watched her much as Malik al-Massrî had watched her. Angry, threatened and threatening, proprietary, making her an object not of desire, but of subjugation. Janx had treated her that way once, and faced with her ire, had treaded a line of caution with comic exaggeration since. Margrit spoke slowly, words more weighted than she intended: "Evil doesn't."

Something unexpected happened in Janx's green eyes, disconcertment fading into surprised pleasure. He held his pose a moment longer, studying Margrit without guile, then brought his hands together and shifted his weight so he could offer a flourished bow from the waist. "What peculiar honors you do me, Margrit Knight. For your kindness, I'll give you what you haven't asked for—advice."

"Are you going to tell me to walk away?"

"No." Janx gave her a toothy smile, letting it linger so her gaze was drawn to too-long canines. Daisani should have those teeth, she thought for the dozenth time. The vampire should have a mouthful of weaponry, not the dragon. "No, my dear. You're a lawyer. I'm going to tell you how to handle Alban's forthcoming trial."

ELEVEN

MARGRIT'S CELL PHONE trumpeted the *William Tell Overture,* startling her into a flinch and earning a shift of surprise from Janx. Habit drove her to her feet as she searched her purse for the phone, and sent her walking a few feet away, as though doing so would render Janx incapable of hearing her.

"I wouldn't, if I were you. If you're getting reception, you'll probably want to stay exactly where you were." Janx nodded to the chair she'd abandoned and Margrit came back to it, thumbing the phone on.

Her mother's voice, distorted with static, came through. Margrit put a finger against her opposite ear, trying to hear better, then muttered a curse as the connection dropped entirely. "It never rains but it pours. If I don't call her back, she'll think something terrible has happened. Can you show me the way out of here?"

"I can," Janx admitted languidly. "Whether I *will*…"

"Well, your other option is keeping me locked up like Bluebeard's wife."

"Like Beauty, I should think." Janx collected Malik's

cane and pushed to his feet, still more stiffly than she was accustomed to. "Are you certain you have to go now? We were doing so well."

"You've met my mother. The grapevine's probably told her I wasn't at the trial this morning, and she knows the only thing that would keep me away would be dismemberment or death."

Janx gestured at her. "At least you look the part."

Margrit looked at herself again and groaned. "I hope I have time to get home and shower before she sees me."

"I could come along," Janx offered hopefully. "Distract her."

"Absolutely *not*."

"I can be very distracting," he promised.

Despite herself, Margrit laughed. "Yes, you can be, but you may not be. Just tell me how to get out of here before Mom uproots half of Manhattan trying to find me."

"Allow me to escort you, at least. Grace prefers not to have random interlopers wandering her tunnels."

"That's another reason it wouldn't hurt for you to move on. This is her territory." Margrit took the dragonlord's elbow when he offered it, matching her pace to his unusually slow one. He'd made deliberate haste in leaving the warehouse, had moved then with all his customary beauty, and now, she thought, he was paying for that arrogant performance.

"So concerned with territory and belonging. Are you like this in all aspects of your life, or just when it comes to us?"

"I think it's just you." Margrit frowned down the tunnel, trying to recognize features. "The battles I fight aren't usually about territory. They're about money or power or passion. It's just with you that land wars come into the equation. Grace has worked hard to make a safe place for those kids down here. You and what you do are the exact opposite of what she's trying to achieve."

"You could always ask me a favor." Janx's voice was too light, as though the question was a test. "I do believe I still owe you one."

Margrit paused, drawing him to a stop, and studied him. "One," she said slowly. "You owe me the one we agreed on. Then again, I very likely saved your life this morning, Janx. That makes two favors you owe me, and if I've learned nothing else, I've learned that the Old Races count coup. You could've told me how to deal with Alban's trial as a balance to the attack this morning, but you handed that over for free. For my Grace," she echoed softly. "What would you do, dragonlord? What would you do if I asked you to leave Grace's tunnels, to leave New York, in exchange for your life?"

Janx's jade eyes grew paler and cooler as she spoke, and when he replied, it was less with anger than a mark of respect Margrit thought she had only just earned. "I wouldn't have expected you to call in that marker, my dear. I find myself caught between awe and dismay. Do you really believe my position here can be traded away so easily?"

"You wouldn't be dismayed," Margrit said, "if it couldn't. So now I have my answer."

Janx's lips curled, showing teeth. "You've learned too well for my tastes, Margrit Knight. This is your exit." He stopped shortly, making a gesture of fluid chagrin. Margrit put a palm against the ladder he'd brought her to, glancing up, then pulled herself onto the first rungs before looking back.

"I haven't asked."

"No." Janx's expression turned dour. "You haven't asked *yet*."

Margrit's cell phone rang again as she reached street level. It was midafternoon, a deceptive amount of time having passed with Janx in the unchanging light below the streets. She took a breath and held it, then, hoping her voice would sound normal, answered with a cheerful, "Hi, Mom."

"Margrit Elizabeth, what on earth is going on? I've been trying to call you all morning. Are you all right? Why aren't you in court? What were you doing in Harlem this morning?"

Margrit's eyebrows shot up so hard she rubbed her forehead, feeling like she'd sprained something. "Who told you that?"

"Tony called me."

"Tony called you?" Margrit couldn't put enough emphasis on the words and fought off the urge to repeat them with the stress on a different one each time. Anthony Pulcella and Rebecca Knight had suffered a kind of long-running standoff in the years he and Margrit had dated. *Disapproval* went too far, but for Rebecca, Margrit's decision to date a man not of her own ethnic background was as much a political statement as a romantic one. Rebecca's capitulation, only two weeks earlier, had co-incided perfectly with Margrit and Tony's breakup, though in her mother's defense, Rebecca hadn't known that when she'd finally given up the fight. Still, Tony calling Rebecca was well outside Margrit's expectations. "What'd he do that for?"

"He's worried about you, Margrit. So am I. He said

he saw you leaving the site of the dockside fire this morning. Did he?"

Margrit found herself staring sightlessly down the street, humans and vehicles a blur against the backdrop of tall buildings. She heard her own thought distantly: *humans* and vehicles. Not *people,* but humans. Some morning she was going to wake up and not quite recognize herself anymore. Maybe this morning, in fact, though she hadn't been to bed and therefore morning hadn't been properly introduced. The recollection made her yawn and heated her eyes with tears, helping her shake off her stupor. "Mother, what would I be doing at the docks?"

"I don't know, Margrit. What would you be doing not in court today?"

"Trying to stop the mess at the docks," Margrit said, more honest than wise. "Tony was right. I was there. I'm fine, though, so don't worry."

"Don't worry? Margrit, how can I not worry? Your behavior has been erratic since Russell died. I don't want to pressure you, sweetheart, but I think you should talk to someone."

"I talk to people all the time, Mom," Margrit said, a smile starting, and then the expression was choked off in a burst of absurdity bordering on offense. "You mean, a psychiatrist?"

"I was thinking a psychologist. You don't seem to be depressed, but someone to talk to about this sudden decision to change careers and going to work for Eliseo Daisani, of all people, and missing court dates, and this delusion of being able to stop fighting and striking workers at the docks—"

"Mom. Mom! *Mother!* I'm fine, Mom. I really am. Look, I'm working on something bigger than I am, and that's all I can tell you. I know it seems as if I've been acting strangely lately—"

"Seems?"

Margrit blew her cheeks out. "All right, I have been. But I have reasons, and if I ever can, I'll tell you. Okay?" She bared her teeth as she recognized the promise as one she'd given Tony too many times. "I'm sorry I can't tell you now," she added more quietly. "I wish I could. But I'm being as careful as I can be, and everything's going to be all right." She sounded confident and reassuring to her own ears, and hoped that her mother, at least, would believe it.

"Margrit, does this have anything to do…" Rebecca fell silent a long moment, then let go a quiet breath. "Never mind."

"It does." Margrit swallowed, hoping she'd interpreted her mother's unasked question correctly. Rebecca Knight had twice seen—or experienced—Daisani's inhumanly fast ability to move. Unlike Margrit, she seemed reluctant to pursue the *how* behind his talent, even when she owed her life to it. That she and her mother lay on opposite sides of such a narrow divide made Margrit's chest ache with loneliness. "Mom—"

"I see." Rebecca's voice turned to a professional briskness that told Margrit she'd once again lost the moment to pursue a thread of connection between them. "Please be very careful, sweetheart. I'll tell your father I spoke to you today. We both love you."

"I love you, too." Margrit folded her phone closed and directed a frustrated glare at the street, as though somewhere below, Janx would feel its heat. "If I haven't made my choice, I'd like to know what the hell else this is."

"The consequence of living," an auburn-haired woman replied as she brushed past. Margrit blinked and the woman threw a bright smile over her shoulder. "Never could resist a rhetorical question." She disappeared into the crowd, leaving Margrit still blinking after her.

Tony Pulcella was waiting on her doorstep when she got home.

Margrit slowed halfway up the block, unexpected cheer from the woman's comment fading as she saw the detective. There was nothing she could say that would satisfy him. For a moment she looked around for an escape route, but by the time she looked back, he'd seen her and was rising to dust off his pants. Margrit sighed and joined him, itchingly aware she was still grimy from the encounter at the warehouse.

Tony looked exhausted, though he was cleaner than Margrit. For a moment they stood there looking at one another, before Margrit shrugged and tilted her head at the building's front door. "Want to come up?"

He nodded silently and Margrit opened the door, and, out of consideration for his weariness, took the elevator to the fifth floor, neither of them speaking until they'd entered Margrit's apartment. Then Tony said, "You're okay," and, "You know where he is," as though the two comments— not, Margrit noticed, questions—were related.

"I'm fine. You look like hell." Margrit toed her shoes off and padded into the kitchen to open the fridge so she could offer Tony a Coke. He accepted and drained it without speaking, then turned an expectant gaze back onto Margrit, who shrugged and addressed the other half of what he'd said. "I know he's down below the city. I doubt I could find where he's staying. I'm not much help there. Sorry."

"How long've you known?"

"This is the first time I've seen him since you raided the House." Both true and evasive, the same kind of answer she'd been giving Tony since she'd first encountered the Old Races. He'd been more than right to make a final break in their relationship. Margrit released her hair from its bonds and scratched her hands through it.

"So what were you doing there this morning?"

"Cara Delaney was hurt in a fight down there yesterday. She asked me to go reassure her people. I had no idea Janx would be there." That, at least, was true.

"And you left with him because…?"

The corner of Margrit's mouth turned up. "Because I didn't want to sit through the third degree, I guess." She hesitated, then admitted, "Because I figured you'd cover for me."

"So you did see me." Neither surprise nor anger colored Tony's voice, cool professionalism in place instead. Regardless, recrimination stung Margrit as she nodded. "I thought you had. You're right. I did cover for you. Maybe you can tell me why."

Margrit drew breath to answer and Tony held up a palm, stopping her. "Better yet, maybe you can tell me why damned near every security camera we've found dockside is fritzed out and why on the handful that aren't, the images are smeared."

"Smeared?"

"Like in the cameras from the Blue Room."

"Oh." Vivid memory played up as though she watched the videos again. Pixels had stretched and distorted behind Alban, making shadows when nothing was there. Only later had she realized that the camera had picked up some hint of Alban's true shape, and that she had been looking at his obscured wings. Janx would presumably generate such a blur of raw pixels that the man at their center would be rendered completely invisible. Then curiosity straightened her spine. Daisani did regular television interviews, and Kaimana Kaaiai had been filmed, neither of them with the distortion she'd seen in the dance-club camera recordings. She would have to ask the vampire how that was. Maybe something to do with converted mass. Though she'd only seen a baby selkie transform, Deirdre Delaney's size had seemed comparable in both shapes. Perhaps vampires and selkies had less to hide, so to speak.

"You going to share that thought with me?" Tony folded his arms over his chest, brown eyes dark with anticipation of disappointment. Margrit's answer caught in her throat and Tony's expression shuttered further. "You said al-Massrî could disrupt electronics, Grit."

Margrit tilted her head back, swallowed and reversed her gaze. "He could. He had one of those weird electric fields you read about. He fritzed my cell phone out."

"That's not what you said."

"Oh, come on, Tony, I said a lot of crap that night. I was upset." In frustration on both her own behalf and Tony's, she'd laid out the alliances and natures of a group of gathered Old Races amongst whom she and Tony had been the only humans. That every word she'd spoken had been true made no difference in Tony's ability to believe her.

Tony shook his head. "You think fast, Grit, and I know you're a good liar. But you've never made things up."

Margrit eyed him. "Isn't that what lying is?"

Sour humor quirked his mouth. "Technically, yeah, but I'm talking about the kinds of things you said that night. Dragons and vampires. That's not the kind of lying you do."

Alarm rooted Margrit to the floor, making her feel heavy. Tony was right: it wasn't the kind of story she told, but she'd never dreamed he might invest himself in considering that. Pursuing what she'd said in a moment's heat could far too easily cost the detective his life. "So I was telling the truth? Tony, that puts at least one of us up for some new and exciting kind of lunacy charges."

"Does it?" He studied her for long moments, eyebrows drawn down before he sighed, shrugged and looked away. "I guess it does. But there's something wrong when you spouting fairy tales is the only way to make sense of anything, Grit. I want to know what's going on, and you're the only piece I've got access to."

"So why aren't you arresting me for obstruction of justice?"

Tony's mouth soured further. "Because you're about to go work for Eliseo Daisani and there's no point. He'd get you walked out of there and the stupid son of a bitch who walked you in would be busted to traffic duty for the rest of his career."

"I wouldn't let him do that."

"You volunteering to be arrested?"

Margrit ducked her head. "Not when you put it that way."

"So help me out here. Anything. There's got to be something."

"Nothing that's going to help you understand." Margrit pressed her lips together. "But if things haven't settled down at the docks in forty-eight hours, I'll give you everything you need to settle it yourself."

Tension lanced through the detective, bringing him to attention. "Like you handed me Janx's bust?"

Margrit wrinkled her face, unwilling to argue her place in the House of Cards's downfall. "A little like that."

"If you can do that, Grit, why not do it now? Why wait another two days? People are getting killed out there."

"Because I made a promise." Margrit winced again, far too aware of how little weight her promises carried with Tony now. "It's the best I can do."

Tony, jaw knotted, turned toward the door. "Fine. Two days. Just remember, any deaths between now and then are on your head."

TWELVE

A CAREFUL STUDY of the calendar told Margrit it was Thursday afternoon. She'd gotten up at four in the morning on Wednesday and hadn't gotten any meaningful sleep since. She thought regretfully of the calendar her coworkers had made, with only nine or ten hours left on it. Responsibility told her to go in to work, to do what little she could, but instead, burdened more by Tony's curse than fatigue, she showered and crawled into bed.

She woke up what felt like only minutes later when her phone blared. Feeling unexpectedly invigorated, she glanced toward the clock, discovering it was after seven, and answered the phone to hear Daisani, with a hint of Bela Lugosi in his voice, say, "Good evening."

Margrit laughed. "Are you drinking, Mr. Daisani? Never mind. What's up?"

Daisani was silent a moment before saying, "You recall how you accused me of showing off, Margrit?"

"I do." Margrit threw the covers back and climbed out of bed to look for running gear. "You said it wasn't that hard to resist, most of the time."

"It's far more difficult to resist replying to that line with the appropriate response," Daisani informed her dryly. "Yet somehow I can never quite let myself do so. It seems like such a cheap shot."

"It is, but sometimes they're worth it. Did you call to discuss vampire movies with me?"

"I did not. I called to ask if you were aware that Alban's trial is tonight."

Margrit's throat constricted around her previous good nature. She dropped her running tights and sat on the bed, staring across the room. "Tonight? They got here that fast? It's only been one night."

"The nearest and largest enclave that I'm aware of is in Boston, which is hardly an insurmountable flight."

"But somebody would've had to go tell—" Margrit stopped her own protest, seeing its flaws. "Alban carries a cell phone. I suppose they all might."

"And if not, they have more esoteric ways of communicating."

"Not Alban. Iron stops the link to the memories. Someone else would have had to have called, or gone to get them. The sun hasn't set yet. How do you know they're here?"

Daisani's pause was interested. "It breaks the link? Are you certain?"

"Forget I said that. Are you sure they're here?" Margrit switched the phone to speaker and got up to pull regular clothes out of the closet, wiggling into jeans and a light sweater.

"Chelsea Huo just called to inform me, so yes, I am."

Margrit stopped with one sock on. *"Chelsea?"*

"She suggests that we make haste."

"We?" Margrit pulled her other sock on and found a pair of boots as she eyed the phone.

"Alban Korund is an old friend of mine, Margrit. You don't expect me to stand by and let his trial go unattended, do you?"

"Somehow I doubt you're volunteering out of the goodness of your heart. What interests are you protecting?"

Caution clamped her lips together as memories of Sarah Hopkins surfaced again. She and her child were the secret Alban bore for Janx and Daisani, and she would be the reason Daisani was concerned with Alban's trial. Hidden stories could too easily be revealed in the midst of such proceedings.

But Daisani dismissed her suppositions with a soft answer of, "Nothing that has any importance any longer. The best and only reason I have for attending Alban Korund's trial is friendship. Once upon a time, and not so long ago, that might have been different, but you've changed our world so much. Give me some credit, Margrit. Time makes relationships complicated, but we rarely forget where we began. Now," he said after a moment's silence, "shall I come around to pick you up?"

"Please." Margrit's voice scratched, throat too tight for words. It was too easy to forget the Old Races weren't human, at least for brief spaces of time. They moved too fluidly, but the eye became accustomed to that, and in their human forms, that was the only thing to truly mark them apart. The only thing, at least, until age and regret and pain showed in a vampire's gaze, undoing all his humanity with a glance. Daisani had cut her open with honesty more than once, and Margrit doubted she would ever learn to stand against the inhuman depth he could show. "Please," she whispered again. "That would be nice. Thank you."

"Not at all. We should be there in good time for the awakening."

Sunset, once a moment of freedom, was now only an awakening to a new, more dreadful prison than the one that kept him safe in daylight hours. Alban clamped down on a roar, wrapped up the impulse to reach out for comfort and clawed his hands against chains as he panted for breath. Iron did more than bind him: it seemed to weight him, making air harder to draw in, as if his lungs were full of cold metal. It denied him the simple ability to touch another gargoyle mind with his own, and for all that he'd given up that intimacy centuries earlier, being *unable* was a far worse fate than being unwilling.

Not that there was anyone beyond Biali for him to contact, and Alban had been barely more than a child when he and Biali had last been friends. Head lowered, hair falling in white waves around his cheeks, Alban dug taloned toes into stone and willed himself to stop trying to transform; to stop trying to escape thrums of pain. It was unnatural for a gargoyle to resist so much. Stone endured. Elements could leave their mark, but throughout time stone sat and waited, embodiment of patience.

A laugh he barely recognized as his own grated Alban's throat. In the brief span of time since Margrit Knight had come into his life, she'd infected him with human impatience, a desire to see things done, and done now. His sympathy for that plight spiked. Once freed of restraints and set on his own lonely path, he would have to try a little harder to live his life at her speed.

At least he knew she would still have him. The frustration that had built in her at his adamant stance against speaking for himself pinched him as thoroughly as the chains did. She'd forgiven him even through the midst of her irritation, proving yet again that humans adapted quickly, even to the impossible. The weight of regret bowed his shoulders, and for a few seconds he ceased struggling against his chains, consumed by worry for mistakes made.

The door opened, bringing Grace in on a breath of cooler air. "Better today, love? You're not fighting so hard."

"Perhaps I've nothing to fight for." Alban lifted his gaze but remained in his crouch, his eyes at the level of her ribs as she paced the room. "You're agitated."

"I am." She came to a stop in front of him, then crouched, as well, making herself diminutive in comparison. "Grace might be able to get you free of those chains, Korund. But it'll hurt like hell if it works." Her eyebrows shot up. "It'll hurt like hell if it doesn't."

"You think Biali won't free me when the tribunal meets?"

"I think he wants to see you enter in chains, already condemned. He's brutal, not stupid. First impressions count. He'll want them to see you as a prisoner."

"I am a prisoner, and rightfully condemned."

Grace sighed in exasperation. "You're easy on the eyes, but I don't envy Margrit in dealing with you. Not all of your people are martyrs. Why are you?"

"Believing in our traditions doesn't make me a martyr." Alban tried without success to keep offense from his voice.

Grace, pacing again, spat a sound of disbelief. "You tell me, then. Are you so eager to walk in chains that I won't try, or will we see what I can do?"

"My damaged pride would like to see Biali's face when he discovers his trap didn't work," Alban muttered. "But if you can do this, why did you wait until now to offer?"

"Because Grace has secrets to keep, too." The blond woman's answer was hardly louder than his own. "You'll close your eyes, gargoyle, and keep them closed. It'll hurt."

"Closing my eyes will hurt?" Alban asked lightly, then glanced over his shoulder at Grace, whose lovely features were drawn tight with anticipation. He murmured, "Forgive me," then settled back into place. "They are closed."

"Try to not lash out, then, love, and we'll see what Grace can do." Grace put her hands on his shoulders as if in warning. Alban grunted, tension rising even as he tried to stop it, but he nodded agreement.

Where Grace touched him turned to ice, burning cold that sank through him like a stone in water. It drew a gasp: gargoyles were not especially susceptible to temperature. To feel such chill with no warning or transition was as shocking as the cold itself. Grace, sharply, said, "Hold that," and Alban inhaled again, breath catching in his lungs and holding there.

Cold flowed through him, worse than ice water in his veins; that, at least, would follow the pulse and beat of blood. This frozen touch sank in through muscle, through blood and bone, moving against nature and spreading as it moved. It clawed at his throat, digging into the iron that had become a part of him, and the iron turned to links of frigid crystal.

Stone crumbled under Alban's feet, the floor tearing beneath his talons. His eyes had opened against Grace's orders, but he saw nothing but gray in front of him; gray and tear-blurred dancing images of his own forearms, muscle cording and shuddering white with stone.

Pain did not begin to describe it. Cold transcended agony and left the middling discomfort of being bound by iron far behind. It tore down stone walls, and with their tumbling came a lifetime of emotion that he had carefully left behind.

He did not, of course, remember the first time he saw Hajnal, for she was his elder, and had always been a part of their mountain-born tribe. Small, for a gargoyle, and very dark for one of their kind. Her family name was Dunstał, black stone, and they shared an affinity for glassy obsidian and other black rock spat from the heart of the world. Their physicality reflected that, amber skin tones and black hair, making them stand out against a people whose coloring tended toward the pale. She had always been there, petite and lovely amongst her ala-baster kin.

And Biali had always been nearby, a broad hulk of a gargoyle who rarely smiled, but always danced at Hajnal's whim. Alban had become the younger brother to their duo, chasing after, laughing, learning: being a child, loved and safe in the tall, gray mountains. A score of years had gone by, until one day he was no longer a child, and his heart leapt to see Hajnal winging above their mountain retreat. Until he'd joined her in the sky and found more than friendship beneath diamond-cut stars.

The span of a human life passed in a blur, memories clouded with time. Alban grew older and broader and wiser, losing himself in his people's histories, discover-ing the world beyond their mountains through memories shared by others. He became a warrior, trained by memory and by skirmishes too focused to be playful, but never intended to be made real. Even now, under a song of pain, his muscles flexed with the movements he'd learned, battle built into his body. But there was little enough to fight over, and he had more important things to think of, like the dark-haired beauty at his side.

He had not yet seen a century when it became clear that humanity, all unknowing, would hound his people into hiding and desperation. Even high in the mountains, mortals encroached on their every stronghold, and there were bitter arguments on how to survive them. Some counseled war, and Alban found himself on the opposite side, standing and speaking of tradition and the need to keep the histories safe. He did not doubt his prowess in battle, and, looking from face to face, he saw that no one else did, either.

No one, save one.

Alban, caught in a whirlwind of icy anguish, whispered, "No," with what little breath he had left, and shuddered beneath the weight of unrelenting memory.

Biali should have won. Should have, with his age, his experience; with what he perceived as having to lose. But he had lost Hajnal long since, and Alban fought for her, and the future of his people, and when his blow shattered Biali's face, Alban fell back and refused to fight anymore. Not for fear of exile, though Biali's death would set Alban on that path, but because they were so few, and forgiveness, surely, could come with time.

It was not exile, then, that drove him from his mountain home, but a hope of understanding humanity; of finding a way for his people to live amongst them in safety. Hajnal joined him and they left the mountains, left the valleys, left the landmass humans called Europe, and on the continent's western archipelago they found friends, both mortal and not, whose secrets would change Alban's life forever.

Arguments, fresh and sharp, rose up through memory: Hajnal's distress at Alban's choice to step outside the gargoyle collective in order to protect a child born out of species. She knew, of course; had known Sarah Hopkins, as she had known the fiery-haired dragonlord and the smooth, dark vampire. But it was Alban who had linked to their minds, Alban who had become so intimate with them, and Alban whose memories would condemn them if they were exposed to the depths of history. Hajnal's, riding closer to the surface, carried far less weight, and could be kept from the gargoyle memories with a modicum of effort. She didn't have to—didn't choose to—exile herself from their people in the way he had. But as long as she remained with him, he wasn't *alone*.

Hajnal's death ricocheted through that, tearing chunks of Alban's heart away and leaving emptiness in their place. Biali, as deeply wounded by it, had never, would never, forgive the lost battle that had paired Alban and Hajnal for life. That had, in his mind, set Hajnal on the road that led to her death.

Exquisite, the memory of that death. It was made of icy razors, cutting apart Alban's every heartbeat as he roared her name helplessly. As she told him to leave her, and, most terribly of all, as he did, and in doing so, condemned her.

Generation after generation of humans passed while he stood apart, the scant handful he dared watch over always dying violently, until Margrit.

The bright memory of her presence in his life seared through him, hotter than even the ice. Something cracked within him, vast shattering like stone too long under duress. A terrible shout broke free, the clap of stone breaking apart, and ice released him.

Alban collapsed forward, trembling with exhaustion and the weight of too many memories. Every part of his body ached, as though he'd been splintered and put back together again by some rough stonemason with Pygmalion dreams. Stone did not weep easily; not often; not at all; and he could reach no further than a wish for that release. Not sobs; that was beyond him, but the weary slow slide of tears down granite features would be a relief, if only he could find his way there.

Instead he pushed up to hands and knees, then shoved back into a crouch, one hand planted against the floor to balance the empty shell his body felt like it had become. That was all: he could do nothing more. To have done that much seemed a triumph. His chin rested against his chest, eyes too heavy to open. Rest would come with dawn, no sooner. Iron bound him to his waking form, forbidding him the release of silent stone. He held on to that thought, concentrating on it beyond fatigue that came from his very bones.

Grace moved from behind him, soft brush of leather and silent breath of air. "Korund."

"Leave me." It took effort to form the words. Too much effort to open his eyes and meet her gaze. "I only wish for solitude, Grace. I have nothing left to spend."

"Alban." She moved again, her scent coming closer, leather creaking with action. "Open your eyes, gargoyle. Let's have a look at you now."

Weary beyond words, Alban forced heavy lids to part, and stared without comprehension at the long links of iron chain in Grace's hands.

"D⊕N'+ ASK," GRACE murmured, long before Alban had the presence of mind to do so. Only when she spoke did he lift a hand to his neck, mind still empty of understanding.

No thickness of chain distorted the flesh there. Aches faded from his body, no more distant song of iron knotted in stone. Alban shifted to his human form, muscles clenched in anticipation of pain forbidding the transformation, and instead Grace squinted at the soft implosion of air as his mass changed. She looked drawn and haggard, fine lines he'd never noticed before standing out around her eyes and mouth. "You freed me."

"That was the plan, wasn't it?" Grace stood, all languid poise, and Alban came to his feet to catch her elbow as she swayed. She said, "Thanks" without a hint of grudgery, while Alban gazed down at her, trying to remember if he'd ever heard that word pass her lips before. She smiled faintly and made as if to shake him off, though she didn't protest when he maintained his careful grip on her arm. "I wouldn't want to do that every day."

"Grace, what did you—"

"I said don't ask, didn't I?" The vigilante woman pulled away, more awkward than he'd ever seen her. "We all have our secrets, Korund. Let me keep mine."

Alban let his hand fall. Grace stopped on the far side of the room, arms folded beneath her breasts as she turned back with challenge in her gaze. "Margrit asked what you were," he said softly. "The first time we met, under my Trinity chambers. I said you were human. I wasn't wrong." The last words formed a question, though the inflection supported Alban's confidence in Grace's answer.

She shook her head, one sharp motion, and after a moment, Alban nodded. It took longer to quell curiosity and bow to her wishes rather than ask more questions. Margrit would be proud of him for at least wondering. The thought brought a brief smile to the fore as he spoke. "Very well. I'll only thank you, then, not press you." He folded a hand at the back of his neck, massaging muscle that still held strain from captivity. "But perhaps I'm coming to learn that some burdens are easier borne when shared."

"Ah, and don't I know it. But you're not the one for Grace to make her confessions to, gargoyle. Someday, maybe, you'll hear it all."

"Until then I am in your debt."

Grace tweaked a smile that did away with some of the fatigue written on her face. "Now that's a thing I like the sound of, Alban Korund. Pity there'll be no collecting that debt in the ways that would be most fun."

"You are incorrigible, Grace."

"A girl's got to have her fun somehow." Grace flashed a brighter smile, clearly recovering from whatever she'd done to free him, and just as clearly relieved Alban had agreed not to pursue it. He thought she would have to find some kind of answer to offer the tribunal, as a woman with the ability to break a captive gargoyle free would be of interest to all of them, but he, at least, could respect her wishes.

"Are you ready?"

"No." Alban exhaled, then shook off his human form for the gargoyle. "No, not at all, but it seems I have very little choice. So be it. Take me to my leaders."

Grace was still chortling over that as she led him into the trial chamber, the same room he and Margrit had been brought to a few months earlier when Grace had first apprehended them in her tunnels. Now, though, there were no human children littered about, but, rather, more denizens of the Old Races than Alban had seen in one place in centuries, save the selkie show of strength a few weeks earlier.

Six gargoyles presided, none of them friends. Amongst them, dividing them, sat Chelsea Huo, her apple-wizened face calm and her nut-brown eyes dark with sorrow.

Janx and Daisani sat together, an unusual show of camaraderie for two ancient rivals. The gesture filled Alban with pleased bemusement; he had hardly expected to see either of them, much less presenting a front. Both inclined their heads in acknowledgment as Alban entered; it was more than the tribunal itself had done.

Opposite them, on the other end of the gargoyle arc, stood a scattered handful of djinn and selkies. Alban knew none of them, save one: the amber-eyed male who had recently held Rebecca Knight's heart in his hand, and who had only been stopped from doing murder by a vampire's blood. That he was there; that anyone beyond the gargoyle tribunal was there, sent a warning through Alban. There was more at stake than just his exile.

Grace was the only human in the room. Regret seized Alban's heart and held it a long beat, then slipped away in a moment of clarity. It was better, perhaps, for Margrit to not attend. She would only be frustrated with his course of action, and he had no real wish for her to see him condemned. That he stood so bore less shame than watching her as his people made it moot.

A shift signaled the last arrival's entrance. Alban followed a dozen people's attention as it turned to the other door in the room, knowing who he would see. He stood, in part to lord his height over Biali, and in part to make certain the other gargoyle saw Alban was free of chains.

The scarred gargoyle faltered in his stride as he entered, curled lip losing some of its sneer as he took in Alban's unbound form. Alban permitted himself a faint smile that darkened Biali's countenance again, and he stalked across the room to take up a position opposite Alban. For a few seconds the room was still, each being present sizing up the others and assessing the power balance. Then one of the gargoyles shifted, drawing attention to himself, and spoke in a voice like flowing lava, hot and deep.

"Who calls this tribunal?"

"I do." Grace stood, all human cockiness and casual challenge. "I'm called Grace O'Malley, and it's me who's brought you here to decide Alban Korund's fate, and Biali Kameh's, too. These are my tunnels, gargoyle. I'd ask you to name yourself, so me and mine might welcome you."

"I am Eldred of the clan Casmir, and as eldest of the gargoyles present, accept your call and your welcome." Eldred bowed his head in polite admission while Alban studied him, interest piqued well outside the matter of his own trial. He had harvested the gargoyle memories for the histories of the selkies' disappearance, and it had been this resplendently voiced gargoyle who was the last to speak with those people before they went into the sea. The memory Alban had investigated had been from Eldred's point of view, and Eldred himself unseen in it. Still, Alban had gathered a sense of the gargoyle, and he seemed aged with sorrow, tempered with more compassion than he had been centuries earlier when he'd bid a friend goodbye.

"Who brings complaint against Alban of the clan Korund, called the Breach?" Eldred went on without heed to Alban's consideration, and Biali stepped forward, radiating smug anger.

"I do. Biali of the clan Kameh, and my complaint is the death of one of our own."

Though they had to know the charges being brought against him, the gargoyles hardened, interest draining from their gazes and leaving stony outrage behind. "You wouldn't have known her," Biali growled. "She was Hajnal's daughter, called Ausra, and grew up outside of our enclaves. She died at Korund's hands, for attacking a human. I have it from his memories, and offer them to the histories as proof."

Eldred turned to Alban. "What say you to the charges?"

"They're true."

Astonishment rippled through the watchers, gargoyle or not, so palpably that unexpected humor burst within

Alban's breast. He had never considered speaking anything but the truth; it seemed others had never imagined he might, or that such a crime could be committed. Janx's mouth tightened, less with surprise than caution, and sympathy burned Alban's humor to a cinder. Alban's condemnation for Ausra's death could too easily lead to an inquiry of Malik's, and the guilt there was spread wide. Eldred lifted a hand, silencing the gathered Old Races, and considered Alban. "Have you nothing more to say?".

Alban turned his palms up. "I believe madness held Ausra in its grip, and that all our people were endangered by her, but that wasn't what drove me to act. She'd murdered four human women in a matter of days and a score of others over fifteen decades. She had another human life in her hands, and I chose the human woman over her. I would do so again," he added more softly, then raised his voice again to say, "but we've never, as a people, considered motive, only results. I am guilty of the crime as accused, and moreover, will not stand the trials."

Fresh shock rocked the meeting room, disbelief erupting from the gargoyles and quiet disapproval marking Chelsea Huo's expression. Daisani danced fingertips against his lips as if hiding a smile, and Janx, beside him, did smile and gave Alban a slow nod of appreciation when he glanced that way.

Biali's fury roared above the others, cry of a man denied his vengeance. Eldred, too dignified to shout, stood and waited on his presence to calm the chattering group. "Unusual, but not unprecedented," he murmured. "I must then ask if there is another who will stand in your place as your second."

Alban drew breath to deny it, and then finally, finally, finally, came Margrit, her voice clear and steady over the tribunal's murmur and Biali's open scorn. Aghast, Alban turned from the tribunal to look toward the doorway she was framed by.

Grace had to have helped her with the clothes. He'd never seen Margrit dressed in leather before, but her easy, confident stance made her a creature of desire and caution all at once. All that was feminine had been left behind, leaving only the female, deadly in appearance indeed.

Her thick hair was tamed and knotted into a twist at the back of her head, showing off the strong lines of her face. The jacket she wore was fitted but not constricting, leather old enough to move easily, heavy enough to protect. It was zipped now, and a pattern of silver studs splashed over the arms and chest, marking it as belonging to Mariah, Alban's favorite among Grace's teens. Alban was torn between gratitude that the girl's clothes fit Margrit, and dismay that she had cause to don what were all too clearly fighting leathers. She wore pants of the same well-fitted, heavy material, and boots sturdy enough to add an inch or more to her height without in any way being heels. She was dangerous and beautiful, and broke away from the framing doorway to stalk before the tribunal, and repeat the words that had shot dread through Alban's heart.

"I will."

FOUR+EEN

⊕NE GARG⊕YLE AM⊕NGS+ the jury was on his feet, an elegant creature whose stony gray hair and craggy features made him seem older, to Margrit's eyes, than his brethren. He watched Margrit with quiet patience, waiting for the room to fall silent again. She nodded to him and his eyes creased just slightly, as if he was amused or pleased by her acknowledgment.

None of the other gargoyles paid her particular heed, though she was obviously the center of their discussion. There were five of them, ranging in size from two women with Valkyrie-broad shoulders to a lanky blond whose form was so different from the gargoyles Margrit knew he might have been of another race. The one on his feet was heavyset, not Biali's aging prizefighter in form, but bulky in a way that suggested muscle and strength rather than fat running out of hand.

None of them were as pure a pale as Alban, though none of them had Hajnal's loamy tint, either. Margrit fought the urge to look toward Alban, bringing up his alabaster skin tone in her mind instead, and comparing it to the varied shades of light stone the tribunal shared. Of the gargoyles she'd seen and met, only Biali's stark, unmarred white came close to Alban's alabaster, and now that Margrit had others to liken them to, she could tell that Alban's color was delicate, almost translucent, where Biali's was hard and relentless.

One of the gargoyles leaned toward Chelsea Huo to speak to her, and even in outrage, moved with the fluidity that marked members of the Old Races. The tiny bookseller looked at ease amongst the gargoyles, easily as comfortable as she'd been standing with selkies and djinn that morning. Only that morning, Margrit realized with astonishment. The day, even with a nap, had gone on forever.

Daisani was scowling at Janx, who had kicked back and folded his hands behind his head, eminently pleased with himself. Even the handful of selkies and djinn talked animatedly, accusing gestures thrown Margrit's way. She felt unexpectedly at home: she'd spent years as an advocate of lost causes. Law school hadn't prepared her to stand a medieval trial as the defendant, but this was a courtroom like any other.

"Margrit, you cannot do this." Alban's voice, low with strain, came from a few feet behind her. Margrit glanced at the gathering, and, confident they'd continue their arguments for a few minutes longer, turned to face Alban with a rueful smile.

"Actually, I can. Your traditions allow for a second. Very human of you." Her smile grew, cockiness transcending concern. "Or maybe very gargoyle of us. I wonder. Either way, Janx told me about the loophole, so here I am." Margrit bit her lip, wanting to step closer but afraid moving farther would attract the tribunal's attention. Uncomfortably aware there might not be a chance afterward, she was reluctant to break up their brief chance to speak before the trial.

"Had I known you would take this sort of rash action—"

"You would've tried talking me out of it, but you wouldn't have changed your stance, because you believe you're right just as much as I believe I am. I've got to give you credit for consistency, anyway." Margrit moved closer after all, offering Alban her hand. He took it as though she were fragile, rubbing his thumb against her palm. She shivered at the spill of warmth and relaxation, a core of heat lighting at the touch. Folding her hand around his, she lifted it and kissed his knuckles, leaving her mouth against his skin as she spoke again. "You drive me crazy, you know that? Sticking with your traditions, upholding your laws, believing in them regardless of personal cost, or, yeah, maybe because of personal cost. I'm going to have to learn to live with that, aren't I?"

Alban lowered his head toward hers, making a private space between them. His scent wasn't as clean as she was accustomed to, with a hint of aged dust and stone, but its familiarity, like the courtroom setting, was comforting. "I'm afraid so."

Margrit nodded, then tipped her chin up to smile at her serious-gazed gargoyle. "I can do that. But I can't stop fighting for what I think is right just because we disagree." She kissed his knuckles again and stepped back, eyebrows arched in mild challenge. "So I'm going to do my damnedest to clear your name, whether you like it or not. You can figure out your retribution later."

"Margrit, my retribution isn't what you should be concerned about. You cannot fight Biali. He'll kill you."

"I don't think so." Margrit spoke with more assurance than she felt, hoping Alban couldn't read the tremor that ran through her. "He said once he preferred fair fights, not ambushing women in the dark."

"You put too much faith in our honor. First Janx, now Biali. It's—" Alban broke off, exasperated rue flattening his mouth before he sighed. "It's a very bad idea."

"You keep telling me that." Margrit lit a smile, bright for the moment before it turned to uncertainty. "It's a bad idea, but it's the best one I've got, and if I put too much faith in the Old Races' honor, it's because I met the most honorable of you first. You're a hard act to follow, Alban Korund."

The noise around them settled, leaving Margrit's last words hanging in the air much too loudly. She pressed her eyes closed as blood rushed to her cheeks, then turned to face the assembly with a grimace. Janx, still kicked back, grinned openly, and her embarrassment faded beneath the desire to give in to a giggle. Reminding herself she stood in a court of law, she dragged her expression back under control and lifted her chin to meet the tribunal's gazes.

"The gargoyle trials have been explained to me," she said before anyone else spoke. "A three-part test of what I understand to be essentially strength, sense and sentiment, to be undertaken to prove innocence in the face of evidence. I'm aware of the risks and willing to undergo the trial on Alban of the clan Korund's behalf. I also gather," she added a bit more dryly as Alban caught his breath to protest, "that having forfeited his willingness to participate himself, the defendant isn't permitted to object to someone else partaking for him."

"*I* can." Biali's voice dropped to a dangerous rumble, like the distant precursor to a rock slide. "My fight's not with the lawyer. I want Korund."

"You'll have me. Margrit, this—"

"You have refused the trial." Eldred overrode Alban's protest implacably. "The decision is no longer yours."

"It is the wrong decision!" Echoes thundered around the concrete and stone room. Margrit flinched, hands knotting at her sides. She was unaccustomed to hearing Alban lift his voice in anger, and it was easy to forget that breadth of chest could lend his words so much power.

"That," Eldred said, "is something you might have considered earlier. You have forfeited your place, and you will remain silent or be removed from the grounds until the trial is over."

Alban growled low in his throat, lifting hairs on Margrit's arms, but he said nothing else. Biali smirked, clearly pleased enough to see Alban put in his place that he clearly forgot for a moment that he, too, had been thwarted. That realization wiped pleasure from his face a few seconds later, and his gaze went hard and calculating as he turned it to Margrit.

Trying to regulate her heartbeat was useless. It leapt out of her control, making a ball of sickness in her throat and flushing her body with heat. Challenging Biali was a gamble. Not a bluff, but a tactic counting on honor that, despite her arguments to Alban, Margrit wasn't certain Biali possessed. He had lost two women he loved to Alban. Margrit's life might seem a fair exchange, a way for him to make Alban suffer the way he had.

His nostrils flared and his mouth thinned with dislike. "You're afraid, lawyer. I can smell it."

"Of course I'm afraid. I'm reckless, not stupid." Admitting it aloud lent Margrit some strength. She pulled her shoulders back, heart rate calming as she drew a deep breath. Then humor and honesty swept her, and she added, "Maybe a little stupid."

A rush of quiet laughter ran around the room, bypassing the gargoyles but touching the others. Frustration contorted Biali's scarred face and he made a throwaway gesture. "Fighting her proves nothing. A human stands no chance against me."

Margrit, hands still knotted at her sides, said, "Not that I'm especially looking forward to being pulverized, but isn't the point of this to see who dominates in the trial? The one who wins two out of three is forgiven in the eyes of God, right? Wouldn't clobbering me put you one step ahead of the game?"

Disgust so profound it bordered on pity wrinkled Biali's face. "It would prove nothing." He turned to the tribunal, a note of slyness coming into his voice. "If a second can stand in Korund's place, then I can request a second for mine."

Eldred and Chelsea exchanged glances, the latter's feather-fine eyebrows rising as she indicated the decision was Eldred's. He nodded, attention coming back to Biali, and the scarred gargoyle curled his lip in pleasure. "Then for the trial of strength I choose a second. I choose *her*."

He pointed a taloned finger at Grace O'Malley.

Grace actually looked over her shoulder before her incredulous laughter broke over an outcry of surprise from the tribunal and audience. "Me, love? Is it your mind you've lost?"

"You're human," Biali growled.

"Sure and I am, but that doesn't mean—"

"Nobody else represents a fair fight." Margrit spoke so quietly she doubted she'd be heard. Her own laughter fluttered at the back of her throat, a thing of disbelief and relief. "You're the only one I'm anything like equal to in a battle of strength. If you don't accept—"

"What if I don't?" Grace spun on a booted heel, facing the tribunal. "What if I say no? Does Scarface there win by default, or do you go through the ranks until you find someone willing to fight?"

"It's unprecedented," Eldred said after a moment. "We would have to debate."

"There's no one else, Grace." Margrit's own voice sounded far away to her. "Any of the rest of them would pulverize me. I'd kind of like to come out of this alive."

Grace turned around, mouth drawn down. "And what makes you think I wouldn't clean the floor with you myself?"

Margrit's eyebrows rose and the fluting laughter at the back of her throat escaped, as if lifting her eyebrows released a valve. "Grace, I can probably outrun you. I seriously doubt I can outfight you. You're bigger than me, you've got better reach and you probably know more about self-defense than I do. But even your best shot's not going to take my head off, which *his* would." She nodded toward Biali, who gave back an ugly smile. "Do me a favor here and say yes, okay?"

"And what does Grace get out of it, love?"

"Some bruises and a sense of righteousness?" Margrit asked hopefully, then winced at the flat look Grace gave her. "Not having to explain to my ex-boyfriend the police detective why my dead body's in your tunnels? No," she said before Grace could object, "I don't really think you're dumb enough to leave me here if I got killed. Look, I'm trying, okay? I'd owe you one," she finished more quietly. "I'd owe you a lot."

Grace's gaze slid toward Janx, then back to Margrit. "You're piling up the debts fast, Knight."

Margrit held her breath a long moment, then let it go explosively. "Keeps life exciting. Was that a yes?"

Grace pressed her lips into a thin line, turning her attention to the tribunal. "Just what kind of fight is this? Can't be to the death, not with the way your laws work. You just put us in the ring and we go until the bell?"

"To defeat," Eldred agreed. "It is…" He looked between the women, explanation lingering on the air as he seemed to search for words. "It is unusual," he finally said. "Unusual to have two combatants whose hearts may not be in the matter."

Margrit muttered, "Mine is," and glanced toward Alban, who rolled his jaw but kept silent. Grace shot both of them a sharp look before eyeing the tribunal again.

"The lawyer's got something to fight for, which means I do, for I don't like to take a beating when I can avoid it. But *you*," she said to Margrit, "you need to think about reforming *these* laws, if you're going to be taking on fights that aren't your own."

"I'll pencil it in." Margrit wet her lips and squared her shoulders again, then folded her hands behind her back to keep them from wandering through the air. "How do we, uh, start?" She'd envisioned battling a gargoyle, somehow; someone, at least, who had sufficient physical strength as to genuinely frighten her, and had counted on adrenaline pushing her past thought into a struggle for survival. Instead she felt a blooming sense of the absurd, as if she was about to take part in an extravagant pantomime.

Eldred gestured toward Grace with such solemnity Margrit suspected he was trying not to laugh at them. "Meet in good faith, clasp hands, and then begin as you will. We will determine the victor and end the match when it is appropriate."

Grace stalked over to her, tall and leggy and alarming as she offered a hand. Margrit hesitated, still feeling foolish. "What about that gun you used to carry?"

"Do you really think I'll be shooting you?" Grace reached for the small of her back, though, and tossed the weapon away. It clattered against the floor, spinning to a stop at the tribunal's feet. Margrit watched it go, then swallowed hard and reached for Grace's hand, surprised when the other woman caught her in a hard warrior's grip, forearm to forearm. "Well met," she said, more formality in her tone than Margrit had ever heard before. She didn't reply, and Grace's eyebrows shot up in expectation, making Margrit jolt with realization.

"Oh. Right. Right. Um, well met. Uh—"

Grace hit her in the face.

MARGRI+'S HEAR+FEL+ BELL⊕W of pain and outrage was cut short by another blow, this one to her
midriff. Grace released her arm and Margrit doubled,
choking. It was only toppling to the side that saved her
from a knee in the face. She hit the floor with as breath-
taking a thud as the fist to her diaphragm had been. For
a bleary instant she could only think how lucky she was
that Biali hadn't set a gargoyle on her, and then Grace's
foot caught her in the ribs and lifted her a few inches up
and back. Margrit heard a thin wheeze and realized it
was from her own throat. She hadn't realized a kick
could actually move someone that way; she'd thought
that was a dramatization of movies, if she'd thought
about it at all.

Oxygen flooded into her starved cells before Grace
landed another kick. Margrit rolled across the floor,
trying to escape the long-legged, heavily booted vigilante. Everything tasted of copper, and when she wiped
a hand below her aching nose, it came away smeared with
blood. It seemed incongruous to the point of impos-

sibility: she had never been in a fistfight, even as a child. To encounter her first one now was absurd.

Grace moved vampire-fast to Margrit's bewildered senses. Instinct curled her in a ball, protecting her head and torso. The fight was over. Tony had always denigrated on-screen fracases, pointing out to Margrit the moment at which the fight would really have ended, usually only one or two blows into the sequence. She'd always elbowed him in return, telling him it was fiction and to be quiet and enjoy the choreography. Nothing about an extended battle seemed enjoyable now. A kick smashed into her forearm, pain a blinding reminder that that arm had been recently broken.

She felt it like a switch flipping. Determination colder than anger or fear rose up in a ruthless refusal to be as helpless now as she'd been against Ausra. Margrit coiled tighter, rolling onto her knees with her hands still knotted protectively over her head. She was suddenly aware of how that opened her ribs up for attack, and Grace obliged, kicking her again. Margrit twisted away, skittering far enough to the side that the kick had less impact than its predecessors had, and putting Grace's booted feet almost directly in front of Margrit.

She shot out of her ball headfirst, regretting that she didn't have time or leverage to get her legs fully under her and use their strength to drive herself upward.

The top of her head crunched into Grace's groin. For the first time since the fight had begun Margrit heard something outside her own labored breathing: a gasp of horror and surprise and approval rushing around the audience. Grace herself, always peaches and cream, whitened further and staggered back a few steps as Margrit scrambled to her feet.

She knew *nothing* about fighting. Rather than dwell on that, she let momentum carry her forward, all her energy redirected as she charged Grace and caught the taller woman in the rib cage with her shoulder. The tribunal scattered as Margrit crashed toward them, slamming Grace into the wall that had seconds before been at the tribunal's back. Grace made a small pathetic sound, then shoved her hands between bodies and forced Margrit away, using the wall to brace herself against.

Some quick instinct warned Margrit of what Grace intended. She ducked her head, and when Grace's forehead smashed down, it wasn't against Margrit's fragile nose, but the solid bone of her cranium. White light exploded through her vision, sparked with red and blue, tiny bits of dancing color.

When she could see again, streams of brightness still shooting through her sight in time with heartbeat-paced throbs of pain, she'd released Grace and had staggered back a few feet. Grace still sagged against the wall, no more functional in the aftermath of a failed head butt than Margrit was. For a moment rationality took over and Margrit wondered what in hell she was doing, but then Grace's expression cleared, turning feral with primitive delight, and she charged Margrit again.

They hit the floor together, rolling and kicking, elbows and fists flying everywhere. Margrit threw a punch she was sure would land and it skittered by Grace's cheek, so close it seemed to have gone through the vigilante without touching her. Outrage at her miscalculation shot the fight beyond any clarity of thought and into a mindless search for vengeance: a chance to get back at someone, *anyone,* for the chaos Margrit's life had become. Yes, she had welcomed it in many aspects, but Cole's fear and anger rose up, reminding her of what was unwelcome. The attack on her mother drove her onward, taking what comfort she could in something as useless and ill directed as a physical battle. Russell's death gave her reasons of her own to hit, and hit, and hit again. There were no answers to be found in bloodying Grace's nose or taking a fist so hard she felt her jaw slide dangerously out of socket, but it was *something,* action permitted where she had been useless before.

Until she felt tears that had nothing to do with her own pain sliding down her face. Hot tracks cut through grime and blood, Grace's features swimming into view for the first time in whole minutes. The beautiful blonde's face was beginning to swell, bruises and muck ruining its lines. Margrit could see in Grace's eyes the battle madness that had overtaken Margrit, the need to dominate that had nothing to do with why they were fighting or what ends they sought. It was simpler than that, one animal trying to survive an encounter with another.

But Margrit's pain was fading, blood no longer flowing from scratches or her bruised nose; her ribs no longer hurting from the blows Grace had landed. Even the headache from smashing skulls together had faded, and a simple clear thought finally broke through.

Grace couldn't win.

Grace couldn't win, not with Daisani's blood flowing through Margrit's veins. Margrit would heal too quickly, and Grace would never stop fighting. That thought seemed suddenly, briefly, to define the blond vigilante, and Margrit liked her for it. Admired her for it, even though the mindless rage in Grace's eyes was currently for her. They could kill each other on the match floor, but Grace would never yield shy of that, and she could not, in the end, defeat Margrit.

Margrit took a deep breath, and when the next hit came, let it spin her away into oblivion.

Darkness didn't last nearly as long as she pretended it did.

At first it was for Grace's sake. If Margrit's eyes popped open again a few seconds after she'd gone down, the fight wouldn't be over. Then it was for her own as she lay in a boneless heap, listening to voices both worried and angry rising around her as her body knit itself back together. That felt distinctly horrible: bones that were slightly out of place, though not broken, seemed to jerk back to where they belonged, making twisted pops. Nausea rose in Margrit's belly and she worked not to swallow against it, afraid that would look too awake. A spurt of coughing took her so hard she had nothing left but to collapse again when it was over, and that was as much a relief to her as it concerned those around her. Exhaustion sat on her like a living creature, weighing her down and slowing her thoughts.

She'd been exposed to more violence in the months since she'd met the Old Races than in her entire previous life, at least on a personal level. What she'd encountered before them had been violence done to or by others, and she had abhorred it without entirely understanding it. Human nature took ugly turns; that she could comprehend. She recognized the impulse in herself often enough, reaching for the least palatable, most extreme solution in moments of exasperation or frustration. It was recognizing them and choosing not to act on them that made the difference between a man and a thug. Very few people managed to stay on the side of the angels all the time. Margrit could pick out too-clear moments in the past months when she'd failed to, some of them sending squirms of embarrassment and apology through her. She'd never imagined her veneer of civility could break down as far as it had in the last few minutes. If she could convince herself she'd fought for Alban's freedom, she might believe she'd at least had the moral high ground, but that comforting lie was beyond her. She'd fought and hit and beaten Grace mostly out of fear and anger and a desperate wish to come out on top just this once.

Margrit opened her eyes, looking up at the cut-stone ceiling above. Biali's scarred face intruded on her vision almost immediately. "You threw that fight, lawyer."

"Yeah." Margrit croaked the word, then wet her lips and nodded before she tried again. "Yeah, I did." She flexed muscle, testing for pain or discomfort and finding none. Daisani's gift was fine-tuning her healing abilities further every chance it got. She still wouldn't want to face a gargoyle, but neither would she want to pit herself against anyone without her advantage. Not, at least, if she learned to fight.

"Why?" Biali sounded justifiably bewildered. Margrit pushed up on her elbows, looking for Grace. The blonde was on the other side of the room, recounting her victory with great sweeps of her arms as one of the selkies tried, without success, to treat Grace's injuries. Margrit chuckled, low dry sound, then looked for Alban, who still stood apart. He watched her with knowledgeable sorrow, and Margrit's mirth faded.

"Because she couldn't win, and I didn't deserve to." She got up, stiffness announcing itself after all. Biali backed off, scowling at her more deeply than she thought warranted, given that he'd just taken the first of the trials as his own.

With her awakening, the room came to more attention, even Grace falling silent and submitting to the selkie's treatment. Margrit put her hands in the small of her back and forced herself straight, wincing as she did so. Daisani arched an eyebrow and she caught herself before making a face, though there was apparently enough play in her expression to give her away, because amusement darted after his raised eyebrow. No one spoke, though the tribunal arranged itself before her, Chelsea Huo the odd man out amongst the gargoyles. Margrit stared at her a moment, trying again to determine her place in the Old Races, then passed a hand over her eyes. "Okay. What's next, brains or benevolence?"

Janx's staccato applause broke the air, his laughter following it on a swirl of blue smoke. "Strength, sense and sentiment, now brains and benevolence. Whatever would strength be in your alliterative little world?"

"Brawn, obviously. Just don't ask me to come up with another trifecta. I don't think I'm that smart right now."

"A shame," Eldred murmured, "as 'brains' is the next challenge."

"Of course it is." Margrit folded her hands behind her back rather than let them wander any further; she had already given a court case's worth of tells to the tribunal and its audience, and seemed unable to stop herself from offering more. "What's the format?"

It shouldn't, she thought a moment later, have surprised her that they brought forth a chess set.

* * *

It wasn't one of the selkie-and-djinn sets that she'd become familiar with. Margrit crouched at the table they set up, studying the figures. Not tiny figures: the tallest were the height of her palm, and the smaller ones more of a size she was accustomed to seeing king pieces in chess sets carved as. There was an enormous array of fanciful creatures, the entire line of pawns individualized on each side. Coiled sea serpents, delicate mermaids, thickset hairy men, clawed and scowling bare-breasted women, all done in varying shades of marble, so the pawns made a near rainbow of color across the board.

Behind them stood the denizens of the surviving Old Races, stolid gargoyles holding the rooks' positions, slithery dragons in the diagonal-moving bishops' places. Unfettered djinn stood as queens, able to move any direction they chose, and the most populous of all, the selkies, were given the king slots.

The knights, on both sides of the board, were slim, beautifully carved representations of Margrit herself.

"There are no vampires." Margrit's voice came out hoarse as she tried not to look too hard at the chess pieces of herself. The last time she'd seen such a thing it had nearly spelled her death, and a childish voodoo fear caught her by the throat and held on. Worse than a soul being stolen by a photograph, this was the whole of her captured in tiny relief.

"No one sees a vampire's natural form and lives to tell of it," Daisani said very softly. "There is no one to carve my people, and we would not stand amongst our brother chessmen forced into a human form."

"But the windows…" Margrit looked toward Daisani,

glad to be able to take her eyes off the chess set. Daisani smiled, such a gentle expression Margrit jerked her gaze back to the safety of the game pieces.

"A conundrum, is it not? Perhaps an artist's fancy."

"Or maybe a vampire's creation," Margrit ventured. Daisani smiled again, and beside him, Janx chuckled.

"You might be better off considering your strategy rather than the mysteries we keep from you, Margrit Knight."

"My strategy. Should it be something beyond 'win the game'?"

Discontent rippled through the room. Margrit followed it, watching frowns of uncertainty. "What am I missing?"

"For a—usual challenge, one with our people and our people alone, the game pieces would be…symbolic. They would guide us through our memories—you know of the gargoyle memories?" Eldred's rich voice sharpened and Margrit wondered whether an affirmative or a negative would be the preferred answer. She nodded regardless and Eldred echoed the action, expression inscrutable.

"They would guide us through memories to some moment of wisdom or insight amongst our peoples. The gargoyle who delved deepest, found an unremembered time that most clearly helped to guide us forward as a people or whose recollection most obviously bore reflection on the matter at hand, would be considered the victor in the battle of intellect. But we have never before faced a second who did not belong to our people. The game itself must be the deciding factor," he said reluctantly. "I see no other choice."

Margrit swung around to face Alban, feeling as though her body had taken on the shape of a question mark. He kept his gaze downcast for long moments, only lifting it grudgingly, and then to give Margrit an almost imperceptible nod. She clenched a fist in triumph and turned back to the tribunal.

"I take it you're uncomfortable with pushing the boundaries of your traditions that far." At Eldred's nod, she tightened her fist again, using the action to keep herself from crowing in delight. "I might have a solution."

This time the whispers that ran through the room were full of curiosity. Margrit waited on Eldred's acknowledgment to continue, trying to keep her voice steady in face of rising excitement. "Alban and I discovered I'm susceptible to your telepathy, or whatever it is you call it that allows you to share memories so clearly. I don't know if all humans are, but I've ridden memory with him more than once. I—"

Babble erupted all around, drowning out Margrit's voice and her arguments. She fell silent, knowing better than to try to outshout a boisterous courtroom. Eldred brought it back under control after a full minute of outrage and exclamation. Margrit bobbed her head in thanks as he gestured for her to continue, and went on, feeling bold and weightless.

"I know it works with other gargoyles. I've caught an unguarded thought or two from Biali." And for that, she sent an apologetic glance his way. Too much surprise creased his features for anger to have taken hold yet, but Margrit had little doubt it would, in time. "And I rode memory with Hajnal's daughter, Ausra, the night she attacked me," she said more quietly.

This time the explosion of sound was concussive. Margrit held her ground only through years of training, and even that didn't quell the urge to step back and make herself smaller amidst the uproar. She lowered her head and bit her lower lip, watching Eldred through her eyelashes. He was her litmus, out of the tribunal members. Biali was too angry in general, and Alban too determined to let old laws have their way, for either of their reactions to tell Margrit how to gauge the gargoyles as a whole. When tumultuous noise began to die down, Margrit lifted her voice, this time taking center stage without Eldred's leave.

"I'm willing to allow the gargoyles access to my memories of that night, after the trials are complete." Margrit waited for the third time for order to restore itself, half wishing she was in an actual courtroom. This was trial-of-the-century stuff, law as theatrics on a massively satisfying scale. The fact that the judge, jury and audience was made up almost entirely of inhuman beings, made no difference at all: building arguments, taking risks, presenting theories and new ideas, were the lifeblood of her career. Margrit would have dearly loved to see a few of the moments she'd just passed shown on the six-o'clock news as the entertainment it rightfully was.

"In the meantime." Her voice cut through the falling chatter and quieted the room. "In the meantime, it's possible that if one of you allowed me access to the memories through your mind, I might be able to participate in the trial the way you've always done it."

"How would we know that it was your wits and not your passageway's that guided you to wisdom?" One of the female gargoyles spoke, her voice lighter than Margrit expected as she voiced the question Margrit imagined Biali badly wanted asked.

Margrit shook her head. "You'd have to choose somebody you trusted, or..." Dismay wrinkled her face as she considered the other possibility. "Or grant me access through somebody who has no reason to want me to succeed. Someone like Biali."

"IF Y⊕U +HINK I'm sharing my memories with you, lawyer—" Biali's offense cut through the rest of the noise with a clarity seconded only by Alban's splutter of disbelief. Janx chortled with pleasure, while the selkies and djinn snapped at one another, their din focused on whether Margrit's offer to share her memories of Ausra's death could be construed as invitation to investigate Malik's, as well.

Margrit, not expecting anyone to take heed, said, "It's not my first choice, either," and sat down at the chess table, body weary enough after the fight to want the respite even though intellect said she should probably remain on her feet. Intellect hadn't taken the pounding her muscles had, though. It might want rest after this next challenge, and she deemed it wise to give in to her body now so it wouldn't rebel later.

"Who *would* you choose?" Eldred's deep voice slipped through the hubbub, drawing Margrit's attention for all that he spoke softly. She sighed and gestured around the room.

"Alban, ideally, but I doubt that's really an option. I don't know the rest of you at all, so any other choice is more or less meaningless. That said, probably you."

"Why?"

"Because I know your name? Because you're the head of the tribunal and because that makes you the final judge in my mind." Margrit reached out to touch one of the pawns, then dropped her hand again. "Judges are supposed to be impartial, so you seem least likely to sway or be swayed by someone drifting through your mind."

"If you undertake this task, Margrit Knight, you will need to burrow, not drift. This is not a game to be taken lightly." Eldred retreated, leaving Margrit alone with the chess pieces and a room full of Old Races.

Debate went on longer than she anticipated, less for the matter of permission than the appalling idea that humans could perceive the gargoyle memories. Margrit heard talk of battle and of treaties, all of it idealistic with the first blush of conception. Neither was a wise choice, not that she could think of a way to stop a cadre of gargoyles from exposing themselves in the human world if that was their desire. Letting their discussion fade into white noise, she pushed a pawn forward so she could see it better, examining the individually carved scales on the serpent's hide.

A second pawn across the board was pushed forward by a taloned finger. Margrit looked up, startled, to find Biali sitting down across from her. "They'll be at it all night."

"Inconvenient," Margrit said under her breath. "What with you turning to stone at dawn and all. I'd hoped we could do this in one day. Night. Whatever." Since he was there, she prodded another pawn forward, resisting the impulse to pick it up and study the feathery wings on the clawed woman's back. "What race is this one?"

"Harpy. They lived in what you call the Amazon, and

nine out of ten of 'em were female. Never stopped fighting amongst themselves, and when the humans came, they couldn't organize to fight outsiders." Biali pushed one of his hairy men forward. "Still, they did better than the yeti. They at least fought. The yeti only ran. What memories?"

Margrit went still, a hand above the dragon-cum-bishop. She'd cleared a path for him to angle out, but she left him where he was, sorting out Biali's question. "Hajnal, mostly. Last weekend when we danced at the ball. I saw her through your eyes for a moment. Saw, or remembered, how much you loved her." She'd even felt a flash of desire, unexpected heat in looking on a feminine body. Sharing memories was disconcerting. "I didn't mean to intrude. Sorry."

"You mean that, lawyer?"

"What, that I'm sorry? Yeah, of course I do. It's not polite to pick up on other people's memories without them knowing about it. I just don't know how to brace against it."

"Keep playing," Biali said after a silence. "I'll teach you."

She wasn't certain when the chess board had become slippery and malformed, like a thing out of dreams. Peaks and valleys rose, black squares and white distorted and stretched among them. Far too many of the playing pieces slipped away, plummeting to their doom in craggy rents that pulled the board apart. Margrit clutched at them, trying to save what she could, but they slid through her fingers, insubstantial and screaming as they fell. She lunged after them, unaware of her own danger until someone, grumbling, thrust a hand at her and dragged her back from a precipice.

"No point in going after what's gone, lawyer. You'll only die trying."

Biali's presence stabilized the world, chess colors fading into night shades along a mountain range that went on as far as Margrit could see. Trees, gray-green in moonlight, offered softness to the landscape, and a silver river far below glittered as it cut its way through the stuff of memory and made a living place of it. Biali glowed under the hard blue-white light, so bright Margrit cast a glance at the moon, half expecting it to be blue itself, like an ultraviolet light at a dance club. Everything around her had a sense of expectation, as if each thing she did was anticipated, considered and recorded. As if the world was a living, thinking thing, far more connected to its denizens than the one she lived in was.

"It is," Biali said gruffly. "These mountains are our memories. They live while we do, growing and changing, all our histories built tall and wide for delving into when we need. You're the first human to stand here, lawyer. Enjoy the view while you can."

"That sounds ominous." Margrit dragged a breath of crisp night air in, marking how different it tasted from the muggy warmth of Grace's below-city tunnels. "And I didn't say anything aloud, did I?"

"There's no privacy here, not unless you learn to close up your mind and keep your thoughts to yourself."

Margrit, not deliberately, thought of a box—a Chinese takeaway box, white with red painted letters on the sides and a fragile metal handle squared over its top—and folded it shut, trying to tuck her thoughts away. Biali laughed, startling her.

"Not bad. Not bad at all, lawyer. You're leaking a bit, but you've got the right idea. Now, what've you got in your hand?"

Margrit clenched her hand, hard carved edges of a chess piece cutting against her palm. Feeling childish for asking, she said, "Does telling you give you some kind of advantage?"

Biali stared, then barked another laugh. "You're in trouble either way, aren't you? Nah, even if we're carrying the same token the memories will carry us down different paths. Don't tell me if you don't want to. You'll get free when you've done as much as you can whether I know where you're off to or not."

Margrit nodded stiffly, then looked around again. "This is your memory?"

"All of ours. You're in the heart of our people."

"Why don't I see anyone else, then? People who are important to you, anyway?"

An image bloomed behind her eyes, drawn there as though it came from within her: her takeaway box, all white and red and faint angles. Then white granite grew up over its sides, sealing it off in flawless stone. The pictures faded and Margrit pursed her lips, looking down. "Oh."

"Any other questions?"

"Yes." Margrit lifted her eyes again. "What do I *do?*"

Biali shrugged his massive shoulders. "Just follow the memories, lawyer. They'll take you where they want you to go."

"One more question. Why are you letting me in?"

Biali shrugged again, turned away, his form fading

faster than distance could take him away. "I told you once. You're not bad, for what you are."

Then he was gone, leaving Margrit alone on the mountainside.

She began to open her hand, then suddenly clenched her fist around the chess piece instead. If what Eldred and Biali had said was true, she might find her way to whatever bit of wisdom she was meant to bring back without looking at the piece. She knew from feel that it wasn't one of the winged harpies, nor one of the hunched gargoyles: it was too tall for that, and too narrow. It might have been almost any of the others, though not, she thought, one of the yeti; it didn't seem squat enough. If she needed its guidance later she would look at it, but for the moment she tightened her fingers and studied the mountains.

Openness and height spread out, reminding her that she hadn't gone for a run in days. The leather and boots she wore were completely inappropriate for exercise, but Margrit glanced down at herself with a grin. Memories and dreams weren't exactly the same thing, but they were kin to one another. If the gargoyles could shape the whole of their memories into a mountain range, she could certainly dress herself in running gear for the duration of her stay there.

A moment later she went bounding down the mountainside, feet light in her running shoes, hair flying into her face as she bounced from one smooth rock face to another. Stone turned to trees to dart around, long strides eating up the ground, and trees became meadow as Margrit stretched and laughed and ran more freely than she'd done in weeks.

She came upon the river with no warning, and with even less thought dove into it, gasping with shock both at her choice and the cold as a current swept her downstream. It pulled her deeper than she thought a river should go, the surface growing darker and farther away even as she struggled to reach it again. Panic seemed curiously missing as her lungs began to ache, as if a part of her mind disbelieved what was happening, and refused to accept she needed air within memory's confines.

A shape came out of the water, lithe and quick and swimming against the current as though it hardly existed. Human hands caught her, a humanoid face coming close to hers. Masculine, she thought, though with peculiarly large, double-lidded eyes that blinked rapidly at her in the gloom. Not so dark she couldn't see, though after a few seconds she began to think the creature who'd caught her glowed with his own bioluminescence, a waft of electric blue in the dark.

He lifted his hands to her face, drawing her closer still, then tipped his head and, without invitation, covered her mouth with his own. Margrit squeaked a protest in the back of her throat, so surprised she could do nothing else before agony ripped over her.

Memory seared her, changing her concept of herself from a human creature to something born of the sea. When she dragged in a breath, cold water flooded her ribs and throat, and when she gawked at herself in horror, it was to discover tremendous gills lining her torso. Her vision had cleared, leaving her able to see that her rescuer *did* glow, and that his hair was the same electric color as the aura he gave off. Like her changed self-perception, he too had gilled ribs, and now that she could see more clearly, fluttering gills at his throat, as well. His eyes were enormous, and his hands less human than she'd believed, with webbing between the fingers.

A grin split her face so widely it hurt as she backed up to look at the rest of him. Despite the gills, he looked mammalian in form: the heavy, brilliantly colored tail had no scales, only soft-looking hide like a whale's, and horizontal fins at the end, more like a dolphin than a fish.

A trill of laughter escaped her throat and she tried for words, uncertain if she could make them underwater. "I get mermaid memories? Really? That's so cool."

"I am only your guide." The mermaid—merman—siryn, Margrit settled on, remembering the Old Races' name for the undersea peoples, and feeling absurd using *merman,* which seemed even more made-up than *mermaid.* The siryn's voice was musical, catching Margrit by the heart and tugging her whether she wanted to follow or not.

Alarm spiked through her, abrupt recollection of the siryns' reputation. Margrit backpedaled, only realizing as she did so that she, too, wore a mermaid's tail, hers of rich coppery brown, like an impossibly vibrant shade of her own cafe-latte skin. "You're not going to drag me off and drown me, are you?"

A few powerful strokes of her benefactor's flukes sent him around her in quick, irritated circles. "Would I have given you the memory of how to breathe and swim beneath the water if I intended to drown you? I am your guide, not your doom." Even in pique he sounded like rainfall on crystal, voice shimmering with beautiful offerings. Challenge laid down, he flicked his tail a few times and surged away, leaving Margrit to follow or not, as she saw fit.

A mixture of wanting to apologize and sheer delight at the scenario sent her after him, her hair clouding around her when she caught up. Like the tail she'd been granted, it was more brilliant in color than she was accustomed to, though not as unearthly as her guide's. "How are you giving me the memory? Can siryns do that, too?"

"No. This all takes place within the gargoyle histories. I utilize their ability to share memory in order to make you more comfortable. You could traverse this realm in your own form, if you so wished."

"In other words, this is all happening in my mind." Margrit drew another deep breath, feeling water flood her ribs, and smiled against the coldness. "Guess I might as well enjoy it. Where are we going?"

"Where does your heart tell you we are going?"

"To the heart of the world," Margrit said promptly, then coughed on her own pomposity. "I don't know why I said that."

Laughter washed through the siryn's voice, high notes on a piano rendered into something impossibly pure. "Because your heart told you to. Now, hush. We will not want to speak as the pressures grow stronger. The depths are not comfortable, even for our kind, and we need what air we can steal from the cold, black water."

It wasn't until she didn't find it that Margrit realized she had truly expected to see Atlantis when her blue-haired guide finally drew to a halt, closer to the dark ocean floor than Margrit had ever imagined being. Instead of the fabled city, though, there was merely a rent in the earth, so broad and deep that both heat and light rose from it even in the icy depths. A primitive impulse to run—or swim—as fast as she could, as far as she could, set Margrit's heartbeat racing until she felt dizzy from it. This was not a place humans were meant to be, and the sensation that a price would be paid for intruding weighed on her as heavily as the ocean pressure did. Hell had much in common with this stretch of barren undersea land. Even the juxtaposition of hot and cold promised to punish the wicked with one form of misery, then another.

When a serpent of impossible length and breadth slithered free of the torn earth, Margrit laughed, then shoved her hands against her mouth as though she could push the sound back in. There would be a serpent; of *course* there would be a serpent. She could hear the hysteria in the laugh she tried to swallow, and dared not follow her own thoughts too closely for fear of finding madness in them. She knotted her hands more tightly, and realized something cut into one palm.

A sea-serpent chess pawn floated a few centimeters away when Margrit opened it, caught in the current its make-sake created as it swam. The tremendous serpent circled her and her companion, watching them as it wound around time and time again. Its great length putting Janx's dragon form to shame: it was as though it had been born at the beginning of time, and had grown slowly, constantly, ever since. It had too many, or too few, colors to name, all of them shimmering and changing as the creature made a whirlpool of itself around Margrit and her guide. They were turned in its vortex, unable to meet the monster's eye with their own.

Its miniature representation floated away, just out of Margrit's reach, insignificant beyond words in comparison to its model. The carving looked like the toy it was;

the real serpent looked like a limbless dragon, broad-snouted with wide-set eyes, a Norse carving come to life.

"Oh." Margrit's voice cracked even on that single word. "Oroborus. My God." She heard more fervency and devoutness in her near prayer than she'd ever heard in her life, and wondered what her mother, her father, her kindly priest at her church, would think of that. Her chest ached, delight borne from someplace so deep within her she had no idea where it began. It stole her breath, stole the form she'd been given and left her dangling in the water as a mere mortal, ordinary human. Warnings whispered that she should be frightened, she should be drowning, she should be crushed, she should be dead, and none of it, not one of those true and dire thoughts, could unman the consuming, heartbreaking joy that welled inside her.

She stretched her hands out, not so much daring to touch the monster from the heart of the world as in worship, felt more deeply than she had words for. "My God, look at you. Thank you. *Thank* you for letting me see you." She caught the tiny chess carving and held it up in her fingertips. "This is for you," she said impulsively. "We do remember. Even humans. We do remember." That the serpent in her personal mythology was most often passed off as a thing of evil seemed shallow and absurd in face of the great Leviathan. That it had offered the path to knowledge seemed the important part.

The serpent's swirling vortex slowed as it brought its head in to examine the chess piece. Its eye was taller than she was; taller than herself and her guide put end to end. Margrit had no way to give words to the creature's size, only that it dwarfed any living thing she'd ever imagined, and that she thought the earth's molten core would look small in its coils. It studied her and her gift with inexpressible calm, then with great and slow deliberation, opened its mouth.

It did so very carefully, as if aware that it would suck Margrit, her guide, everything around them and half the ocean's water in if it were to do so quickly. Even with its jaws barely parted, its gaping maw was cavernous, so dark and huge it couldn't conceivably be something alive, but had to be some new-born formation torn from the ocean's bed. Margrit hung in the water, frozen in bewildered incomprehension before realizing the vast serpent was accepting her gift. Trying not to laugh with terror, she kicked forward and very, very cautiously dropped the chess piece into the serpent's gum beside a tooth so large it reached a vanishing point when she craned her neck to look up at it.

With a delicacy that belied its size, the serpent dipped its tongue—forked and unbelievably long—into its gum, wrapping it around the minuscule carving and flicking it back into its throat. It swallowed once, an action that slid along forever, then, with what seemed to Margrit to be incalculable amusement, flicked its tongue a second time, this time at her.

The world spun head over heels, and she opened her eyes in Grace's council room to find she was soaked through and through, and that she held nothing at all in her hand where the chess piece had been.

THE SILENCE IN the audience chamber was as impressive as the crushing pressure of the ocean depths. Biali, still across the table from her, stared wordlessly at her clothes. He looked as he had before their journey into memory: scarred and angry, but now also confused. Margrit stood up, water spilling down her thighs to puddle at her feet. "What the hell happened to me?"

"We thought you might tell us that yourself." Alban, voice dry to hide concern.

Margrit turned to him helplessly, then back to the others. "I take it I'm not supposed to come back soaking wet."

"It has never happened before," Eldred allowed. "What memory did you follow? What words were you given?"

"Words? I— Ah, crap, I forgot all about that part of it. He—it, whatever—didn't say anything. I don't even know if it could talk. It probably would've vibrated me to pieces if it had." Margrit closed her mouth abruptly, stemming her babble, then said more carefully, "I had a serpent in my hand. What was I *supposed* to see?"

"One of my long-lost brethren, presumably." Janx

opened his hands expansively, as if inviting the whole of the room to fall into that category. "One who might perhaps share some salty bit of sea wisdom to guide us all with. One who might tell you if any of his kind still live," he said more quietly, and more sharply. Margrit's face crumpled.

"No, sorry. None of that. What about you?" She turned to Biali, water droplets flying with the vigor of her motion. He passed a hand over his shoulder as if he'd brush water away, though she didn't think she'd sprayed him. Then he opened that same hand, revealing one of the gargoyle rooks.

"I saw Hajnal, who reminds me that there is no greater force than the beating heart. Love conquers all," he said, bitter growl to the words.

"Or life does." Margrit dropped into her chair again, squelching, and curled a lip at the coldness of her leathers. "Sounds pretty sage to me."

"And so it is," Eldred said. "But your journey must be more fully explained, Margrit Knight. No one has ever come back wet. Where did you go?"

"The heart of the world." Margrit repeated what she'd said to the siryn male, feeling as absurd to voice it now as she had then. She wanted flippancy in her voice, but instead she sounded as she felt: awed and very, very small. "I met an oroborus who'd let go of its tail, and gave it my chess piece." She turned her empty palm up again, then let her hand fall. "It didn't say anything, just ate the carving and sent me back home."

With her last words she realized the profundity of silence that had fallen over the room, and twisted to look at the tribunal and its audience. To a being, they had the stillness that only the Old Races could accommodate, and of all of them, only Chelsea Huo watched Margrit.

The rest watched Chelsea.

She had risen at some point, perhaps while Margrit spoke, and now stood as if rooted deep in the earth, unmovable, unswayable, her apple-wizened face so neutral as to be terrible. Under that gaze Margrit felt as small as she had beside the oroborus, pinned in place by great weight and age and strength.

Chelsea did not, in actuality, shake herself, though some infinitesimal shudder ran through her and broke the stillness that held her captive. "You saw the serpent at the heart of the world? You offered him a gift?"

"Was that bad?" Margrit's voice quavered and she cleared her throat, trying to embolden herself. "It seemed like the right thing to do at the time. He—he? He seemed pleased. What—who—is he?" Her palms were damp with sweat, but wiping them on her leather pants would've done no good even if the pants were dry. Margrit tried anyway, then hugged her arms around herself, feeling as though Chelsea's answer might be a headman's ax.

"He is the Serpent." Daisani answered when Chelsea's silence had gone on too long, and drew all eyes to himself by doing so. To Margrit's astonishment, the vampire sounded very nearly reverent as he spoke, but recalling her own emotional reaction, she understood. "The same who litters your holy books and the same who entwines your healing staves. He is more than one of us, more than one of anything you might quantify. He is the beginning and the end of time, eternal in a way no other thing is. And he never lets go of his tail," he added more prosaically, which earned a snort from Chelsea.

"He's never had hold of his tail," she said briskly, then shot a sharp-edged smile toward Daisani. "But they do say he knows the truth about where the vampires came from."

Daisani's gaze narrowed. Chelsea huffed an unimpressed breath, but Janx took attention from them with a murmur as soft and awestricken as Daisani's own.

"They say he's the counterpart to the mother of us all. That one can't exist without the other, and neither of them can die until the end of the universe. No one in the history of the world has ever spoken with him."

"The mother of us all? There's a mother of us all?" Margrit came to her feet, her boots and clothes squishing.

"You would call her Gaia. Mother Earth," Chelsea said with a degree of impatience. "A legend from which everything is born."

"Her—mother—but—!" Margrit reined in her spluttering and lifted her hands to her head. "And this serpent is her counterpart? What, the death of us all? And I found him in the gargoyle memories? How's that possible if nobody's ever talked to him?"

Chelsea rolled her eyes. "Dramatics. First, he's touched many people through the aeons. Your mythologies come from somewhere, after all. Second, I think it's clear you went well beyond the gargoyle memories, Margrit. No one returns from those adventures drenched in seawater or missing items they took with them into memory. It's a psychic journey, not a physical one. However." Her voice sharpened and Margrit came to attention, feeling young and small all over again. Chelsea repeated, "However," more gently, and smiled. "Insomuch as anything can be, the serpent is the truth at the heart of everything, and if he accepted a gift from you,

you've been honored beyond any other living being in
this world."

"Oh," Margrit said faintly, and all the other questions
that had been raised fell away. "Does that mean I win?"

Even Biali conceded, grudgingly, that it did, and
Margrit left the tribunal chambers to the argument of
what wisdom was meant to be derived from her experience. Grace led her back to Alban's room, where Margrit
dried herself and changed into her own clothes, now that
the protective leathers were no longer needed for fighting.

Grace was still waiting when Margrit emerged,
toweling her hair dry. The tall vigilante was more swollen
and bruised than Margrit: she'd caught a glimpse of
herself in a mirror, and Daisani's gift was doing its work.
By morning she doubted she'd see any marks left from
their battle. Grace noticed it, as well, and looked sour.
"Vampires."

Caught off guard, Margrit laughed. "The worst thing
about living in Santa Barbara."

Grace's bruises creased with confusion and Margrit
waved it off. "Never mind. I'd think you were the right
demographic to have seen— Well, never mind. Are you
okay?"

"I'll heal. Didn't know you had that much fight in
you." Grace gestured toward the hall and took the lead,
much to Margrit's relief. She still hadn't spent anything
like enough time in Grace's domain to know where she
was going, though at least a few hallways were beginning
to look familiar.

"I didn't know I had that much fistfight in me, anyway.
I kind of wish I still didn't know."

"Sometimes it's good to know how far you'll go."

"Yeah? How far will you go?"

Grace paused outside the chamber door, leaning on the handle as she gave Margrit a light smile. "To the edge of heaven, so I can earn the kiss of angels, love. And yourself?" She pushed the door open, ushering Margrit in before she could reply.

The air within the meeting room felt like Janx's alcove often did, as if it had a personal grudge and intended to hold Margrit back. Margrit caught a quick sharp breath, gaze skittering from one face to another as she tried to ascertain what she'd missed. Biali scowled furiously, arms folded against his thick chest; Alban looked poleaxed, his own gaze roving from one member of the tribunal to another. The selkies and djinn whispered amongst themselves, while Janx and Daisani eyed each other as if one had done something unspeakable, and the other didn't wish to speak of it, but couldn't let it go. Behind Margrit, Grace let go a soft whistle. "Wonder what we missed."

"Enter, Margrit Knight." Eldred's dark, chocolate voice rolled over her and Margrit scurried forward, feeling as though she'd turned up late for an important test. She bobbed her head, nearly cutting a clumsy curtsy when she came in front of the tribunal, then bit back a laugh at her own nerves.

"Sorry if I—"

"Silence."

Margrit swallowed hard enough to hurt her throat trying not to repeat her apology. She still had the towel clutched in both hands, giving her the silly but reassuring idea that everything would be all right. Eldred waited on her for long moments, clearly expecting his edict to be broken, but Margrit remained quiet, and the djinn and selkie whispers died away. Margrit regained some measure of composure, familiar enough with gimlet-eyed judges to be comfortable in Eldred's imposed hush. Finally the silence grew sufficiently profound that even Janx and Daisani broke off their wordless exchange to pay heed.

Eldred, with the art of a showman, held his place and the quiet to the breaking point, waiting until Margrit, at least, fidgeted internally, though she didn't let it seep through physically. Then, sonorous and deep, he announced, "The trial is ended—"

"What?" Despite her best intentions, Margrit's voice shot up. "I only went to change clothes! I haven't stood the third—"

"Margrit." Alban spoke from behind her, soft and calming. Margrit knotted her hands in the towel and set her teeth together, forbidding any more words from escaping. Eldred glowered at her until satisfied she wouldn't interrupt again, then started over.

"The trial is ended. We demand tests of strength, of wisdom and of compassion. Of these tests two are decided at the heart of the tribunal, and we name those two as strength, gone to Biali's champion, and wisdom, gone to Alban's. But for the third, the trial of compassion, we must look beyond our trials and determine the larger actions of our combatants.

"Margrit Knight has, at great risk to herself, taken Alban Korund's place in this trial. Why have you done this?"

"Because it's wrong not to fight for what's right," Margrit replied, then winced at the rhymed phrasing. Eldred, though, nodded acceptance, so she pressed her lips shut against trying for more eloquence.

"Biali's champion should not have won the battle of strength. Why did she?"

Margrit shot a guilty look toward Grace, whose expression remained neutral beneath the bruises. "Because I threw the fight, Your Honor. Eliseo Daisani gave me a sip of his blood a while ago, and I heal faster than any human should. Grace couldn't hurt me enough to win, but she wasn't going to betray Biali's honor by not trying. *I* wasn't going to let her kill herself on the moral high ground."

Eldred nodded a second time. "And why are you part of these proceedings at all?"

"What, beyond Alban throwing himself on his sword? Because he needed help a few months ago, I guess. Because he asked me to help clear him of the suspicion of murder." Her answers had none of the polish of a prepared ending argument, and the lawyer in her cringed at how raw and inexperienced she sounded. But once more, Eldred nodded.

"And are you willing to have these answers, these memories, recorded for our histories, so that we might all feel and see their truth?"

Margrit blinked. "Sure. What do I have to do?"

"You've joined our memories. The process of us entering yours is somewhat different." Eldred broke off, glancing at Alban. "Unless the exchanges have gone both ways?"

"No." Alban shook his head, as though the deep, rumbled word was insufficient. "She's been an inactive participant in our joinings."

Scarlet leapt up Margrit's neck to burn her cheeks, tears of laughter and embarrassment and half-real offense carried on the heat. She knew what Alban meant, but couldn't help taking it wrong. Beneath blood rushing in her ears she heard Janx chuckle. "What a dreadful thing to say to a lady, Stoneheart."

The weight of two dozen Old Races' gazes landed on her. Margrit's blush grew hotter and she clapped her hands over her cheeks, wishing she had the skin tones to hide such furious color. Unable to command a full voice, she croaked, "You're not helping!" to the dragonlord, who laughed aloud.

"Do forgive me, my dear. I only thought to chide our friend for his careless words. Pray continue," he added brightly to the silent onlookers, and after shooting Margrit a pained look of apology, Alban did.

"It's been much as any sharing of memory with one who is not a gargoyle, save that Margrit seems to be susceptible to my unguarded thoughts. That, I think, is unprecedented among the Old Races." He hesitated, waiting for correction, but Eldred urged him to continue. "Her memories have been closed to me, as would be any of theirs," and with the word he gestured, including the other Old Races with a circle of his hand, "if I wasn't invited to explore them."

"Then the ritual of request will suffice to allow us access to her memories?" Eldred's rich voice held a mix of fascination and dismay.

Alban shrugged. "It's entirely possible her memories will be cut off from us entirely. We haven't tried."

Margrit said, "Um," and her voice cracked on the syllable. Another blush rose as the gathered Old Races turned to her again. "There was that one dream…"

Alban blinked at her slowly, and then to her delight, color flushed *his* pale face, the first time she'd ever seen him blush. "I assume that contact was initiated by my thoughts of you," he said quite formally.

Suddenly cheerful with camaraderie, Margrit flashed him a bright smile that helped beat down the heat in her face, then turned to the gargoyle council with open hands. "So let's try your request ritual. What do I do?"

"You may wish to sit comfortably." Eldred gestured to the chess-table chair, and Margrit, relieved she'd dried off and changed clothes, set her towel aside and sat.

"Who'll be in my head?"

Eldred's hesitation was barely perceptible. "I will. But in such cases it's traditional for the entire tribunal to follow, so we can all experience the events as clearly as possible."

Goose bumps shot over Margrit's arms as she looked from stranger to stranger, finally bringing her eyes to Alban's. He inclined his head, small movement of reassurance. She dragged a deep breath and nodded, looking back at Eldred. "What about—" She tilted her head at the gathered selkies and djinn. "Will everyone be watching, or just the gargoyles?"

"Only the gargoyles. Sharing thoughts with the others requires repeating the welcoming ritual with each of them. I see no need to risk a greater link, particularly when we've never shared with a human before."

"Did you have to say *risk?*" Margrit made a face, then brushed concern away: she'd ridden Alban's memories with no ill effects. "How do I guide you?"

"By focusing on the events in question. We will not sift your memories, searching for things you don't wish to share, but you should know that this is not a…" Humor curled the corner of the elder gargoyle's mouth. "Not a surgical procedure. I can't promise you your privacy."

Janx, just within Margrit's peripheral vision, shifted enough to be seen, making himself a deliberate reminder of things that should remain hidden. As though she could forget. Margrit quelled the urge to scowl at him and only nodded to Eldred. "I understand. You said there's a ritual?"

Eldred sat across from her, moving chess pieces out of the way so he could place his elbows on the table and put his hands palms up, like an offering. "Your hands over mine, please, but not touching. And, perhaps, the name you go by."

Margrit put her hands above the gargoyle's, laughing softly at their comparative dark daintiness. With her fingertips above the heels of his hands, his fingers extended well past her wrists, talons making a thick and dangerous-looking cage. "My full name is Margrit Elizabeth Knight. My friends call me Grit."

Another smile curved Eldred's mouth. "Very well. Margrit Elizabeth, called Grit, the gargoyles ask to share memory with you, so that it might be recorded in the history of our peoples for all time." His voice deepened, becoming more sonorous as he spoke. Prickles waved over Margrit's nape, then soothed again as she relaxed into his words. "I am Eldred of Casmir. If you grant us this sharing, I will be your conduit into our memories, my eyes to yours, my hands to yours, my heart to yours, your eyes to us, your hands to us, your heart to us. Do you consent?"

Margrit, too aware of another ceremony, answered with the same words, heard herself say, "I do."

Eldred closed his hands around hers.

Impossible noise took off the top of Margrit's skull.

EIGHTEEN

AT EIGHT, a stick of a thing with corkscrew curls lightened by the summer sun, she could outrun her best friend, a boy of the same age, with laughing ease. By eleven, he'd outgrown her by several inches, his legs seeming to go on forever while hers were stubby and short by comparison.

She could still outrun him.

She could at fourteen, too, though by then she was resigned to a diminutive height and beginning to grow into curves that most professional female athletes never saw. It didn't matter: she ran as fast as she could, losing herself in the rhythms and challenges of speed.

One day she ran so fast she began to fly.

Winter nights slammed into her as she spread her hands and soared through the city sky. She was made of wind, or maybe ice, and then of glass, thin and fragile in the sky, but full of vibrancy and color. Her vision bent and telescoped, glass shaping to show her all the moments of her life.

A fraction of her that stood outside the colored glass whispered concern: there were connotations to your life flashing before your eyes, and with the pounding white static filling her mind, the idea that she was dying felt too close to possibility.

Luka Johnson folded as the jury declared her guilty of murder. Margrit caught her, prepared for the possibility of both the verdict and the fall. Her youngest daughter, a babe in arms, darted through Margrit's memory like an old hand-cranked film, flickering and jumping from one age to another until she was three years old and her mother, finally granted clemency by the state governor, swept the little girl into her arms.

Glass fragmented, shards of stained color shattering out. One twisted as it fell, showing a dark-haired woman whose hand curled over her belly protectively. When the piece hit the floor, it broke in three, splitting apart a trio of men whose colors were those of life and death and blood: white and black and red.

Panic surged through Margrit, so raw it barely felt like her own. She kicked the shards aside, knocking them under a brightly woven tapestry that lay crumpled on the floor. The tapestry exploded with the sound of glass raining, and in each colored droplet lay a memory. Like came to like, bundling school together in a blur of youthful dreams and heartfelt promises; in hours of heavy-headed studying and searing moments of freedom found in long runs. Beyond school, Tony Pulcella, gloriously cast in warm, rich color, sent daggers through her heart for chances lost and promises broken.

She flew again, high and free, with someone else's warmth cupping her body. Heat surged in her as she reached for that memory, eager for a strong touch and loving hands to encompass her and take away thoughts of the world with sensual, exciting exploration. She arched beneath the gargoyle's body, and then, unwelcome in the midst of growing need, she heard his voice.

Concentrate, Margrit. Focus your thoughts. He sounded strained, as though he spoke from a great distance and through a barrier of immense proportions. *Think of Ausra.*

Fear and anger razed any memory of desire. Ausra, petite and loamy and beautiful, raged through Margrit's memories. Every moment of her brief encounter with the half-gargoyle woman played through her at once, sparking pathetic whimpers of pain that reverberated as harsh, black streaks through stained-glass color. Terror bled orange and red, like fire, and then glassy flame consumed her, the blaze reflected and refracted everywhere she turned.

As in her nightmares, Malik died in the flames. Images fragmented again, the ridiculous first-person view of a neon-green watergun being fired; a wounded dragon in profile, roaring, frozen in time. A pale streak within the flame, crushing weight collapsing a djinn bound to his physical form. The bits of memory melded together, rewound, replayed, with acrid heat and the scent of hot steel filling Margrit's senses. It was more inescapable than her dreams, a waking horror she couldn't run from.

She scrambled backward, trying to hide within the white noise generating inside her own head. Flame was doused by static, the rush and color of hissing snow reminding her again that her focus was the gargoyle; was Ausra. Memories of the woman formed in the whiteness, stalking toward Margrit as she felt her left arm snap again, pain howling through her body. Memory flashed forward to the hospital: Daisani rolled up his sleeve in tidy motions, and the sugar-sweet coppery taste of his blood clogged Margrit's throat. She would never be quite human again.

And back, reminded of Ausra once more by *not quite human*. The memories that barraged her this time were the gargoyle's own, histories of a broken mind. So many human women dead at Ausra's hands, so many women whom Alban had dared to watch over, dead for a vengeance that was never Alban's to pay. Pain crackled through Margrit's body as she remembered, experienced, the first morning Ausra had stood against the sunrise and seen gold fire glimmer over the horizon before she succumbed.

That image caught in glass, so gorgeous and deep Margrit gasped with it. Pity surged in her for the first time and she reached toward the frozen memory. But the glass began to crack, thin lines of strain a too-clear representation of Ausra's mental state. Perhaps it hadn't been her fault; Hajnal had died birthing her, and a family's worth of memories had cascaded into an unformed, unready mind. Madness had been the only path open to her; revenge against the gargoyle she believed must be her father, who had abandoned her and her mother, the only choice she could see that she had. So many flavors of despair, all prismed in glass so they could reflect and shine on roads taken and decisions made.

One bright shard lit Biali, who stood at Ausra's side and did not stop her from becoming what she was. Perhaps he had helped shape her; perhaps he couldn't have saved her. The memories Margrit held of the gargoyle woman ran too shallow to answer that question. For the first time, she felt pity for the creature who'd tried to kill her, but as she touched the glass, it fell into slivers, cutting deep into her fingers.

Drops of blood scattered, carrying with them moments of her life. Afraid she would give herself away, Margrit scampered after them, trying to collect droplet-shaped bits of crimson glass. They fell through her hands instead: a first Communion and the turning of her tassel as she earned her law degree; her first kiss and her most recent, twining together so one became the other. Frantic, she tried harder to pick them up, losing bits of her life in the process.

Ausra reared up above her, a promise that those precious seconds would never be regained. One blow; that was all it would take to end Margrit's life. She would watch it fall, not out of bravery, but because she couldn't make her eyelids close, and when a roar cut through the static, her only thought was, *so that's what dying sounds like.*

And then her life was spared and Ausra's ended, a reversal of fortune against every law the Old Races held dear. A human life over an ancient one; human awareness of their people allowed to persevere where immortal hope ended; a child of two worlds destroyed because there was no other choice.

Sarah Hopkins, dark-haired, pregnant, afraid, alone, became a cutting edge of color, wedging her way through memories Margrit was only too glad to let go of. That same triumvirate of men surrounded her: Alban, tall and calm and dressed in quiet colors complementary to his paleness; Janx, gaudy and bright and gorgeous as he always was, a peacock in supersaturated shades; Daisani, small and lithe and exquisitely outfitted in sober tones, and all of them in the fashion of Sarah's century, nearly four hundred years gone.

Then heat shattered the glass, breaking away Sarah's image. Beautiful colors blurred together and turned to brown in the wake of the fire that burned London down and down and down. She was gone from them, lost to fire, lost to flame, and each day it burned higher, fueled by rage and grief, as she was nowhere to be found. Janx and Daisani stalked the city together by day and by night, never followed by a pale shadow, too united in their sorrow to trouble themselves with the absence of their third.

And so all unknown that third slipped away so easily, a human woman borne in his arms, her belly cradled in her hands as London burned beneath them.

Margrit, steady and ready as she always was, touched her palms to Eldred's, and chaos erupted in Alban's mind.

Gargoyle memory stretched back inconceivable years, touching the minds and hearts of the Old Races. Their discipline retained histories that no other recording method could so faithfully keep. Often it was by stories shared, but the ritual invoked by Eldred was one well known to all their peoples, and it let breath and bone and body become one with the memories.

Not in all the history of five races and more now lost to time had opening a path from one heart to another torn the roofs off all the minds in contact with the story-giver.

Not in all the history of five races and more now lost to time had a gargoyle ever tried to join minds with a human.

He should have known. Beneath the screaming blur of emotion and memory that poured from Margrit, Alban's self-directed recrimination bit hard, then lost its teeth. He couldn't have known; there was no way *to* know a human mind didn't hold information in the same structured,

stylized way the Old Races had learned to retain their
own memories. Humans had so little time to learn, so
little time to remember; it made sense that they had less
need of the formalities of recollection that allowed the
oldest of the immortals to remember their own lives
without resorting to gargoyle tales. It made sense, but
Margrit's easy ability to ride gargoyle memory had made
the possibility of the reverse seem easy, too.

Details of her life washed over him, intimate and
sweet, a gift he wanted to savor. An early memory, child's
irrefutable logic wearing down her mother, who in her
youth had been luminous, and who in maturity was, to
Margrit's adult mind, mixed with the childhood memories, intimidating. Her father's rich laugh mingled with it
all, warm voice promising, "She'll grow up to be a lawyer
if we're not careful." The memory's soft edges told Alban
that Margrit didn't consciously remember the comment,
but the way it hooked and pulled and weighted other
memories, becoming an epicenter, said that it had affected
the choices she'd made in her life.

Alban flexed his shoulders, feeling wings stretch and
fold, reminding him of who he was. Helping him to break
out of the phenomenal static rush that Margrit's life,
pictured in moments, made up. Only just then aware his
eyes were closed, he forced them open, and let go a
rough, low sound of astonishment.

The gargoyle tribunal had joined with Eldred before
he'd completed the ritual to enter Margrit's thoughts.
That *they* should be enthralled was to be expected.

That Janx and Daisani, that the gathered selkies and
djinn, that even Grace O'Malley, should all stand slack-
jawed and silent, was *not* expected. Mutable expression

slid over vacant faces: fear and anger, dismay, outrage, hope, delight, all tangled with the endless rush of memory pouring from the dark beauty at the room's center. A shard of panic sparked powerfully, not from Margrit at all, but, if Alban read its flavor correctly, from Janx or Daisani. Of the two Janx was the more likely to revel in such raw emotion, strong enough to alter the path of recollection Margrit followed.

Keeping his own thoughts unclouded was difficult. Margrit's memories were as forceful and brisk as her personality, and the new thoughts she lingered on were deliciously seductive.

And hardly to be shared with others. *Concentrate, Margrit. Focus your thoughts. Think of Ausra.* He formed the thoughts with caution, uncertain if she would hear him in the chaos. Her mind was alight with fire, leaping easily from one scene to another, as quick and light as flame jumping a river. There was too much to take in, too much to hold on to in the quicksilver way her human mind processed images and discarded them.

Flame went still for a few long seconds, as if caught in ice. Caught in glass, he realized, seeing Margrit's metaphor more clearly for an instant. The brief moments he and Ausra had encountered one another encompassed him, entangling Alban's own memory with Margrit's so thoroughly he staggered, uncertain whose life he was experiencing. Margrit poured detail into the gestalt, moments seen from two places at once and none the easier to bear for having been shared. They ended with the hideous firecracker noise of Ausra's neck breaking, a sound that sickened Alban even in memory, and one which would never let him go.

But Margrit's thoughts whirled again, dragging down through time and promises to unearth other moments of shared truth. Noise rushed up around him again, though whether it was his own attempt at protecting old secrets or simply the chaos of human memory trying to pull him down with everything else, he could no longer tell. He gave up trying to process her thoughts or guide her memories and instead worked his way forward step by slow step, reminding himself with each movement that he was a gargoyle, a creature of stone. Gargoyles did not lose themselves to mercurial passions so easily.

At last, at long, long last, he reached her and dropped to his knees beside the table. Cupped her face and turned it toward him, whispered her name to eyes gone white with the weight of memory, and then offered a kiss, soft and simple and sweet, to break the spell.

Margrit came awake with an indrawn breath bordering on a shriek and yanked her hands from Eldred's before she even knew Alban was at her side, holding her, protecting her. Her skull raged with pain, as if someone'd poured glass shards into her brain and stirred vigorously. She stared at Alban, wide-eyed, then heard a high-pitched giggle that went with wondering whether Daisani's gift of healing blood could cope with a brain razored to bits. Only when the sound repeated, piercing her headache and sending it to a new height, did she realize it was herself making it. With a cry half of embarrassment and half of pain, she tumbled out of her chair and collapsed against Alban, fingers curled in his shirt as she struggled not to whimper.

Even the beating Ausra had given her hadn't hurt as

badly as her head did. Needles of ice slid in her ears and under her nape, stabbing inward and creating more too-loud static that lifted hairs all over her body and made them feel pain, too. Margrit folded her arms over her head, trying to protect herself *from* herself. "What happened?"

The silence that followed was filled with shrieking static. "It seems human memory is not meant to be read by gargoyles," Eldred finally said, so dryly Margrit let another too-high giggle of pain escape. If she could only hold her head hard enough, she thought she might squeeze the ache away.

"Tell me you got what you needed."

"We did," Eldred began, but Janx, sibilant and angry, breathed, "Oh, yes, Margrit Knight. We did." He glided up behind her, great weight and heat making the air so heavy she couldn't breathe. Her head throbbed harder and she stuffed a fist in her mouth, trying to hold back a cry as she bit down, then gasped raggedly for air and twisted to look up at the dragonlord.

Daisani accompanied him, expression bleak with anger so old it looked as though it had been banked for centuries and only now brought to the fore. "You let us believe she had died, Alban." The vampire's voice was impossibly soft, barely disturbing the static in Margrit's mind, and then rose to a sound so sharp she thought she couldn't hear it with her ears: "You let us believe *she had died!*"

NINETEEN

"I† WAS WHA† she wished." Alban's sorrow was heavy enough that Margrit felt it as her own. She sagged against the gargoyle's broad chest, relieved to tears that the two immortals' anger wasn't directed at her. Through a headache renewed with every heartbeat, she listened to Alban's soft words, heard reassurance in his voice and felt exhaustedly, inexplicably safe. "After you fought, after the fire began…" The gargoyle shrugged, large motion that shifted Margrit against him and made her feel tiny and fragile in his arms. "She could not live with what we were."

Margrit could almost hear the words Alban didn't say, the choices he made to spare Daisani and Janx what Sarah Hopkins had said centuries earlier. Not what *we* were, because Alban had been fond of the woman, but had never loved her as his friends had. What *they* were; what they *are:* those were the words Sarah had spoken all those years ago. She could not live with what Janx and Daisani were, for all that she had loved them, too. Alban's memories flowed unchecked now, a quiet river of regret. Despite her pounding head, Margrit gathered them up and held them close, seeing deep parallels between a woman born almost forty decades earlier and Margrit's own family. Rebecca Knight had turned away from learning Daisani's true nature, a cut that wounded the vampire more deeply than reason explained. Perhaps it stemmed from a love lost in a far-gone era.

"What of the child?" Janx's voice scraped low, each word so precise it stood on its own, a threat instead of a question. "Did the child live, Stoneheart?"

Alban sighed and folded his head over Margrit's, new and ancient grief welling inside him. She closed her eyes, feeling the answer within him, and the weight of the promise he'd made to Sarah Hopkins: a promise of silence, no matter what the cost and no matter what truths might be revealed or hidden. And yet, after nearly four hundred years of keeping that silence, he drew breath to answer.

Tariq, hissing fury, burst in to steal Alban's chance. "Forget your ancient grievances. Is what was seen in the human's memory *truth?*"

Margrit, numb with foolishness, opened her eyes and said, "Yeah," even as Alban tightened his arms in warning.

As one, the djinn exploded in a whirlwind of outrage, their combined strength enough to knock the strong-bodied selkies and slender vampire from their stances. The gargoyles remained unmoved, and Margrit, safe in Alban's arms, did, too. Janx, even weightier than the gargoyles, looked unimpressed and insulted. Margrit shot a worried glance toward Chelsea and Grace.

Both returned her gaze with unruffled calm. Chelsea still sat in her council chair, looking tidy and patient and sad, and Grace stood with her legs wide and arms folded over her breasts, a platinum superhero in black leather.

Static rushed up to fill Margrit's head again and she turned her face against Alban's chest in confusion, certain that if she wasn't safely ensconced in his arms, she'd have been whipped around the room. The djinn were settling now, their display having earned too little awe, or maybe they simply couldn't *talk* in their air forms, and, like angry children, wanted to be heard more than they wanted to indulge in excess.

"Then we know who Malik's killer is." Tariq spoke almost before he'd finished forming, making his words airy but full of spite. "No wonder you offered us so much, mortal. You bargained for your own life."

Margrit lifted her eyes, oddly relaxed in the face of his challenge. It was partly Alban's presence that gave her confidence. His gentle strength was a well to draw from when her own ran dry, and his compassion ran ever deeper than she'd known. She could feel his breath, her own so slow as to match it, making the two of them one.

More prosaically, her head also hurt too badly to allow for fear or anger or any high-pressure emotion, and so she felt only detached reserve as she met Tariq's eyes. "I offered you as much as I did because I believed it was right. I still do, and the offer still stands. You have another day to consider, and then if you insist, my lord djinn, we'll take it to the mat." The last words rather lacked the dignity she'd hoped for, but they were at least spoken with the same tranquillity as the rest of her statement.

"Margrit?" Daisani's voice scraped as badly as Janx's had a moment earlier, his astonishment even deeper than Tariq's. "*You* took Malik's life?"

"I did." Alban interrupted as Margrit drew breath to explain. Daisani's expression went ever more incredulous, and Margrit said, "He had help. They can't change if they get soaked with salt water. I had a watergun." She lifted one hand to mock squirting, then realized what she'd done with dismay. Not the confession, but the playful pull of an invisible trigger. It lacked all the formality that her exhausted headache was trying to settle on her.

"In their defense," Janx said unexpectedly, "the thing was done in *my* defense. Malik was trying very hard to kill me, and very nearly succeeding." He spun the corundum cane in a theatrical circle, apparently having forgotten the anger that had held him in its grip only moments earlier. "I know, my old friend, that you swore an oath to keep the djinn safe, and to make restitution against anyone who might breach your word. Perhaps this once we might…forgive old vows, and leave the game to continue."

Daisani shot the briefest of glances at Tariq, who curled his lip as he looked at Janx. "Do as you will. *Your* vengeance is not ours." With a twist as dramatic as the dragon's, he whipped himself into a dervish, the other djinn following suit. In a moment they were gone, leaving nothing but a rattle of dust in the air, and then even that faded. The youthful selkie who had spoken to Margrit at the meeting that morning gave her a look of angry scorn, and with no more commentary, led his people from Grace's audience chamber.

Margrit mumbled, "I'm going to have to talk to Tony," and turned her attention back to Janx and Daisani.

They stood as though locked in ancient combat, both so still they seemed all but lifeless. Neither looked happy, though Janx's face was so accustomed to wearing merriment that a hint of it lingered and marked him with a profound sorrow, as if the exaggerated lines of a comedy mask had been peeled away to show its tragic partner underneath. "Very well," the dragon finally whispered. "If it is not so easy as that, we will make do as we must, my friend. As we always have and as we always shall." He swept a less insolent bow than any Margrit had ever seen him perform, though it wasn't precisely respect that marked the gesture, either. Acceptance, maybe, or resignation.

Then, as one, the two men turned to Margrit and Alban, and this time it was Daisani who murmured, "The child, Alban. Tell us of the child."

"He can't." Margrit's voice sounded light and distant to her own ears. The headache made her feel as though her skull had been stuffed with cotton. "He promised her. You must know that. He promised her that whatever happened, he would never tell either of you. If I didn't have such a messy mind, you wouldn't know now."

Daisani, startlingly, bared his teeth at her. For all that they were flat and ordinary, Margrit flinched back, heart rate spiking at the show of aggression. Her headache flooded back and Daisani's voice grated across it: "The child would be one of ours, Margrit Knight. After all you've done to change our people, you *dare* make mockery of something this important?"

"I'm not mocking." Margrit's pulse fluttered in her throat, bird-quick, distressing her with its vulnerable show. "I'm just saying he can't tell you. You know how gargoyles are."

"Margrit," Alban murmured. She smiled, trying not to wince as moving her face redoubled the pain in her head.

"Am I wrong?"

He huffed, answer enough, and Margrit's wince-

inducing smile repeated itself as she looked back at the
ancient rivals standing above her. "She lived. *They* lived.
There were two of them, both girls. Sarah named them
Kate and Ursula. They lived," she said again, and this
time her smile didn't hurt. "Congratulations. One of you
has descendants."

Something too weak to be rue flooded through Alban
as Margrit blithely, deliberately, took the onus of silence
from him and shattered it with a handful of simple words.
Gratitude that she would do such a thing colored with wry
acceptance: *nothing* was sacred to Margrit Knight, no
secret precious enough to be kept when it could be played
as a hand. Whether that was the lawyer in her or the
human amidst immortals, he was uncertain, but the why
hardly mattered.

Janx and Daisani stared at the woman bundled in
Alban's arms as though she'd thrown a lifeline they were
incapable of grasping. "They were born in the spring,"
Margrit rattled on. "Alban was there to make sure Sarah
was all right, that she had money and a home and a nurse,
and then he left them. They didn't look like much, just
little and red and squalling. They were very small." She
cradled her arms, familiar gesture, but somehow conveyed Alban's size to the newborns', and how extraordinarily tiny and fragile they were to him. It was rare to see
a gargoyle act out moments shared through memory; to
see a human do so bent Alban's mind out of shape with
astonishment.

"It was too dangerous to go back." Margrit's voice was
high and soft, words a singsong. "Sarah wanted a quiet
life, one not ruled by the Old Races. The only way to give

her that was to leave her alone. And when you left London and he did go back, years later, to check on her, they were gone. She was clever," Margrit said in a voice more like her own. "I'd have a hell of a time running from you, but it wasn't that hard in the seventeenth century, was it?"

"Margrit," Alban murmured with a note of quiet dismay. She turned a smile edged with pain up at him.

"Sorry. Talking distracts me from my head. I don't really understand what's happening to me."

"It was what you might call a feedback loop." Eldred spoke, making Margrit startle within the compass of Alban's arms. She peered over his biceps, fingers curled against it.

"I forgot you were here." A moment passed and she added, with greater concern, "I forgot about the trial." She struggled out of Alban's arms, pushing to her feet and putting on a veneer of professionalism that belied the grayness of her skin tones. Alban, watching her, *knew* she was in pain, could see the lines of strain in her face, but as she relaxed into her courtroom personality he doubted what he knew. "I'm sorry," she said far more briskly. "I didn't mean to create this kind of disruption."

"It was hardly your fault. None of us anticipated this."

Margrit nodded once, still briskly, before a little of her facade crumbled. "What happened? It felt like the top of my head came off. Still does." She touched her hair and flinched, then dropped her hand again, clearly unhappy with what she'd just given away.

"I think, in any practical terms, that's precisely what did happen," Eldred said ruefully. "Your susceptibility to our ability to share seems to…amplify, upon creating a true bridge between minds. And your thoughts are not patterned as ours are."

"You took off the tops of all our heads," Janx murmured. His gaze on Margrit was hungrier than Alban had ever seen it, sending a surge of protectiveness through the gargoyle. He pushed out of his crouch, not moving from beside the chess table or Margrit, but there was no need to. Janx and Daisani had come close enough that simply standing expressed Alban's size in comparison to the other two. Only in his dragon shape could Janx rival Alban's gargoyle form, and he doubted Janx would make that shift in this company.

"So the ritual opened my mind and you all rode my memory." Margrit's voice was strong with comprehension, though she added, "Oh, God," much more softly as the implications of that intimacy set in. "But you have my memories of Ausra. Of what happened. What do we need to do to conclude the trial?"

"Biali shared his own memories while you changed clothes," Eldred said quietly, then sighed as he turned to the gargoyle whose actions had begun the tribunal. "And so I suppose we may as well complete the forms. Why did you, Biali of the clan Kameh, bring us to this tribunal?"

"To see justice done for Ausra. For Hajnal," he growled, glaring at Alban. Alban, stung by understanding, lowered his gaze. He had no room left in him for hate, if he ever had. For him, only regret colored their dealings now, though Biali still spoke with anger. "Cut the farce and get to the heart of it."

Sorrow passed over Eldred's face, deepening his voice further. "We have already taken Biali's memories into our own, and there can be no doubt that the trial is decided. Margrit Knight has chosen compassion time and time again, even when it was to the detriment of her own cause. Biali's choices were perhaps born from love, but have taken a path of vengeance. There can be no forgiveness for enslaving one of our own, just as there is full acceptance for one whose true heart is proven in our court.

"By right of trial, Alban Korund is free and a welcome part of our community. Biali Kameh will walk alone."

"Are you *nuts?*" Margrit surged forward, disregarding her headache as she put herself mere inches from a startled Eldred. "What are you *doing?* You can't exile Biali, not after all of this. The whole point is that this is a stupid law, exiling people from tiny communities. Biali made a mistake. He made a huge mistake, but didn't the lesson he came back with say love conquers all? He acted stupidly, he chose badly, but Hajnal wasn't just talking to him when she said a beating heart is the strongest force on earth, right? Isn't that what you said? That you're all supposed to listen and gain wisdom from what's found in the depths of the memories by those on trial?"

Protests rose around her, but outrage had Margrit in its grip thoroughly enough that she couldn't hear their words, only that they spoke. Her head felt as though it would fly apart with every breath, adding insult to her indignation.

The remaining tribunal members gathered around her and Eldred, wings half spread to make both a private area and, some primitive part of Margrit's brain recognized, to threaten her with their size. She was small, they large; she should retreat, not fight. Her anger burned through any sense of menace and she continued shouting at Eldred, confusing her circle of jailers enough that they fell back a little.

"You do not understand our ways," Eldred said

below her invective. Margrit threw her hands up, sheer exasperation.

"Of course I do! You and goddamned Alban, determined to stick with the rules against anything even vaguely resembling sense! God, you all deserve one another! All right, fine, you want to play it your way? I'll play it your way. I demand another trial to determine Biali's proper place within your society." Red spiked through Margrit's vision as she shouted, and she wished she had a gauntlet to throw down; the gesture would be wildly satisfying.

The gargoyles surrounding her fell back farther, astonishment driving them apart. Eldred gaped, then tilted his head back and laughed, a warm, rich sound of genuine amazement. "Who do you challenge, Margrit Knight?"

"You," Margrit snapped. "All of you. Anybody. Whoever I have to, as many times as I have to. This is a *stupid* law, and I'm not going to stand for it."

"Do I get any say in the matter?" Biali asked from somewhere behind her, voice as dry as desert sands.

"No. You're causing all these problems. You can just be quiet while I save your big, broad ass. Chelsea!" Margrit elbowed the gangly gargoyle out of her way and emerged from their circle to glare at Chelsea. "That serpent, you said he's basically the truth at the heart of everything, right? And I'm about as favored as it gets in his eyes right now?"

Chelsea's feather-thin eyebrows rose. "I did, and you are."

"Hah!" Margrit turned back to the gargoyles, heat rushing through her veins in buoyant triumph and passion. She could ride it through the pain, especially if she tried not to breathe too deeply. "So if we're reducing those journeys to platitudes and clichés, then Biali's got *love conquers all* and I've got *the truth will out.* I'm *right,* and right now I've got the serpent at the heart of the world watching over me. You really want to go up against me with that kind of linebacker on my side? Because if you do, I'm ready and willing."

Silent gargoyles exchanged glances before Eldred surprised Margrit by turning to Chelsea. The tiny woman cocked an eyebrow again, as if disavowing responsibility. Eldred looked toward Biali, then lifted his voice. "Alban, what say you?"

Biali's scarred face contorted and Margrit remembered abruptly that he had more than once expressed disdain for the mercy Alban had shown him in battle. Alban's answer was a long time in coming, and left its mark on Biali's face, as well. "I have no need or desire to see another of our kind exiled. I hold no grudge, nor any lasting damage. Let him belong." Far more softly, he added, "It is what Hajnal would have wanted."

Eldred's nod of acceptance was stiff. Margrit flung herself into one of the chess-table chairs, skidding across the floor in triumph. The action jarred her skull and a pained blush heated her face, but for the moment, she didn't care.

"Margrit." Though she hadn't noticed his retreat, Janx spoke from the door, where Daisani stood at his side. "I think Stoneheart would not answer this, but you've proved wonderfully indiscreet. What of Sarah, Margrit? What of Sarah Hopkins?"

Margrit turned her head, hearing stiff muscles in her neck creak. "It's been three hundred and fifty years, dragonlord. I'm sorry."

Janx hesitated a long moment, then nodded. It was, for once, Daisani who sketched a brief and acknowledging bow, and then the two rivals exited together, bound by one more ancient grief.

One by one the tribunal shifted forms, becoming human, and Grace guided them out. The door banged shut behind them, leaving a hunch-shouldered Biali in Margrit's line of sight. "What'd you do that for?"

Exasperation bubbled up so strongly Margrit hissed through her teeth. The impulse to stamp her feet and fling her hands around in a tantrum of frustration, was barely alleviated by the steam-engine eruption of sound. "Because it's a stupid law. Because you did a stupid thing, maybe even a lot of stupid things, but insofar as there's a right reason to do stupid things, you did them for the right reasons. You did them because people you loved died, and that hurt got twisted around with justice and turned into vengeance, but you're not evil and you don't deserve to be shut away from your people. And there are only a few hundred of your people *left,* and if you all want to survive, they need you, as much as you need them." All the passion drained out of her, leaving her slumped in the chair and a bit wry. "Besides, why go for a partial victory when you can take the full sweep?"

Biali grunted, Margrit recognizing the sound as something as close to a thanks as she would probably ever get. Then he looked beyond her. "Korund."

"Biali." Alban's voice sounded unusually soft in the empty chamber. After a long moment Biali nodded and stumped out of the room, leaving Margrit alone with Alban.

TWENTY

MARGRIT PUT HER elbows on the chess table and slid her fingers into her hair, massaging her head. "Sorry. I shouldn't have gone off about Sarah, but they weren't going to let it go with no answers, Alban. I thought it'd be easier if I broke your promise for you. God, my head hurts."

"Are you so certain I wouldn't have spoken?" Mild amusement filled the gargoyle's voice.

Margrit lifted her gaze, still rubbing her temples. "I could tell you wanted to, but you take your promises seriously." She stood, taking a deep breath, and wiped her hands against her jeans. "How angry at me are you?"

"Angry?" Alban spread his hands helplessly. "You're the most principled, bravest, foolish woman I've ever met. You just challenged an entire host of gargoyles to combat." Laughter shook his shoulders and he extended his hands toward her. "Thank you, Margrit. Thank you for my place among my people, for breaking promises I no longer wished to hold, for risking your life for mine. For ours."

"Oh, stop it." Margrit lurched from the chair and took the few steps to him in a clumsy run, crashing against his wide chest. He was warm, like well-sunned stone, the sour scent of iron fading from his skin. "I'm not the principled one," she mumbled. "You stick to your guns even when you're wrong. I make compromises and wheel and deal. We're hardly birds of a feather."

Alban flared his wings, chamber lights glowing through the translucent membrane. "I have no feathers at all. Margrit, you've paid a high price for what's transpired tonight."

"What I've paid isn't anything like what's coming." She tilted her head up, twinging again at the movement, and saw concern come into the gargoyle's pale eyes. "I'm okay," she promised. "My head's been throbbing since Eldred took my hands."

"It was the bruises that concerned me." Alban traced taloned fingertips just above her skin, outlining bruises that she hadn't noticed until he followed their shape. Even then they were merely uncomfortable, nothing compared to the still-shouting static in her head.

"They'll be gone soon. I meant it when I said Grace couldn't beat me. I was healing during the fight. I could feel it. Alban—" Margrit broke off, wanting to say so many things they tangled her tongue. "Your chains are gone," she finally said, awkward with not knowing where else to begin. "I didn't think Biali'd let you go before the trial."

"He didn't." Alban shook his head as Margrit's eyebrows drew down with confusion. "Grace freed me."

Fresh static burst in Margrit's skull, whitening her vision. "Grace? How?"

"I don't know." He hesitated, a gentle touch against her cheek felt before Margrit could see clearly again. "She touched me—touched the chains—and there was a terrible coldness and a great deal of pain, and then I was free. My people will want to know how, once they're made aware. We haven't often been enslaved, it's happened, and someone who can free us…"

"You didn't ask?" Margrit's voice shot high. "I thought she was human. I thought—"

"I did ask," Alban said. "But she didn't want to tell me, and given that I was in her debt, I chose not to press her."

"And you can just live with that? You can just live with—with not knowing how she did something impossible and took iron that had bonded with your flesh out of your body? You can just live with the vampires saying they're not from this world at all, and you can just live with whatever the hell it is that makes you all jump when Chelsea Huo says to? Alban, do you have *any* answers?" Margrit pulled her voice down from a shout, half aware she was trying to drown out the white noise within her own mind. "How can you live with not knowing?"

Bemusement crossed Alban's stony features as Margrit put her hands against her head. She closed her eyes against the gentleness of his expression, trying to gather herself, and only spoke when she thought she had control. "Sorry. My head hurts a lot." It was another moment before she dared open her eyes to find sympathy in Alban's gaze. "I have so many questions, and nobody wants to answer any of them. Janx said I can walk away from the Old Races much later than I could ever imagine, and I can see where it might be tempting, if I'm always going to be standing here on the outside, looking in. Why does everybody kowtow to Chelsea, Alban? Why can you simply accept that Grace pulled iron out of you without wanting to know how?"

"I do want to know," Alban said mildly. "But I said I wouldn't ask, and I'm not as bedeviled by curiosity as you are. I don't want you to walk away from us, Margrit," he added more softly. "I don't want you to walk away from me."

Margrit sighed and put her forehead against his broad chest. "I'm not planning on it. But don't think I haven't noticed you didn't answer any of my questions just now, either."

Alban chuckled. "You notice everything. Most of your questions aren't mine to answer, or I *have* no answers. Even the gargoyle memories tell us nothing more about the vampires than that they claim to be not of this world. It's an affectation, but…" He trailed off, and then a smile came into his voice. "You may have noticed that we Old Races, as a rule, tend a little toward affectation."

"No, really?" Margrit tipped her head up, mouth twisted into a smile that faded away. "Will I ever get answers? Am I always going to be the human stuck in the middle of a fairy tale?"

"You can route any comer, defend any stand, argue any case. The Old Races fall before you, and no," Alban said with a lift of his brows, "I am not teasing you. I think you'll get your answers in time, Margrit. You may have to earn them from each of us as you go along, because we aren't prone to sharing secrets, but give us time. Give yourself time."

"Easy for a four-hundred-year-old gargoyle to say."

"Almost five hundred," Alban said lightly. "Your haste has already shaped our world. You can afford a little patience. It's been barely three months since you discovered us at all."

Margrit opened her mouth and closed it again, surprise washing out the ache in her head for a moment. "Okay. All right, you're right. I can probably stand to wait another three or four before I know everything about all of you. But I will want to know, Alban. I have to know everything I can. I'm never going to be one of you. Understanding who I'm dealing with is the only compensation I've got."

"I rather think you might understand us better than even I do, who have stood apart for so long."

Margrit shook her head. "You're not alone anymore. You're with me. You're part of your community again. Just—don't pick any fights with Biali."

Alban brushed his knuckles against her cheek and a thrill of warmth suffused Margrit. Still damp, exhausted and hoarse from arguments, she was more fully at home within the circle of the gargoyle's arms than she could ever remember being elsewhere. It went beyond sensuality, beyond happiness, into something so complex and profound it seemed absurd that a single word could encompass it, yet one did. *Content.* She was content, and had never known that emotion could fill her so completely.

Seeing her smile, Alban dipped his head to touch his lips against hers, then his forehead to hers. They stood that way, both smiling, as he spoke. "As you so assiduously tried to tell me, and I so fervently refused to hear, I have not been alone since you came into my life, Margrit. I believe I will stop trying to convince myself I am, for fear you'll move whole mountain ranges to block my way when I try to leave."

"That's more like it." Margrit wound her arms around Alban's waist. "We should be together, and on the same side. The djinn aren't going to let Malik's death go. I'm sorry." She set her front teeth together delicately, lips peeled back in a show of frustration. "I've been playing both sides against the middle for two days, not letting anybody know how he died, and now—"

"You could hardly have anticipated what would happen when you offered memories to the collective."

"A feedback loop would've been bad enough. I turned into a broadcast tower!" Margrit wrinkled her face as her own pitch made her head ring. "I blew the top off every secret I knew."

"No," Alban said with sudden clarity. "Not every secret. You buried one with an avalanche of others." He glanced toward the door, and Margrit followed his gaze, knowing which two of the many who'd passed through it he was thinking of.

"Yeah. I told them everything, but I didn't tell them you'd found her again."

Even with static rushing in her head, it was easier to ride memory now, as though new channels had been opened up in her mind. She knew that it was Alban's memory she recalled, but she felt very little dichotomy, no confusion of one body or another. Wings spread beneath the moonlight felt natural and strong, and wearing his broad body, meant for flying, felt natural, with no confusion as to what had happened to her own smaller form.

Forty miles outside of London, in the midseventeenth century, might have been four thousand in the modern world. It was an easy night's flight, even there and back again, as long as the winds were with him. Janx and Daisani had taken the broken pieces of their hearts and left the city that had disappointed them years since, and Alban had waited until he thought even Sarah's memory had faded before he winged north to the farmstead she'd owned.

He knew it had been abandoned before he landed. The land was unfurrowed and weeds choked those vegetables left to grow on their own. No smoke rose from the chimney, and no scent of it lingered on the air to say a fire would be banked high in the morning. There was a stillness to the house that said it was unlived in, and when he first opened the door, it was to a room stagnant with disuse.

A cradle, long since too small for the girls' use, was tucked against the wall beside the fireplace; opposite lay a straw bed molding with age. The twins would have altered their hours in the cradle and bed, one suckling while the other slept, but neither had done so for a long time.

Everything else was gone from the cottage: no pot hung over the fire, no blankets lay to rot with the bed. Even the kindling was gone, perhaps to be made use of on the road. Alban crossed to the cradle and set it to rocking, a little surprised it hadn't been broken apart to be burned, as well.

A patterned piece of fabric lay at its bottom, little more than an off-colored shadow in the moonlight from the open door. Alban lifted it, finding the pattern to be stitches, and, frowning with curiosity, he brought it into the light.

A crude shape was picked out on the fabric, a rough oval with a handful of divots breaking into its form. Near the bottom was a tiny stitched house; at the top, another. The piece's edges were ragged and frayed, as though it had once been a child's chew-thing. Bemused, Alban tucked it into his fist and carried it back to London.

Hajnal gave the scrap a bare glance and, with a look

of fond exasperation at him, said, "It's the island, Alban. England and Scotland and Wales. She's gone to live in the north." Then amusement had sparked in her eyes and she'd added, "It's very like our way of making sure we won't lose each other, isn't it. Our promise to meet each other at the highest point we can find. Did you tell her about that?"

Alban, flummoxed, admitted he had, and Hajnal looked knowing. "The top of Scotland is as high as you can go without leaving this island. It's a clever bit of work."

Nearly four hundred years later, Margrit felt Alban's rise again in both memory and the present, pure bewilderment as he said, "But how do you *know?*" And in memory, she thrilled at the warmth of Hajnal's responding laugh.

"I know because Sarah would leave a message only one man could read, and you're him. You'd have come to it in time."

"Your faith is ill placed." Alban pulled his lifemate into his arms, and memory faded into another time.

Not so very much later, but long enough. Winter, for ease of traveling through the long nights. Two gargoyles winged through cold starry skies, full of joy at living and exploring and togetherness. The northern coast of Scotland was an expansive area to search, but there was little hurry. Children grew up quickly, but not *that* quickly, and a woman alone with two young girls would eventually be found.

"She might have married," Alban said one night, and Hajnal, warm with firelight under the stars, shook her head. Bemused all over again, Alban said, "How do you know?"

Hajnal shrugged. "Her daughters' father is one of the Old Races, and there's no telling how that will show up.

Not even the memories tell us that, Alban. Perhaps the winter slaughter will bring out a hunger and a speed and a darkness from them, or a bit of bright coin will trigger need and an impossible new form. Sarah wouldn't risk the girls being exposed to a husband." Hajnal went silent a long time, playing with a piece of obsidian, catching flame in it and releasing it to the night again. "But that's only the pragmatic reason. Sarah Hopkins loved them both, my love. It takes an unusual woman to draw a dragon's eye, and a rarer one still to dare turn away from the love of a vampire. Perhaps I'm wrong, but if they had been the men in my life, and I had been only human, I think I would not look for anything more after them. I think the memory would be sweeter, and more bitter, than any other life I might find in their wake, and I think that I would be happier with the dream of what was than the possibility of a new future."

"How maudlin," Alban said with a smile, and Hajnal laughed again, protesting, "Romantic. It's romantic, not maudlin."

But there was no husband when they found her, only Sarah and twin girls, rangy now with young women's years. They were slim and tall and quick and not alike at all, but for a sense of raw command about them both. Sarah, a dozen years older than she'd been when Alban last saw her, had weathered the time well, and watched the girls with pride.

"But I'm not like them," she said. What had once been a thick London accent was marred by a burr now, misplacing her wherever she went. "You'll look after them when I'm gone, Alban? I have some years left in me, but they're special. They'll need watching. They'll need—"

"Hiding," Alban finished in an acknowledging rumble. "They're not supposed to be, Sarah. Not according to our laws."

"Do you believe your laws are right?"

"I believe I flew you out of London when you asked me to, knowing you were pregnant, knowing you would birth a half-breed child. I believe our future is difficult enough without losing ourselves to the human race, but I don't believe it enough to let you fall, or your children suffer. Are you sure this is where you want to live?" he asked more solicitously. "It's a hard life here, Sarah. Hajnal and I could make it easier for you somewhere warmer and finer."

"Somewhere that they would be more likely to find us. The only years of my life that haven't been hard were those times in London with them. I don't mind, and it's safer here for the girls. In a city, if anything happens, someone will notice. Here…" She opened a hand, trailing it across the windswept hills. "No one will see but the cattle."

"Leave another message," Alban murmured. "When you move on, so I can find you."

"The girls can write and read a little already," Sarah said with pride. "Send us letters, and we'll keep you in the know."

"But you never asked." Margrit's voice sounded muzzy to her own ears as she shook off the weight of memory. Some of her headache cleared with it, blessed relief. "You never asked which one of them was the father."

Alban looked down at her, solemnity marred by a spark in his gaze. "It must be something about women. Hajnal was always annoyed that I hadn't asked, too. How does one ask such a thing delicately, Margrit? I could never decide."

"You say, 'So who's the father?'"

"That is *not* delicate."

"You've obviously never heard girlfriends go out for drinks without the men in their lives. Women can be just awful. You should've made Hajnal ask."

"Hajnal and Sarah weren't friends," Alban said thoughtfully. "I never fully understood why."

"Aside from the fact that all of you men doted on her?"

Alban looked affronted. "I did not."

"Alban, you snuck out in the middle of a raging fire to fly her to safety, and let her lovers believe she'd died to protect her. It's the stuff of fairy tales. Everybody gets a little jealous when someone else gets to be the princess."

"We shared memories," Alban said, still offended. "She knew she had no cause for envy. I liked Sarah, but I loved Hajnal."

"You're right." Margrit smiled up at him. "You'll never understand. Well, we're going to have to find them, so maybe I'll get a chance to ask."

"We have to what?"

Margrit rolled back on her heels, eyebrows lifting. "You don't really think Janx and Daisani are going to let this lie, do you? They have *children,* Alban, maybe grandchildren or more out there, or at least one of them does. There's no way either of them is going to let that go. Look at it from their perspectives. For one thing, it's a link back to a long-lost love. For another, one of them has descendants. One of them's going to want to use those descendants against the other, and the other's going to want to protect them. For a third, half-blood children have just been legitimized. They could have potential dynasties out there, waiting to be exploited."

"That hardly encourages me to reveal them."

"Then they need to be protected." Margrit folded her arms in triumph. "One way or another, we have to find them."

"Fortunately," Alban said with a sigh, "they're in New York."

TWENTY-ONE

MARGRIT LET ASTONISHMENT out in a sharp laugh. "They are? And Daisani and Janx don't know?"

"How could they? More than a century passed between Sarah's death in London and the girls' arrival here. They've lived quiet lives, moving from district to district, sometimes out of the city and back again. I've kept watch over them, sent money to bring them to America after I left France. We see each other often enough to know we're well, and little more than that. Janx and Eliseo have been interested in my actions for too long, and I've never wanted to risk exposing the girls."

"Well, come on! Let's go see them!"

"At this hour?" Alban's heavy eyebrows rose in gentle teasing. "Even if they're awake—"

"Do they sleep? Janx and Daisani don't seem to." Margrit put the heel of one hand against an eye, adding, "Neither do I, lately. I thought Daisani said the healing blood wouldn't negate my need for sleep. Maybe that's why my head hurts. What day is it, anyway?"

"Friday," Alban replied equitably. "The early hours, but Friday. When did you last sleep?"

"I napped before coming to the trial. Besides that, not since before Biali snagged you." Margrit shook herself, drawing a deep breath that seemed to loosen some of the static in her mind. "Never mind, I'm okay. Do they sleep?"

"They did as children. I assume they still do. It may be, Margrit, that this particular venture should be yours alone."

New astonishment swept her. "Why?"

"Because the sun will rise in a few hours, and it may be more important to warn them than for me to make proper introductions. It's hard to imagine how they might find them, but even crippled, Janx has resources, and Eliseo…"

"Is Eliseo Daisani. All right." Margrit shrugged, small, helpless movement. "I'll go as soon as it's light. Or— Ah, hell. There's no way I'm going to work, is there. Dammit. Cara was right."

"About?"

"Managing the Old Races is my job. It's more impor- tant to me than the one I'm doing at Legal Aid. I really never imagined that could happen." She pulled away, searching the empty chamber for water bottles and finding none. Daisani's posh office would have them, but the idea lost its irritable edge as she realized its absurdity. Grace's underground hideaway was a far more likely location for midnight tribunals than the business mogul's penthouse work space. "Janx says I'm not really commit- ted to the Old Races yet. What more does it take?"

"Sarah Hopkins bore children to the Old Races and still walked away. The measures that hold you to us are many, but they're not impossible to break, Margrit. Janx might not let go of the third favor you owe him, and until that bond is completed, it might be more difficult to leave us. But if you truly want to sever all ties with us, it's within your capability. I've told you that since the beginning."

"And I've never wanted to." Margrit turned back to him. "Part of me is sick at the idea that I'm this ready to choose your people and your problems over the career I've been working toward my whole life. The rest of me still says that if I want to make a difference in the world, being your advocate is the most profound thing I can do. Nobody will ever know, but…"

"You'll know. Perhaps that's enough."

"Maybe." Margrit drew a deep breath, feeling her heartbeat flutter with nerves. "Before I go see the girls, Alban, I need to ask you a favor."

"You should know by now that I'll refuse you nothing."

It was true: he would refuse her nothing. But for one brief moment, Alban wished that he might have refused *this*.

He held himself deliberately still on the rooftop of Margrit's apartment building. She'd gone in to rouse her housemates, grim with a promise made to the male of the couple. Cole had glimpsed Alban's true form and had been both frightened and angered by what he'd seen, but Margrit was right in one thing: it would not do to ask Cole to bear that secret when his lifemate was kept in the dark. Margrit's own relationship with a human detective had fallen to pieces in part because Margrit was willing to keep Alban's secret. Tony Pulcella had lost faith in her, and rather than restore it, Margrit had chosen to protect the Old Races over her own ease. Asking Cole to do the same was beyond reason. Alban understood that.

Comprehension did nothing to slow the unusual rapid beat of his heart, or the grinding worry in his belly. He'd shown himself to Margrit out of necessity and an irrational belief that she, who ran through the park fearlessly at night, would somehow be able to understand and accept him. There was no such hope with Cole or Cameron.

So he held himself still in order to not betray nerves, wishing he still wore his gargoyle form so that he might wrap wings around himself and feel protected from exposure. He'd agreed it was easier and safer to present him in human form first, but he felt vulnerable.

The rooftop door opened with a whine, Margrit's quiet "Alban?" carried on the wind. He stepped away from the edge he'd sentried himself at, hands deliberately loose in his pockets as he came to meet Margrit and her housemates.

Cole, dark-haired and handsome, radiated distrust and fear. He held Cameron's hand too hard, adding to her frown. She was taller than he by some inches and held her long, blond hair in a fist over her shoulder, trying to keep the wind from lashing it into her face. Both were dressed and bundled in warm jackets, though Cameron's tennis shoes were untied and she looked bemused. "I know you don't come out in the day, Alban, but couldn't you have come by in the evening? 5:30 a.m. isn't exactly visiting hours." She leaned her head against Cole's shoulder, a few strands of hair escaping to plaster themselves across Cole's face. "What's going on?"

"I apologize for the necessity of meeting at this hour. Margrit and I have something we needed to tell you—"

"Oh my God." Cameron straightened and reached for Margrit's arm, letting her own hair go in the process. It whipped around and she snatched at it, then gave up and seized Margrit again. "Oh my God, are you *pregnant?*"

Alban, accustomed to the swoops and falls of riding

air currents, could not remember one that had ever plummeted his stomach so dramatically. Margrit squawked with dismay. "*No!* God, why does everybody— *No!* I'm not pregnant! Jeez, Cameron!"

"Oh." Cameron released Margrit, expression downcast. "Man, that would've been worth climbing up to the roof in the cold and wind. What else could be that important?" She looked between Margrit and Alban expectantly. "C'mon, spill it."

Margrit glanced at Alban, who gestured feebly for her to speak. His pulse continued to beat at an impossible rate, churning his stomach in a completely unaccustomed manner. Gargoyles were rarely shocked, but he was beyond words, a peculiar combination of relief and sorrow holding him in its grasp. A child wasn't something he'd considered. To have the idea introduced and rejected in the same moment flummoxed him.

Margrit nodded, then looked at Cole, whose tense expression hadn't changed, and sighed before turning back to Cameron. "Okay. I want you to hear me out, Cam. You're not going to believe me, but I'm asking you to listen until I'm done, and then when you don't believe it, I'll prove it, okay?"

"Okaaaay. This is all very dramatic."

Alban's upset stomach faded a little as he, Margrit and Cole all breathed words very much to the effect of, "You ain't seen nothin' yet," at the same time. For an instant the possibility of camaraderie seemed alive, but Cole's twisted mouth then belied it.

"All right." Margrit inhaled deeply, clearly searching for somewhere to begin. Alban touched her shoulder, hoping to offer reassurance, and she returned a wan smile before saying, "You remember the speakeasy windows. The ones I put together to make into images?"

"Yeaaaah. We had this conversation already, Grit."

"Yeah. Um, right. I just kind of didn't follow through on it." Margrit pulled her own hair out of its ponytail, then knotted it back up fiercely. "All of those creatures portrayed in the windows, the dragons and everything. Dragons and djinn, selkies and gargoyles," she said more firmly, suddenly committing herself to the explanation. "That's what they were. The ones you thought were mermaids were selkies, seal-people from Irish legend."

"Okay, sure, whatever." Cameron stuck her head out, a tiny shake indicating Margrit should get on with it. "And man presiding over them all. So what?"

"That wasn't a man, it was…" Margrit trailed off, then looked at the sky and mumbled, "Never mind. The point. The point is they're legendary, but they're not imaginary. All of them, all of those creatures represented in the windows, are real. I've met them all."

"You've met a dragon."

"Yeah."

"And a gargoyle."

"…yeah."

Cameron laughed. "So that's why you can't come out during the day, huh, Alban? You're like that cartoon? I always thought that was a cool idea, even though I never got why they had to go to sleep during the day. Seems kind of pointless. At least vampires get, like, destroyed by sunlight. The gargoyles just turned to stone. Fwump."

"In actuality," Alban murmured, though he knew he shouldn't, "vampires are not destroyed by sunlight. And my people are not especially like the ones in the cartoon, although we do share the transformation at dusk and dawn. Ours is a protective state, a way to help us maintain histories of our people that go back millennia. And now, because there is no way you can believe me otherwise, I'll show you the truth."

Alban transformed as he spoke, soft implosion of air bouncing out as his mass became significantly greater than it had been. Cole hunched and stiffened all at once, angling himself as though he prepared an attack. Margrit thought he didn't even know he did it, that it came from someplace deep and instinctive, a primitive hunter faced with unknown prey. Alban, in face of Cole's pose, held very still, though it wasn't the preternatural stillness Margrit had seen him assume many times before. This, too, was preparation: waiting to see which way the predator would jump. That gargoyles, too, were predators crossed Margrit's mind, and she hoped it wouldn't come to any sort of fight.

All of that happened beneath Cameron's resounding shriek. Margrit knew her friend well enough to recognize fear in her voice, and heard only pure surprise. Before the echoes had died Cameron had jolted closer to Alban, her babble making her sound like an overexcited teenager.

"Oh my God. Oh my *God!* Margrit! Oh my God! *Cole!* Oh my God! Are you actually— Oh my God. Is that— Are you— Are— Holy shit! Can I touch it? You? Him? What are you? Holy shit!" She reached out to touch Alban before getting permission, but before doing so froze, then whipped around to face Margrit, her eyes large as she hissed, "You *slept* with him?"

Margrit bit into her lower lip, trying not to look at

Cole, whose expression blackened further at the reminder. She nodded warily, afraid of Cameron's censure, but the taller woman just seized her shoulders for the third time that morning. "You are so giving me all the details!"

Cole made a sound of disbelief and Cameron turned a wide-eyed gaze on him. "What, don't you want to know?"

"No! Jesus, Cam, look at that thing! It's not even human!"

Cameron looked toward Alban again, and a smile of wonder stretched across her face. "I can see that. My God, it's amazing. He. You. You're amazing. What *are* you? *How* are you?"

Margrit, beneath the rush of breathless questions, murmured, "She's taking this better than I did."

"You were concussed," Alban pointed out. "And I was wanted for murder. I believe the jury would consider a plea of extenuating circumstances." Margrit smiled as he offered a graceful inclination of his head to Cameron. "I trust you mean how is it that I exist, rather than how I'm feeling. We believe ourselves to be simply another evolutionary track, from long before this world settled on its path. There are not many of us left, and I fear most humans aren't as delighted by our presence as you seem to be."

"I don't know why not. You're amazing." Cameron walked in a circle around Alban, a hand lifted like she wanted to touch him, though she didn't, only brushed the air near him. "This is incredible. Am I going to wake up back in Kansas?"

"I wish," Cole said through his teeth. "I've been trying for two weeks. It's real."

"You knew? You did know, that's why you and Margrit

had a fight. She said it was about Alban. Cole, how can you be angry?" Cameron pulled her gaze from the gargoyle again, smile starting to fade as she took in Cole's tight expression. "You really are angry."

"Of course I am! Margrit's screwing that freak and you… Jesus, Cameron, what's wrong with you? That thing is a, a—"

"A gargoyle," Margrit said quietly. Cameron's draining pleasure exhausted her, saddening her immeasurably, just as Cole's anger had done earlier. "And he's a friend of mine, someone I care about a lot, Cole."

"You want to talk about friends, how about Tony? You dumped him over that thing, and I'm—"

"Technically he dumped me." Margrit half regretted the muttered words as soon as they were out, but a spark of vindictiveness was just as glad she'd spoken. It wouldn't help, but damned if she wouldn't have the record straight.

"I would have, too, if I'd found out you were screwing around on me with—"

"Margrit's greatest indiscretion with regards to me was in keeping her silence on my true nature during Detective Pulcella's investigation." Alban cut in, voice low with warning. "I can understand your fear and distrust of me—"

"I'm not afraid of you," Cole spat, scorn so thick it almost hid the note of falsehood in his denial.

Alban shrugged, wings rippling with the movement. "But I think it unfair to impugn Margrit's honor. You've known her for many years. Surely you think more highly of her than that."

"I don't know her at all." Cole turned away, a slash of

hurt and anger against the night. Cameron's shoulders dropped, much of her joy gone, but she turned to Alban with a hopeful smile.

"Thank you for trusting me. Us. I have about five million questions, and I really, really hope I get a chance to ask them sometime. I'm glad to have really met you, Alban." She hesitated, then put out her hand, and Alban clasped it gently with taloned fingers.

"I am glad, as well, and I think we'll have more opportunities to talk." His smile was toothsome and alarming, if she was predisposed to being alarmed, but Cam's answering smile dimpled with a hint of the delight she'd shown earlier. Then she followed Cole, concern in the bent of her body.

Margrit steepled her fingers in front of her mouth as she watched them go. "That went better and worse than I hoped. I thought Cam would be more alarmed, but I hoped Cole would have mellowed out a little by now."

"He may never, Margrit." Alban stepped up behind her, folding his arms around her waist and closing his wings around them both, making a pocket of warmth against the wind. "We don't keep ourselves hidden because we want to hide from reactions like Cameron's. She did take it better than you."

"Well, you *were* wanted for murder. And I'd been hit by a car. Almost. And…" Margrit elbowed Alban lightly as he began to chuckle. "I came around."

"And she had the safety of friends at hand. Yes, you did, a gift which I will never stop marveling at."

Margrit sighed. "Maybe it's a girl thing. We all watched too much *Dark Shadows* and *Beauty and the*

Beast when we were kids and now magnificent creatures hiding in the dark are tantalizing, not terrifying."

"I hate to disagree with such a persuasive argument, but not only were you terrified of me initially, but I believe Janx and Daisani still…"

"Scare the shit out of me?" Margrit offered when Alban hesitated, lost for a phrase. He chuckled and nodded, earning Margrit's rueful smile. "All right, so it wasn't the best argument ever. I should…probably go in and try to talk to them. And if that doesn't work, at least take a shower and try to find the twins before I have to go…"

"To work?"

"That's how that sentence should end. Instead I have to try to keep the djinn from declaring all-out war on you, me and Janx, probably especially me, and if that doesn't work, I have to borrow a pint of Daisani's blood and get the police department to trust me when I say dip the handcuffs in it." Margrit thinned her lips, looking up at the gargoyle. "You've made my life very complicated. Interesting, but complicated."

"I hope you can forgive me for that."

"Probably." Margrit drew a deep breath. "All right. Tell me where to find the twins, and leave me to face my housemates."

TWENTY-TWO

THE SOUNDS OF argument cut off as Margrit closed the front door. Cameron, pink-cheeked with distress, looked out of the bedroom she shared with Cole and whispered, "We didn't think you'd be coming home."

"I thought maybe it would help to talk."

"Talk?" Cole's angry voice sailed past Cameron. "What is there to talk about? When you said it was too much to deal with a couple weeks ago, I thought you meant it was over, Grit." He appeared behind Cam, who turned out of the way so her taller form wouldn't block his view or his conversation.

Conversation. That was an unusually polite word for the exchange. Margrit sighed and went to lean on her bedroom door. Cam, falling into an old pattern, stepped away from Cole to lean against the front doorframe, making an unequidistant triangle between the three of them. They'd spent uncountable time in those doors, standing around talking for hours after they should've slept. A spark of hope lit in Margrit's breast, even though Cole's tight expression told her there was no reason for it. "I think I said I was too tired to fight about it right then and we'd talk about it later. I guess it's later now."

"Yeah? And what do you want me to say? That it's okay you're screwing a freak?"

"No." Margrit's reply was very soft, even to her own ears. "Mostly what I want you to say—to promise—is that you won't tell anybody, under any circumstances, what you know. Because if the rest of them find out you've learned about them, if they think you're any kind of risk, they'll kill you, Cole. Both of you. Their existence depends on secrecy."

"Of course we wouldn't tell." Cameron sounded confident and strong, her expression laced with challenge as she looked toward her fiancé. "Aside from who would believe us, it'd be a death sentence. Not for us," she said as Cole's gaze darkened. "For them. You wouldn't want to be responsible for killing somebody, would you, Cole?"

"That thing isn't a somebody. It's a monster. How do you even know it's safe, Margrit? How do you know it's not going to turn around and tear you apart someday?"

"Because if he wanted me dead, I'd be dead half a dozen times over already." A shiver turned Margrit's skin to goose bumps as she realized how true her statement was. She'd been in more danger in the weeks she'd known Alban than she'd ever known before. "He wouldn't have had to have done anything. He could've just let that cab run me down in January."

"Was that on purpose?" Horror filled Cameron's question and her voice shot higher as Margrit nodded. "Grit, what happened back then? Did Alban kill all those people?"

"No." Margrit glanced upward for strength, then plunged on. "It was another gargoyle, a woman who thought Alban was her father and had abandoned her and her mother. She tried to kill me. Alban saved my life." She rubbed her hand over her forearm, remembering the pain of its break. "He's been protecting me for a long time."

Cole demanded, "How long?" as Cam's worry relaxed a little.

"Years," Margrit replied reluctantly. Cole's expression said the same things she had thought when she'd first learned that Alban had been watching over her: that she'd been stalked by a lunatic. "He doesn't think of it that way," she said to the unspoken accusation. "Gargoyles protect. That's what they do. It's what they *are*."

"At least somebody was keeping an eye on her." Cam's smile wavered hopefully. "I mean, she wasn't out there running every night all alone after all."

"That's supposed to make me feel better?" Cole asked. Cam's tottery smile fell away. "It does me."

"Knowing there was a monster stalking your best friend makes you—" Cole broke off with a sound of fear and frustration, then turned on his heel and reentered their bedroom. The door closed behind him at a decibel and speed just shy of a slam.

Cameron flinched and Margrit dropped her chin to her chest. "I'm sorry."

"So am I." Cam sounded exhausted and bewildered. "Grit, I don't know…"

Margrit lifted her gaze again, tightness pricking at her eyes and throat. "I know. It's one thing to date somebody your friends don't approve of, but this is different. This isn't the guy you think might be violent or have a drug problem or who's just a jerk." She chuckled and put a hand over her face for a moment. "In fact, Alban's about as far from any of that as you can get. But it's a little hard to ignore what he is."

"Would you have told us?" Cam folded her arms across her chest, hugging herself tightly as she watched Margrit.

"Yes. I wanted you to get to know him before I did, because…" Margrit gestured toward the closed bedroom door Cole had retreated behind. "I thought it'd be easier to explain if you already basically thought he was a decent guy. I can't think of a much worse way for Cole to have found out than the way he did."

An image of Alban wrestling with Janx against a backdrop of fire flashed through her mind and Margrit curled a lip. That would have been infinitely worse. Even she'd been frightened and angry. "I would've told you," she said with a sigh, pulling her thoughts back to what had actually happened instead of dwelling on more dreadful might-have-beens. "You guys are my best friends. I didn't want to keep secrets."

"But you did."

"Biding time isn't quite the same as keeping them." Margrit brushed away the cautious suggestion. "No points for lawyering my way out, huh? Sorry."

"It's not that I don't understand, Grit…"

"I know. It's just that with things as they are, there's no real way out. I don't think it's anybody's fault." Optimism crept into her voice, but faded before she was finished speaking. "I hope Cole can forgive me. That you both can."

"What if he can't?"

Margrit looked away, regret knifing through her gut and cutting into her lungs. Janx's insistence that she hadn't yet crossed an irrevocable line, that she could still return to the world and life she'd known, rang in her ears. "I know

I'm supposed to say I'd choose my friends, Cam. That I'd choose my life. But I don't know. I really don't know."

Cameron pushed off the doorjamb, sorrow in her face and voice. "Yeah, you do. You just don't want to say it out loud because you don't want to hurt my feelings, and maybe because you're not quite ready to make it real. But you said it the other night, didn't you. Alban lets you fly." She spread her hands, then let them drop as she shrugged. "If he turns out to have wings of wax, I'll try to be there to help catch you when you fall."

At least her headache had faded. Margrit leaned against the train window as it left the station, grateful for the few minutes of dark before it climbed up to ground level, and for the cool, fresh air that blew in from somewhere. Her mind still felt awash with static, though that, too, was less distracting than it had been. Cam's promise, full of friendship and concern, had followed Margrit out of the apartment and still haunted her now. Cole's anger had heavily tempered Cameron's enthusiasm, and Margrit had few illusions as to whose side, ultimately, Cameron would stand on.

Not that she blamed her friend; she, too, was finding herself choosing sides, and leaning toward the one that inevitably cut her off from most of the world she'd known. That her old friendships might not survive cut deeply, but Cam was right: it seemed to be a sacrifice Margrit was willing to make.

As was her job. Margrit turned her wrist up to glance at her watch. It was creeping past seven. If meeting with the twins went extraordinarily well, she might make it back into the city by nine. In hopes of doing so, she had dressed professionally. Even a brief appearance at work was better than nothing. Her coworkers had planned a going-away party for her that night. Margrit wondered if it would still be held if she'd failed to come into work at all for her final two days at Legal Aid. The calendar would read eight hours left, if anyone had bothered to tear off pages while she wasn't there.

The train's automated voice announced her stop and she got off mechanically, glad to hail a taxi and let someone else worry about getting her to the specific address. It seemed as though it had been a noticeable portion of forever since she'd last gone for a run, though careful counting told her it had only been two days. Maybe at lunch, if she had a period of time as defined as *lunch* that afternoon.

The cabbie pulled over at a well-kept brownstone. Margrit studied it out the window for a few seconds, as if she could learn something about the women who lived inside by doing so, then paid the driver and climbed out, hesitating at the walkway for another moment.

Not much could be deduced from their front yard: it was neatly mowed, with a scattering of just-blooming snapdragons and tiger lilies against the house, their scent carried by a brief twist of breeze. There was no evidence of children, something Margrit wouldn't have thought of had there not been tricycles and play sets in other yards. The idea of locating not only a dragon or vampire heir, but an entire litter of grandchildren and great-grandchildren brought a smile to Margrit's lips, and, buoyed, she opened the gate and made her way to the front door. Another quick glance at her watch told her it was still far too early to arrive unannounced on a stranger's doorstep.

Her other choice was to stand there waiting for the hour to grow later. Margrit set her jaw and pressed the doorbell firmly, then took a step back to wait out its ring.

It opened much more quickly than she expected, revealing a snow-haired woman hobbled with age. Margrit blinked in astonishment, realizing she hadn't asked Alban how old the twins appeared to be. She'd assumed they'd be like their Old Races parent: unaging. "Well?" the woman demanded irascibly.

Margrit pulled herself to attention, feeling a blush mount her cheeks. "Hi, sorry. My name's Margrit Knight. I'm a friend of Alban Korund's, and I'm looking for Kate or Ursula Hopkins…?"

"Never heard of 'em." The woman began closing the door.

In a fit of surprised panic, Margrit slapped her palm against it, crying, "Wait!"

The woman stopped, clearly more annoyed than alarmed, and glowered at Margrit, whose blush intensified. "I'm really sorry. I might've gotten the names wrong, but I'm looking for two sisters who used to live here. Maybe you bought the house from them…?"

"I've lived here since 1962," the woman snapped. "Now go away."

"Oh." Margrit fell back another step, confusion and concern bubbling within her. "I'm really sorry. I must've been given the wrong address." She looked at her watch a third time, as though the hour might deny the already-risen sun. There would be no calling Alban for an explanation until nightfall. "I'm sorry to have disturbed you. Thanks for the information." Bewildered, she retraced her steps to the sidewalk and found herself looking both ways, as though a clue might lie within sight. The old woman closed the door with a resounding click, making Margrit jump.

Bad enough that the twins weren't there. Worse, this was a residential neighborhood, one taxis didn't run through every few minutes as a matter of course. Margrit sighed, wishing she'd worn shoes more meant for walking, and pulled her cell phone out as she struck back the way she'd come. At least if she called a cab and was picked up, she could make it to work on time.

An auburn-haired young woman in a bathrobe came out of the house at the end of the row to retrieve a newspaper. Margrit nodded a hello and shook her phone, as if doing so would cause someone to pick up. "Come on, c'mon, why aren't you answering?"

The woman's voice followed her in response: "Sometimes we don't want everything answered."

Margrit twisted around in surprise to see the woman's smile as she added, "Never could resist a rhetorical question."

"You may as well come in," she continued. "Crank your jaw up first. Wouldn't want you to trip on it."

Margrit snapped her mouth shut and said, "Never mind" as the cab company finally answered. She hung up, still staring at the woman. "I saw you a couple days ago in the city."

"Yesterday, actually. Yesterday afternoon."

"Is that all?" Margrit thought back, realized the woman was right, and shook herself. She was losing time badly enough to wonder how the Old Races, effectively immortal, dealt with the slip of one day into another. It seemed possible that the woman standing before her might be able to answer that question, but another one surfaced first: "Were you looking for me?"

The woman's eyebrows rose. "Should I have been?"

"No." Margrit pressed a hand to her forehead, then let it fall. "No, it's just that it never rains but it pours, so in retrospect I thought you might be. You *are* Kate or Ursula Hopkins, right?"

"I used to be."

"I'm sorry," came an annoyed female voice from the house behind the auburn-haired woman. "You got the cryptic twin."

A second woman, this one with darker hair than the first and already fully dressed, came out of the house to elbow past the redhead and open the gate. "She'll keep you out here for a week, being mysterious at you. I'm Ursula." She shot a look at her sister, and, clearly to keep the peace, said, "Or I was." Then, back to Margrit, "If you're a friend of Alban's, there must be something wrong. Come on inside."

Margrit, feeling light-headed, said, "Because Alban doesn't have any friends, or because he's sent one to find you?" and came through the gate.

Ursula latched it behind her. "Both, and on top of it you're here during the day, which isn't when anybody he'd usually call friend could visit. Kate, go get dressed."

"And miss something? I don't think so." Kate padded past both Margrit and Ursula, moving with ordinary human fluidity. Margrit lurched into step behind her, wondering if she could turn the Old Races grace on and off, or if her human upbringing had tethered her to the earth.

Kate led them into a kitchen-dining room at the back

of the house, where a bowl of cereal was growing soggy on the table. She picked it up and dropped into a chair, then gestured with her spoon. "There's water or juice if you want some. Or cereal. Or toast."

Ursula gave her sister another hard look and went to fill a glass with water, handing it to Margrit. "Would you like anything else?"

Margrit curled the glass against her chest and shivered as a draft caught her. "No, this is fine, thanks. I ate breakfast before I came out here."

"All right." Ursula poured granola into a tub of yogurt and joined Kate at the table, inviting Margrit to join them. Feeling slightly overwhelmed, she did, and clutched her water glass as she studied the sisters.

They weren't identical, but nor did Margrit doubt they were twins. They looked to be somewhere in their twenties, younger than Janx and certainly younger than Daisani, though like them, there was something about their hazel eyes that hinted at more years seen than their faces acknowledged.

They shared a high roundness of cheekbone that must have come from their mother: neither Janx nor Daisani had any such roundness to their features. Kate's hair was a flawless shade of auburn, so perfectly caught between brown and red it was impossible to say one or the other dominated. Ursula's was black, reminding Margrit that she'd heard red hair was only one genetic marker off being black. Even though Kate was barefoot, they'd both stood taller than Margrit. Given that they'd been born in an era where the average height was considerably shorter than in modern day, that struck Margrit as unfair.

"So whose are we?" Kate said when she evidently thought Margrit had looked long enough.

Ursula rolled her eyes. "Don't be rude."

Margrit, too curious to be cowed, shook her head. "I honestly can't tell. Don't you know?"

"Of course, but we hardly ever get to ask. What are they like?" This time, despite Kate's bluntness, even Ursula sat forward, a shard of interest changing the color of her eyes.

Surprise thumped through Margrit. "Alban hasn't told you?"

"Of course he has, but he's a gargoyle. Ow!" Kate glowered at Ursula, whose weight shifted again as she drew her feet back under herself. "This woman wouldn't be here if she didn't know about all of us, Urs."

"Margrit," Margrit said. "Margrit Knight."

"I knew that," Kate said with asperity. "You do know about us, right? You see?" she added in triumph at Márgrit's nod. "So tell us about them."

"Katherine, if she's here, she's got something more important to discuss than their personalities."

"Oh, now I'm in trouble." Kate rolled her eyes, making her look even more like Ursula. "She dragged out the full name. Mother got to do that successfully, not you, Urs." She turned her attention back to Margrit, expectation lifting her eyebrows.

"Janx eats up all the air in the room," Margrit said. "Just by being there. It's hard to breathe, as if your chest weighs a hundred pounds more all of a sudden. He likes to tease. Eliseo's sort of more ordinary, except he bulldozes you to get what he wants and you're kind of left wondering what hit you. They both subscribe to getting more flies with honey, but Janx is better at making people laugh. They're lonely," she said, surprising herself with the qualifier. "And they just learned that you survived."

TWENTY-THREE

BOTH WOMEN WENT still with a fullness that removed any question of their heritage. It wasn't a gargoyle's absolute immovability, but it went far beyond human, coming from their centers and moving out until they were wholly encompassed by it. Their gazes were locked together, giving Margrit the eerie sensation that they communicated wordlessly. Twins, she knew, were reputed to share each other's thoughts and mental processes to a greater degree than other siblings. Adding nearly four centuries of practice to that made her imagine their ability to come to silent agreements was quite literally inhuman. A draft spun through the air, chilling Margrit as she watched the two.

Ursula, clearly the dominant of the pair, broke away and returned her attention to Margrit. "What happens now?"

The question, so pointed and pragmatic, surprised her. "I'm not sure. I don't think anyone will come hunting you, if that's what you're worried about. The injunction against breeding with humans was lifted just a few weeks ago." She hesitated, struck by the enormity of what she was about to say. "I think you're basically full citizens now. You could be part of Old Races society, if you wanted."

"And if we don't?" Ursula asked, words weighted and cautious.

Margrit shrugged. "I don't know. Janx and Eliseo are going to start looking for you now they know you survived. But you've got a three-hundred-fifty-year head start on hiding. You can probably keep it up for quite a while."

"But not forever."

More dourly than she intended, Margrit said, "Nothing is forever." Ursula arched an eyebrow and Margrit passed her own moodiness off with a wave. "There are, what, seven billion people on the planet? I honestly don't think that's enough to hide among if Eliseo Daisani really wants to find you. He's got unlimited funds, a great deal of motivation, and he's faster than a bat out of hell. I think he'll catch up with you eventually, and maybe even sooner rather than later. In fact, if you're really unlucky, he's already having me followed and knows where you are. Sorry," she added to two near-identical expressions of shock. "I only just thought of it. I'm not that good at cloak-and-daggering."

"What would you do in our position?" Ursula had evidently been voted spokeswoman in their unspoken discussion; Kate still sat wrapped in a thoughtful silence.

"I'd decide what I wanted from the Old Races and then present myself, fait accompli. Everybody is going to want something from you. You may as well start out as strong as you can."

"When you say everyone…?"

"You can assume pretty much all the Old Races in the city know about you by now." Margrit sat down, explaining how the twins had been discovered as briefly and thoroughly as she could, then outlining the chaotic state that had developed over the past few weeks. The twins absorbed her words with little more than occasional glances at one another, waiting until Margrit finished before Ursula nodded.

"We'll consider your advice. And you won't find us here again, Margrit Knight. Don't bother looking."

"Should I tell Alban anything?"

The not-young women exchanged looks again, Ursula finally replying, "Tell him we've gone home."

"I will." Margrit stood and found herself fighting the urge to bow slightly, as Janx might have done. "I'm glad to have met you. Good luck."

"Thank you."

"Were they glad?" Kate's voice arrested her at the kitchen door. The auburn-haired woman sounded young and uncertain, as if preparing herself for a disappointment she didn't think she could face.

Margrit turned back, one hand on the doorframe. "They were both furious with Alban for not telling them your mother had survived the fire. That you'd survived. They were... I don't know if *glad* is the right word. Greedy. They were greedy for news of you."

Kate nodded, and after a moment Margrit took that as her dismissal and slipped away.

She turned back at the street, looking at the twins' home; looking at the other houses that stood straight and tall alongside it. There was nothing to hint that the women who lived at the corner house were anything less or more than human.

Four centuries of pretending. A shiver lifted bumps on Margrit's arms. She had enough trouble with a few weeks of hiding and lying. Being condemned to a lifetime of it—more than a lifetime—was difficult to contemplate.

But that was what she was signing on for, if she wanted to make a life with Alban. It would be a lifetime of secrets and hidden worlds, and despite some bold words to Daisani weeks earlier, Margrit doubted that the Old Races would ever see the kind of emancipation that slaves once had. Slaves, at least, had been a part of society, ignorable but not actually invisible. It was far more difficult to bring fairy-tale creatures into the light of day and create for them a chance to survive long enough to build tolerance and acceptance. Margrit would be alone in a fundamental way, if she went with Alban.

Less fundamental, though, than what the twins had faced, perhaps. Daisani's gift of one sip of his blood only brought health, not long life: he'd been very clear about that. She wouldn't face the near eternity the twins had already lived, and the Old Races, at least, knew who and what she was. She might have to disguise her life from the human world, but she could belong, as much as any human could, within the hidden world she'd been shown. The twins had been cast aside from both, unable to share their true natures with humanity and forbidden to join the world their father belonged to. Unlike them, Margrit wouldn't be forbidden either world, only forced to be cautious in both.

That, she thought, was a price she could live with.

A sharp gust of wind twisted around her as she finally stepped back from the gate, leaving the brownstone behind. Margrit tucked a lock of hair behind her ear, then slowed, suddenly too aware that the morning was still. Too aware that she'd felt a breeze's touch repeatedly in otherwise quiet areas: cooling her in the subway, whispering around her in the twins' home. Her voice cracked as she whispered, "Come out, come out, wherever you are," and turned, watching the street as though she might be able to pick out an airy form nearby.

Then she was running, toes curled hard against the soles of her heeled shoes to keep them on her feet. Back toward the twins' home, not because a solitary djinn— and she believed it was only one, too little shifting of air for more—not because one could endanger them physically, but because if she had been followed, if their location was known, then the balance had changed and there would be no hiding, not anymore. They would be tracked wherever they went, and perhaps used or manipulated, and the point, the whole *point,* it seemed to Margrit, was to allow these two women to enter the Old Races on their own terms and as their own people. Anything less was a failure.

She vaulted the fence rather than stop to unlatch the gate, and her heel dug into the dirt, clinging and threatening her ankle. Impatient with the human frailty that was her only natural legacy, she jerked her foot free and felt her ankle shriek in protest. For the first time she ignored it, trusting wholly in Daisani's gift: there was no need to walk it off, no need to pretend that the injury wasn't as bad as it felt.

Momentum, nothing more, lent Daisani strength. Her own speed was nothing like enough to knock down a sturdy front door, though the ruckus of her arrival drew both twins to the door fast enough. Kate jerked it open so hard the hinges protested.

"Djinn. Someone followed me, knows where you are—" Urgency, not breathlessness, spluttered her words: the race down the block was nowhere near enough to wind her.

Fire blazed in Kate's eyes, deepening hazel to jade and then through to crimson. Her throat and ribs expanded, contorting impossibly as she drew in more breath than human lungs could conceive of. Wisps of blue smoke appeared, streaming around the corners of her mouth: inhaled, as though she drew heat from the air and turned it deadly. *Janx's,* Margrit realized in a bolt of triumph. She had no agenda tied to learning their parentage, but *knowing,* being the first *to* know, carried its own thrill.

Humans, she found herself thinking, were strange creatures.

Then, in a blur of speed, Ursula smacked a fist into Kate's stomach. The redhead's eyes bugged and she made a sound mixed between a burp and a hiccup that left her discombobulated. Ursula drew her lips back from her teeth, pure animal warning for her sister, then simply disappeared, leaving Margrit agape and Kate still wheezing for air.

Wind whipped behind Margrit. She twisted around, watching a dervish dig a hole in the front lawn, as though a miniature and highly directed tornado had been given the task of landscaping. Flashes of color moved within the whirlwind, moving far too quickly to actually be seen. Kate jolted forward, coming as far as Margrit's side. Without thinking, Margrit lifted a hand, stopping the other woman. Only after she'd acted did she glance at Kate, who lifted a sharp eyebrow at Margrit's audacity, but didn't continue on.

The funnel erupted, expelling a slender body so

quickly it had smashed into the brownstone wall before Margrit could fully register that something had moved. A column of air shot skyward and dissipated, and Ursula slid down the wall of her house to land in flower beds with a dull thud. Kate flowed to her side, the same graceful shift of a large creature's attention from one place to another that Margrit had seen repeatedly with Janx.

"Nothing to hold," Ursula said groggily. Contusions were rising along the arm that had hit the wall and an already-purpling bruise ran down her cheek like overly dramatic goth makeup. "I couldn't get hold. He got away. Sorry, Kay. Sorry. I wasn't fast enough." She put one hand against the brownstone and the other into Kate's, then shoved herself upward. Her eyes swirled in their sockets, dizziness overcoming her, and Kate caught her easily as she fell, scooping her into a bride's carry as though she weighed nothing.

"Nobody's fast enough to hold the wind." Margrit heard wry sympathy in her voice as she stepped forward to offer a hand, though Kate clearly needed no help. "Are you all right? Should I—" Her own words caught up with her and she broke off, staring, then said, "Shit!" with so much enthusiasm she clapped her hands over her mouth. No one was fast enough to hold the wind, but Ursula Hopkins had done one hell of a job trying.

Kate gave her a steady look over Ursula's head. Margrit parted her fingers to whisper, "You're not twins."

"Of course we are," Kate said derisively. "We just have different fathers."

The scornful comment followed Margrit the rest of the day. She'd accompanied Kate back into the house to make certain Ursula was all right, but the twins had resisted her prying into their heritage. Margrit was torn between understanding and disappointment: even if the prurient details were nearly four hundred years old, they still made a good story. They left at the same time Margrit did, none of them under any illusions: the djinn knew both where the twins were now, and whose children they were. They would be unlikely to disappear again, and so their only choice was to decide quickly how to establish themselves, and to do so.

Margrit tried to put those questions out of mind as best she could for the morning, taking second counsel on the trial she'd missed the first full day of. She'd been right: her coworker was well prepared, her presence more psychological reassurance than necessary. Watching him, she was more than aware that her failure to attend the day before had wiped out any confidence she might have provided. Guilt stung her, bringing a wash of tiredness that fed into a cycle. Part of her mind rang with recriminations: she should have been there to do her job. More profoundly, though, lay the awareness that, though she wasn't entirely comfortable with it, she felt more strongly about protecting and guiding the Old Races than she did about doing good for her own people. The two might be one and the same at some juncture, but for now, she had chosen Alban and his people's battles as her own, and had to trust that her coworkers and others like them could fight humanity's wars.

She had wanted to change the world. She'd simply never imagined she might do it in the ways she'd been offered.

Her cocounselor was one of several who took her to a celebratory, bittersweet lunch when the judge called recess. Assuring her he could handle the case, after lunch he sent her back to the office to finish packing and to find a small bouquet of daisies and pink flowers. A card lay at the vase's base, and Margrit read it, then went back to the front desk to smile at the receptionist.

"The pink ones are sweet-pea flowers," he said, before she asked, then smiled sheepishly. "Sweet peas and Michelmas daisies. They're for farewells."

"Sam," Margrit said in genuine surprise and delight. "I didn't know that. You know flower symbolism?"

Sam's smile grew even more sheepish. "Me and Google, anyway."

Margrit laughed and pulled him from behind his desk to steal a hug. "Thank you. They're beautiful, and I'm going to dry them when I get home so they'll last."

"That's not very farewell-like." Sam grinned and returned the hug. "We're going to miss you."

"I'm going to miss you, too." Margrit sighed and passed a hand over her eyes. "I'm going to miss this job. This new thing for Mr. Daisani will give me a lot of opportunities I wouldn't otherwise have, but I'll miss this place."

"Well, we'll take you back if you decide the air up there is too rarefied for your Legal Aid lungs." Sam bumped his shoulder against Margrit's, sending her back to her packing. "You *are* coming out tonight, right? The party's planned. We'll see you off in style."

"I'll be there for a while, at least. I've got another thing later tonight." And there were waters to smooth with her housemates, if that was at all possible. Margrit shook herself and said, more firmly, "Right after work. I'll be there."

* * *

There should have included dinner. Margrit shot a glance toward the door, thinking longingly of the hot-dog stand up the street. It had already shut down, but the idea was appealing after an evening meal made up entirely of red wine. She'd been trying to nurse them, not wanting to face the Old Races at anything less than her best, but the best-laid plans had fallen in the face of raised toasts, and she'd lost track of how much she'd had to drink.

The alcohol, though, hadn't gone to her head the way it would've done even a few weeks before. As with the fight against Grace, she could almost feel her body responding to the wine, metabolizing it and shunting its effects away. It seemed very much like a conscious response, as though because she didn't want to be drunk, she couldn't become drunk, even with wine flowing freely and friends doing their best to see her under the table.

Cameron and Cole had arrived around six-thirty, Cam waving a greeting and Cole at least making an attempt to wipe away a scowl when he met Margrit's eyes. She caught a glimpse of them again and, smiling in unmeant apology to her coworkers, slipped away to try to catch up with her housemates. Someone thrust a fresh glass of wine and an uproarious congratulations at her, and she accepted both with as much grace as she could, then found herself distracted as she searched for somewhere to put the glass down without drinking from it.

Cole cut in front of her unexpectedly, dropping his voice below the general uproar of the party. "So you're really going through with it."

Suddenly glad she still had the wine, Margrit took a fortifying swallow and then handed it to the nearest passerby, who looked startled, then grinned in thanks, toasting her before he moved on. Margrit's returning smile felt pained, and fell away entirely as she looked back at Cole.

"I really am. I thought that Upper East Side apartment would be such a nice move up for all of us…" She'd always anticipated losing her housemates when they got married and moved to a place of their own, but the possibility of losing them more permanently loomed too large now. "Cole, can we get out of here and talk?"

"What are we going to say, Grit? I'm not going to change your mind and I don't think you're going to change mine. I want you to be happy. I just don't think I can watch it, if this is how you're going to get there." Cole sounded tired. "I don't think I bend that far."

Every argument Margrit had died in the making, all of them metaphors that failed on a fundamental level. Humans struggled with skin colors and cultural differences, but it was too easy to see how those could at least be filed under the vast range of human differences, and perhaps accepted and understood. Alban, though, was very literally of another *race*. Inhuman.

She looked up at Cole, trying to find a way beyond the barrier Alban had created between them. "He's a sentient, caring person. Isn't that what should matter?"

Cole sighed and pulled her into a careful hug that felt full of regret. "Maybe." He was quiet a long moment before shaking his head. "That's about the best I can do. Good luck, Grit."

"Thanks." The whisper hurt her throat. Margrit disengaged from the hug and slipped out of the bar alone.

ALBAN REMAINED S+ILL in the first minutes after sunset released him, savoring a subdued sense of belonging that had not been his for well over three centuries. As a youth he would never have noticed the quiet sense of connection that lingered in the back of his mind: the awareness of his people, both physically and mentally. They shared their lives and their thoughts easily, an endless background murmur, and not until he'd cut himself off from it had he realized that it had a sound of its own. Not until he could hear it again did he understand how alone he had been with his own memories.

They still weighed him down. Would always weigh him, as they should. There was still despair when he thought of Ausra's death, though that was tempered with inevitability now. There was still horror at Malik's death, and an awareness that his acceptance within the gargoyle overmind might be short-lived: there had not yet been a reckoning on the matter of the djinn. Only confession, spilled messily into the minds of all the trial attendees through Margrit's dangerous inability to control her thoughts and memories.

Unfair, Stoneheart. Alban's silent chiding came the way Janx would form it, as if he played up the stoniness by scolding Margrit for lacking a skill she had no reason to have. No one, least of all Margrit, could have suspected what would happen if she attempted to share memory with the gargoyles.

And there was a certain relief in all secrets being undone. He wasn't made to keep them, not the kinds he'd accumulated in the past few months. Kate and Ursula, yes; Sarah's life; that secret he had been willing to keep for the sake of children and for the sake of friendship. Killing, done in defense of another or not, done accidentally or not, was too burdensome to bear.

Biali's grumbling presence was nearby, awake and tinged with bitterness. Alban welcomed the familiarity as much as he regretted the divide that parted them. Regretted, but doubted he would try to cross: too many lives, too many deaths, lay between them, and Biali was not by nature a forgiving soul.

Sour humor pulled his mouth long and Alban stretched out of his crouch, admitting the truth behind that thought: *gargoyles* were not by nature forgiving. Stone did not forget easily.

Beyond Biali in Alban's mental awareness, if not actually in physical distance, were the gargoyles of the tribunal. Eldred was the steadiest of those, his sense of self and his roots in the memories reaching down until they became bedrock. Amongst those memories were the last encounter any of the Old Races had had with the selkies before they'd slipped into the sea, becoming, as far as their ancient brethren were concerned, extinct. Eldred had, all those centuries ago, expressed disgust for the selkie attempt at saving themselves; at their decision to breed with humans. It had seemed futile at the time, and the elder gargoyle's opinion had been widely reflected throughout the Old Races.

Their world had changed profoundly since then. Alban had, as he'd foreseen in his youth, watched humanity restructure the world to its liking, and had held fast against those changes, believing tradition to be the only way to survive. That long-held conviction had been shaken under the tidal wave that was Margrit Knight.

Margrit. A smile curved his mouth. She pervaded his thoughts the way Hajnal once had, her actions affecting him so deeply that he could barely imagine his life without her. He'd lost passion to solitude centuries earlier; rediscovering it in her arms was a breathtaking adventure. For all that he couldn't always agree with her, her fire was welcome, warming him after lifetimes of loneliness. Her memory, and the long-lost echo of the gestalt whispering at the back of his mind gave him courage, and with it in hand, he left his chamber to greet his own people at sunset for the first time in centuries.

"Korund." Grace's voice cut down the tunnels, sharp with alarm. Alban turned, surprised, and Grace strode toward him through flickering lights and tall, round walls. "What in hell are you doing?"

Alban glanced down the tunnel, then back at Grace, eyebrows lifted in confusion. "Searching out a meal and the tribunal before finding Margrit."

"Like *that?*" Grace gestured as sharply as she'd spoken and cold curdled Alban's heart. He flashed to human form, hands lifted to stare at them. Talons disappeared into well-formed nails, the one delicate compared to the other, though even in mortal form he had strength beyond anything men could conjure.

"I have never forgotten that before." Disbelief strained his voice. "In all my years, I've never forgotten."

"You're getting complacent," Grace snapped. "Too many things have gone too well for you lately. You're forgetting what you are and what the world would do to you."

"Never," Alban murmured without conviction. "But thank you, Grace." He finally took his gaze from his hands, training it on the curvaceous vigilante instead. The impulse to follow Margrit's curiosity—and his own—caught him for a moment, but he swallowed it with a reminder to himself as much as an acknowledgment to Grace: "It seems the debt I owe you is growing by the moment."

"And I'll call it in some day," she promised. "In the meantime you can get your Margrit to call in her last favor with the dragonlord and get him out of my tunnels."

Alban lifted an eyebrow. "And that's not calling in my debt?"

"That one's Margrit's promise to keep, not yours. Besides, you're the one walking around human territory in your natural form, love. Even if I'd never done you any other favors, you'd owe me large for that one."

"I would." Alban studied the door he'd almost taken, then looked at Grace again. "Tell me what my welcome will be, Grace O'Malley. I was confident a moment ago, confident enough to forget myself. But now I find myself remembering that these men and women were called to pass judgment on me, and while they have granted amnesty and I can once more walk among the memories, I know very little of them, or how they think of me."

"And you think I know?"

Humor quirked Alban's mouth and he quoted, carefully, "'Grace knows more than she should, love.'"

Surprise brightened the woman's dark eyes and she laughed. "There's a spark of cleverness left in there after all. All right, Korund. They're curious, is what they are, which I think you could learn quick enough from the memories."

"I could." Alban hesitated over continuing, and Grace hopped on his pause with a spark of humor in her eyes.

"But it seems like prying, does it, after all this time? Ah, Korund, you're not one of them anymore, but you can't be human, either. Maybe you're well matched with Margrit after all, the both of you forging ahead into new territory." A shadow passed over Grace's face, aging her unexpectedly and making Alban realize he had no idea how old the platinum blonde was. She'd been part of the city's underground for years, according to Margrit, but it hadn't left its mark. Just then she looked far older than even the greatest number of years he could accord her, though it faded and left her as she had been, young in form and face, but somehow ancient in her gaze. "Go on, then, Stoneheart. Join them. See who you are among them, and then move on to see who you are in the world."

"What about you, Grace?" The question held him in place even when he might have wanted to move at her command; to embrace the world as it had become and learn his place in it. "Will you stay where you are while the world changes around you? Will you not move on, too?"

"Ah, sure and you know the answer to that," Grace said

with a sighed smile, and a ghost of humor turned Alban's mouth up at the corner.

"You'll move on when you've been given the kiss of angels, isn't that what you say? What does it mean?"

"Grace'll let you know when she finds out." She nudged him toward the door with a bump of her hips, encouraging him to move without touching him. Alban chuckled again and went where he was bid, putting weight onto the heavy iron door handle that opened the way into the below-streets central refuge.

It opened silently. Grace's territory was inevitably well oiled and smooth-running, far more so than might be expected of a ragtag bunch of teens led by a leather-clad den mother. The group within, though, was wholly different from the youthful faces and chip-on-the-shoulder attitudes Alban had come to recognize and admire over the past months.

Instead an older man straightened from his crouch and turned to look at Alban. He was stocky, not gone to fat, but broad and jowly. White touched otherwise steel-gray hair at the temples, and deep-set eyes were much the same shade as his hair. Alban wondered suddenly if it would be as clear to Margrit that this was Eldred in his human form, or if the ability to recognize one another in any shape was part of what made them unique.

Looking over the others, he thought it took no more than an ability to extrapolate. The lanky youth—younger, certainly, than Alban himself—had a touch of strawberry to his white-blond hair and was as leggy and elbow-ridden in human form as in his gargoyle shape. The two women were as much Valkyries—Margrit's memory intruding, that; Alban wouldn't have chosen the word himself—in mortal form as in immortal, both broad-shouldered and blue-eyed with long, pale hair. They looked like themselves, all of them.

And they were all riding judgment on him. Nervousness that hadn't been present the night before fluttered in Alban's gullet, a reaction that seemed inordinately human. He bowed, as much a slight offer of respect to the elder as a way to hide his own sudden nerves. After an instant Eldred tipped his head in response, gesturing Alban to join them. A mockery of outrage rose to replace worry: this was, after all, Alban's home, and it should be he who offered a place at the table to the newcomers. Only a mockery, though, the thought seeming laughable even as he felt its sting. There were far more pressing matters to be concerned with than whether he was welcomed or welcoming.

"Alban Korund." Eldred's voice was as deep and rich in his mortal form as it had been the night before. "Welcome home."

What had been a trickle of mental touch suddenly became a flood, emotion ranging from reserved to angry and, as Grace had said, to curious. Unprepared, Alban shuddered under the onslaught, the round walls and concrete seating around him disappearing and staggering mountains replacing them.

There was vitality in these mountains, unlike the memories he'd slipped through over the last months. Those peaks had been worn with time, too many lives lost to grow them taller. They had been his family, his closest friends, and they had reflected a dying race.

No longer. Now mountaintops were jagged with change, snow patches glowing blue in moonlight beneath clear skies. The tree line burst with the promise of spring, hints of green in the night, and echoes of voices rang the stone, shivering loose rock into short slides.

Stunned, Alban turned, taking it all in, and when he'd completed a full circle, he faced a campfire, the half-dozen gargoyles in the room with him seated around it. Beyond them rippled hundreds of others, faces and minds joined in the gestalt but not physically present. Challenge was written on those faces; challenge and interest, anger and hope.

"What has happened?" Astonishment pushed his question out before he knew he intended to form it. "We live. We...live."

Biali thundered in, door clapping shut behind him in the real world and carrying ricochets of sound into the mind of memory. He muttered, "You happened," and sat down at the fire, making himself comfortable in a way that seemed beyond Alban to accomplish himself. "You and that lawyer of yours," Biali added, clearly not expecting Alban to put it together himself. "You and that quorum."

"You sat for the gargoyles at the quorum," Alban protested. "Not I."

"Pah. You started it, Korund. Talking to the lawyer. Telling her what you were. Deep quakes send waves across the world." Biali shoved a thick hand into the fire, rearranging branches, and Eldred, looking wry, picked up where he left off.

"We have been dying, all these centuries. You know this." *You* encompassed far more than just Alban: a shift of agreement ran through a thousand faces, swirling back through crowded memories until it had touched them all. "We are slow to change, and have always chosen the safety of tradition over the risk of innovation."

At that, Margrit's image, rife with exasperation, swam before Alban's eyes and made him chuff laughter. That thought splashed through the linked gargoyle minds, making Eldred lift a heavy eyebrow. Alban ducked his head in apology, finding a smile still stretching his face. "I've always held that we were right to stand by our traditions."

"And yet you have disregarded them broadly through your entire life."

Fresh astonishment burned away Alban's humor and he straightened again, agape as he met Eldred's gaze. The elder gargoyle's expression was cool, though beneath it lay a pool of warmth, even admiration, welcoming enough to startle Alban anew. Eldred's sense of self carried a hint of envy, memories shifting and exploring the choices he might have made, all of those thoughts visible to the gargoyle overmind. Hundreds of years earlier he might have embraced the selkies and their decision to save themselves by breeding with humans. Instead he had been repulsed, holding tight to tradition. Now, for all that gargoyles were not creatures in the habit of second-guessing themselves, it was clear that Eldred wondered what changes might have been wrought in the world if he had admired the selkie daring and accepted their choice rather than turned his back on a man who had been his friend for centuries.

"You left our mountains before your hundredth year," Eldred said. "You went to live among humans, to explore the world that they were creating. To try to understand it. Only one of us was bold enough to join you."

"And she paid for that choice with her life," Biali snapped. For an instant tension sang through the gargoyles, Hajnal's loss fresh and painful through the intimacy of memory.

Alban, softly, said, "We've all paid," and after long moments Biali settled back, no longer pressing the point.

Eldred continued as though the brief fracas hadn't happened, his gray eyes turning blue as moonlight spilled over his face. "That in itself was a break with tradition. More so was the friendship you built with Eliseo Daisani and the dragonlord Janx. Dragons and vampires," he said with a shake of his head. "No one befriends vampires. But even that, extraordinary as it might have been, was nothing to the choice you made on their behalf. To separate your memories from all of ours, to make yourself a breach amongst our people, in order to hide half-human children? What—" and he sounded as though he truly wanted to know "—were you *thinking?*"

"That the sins of the fathers need not be visited on the children." Alban turned a palm up, knowing he borrowed human concepts and hoping to placate all his people with the gesture. "They were condemned by their heritage, but innocent in their birth. Their mother loved two men of the Old Races and would have never betrayed the truth of them to the world. I saw no risk in helping them all to live."

"And that," Eldred said, voice filled with granite, "is why you *are* the Breach, Alban of the clan Korund. Your life has not been that of a gargoyle, not in any way that we recognize. You have lived separately from our memories. You've told humans about our existence more than once. You've chosen to allow forbidden children a chance to survive. You have taken the lives of our brethren, and you have made no apology for these choices and decisions."

"I—" Words were useless in the gestalt, memory and emotion riding faster and farther than any vocal construct could, even if Alban could muster them. Eldred was right: there was no apology in him for the deaths he'd caused. Sorrow, yes, and guilt, and regret, but a lifetime, even one as long as a gargoyle's, would not change the fact that he would act again as he had in the heat of the moment. He would choose Margrit over Ausra; he would, in any way that mattered, choose Janx over Malik. Ausra's madness would always be a point of agony, a thing he would never find a way to cease mourning, but Malik had intended to take Janx's life, and for all his horror at causing the djinn's death, Alban knew it had been accidental. He had not done the deliberate murder Malik had intended, and whether the Old Races, whether the gargoyles, whether anyone at all understood that, it was the fine point of difference that mattered to Alban himself.

And that sentiment rocked back through centuries of time. He believed the choices he had made were the right ones, whether they were supported by Old Races law or gargoyle tradition. Sarah Hopkins had not deserved to die for having loved Janx or Daisani; her children had deserved a chance to live, for all that their fathers' people said they were aberrations which should not exist.

"You are right," Alban whispered. "I am not like you at all." Shock made him cold, unusual for a gargoyle, and he stared across the shifting faces within the overmind in a disbelief so deep it was stained with humor. "All this time spent in defense of our traditions, and it seems I have had very little sense of them at all."

"Biali once said you might have led us." Eldred's eyes went to the stark, white gargoyle, and the weight of a thousand more gazes joined him before they all returned to Alban. Even Biali looked up, mouth flattened with irritation. "I believe you have done so," Eldred continued. "Whether deliberately or not, you have led us to this place and time, and to these schisms in what we were and what we must become."

The urge to apologize rose in Alban, but that intent was drowned beneath the weight of Eldred's words. "We have discussed this amongst ourselves, amongst all the clans who are left." Power lifted his words, a tide of tears and fear and joy so profound that it tore through Alban's chest, ripping away the breath there and leaving nothing in its wake. *Anticipation:* the gestalt tasted of it, and his heart began a too-fast beat of uncertainty, as though understanding lay just beyond his grasp.

"We have debated," Eldred said again, "and have found only one answer that we can agree to. We gargoyles number in the hundreds, no more, and our time as part of this world will come to an end if we do not choose to change as the selkies have changed. We are not well equipped to force ourselves down that road, and so for all our people, *before* all our people, it comes to me to tell you that we have, for the first time, chosen a leader for all of our clans, chosen someone to guide us down a path we cannot walk without help.

"So I put it to you, Alban Korund." A hint of humor darted over Eldred's face as he obviously and deliberately formed his question in a fashion not typical to gargoyles. "Will you be our first democratically elected leader?"

TWENTY-FIVE

HUMANS LIVED BY threes.

Through a fog of rage born from fear, through a blur of red and violent white streaks, the bit of trivia gave Margrit something to hold on to. Three weeks without food, three days without water: those were the average extremes that humans could typically survive.

Three minutes without air.

She would have had more confidence in that number if she'd hyperventilated before being snatched.

She'd left the bar clearheaded, Daisani's gift working its magic to wipe away the effects of alcohol. If she'd had a plan, it had been to work her way into the storm tunnels and find Alban. Their worlds were changing in tandem, and she wanted both to be at his side, and to have him at hers as they discovered what new paths lay before them.

Instead, for the second time in her life, someone had grabbed her from behind and turned her into nothing more than mist drifting through the city streets.

Even through blinding fury, she doubted her abductor would keep her misted until she died of asphyxiation. Not that she had any particular faith in her long-term survival chances when a djinn had kidnapped her, but she imagined her execution would be public. Allowing her to die during travel lacked drama, and the Old Races had a fondness for drama. Teeth gritted, Margrit closed her eyes against the smearing colors of the world and waited for the air to become breathable again.

When it did, she was cast away, sent stumbling as though her captor had found handling her as distasteful as she'd found being kidnapped. Half blinded by tears, and gasping on too-thick air, she caught herself on her fingertips against the floor, then scrambled to her feet and faced the djinn who'd captured her.

It was Tariq, standing too far away to retaliate against him, even if she had a way. A bubble of anger burst in her: she should be carrying the ridiculous watergun that had condemned Malik. It was feeble protection, but better than nothing. She'd rectify that mistake if she had the chance.

Behind Tariq stood a group of djinn, held in check by little more, Margrit suspected, than his will. It was less defiance than genuine curiosity that made her ask, "Am I still alive because you wanted an audience?" Her voice scratched and she drew another breath, coughing out the last of the fog. It tasted faintly of acid or blood. Like ketchup gone wrong, she thought, then tried to drag her mind back in line.

She'd been brought to a tall delivery garage. Its corrugated rolling door was closed, rattling as traffic passed outside it. The concrete floor was empty in the center, with boxes and pallets piled around its edges. Those, in turn, were littered with selkies and djinn.

There were more than was easily countable, and they

had split the room more or less evenly, the door's width creating a no-man's-land down the center. Tariq joined his brethren, leaving Margrit alone in a broad, empty swath. She felt suddenly small and remarkably fragile under the eyes of so many Old Races. Unwise impulse drove her to mumble, "You're probably all wondering why I called you here today…."

Over her attempt at humor, far more clearly than she'd spoken, Cara Delaney's voice cut through the room: "No."

Startled, Margrit jerked her gaze up. "Cara? You should still be in the hospital."

Cara stepped out of the gathered selkies with her head held high, though her cheeks were pale. "I dismissed myself. No, Margrit Knight, we are wondering how it is you think it's within your right to offer the djinn control of Janx's territory."

"I could have sworn you told me to avert a war."

"Avert a war, not—"

Exasperation flooded Margrit, drowning any sympathy she might have had for the young woman's injuries. "Give it a rest, Cara. You're not the right person for the job. I'm sure there are plenty of bastards among your people, and you might've gotten a tough-girl badge for getting shot, but you're not hard enough to run this. Seeing as how Tariq was willing to squeeze my mother's heart to a pulp, I'm pretty confident he's got the stones for it." Margrit shot a glance at the djinn. "Does this mean you're accepting my offer?"

"We would be fools not to." Tariq's voice was thick with dislike.

"And what do the selkies do, Margrit? Slink away with our tails between our legs?" Cara's voice remained cold, but a sliver of humor wrinkled Margrit's eyebrows.

"Do seals have tails? Or back legs? They've got flipp—" She broke off at Cara's expression and fought down a smile. "Sorry." Amusement fled and she pressed fingertips over her eyelids momentarily, knowing she gave away signs of strain and not much caring. "You get to not be embroiled in a war, Cara. You get to be fully recognized members of the Old Races. There are tens of thousands of you, and your leader—Kaimana *is* your leader, isn't he?—has a world-market business already. You don't need Janx's empire to establish yourselves as heavyweights among your people. In the name of peace, walk away."

Cara's jaw tightened and she looked imperiously toward the djinn. He tensed in protest, and Margrit sighed. "If that's a 'go away so I can discuss your fate with the human without your interference' look, don't bother. Just say it." Reckless anger flooded her, pushing her beyond the bounds of wisdom. She had a sense of fait accompli, that regardless of her actions it would end badly for her; would very likely end badly for the people to whom she now spoke. Railing at them would probably do her no good and could easily do her harm, but aggravation was more powerful than self-preservation. Especially given that she doubted she could shield herself from whatever sentence the offended Old Races already had in mind.

Cara's voice dropped as if she could disguise her words from the djinn through softness. "Do you understand what they might do if given their heads, Margrit? D—"

Margrit cut her off with an incredulous laugh. "*Cara.* Janx ran a crime empire. He employed murderers as a matter of course. He gave them things to do. He ran gambling houses and whorehouses and drugs and, for all I know, he ran people. I don't *want* to know," she added more sharply, more clearly, as Tariq drew in a breath to speak. "You were a squatter, Cara. You've got to have some idea of how dark the world Janx ran is."

Something flashed in Cara's eyes, a hint of old hurt that made unexpected guilt spike through Margrit's belly. "I know," the young woman said. "I know, which is why I ask if you have any understanding of what you'd unleash by giving the djinn control over this empire."

"Of course I know. Most of my job is defending the bad guys. But the truth is, there are always going to *be* bad guys, and what's more important than who they are is that they establish some kind of control down here. You're on the verge of warfare with humans, never mind among yourselves. You can't afford that. So you either take the deal I offered or I walk out of here and you face the consequences."

"Well," Tariq said softly, "no."

Anticipation rolled through the gargoyles like a living thing, eagerness shared by an entire people. Alban could see them beyond Eldred, hundreds of faces half-present in memory and a scant handful actually there, watching him with hope and curiosity and resentment.

It was to that last, particularly, that Alban responded. His gaze fell from Eldred to Biali, who remained hunkered and glowering into the fire. He was as closed off to the gestalt as was possible, a mere pinpoint of sullen presence with no more hint than that to his thoughts. "It's not a quorum, Stoneheart. It doesn't have to be unanimous."

"I'm sure it isn't." Bemusement filled Alban's voice, spilling into the overmind. That his people could even conceive of such an idea was beyond his expectation of them. They had always been small clans gathered into tribes, passing history back and forth within the family lines. They'd known little in the way of hierarchy; a people able to sense each other's thoughts tended toward agreement without specific leadership. To strive for something as extraordinary—and as human—as an agreed-upon… Words failed Alban as he looked from Biali to their people and back again. He was no king or president, and neither did the sense of their expectations carry that, nor even so much as chiefdom or some other small title. *Leader* was sufficient; *guide* was more appropriate. That word, out of many offered, made Alban nod before he crouched across from Biali.

"You were my first friend," he said quietly. "Perhaps no longer my oldest, but my first. Tell me, Biali, what you think of this idea."

"You're right." Biali looked up, his one good eye hard with old anger. "We're not friends. You're a fool and you're dangerous to all of us. Always have been. Know what's bad enough, Korund? Watching you walk away with the woman I loved and leaving me to make what I could of the rest of my life. Know what's worse?"

Alban shook his head, silent, and waited on the scarred gargoyle's words rather than seek out answers in the overmind. They came soon enough, Biali's voice an angry growl. "Having the choices you made follow me around for centuries. Me, I changed with the world. Went to work for Janx when there was nothing else to do. Found Ausra and hoped there was another chance for me. Didn't look beyond any of that. And now I am. Can't help it. We all are. And what we're seeing is that neither way works, not mine and not theirs." A flickered gesture indicated the silent gargoyle clans. "What we're seeing is the little choices you made are adding up and showing us how the world'll look in another hundred years. What do I think? I think it's a terrible idea."

He finally lifted his eyes again, scowling heavily at Alban. "But it's like I told the lawyer. No point in standing on shifting earth. No point in standing against the tide. You're the only choice we've got. So show us how to live, Stoneheart. Teach us what to do."

Alban breathed a laugh. "You're the one who sat on the quorum and voted for the destruction of all our laws. If I'm to help our people find a new path, I could do worse than to have your advice as we walk it."

Biali's gaze sharpened and disruption shot through gargoyle link. Mountains sprang up around Alban, craggy, impenetrable, and filled with Biali's will. Surprise washed over Alban as Biali came out of the rock, the walls he'd created so much a part of himself that he imbued them.

"I'd forgotten," Alban said almost idly. "I'd forgotten what privacy looked like in the overmind. I've become so accustomed to not needing it, I think I'd forgotten this could be done." He turned, looking at the tall cliffs and the stars that clawed their tops, far away. "It seems I've forgotten a great deal."

"You're a gargoyle," Biali growled. "You don't *forget* anything. You just misplace it for a while."

"Perhaps so." Alban faced his rival again, wondering at the confidence that had allowed him to turn his back on Biali, particularly in a world of Biali's own making. "What are we doing here?"

"Are you just that good?" The last word was sneered, though craggy walls around them echoed with different emotion: frustration; bewilderment; dismay. "Is Janx right? So true and noble as to sicken? Do you hold no grudge, *Stoneheart?*"

Alban fell silent, searching for an inoffensive answer, then spread his wings—his wings; in the sanctuary of Biali's mind, he wore his gargoyle form, for all that it was the human shape that stood in Grace's meeting chamber—spread his wings in dismissal of politeness and acceptance of the truth: "I won, Biali. Come the dawn, I have won…everything. Our battle. Hajnal. The quorum. The trial. A place amongst our people. Margrit. What I've lost isn't so much that I must hold to bitterness and begrudgery for the wrongs you've done me."

"You lost Hajnal, in the end."

"But I was with her for a little while." Alban breathed another laugh, soft sound, and turned again to look at the white mountains rising around him. "A year ago, I think I would have been angrier with you. I was alone then. Melodramatically alone," he added wryly. "Mourning for a life lost two centuries ago, bitter for the chances wasted, angry at the world for snatching happiness away from me, though I wouldn't have admitted to any of that. I would have said I was only doing as gargoyles ought to, standing unmoved against time. The past few months have changed me greatly. This position our people have offered me…I wouldn't have been worthy of it then."

"You always were pompous."

Alban blinked and looked back to find Biali glowering irritably at him. "You wouldn't have had the chance, three months ago. That lawyer changed everything, including you."

"And you?" Alban asked.

Biali's jaw worked before he finally spat, "Don't count on it." The sentiment reverberated from the walls around them, lending it weight.

Alban considered his onetime friend for a long moment, then nodded. "All right. I won't." He crouched and sprang upward, wings catching the air and driving him to the distant peaks. A moment later he broke free of their private conversation and rejoined the gathering of gargoyles, landing amidst them as though he had never left.

Curious faces turned to him, glanced at Biali, and returned to Alban again, unnerving in their solidarity. Alban caught the eyes of those in the room with him, and then the nearest of those in the world beyond as he gathered himself to speak.

"I have, I think, done very little to earn the trust you're offering me. The choices I've made have not been made out of foresight or wisdom, only a belief in what was right regardless of what our laws dictated. If you've changed enough to recognize that we must adapt further or die out, then I think any leadership I might provide is moot. You have already become the change you wish to see. Biali made courageous choices at the quorum, choices I don't know if I would have been bold enough to follow through on myself, even if not doing so might have been hypocritical. I think I feared change more than any of us, but it seems even I've fallen beneath its scythe. If there's any guidance I can offer, then I will, of course, but it seems to me that you would be better served by Eldred or one of the others."

He hesitated, then turned his palms up in supplication. "That said, there is one thing I think we as a people should do. The djinn have it in their hearts to make war on us over the death of one of their own. I'm responsible for that death, and will not hide from it. But I still believe that our third law must hold sway. We Old Races cannot be allowed to turn on one another even when something as terrible as Malik al-Massrī's death rocks our ranks. If exile is to be the price, so be it. I will pay it willingly enough. But we cannot permit this to come to war. Bloodshed is too costly for any of us. So I would ask, if I may ask anything, that some of you join me in finding the djinn and designing a peace accord out of this tragedy before it escalates out of control."

Biali cracked his knuckles over the fire and shoved out of his crouch. A smirk shadowed his scarred face as Alban looked askance at him, and he shrugged his thick shoulders. "What? Pretty words don't disguise that you're going in looking for a fight. I'm not going to miss this one, Stoneheart. It ought to be good."

Ice slid through Margrit's veins, holding her in place as Tariq continued, his voice so soft and steady it seemed that what he was saying must be reasonable. "There is still the matter of Malik al-Massrī's death."

"It was an accident. Would you be persecuting Malik if he'd managed to kill Janx? Or Janx, if he'd killed Malik to survive?"

"Irrelevant questions. The glassmaker lived and Malik died at your hands and the gargoyle's."

Recollection struck a chord. "Glassmaker, that's right. You two know each other, don't you? He knew your name."

Tariq's amber eyes darkened. "Also irrelevant. You will not save yourself by changing the subject, Margrit Knight."

Margrit muttered, "It was worth a shot," then, more clearly, said, "Do I get a trial? Alban got one." Her body was still cold, but her thoughts, at least, seemed to be moving at their usual pace, searching for a way out, or at least an extension of the brief minutes she had left.

"Alban Korund is a gargoyle, and faced a gargoyle tribunal for the death of another of his own kind. Their traditions are different from ours, as he will discover when we mete out punishment for Malik's death."

"So no trial." Margrit bit down on further response, realizing fear was translating itself into sarcasm. Her gaze went to the steel delivery door and slipped away again instantly: even if it was open so she could make a run for it, outrunning a djinn was quite literally impossible. Quick as she could be, she simply couldn't outpace someone who didn't need to travel the distance between two places.

"Do you deny your guilt?"

Startled, she looked back at Tariq. "I—" Complicated emotion arose, embodied in flashes of the House of Cards on fire, and Malik's destruction in the flames. Picking her words carefully, she said, "I deny that I am guilty of murder. I do not deny that I'm partially responsible for accidental manslaughter, and I don't deny that I'll regret that for the rest of my life." *However long it may be,* she added silently.

"Then even if we were so inclined, there is no need for a trial." Tariq nodded and two djinn appeared at Margrit's sides, hands on her shoulders, forcing her to her knees.

Fear finally caught up with her, making the fall thick

and heavy. Tears burned her eyes, whether from terror or pain, and the whole of her body was cold. Tariq put his hand out and a third djinn placed a scimitar in it, then backed away as he unsheathed it with the too-familiar sound of metal on leather.

Margrit's throat clogged, choking off her breath as Tariq approached. Water swam in her eyes, but she couldn't bring herself to blink the fog it produced away, irrationally afraid of missing the strike that would end her life. Out of nowhere, she recalled an article she'd read about decapitation, possibly one written during the French Revolution. The man scheduled to die had promised his friends that he would keep blinking as long as he could once his head left his neck, as an experiment in determining whether death was instantaneous or not.

He had blinked for twenty seconds before finally going still.

She did not want to *know* that she was dead, not like that. Horrifying enough to die young and badly, but far worse to face even a few seconds of knowing her life had already ended and she was only waiting for her damaged body to realize it.

"Cara?" Panic turned Margrit's question into a chalkboard shriek.

"Yes, of course." Cara stepped forward, still pale, and executed a careful half bow toward Tariq, who turned to her with the infinite patience of a man certain of his control.

Cara met his eyes. "I don't like it, but to avert a war that would destroy us all, I agree to Margrit Knight's terms. The docklands and Janx's empire are yours. I hope we may come to some new agreement on working together, but even if not, the selkies will not stand in the way of the djinn. Nor," she added a little more coolly, "will we support you if you should pursue your vendetta over the matter of Malik al-Massrī's death. If you choose to war against the others, you do so alone."

Tariq returned her hard gaze a long time before a sharp smile twisted his features. "We accept *your* terms, and in exchange will allow the life of this human to stand in the place of any of our brethren against whom we might otherwise hold accountable for unfortunate events."

Cara looked down at Margrit, then nodded and stepped back.

Disbelief clenched Margrit's stomach, forcing a frightened laugh free. Tears finally fell, scalding lines down her cheeks, and she shook her head savagely, trying to splash the droplets of salt water on the djinn holding her. Neither so much as flinched. Margrit twisted her head to the side, biting down violently on one of their hands before a blow across the face dizzied her. The injured djinn knotted his hand in her hair and hauled her head back to expose her throat to Tariq's sword.

A rumble arrested all attention, making Margrit's tormentors turn toward the delivery door as it shuddered open. Headlights flared outside, silhouetting two slim figures against the night before the door rolled shut again. Cara took one step farther back from Margrit, shoulders rigid.

Ursula Hopkins folded her arms across her chest and stared boldly at each group gathered in the room: selkies, djinn and the little crowd around Margrit herself. Kate, like a crimson shadow, leaned on the garage door, a foot cocked against it as she studied her fingernails with a deliberate insouciance.

Despite everything, amusement rose up to strangle

Margrit. Janx himself couldn't have looked more non-chalant, and she fought back the urge to suddenly begin wild applause.

Instead all attention hung on the two young-looking women. Silence stretched until Tariq snapped it with, "What is this? We have business, and you—"

"Business?" Kate glanced up with flawless ingenuity, eyes widened to see a hand tangled in Margrit's hair and a blade at her throat. "Oh," she said, as if in genuine surprise, and then smiled. "I wouldn't do that if I were you."

"Half-breed." Tariq spat the word. "You would shy from spilling the blood of your mothers. Even the selkies aren't so weak as that." The blade's curve remained steady a few centimeters from Margrit's throat. She thought her pulse must be reflected in the bright metal, panic and sour relief giving it wing.

Kate minced forward, managing to put on the air of a prissy schoolgirl despite wearing heavy boots, cargo pants and a leather jacket thrown over a torn white tank top. Like Janx, she was exquisite in her portrayal of *otherness;* what the eye saw was not at all what was really there. Everything Margrit could see screamed of innocent curiosity, and it was all a gorgeous falsehood. This was not the woman Margrit had met that morning, though whether this Kate or the other had been closer to her true self, Margrit had no idea.

"Oh," Kate said in the same sweet trill, "oh, is that what you see? You think our heritage makes us more constrained, not less? Such a pity." Her voice changed with the last words, gaining a depth far too profound for an ordinary human woman to achieve. "Release Margrit Knight or reap the whirlwind."

Margrit, afraid to move more than her eyes, jerked her gaze to Tariq and saw avarice light his features before a smile slid into place. "We *are* the whirlwind."

Like Janx, like Alban, Tariq was not so fast as Daisani. In the end, it seemed he didn't need to be.

It was an easy movement, really. Margrit saw it with full clarity, the way he straightened his arm the last half inch and drew it across in one short stroke. It looked brutal and efficient, the sort of thing that might be used to kill a goat or a cow.

Not until the pain set in did she realize that no, in fact, it was the sort of thing that might be used to kill *her*.

SΘMEΘNE SCREAMED. MARGRI+ was certain it wasn't herself, because she was trying, and could only produce a bubbling gurgle. The two djinn whipped into dervishes and, released from their hold, she lifted both hands to her throat, clutching the wound, then staring without comprehension at the blood coloring her fingers.

The pain was becoming extraordinary. Salt in the wound, she thought; salt from her hands, both at her throat again. She began to blink, counting each one and wondering if anyone watched to see how long she survived. Someone ought to be paying attention. Dying without even being noticed seemed worse than just dying. Somehow outraged by the thought, she looked up, searching for anyone who might care that she had fallen.

The screaming came from Cara. Too little, too late, Margrit thought, and wished she could voice the accusation. She supposed she should be pleased someone was paying attention, but the selkie girl wasn't the one she'd hoped for. Twenty seconds, she thought, and couldn't remember how many times she'd blinked. It didn't seem to matter as much as she thought it would. She was falling now, toppling over sideways with her hands still wrapped around the gaping wound in her throat.

Flame gouted over her. Dizzy with exhaustion—that was the blood loss, she thought clinically—she kept her eyes wide even when the world blurred. She would at least watch what happened around her as she died. No one would know, but she would.

The docking area was on fire. That was appropriate: Malik had died amidst flame, and so would she. Everything seemed terribly *slow*, even her thoughts, each of them drawn out with crystalline clarity. She'd thought dying would be more frightening, but instead it was simply…interesting. The last moments should be. She was glad she felt no fear, and then gladder that she'd visited her parents the previous weekend and gone to church with them. She wished she could reach out to them, to promise they would see each other again; to tell them she knew it would be such a long and hard time for them, but that for her only a moment or two would pass, and then they would be together.

They would never understand how she came to die in a back-lot loading zone near the docks, assuming that was where her body was found. Assuming her body *was* found. No, it would be: Tony would never allow her to disappear. Even after all their troubles, he would never let that happen. Perhaps Alban would break the Old Races covenant of secrecy and tell him what had really happened.

Alban. Regret too large to hold in overwhelmed her, pulling her toward darkness. Words and thoughts were too small to encompass the loss of a chance of a life with the gentle gargoyle. She wondered, briefly, if his people believed in an afterlife, or if the memories the gargoyles held so close ensured they would always be remembered, and negated a need for a world beyond their own in which they might meet again.

Fire scored the air above her again, sending djinn tornadoes spinning across the room. Determined not to miss the last seconds of her life, Margrit turned her attention outward, and watched the world come apart.

The Old Races had two forms: the elemental, alien shape and the humanoid form they used to interact with the mortal world.

Kate Hopkins held her ground in the middle of both of those, jaw unhinged to spout flame across the room in huge bursts. Traces of humanity remained in her face: a woman's hazel eyes over too-flared nostrils, more like Janx's dragonly ones than a human's. Her chest was broken open, too large for a person, too small for a dragon, and she dragged in enormous gusts to power her flame with. Her arms and hands were nearly normal, perhaps more strongly muscled than usual, and she had somehow captured a djinn, throttling him with enthusiasm as she hung in the air. Wings had erupted from her back to whip her fire into frenzies, and a tail lashed, taking out selkies who came too close. Legs, half human in nature, kicked and clawed, deadly weapons even if they weren't fully dragon.

The djinn she held was smeared in blood and hung on to her wrists with all his strength, trying to break her grip. She dropped her jaw farther, serpentine tongue flickering out, and then white flame spurted again. The djinn's screams, and then his life, were lost beneath its roar, and Kate dropped a melted, stinking pile of flesh onto the floor.

Tariq blurred with rage, scimitar glinting red with fire. He couldn't fly, but he materialized in the air behind Kate, dropping down with the blade preceding him.

It looked like a puppet being yanked offstage: one instant he was falling, and the next he slammed against the wall, Ursula Hopkins's hand crushing his throat, both of them yards in the air. They slid toward the floor, Kate's body blocking them from Margrit's view, though she heard Ursula's hiss of fury through the chaos.

Then, appallingly, Cara moved. Not swiftly, not as the vampires could do; not as Janx or Kate could do. Not swiftly, but with grim intent. One of her followers knocked her away, shouting a protest over the roar of sound in the loading dock. Fresh blood seeped from the gunshot wound above Cara's kidney as her protector spun around to lay hands on Kate. Half-formed scales glittered across her body and he dug his fingers deep into one, as Alban had once done to Janx. It began to peel back, tearing skin and scale alike, flaying her. Margrit reached for a scream and found it blocked by blood, still nothing more than a hideous gurgle.

Ursula appeared again, grabbing the selkie who attacked her sister. She dragged him close and he made no protest. Then she lashed forward too fast for Margrit to comprehend, her jaw dropped open in attack.

He was not fast, perhaps, but he was certain. Ursula's blur of speed met a downward smash of the selkie's head, and when she staggered back, her nose was crushed out of shape. Djinn swooped down on her, spinning a vortex that lifted her from the ground and forbade her the purchase that might allow her to escape.

Distant and clinical as the rest of her thoughts, Margrit

realized she was far from the only one to die tonight, and
wondered if selkie and djinn bodies were sufficiently
unusual to betray them to humanity. She didn't believe
Ursula or Kate would be captured or killed, though as
Ursula spun in the djinn maelstrom, it began to seem less
likely that she would survive.

It was happening so *fast*. Margrit knew it was fast,
though she could see too clearly, as if the brief seconds
were clarified and elongated for her so she might not
miss anything. That was the reward, perhaps, for the
blood draining out of her body; the last moments of her
life would seem to last forever.

Kate exploded, air concussing with such force it drove
the djinn out of their whirlwind. Ursula fell to the ground
and landed astonishingly catlike, her weight spread on all
four limbs and her body low and tight. Her skin rippled,
a black flow of oil, and she leapt out of her crouch with
the grace and accuracy of a panther, bearing down on one
of the djinn.

He dissipated and she fell through where he had been
to flatten a selkie whose reflexes weren't as fast. Kate
dropped to the floor, massive dragon bulk blocking
Ursula and her victim from Margrit's sight.

The selkie who'd tried flaying Kate had been flung
away by the force of her transformation. Now she prowled
toward him, gorgeously sinuous. Like Janx, her scales were
burnished red, but unlike his silver lining, she was graced
with black. She was perhaps a quarter of his size, though
still significantly larger than a selkie or even a gargoyle.
She lifted a heavily clawed foot to pin her tormentor against
the wall, and the dancing whiskers along her face pulled
back in a grin as she opened her mouth to breathe flame.

Tariq reappeared, dropping from above a second time, this time landing on Kate's neck, just above the roll of muscle that joined limb to body. Selkie forgotten, she snapped at the djinn, twisting herself into a cat's cradle as she tried to bite or claw him off. He wrapped his legs around her neck, stabbing ineffectually with his sword, and held on as though she were a bronco at the rodeo.

Margrit, sleepy, thought the dragon's eyes—still hazel in this form, though burnished with deep red flame— were the best target, and unwisely tried to whisper that across the room. No one could hear her; that was just as well. She had forgotten Kate was on her side, that the half-human children of the Old Races had come to rescue her. The heat and destruction, though, were so great that it seemed as if all the fighting should stop, no matter how it had to be achieved, or what the cost.

Selfish, she scolded herself. Just because *she* had lost didn't mean they all should. The admonishment amused her, and she found herself pleased that she would die happy. She had long since forgotten to keep blinking, but the time had to be running out. Too bad. There had been so much she wanted to do.

It wasn't that humans couldn't hear the sounds of battle from within the office-building loading dock. Anyone on the street might hear the shouts and screams, might recognize the roar of flame beneath the rumble of traffic. Nor was it that human curiosity sat up and took note of wisdom and left such dangers unexplored. No; it was only good fortune that brought the gargoyles to the battle before humanity discovered it; good fortune and perhaps a modicum of weariness from mortals already besieged by immortal warfare.

They had begun at the burnt-out shell that was the House of Cards, half a dozèn of them radiating away from that center point. They were looking for a gathering, not a brawl, and the lanky gargoyle had found one in a loose arc of selkies and djinn in a loading-dock parking lot. Knowledge transferred instantaneously through the gestalt, and within minutes, the gargoyles converged on the parking lot, all of them finding shadows to transform in before coming into the light. There was no resistance from the selkie and djinn guard; formidable fighters or not, they were no match for gargoyles. Had Alban been a human passerby, he would have ignored the sounds from behind the closed garage door, too, and allowed whatever went on there to continue without his interference.

Or he would have before he met Margrit Knight. Now he was uncertain of what he might do; it had not been long at all since he'd considered the ways of the world, whether human or not, to be beyond his caring. He would not have shoved his way through a locked door to discover what sort of disaster raged on its other side.

Only the host of gargoyles at his back kept him moving forward as the door slammed open and revealed anarchy. The smell of burning flesh billowed out, oily smoke and dark flame carried in excited eddies on the fresh air the gargoyles brought with them.

For an uncomprehending moment Alban thought Janx dominated the room, serpentine form whisking through the fire with claw and tooth at the ready. Something was wrong with the dragonlord, though: his color was wrong and his size far too small. As Alban watched, the dragon bit the head off a selkie who attacked his scales with a crowbar. Janx had never done anything so brutal, not to one of the Old Races. Alban staggered to a halt, disbelief numbing him.

Gargoyles flooded past Alban, knocking him aside. One of the females flung herself on the dragon, arms wrapped around its slender neck, wings beating to help her balance as she strangled the reptilian monster.

A blanket of night fell from above, its shape shimmering with black oil, changing so subtly and quickly that Alban's eyes slid off it, unable to grasp what he saw. It landed on the gargoyle who'd attacked the dragon, a maw of darkness opening up with screaming, outraged hunger. Gashes appeared on the Valkyrie's shoulders, stone cut deep enough to bleed, and she released the dragon to struggle with the writhing piece of midnight.

Djinn, furious with battle, fell upon the newly arrived gargoyles, whipping up storms as they waded into the fight determined to subdue first and understand later. Their whirlwinds cleared a path through the garage, all the way to its back wall.

Margrit lay sprawled in a still-spreading pool of blood, hands curved at her throat.

The shout that ripped from Alban's throat shamed the dragon's bellows, though it wasn't enough to pause the fight. He leapt over the combatants, transforming into his gargoyle shape without thinking so that when he crashed to his knees beside Margrit's unmoving form, his bulk shielded her from the battle.

Protected her, as though she still required guarding.

Alban's heartbeat smashed through him, carrying a tide of denial and disbelief matched only once in his existence. It had been raining then, but tonight was clear, a handful of stars scattered across the sky. Dawn was a whole nighttime away, and wouldn't bring healing stone, not this time, not for this woman. "Margrit? Margrit, you must…" *Wake up.* The words whispered beneath his skin but went unspoken, grief emptying him to even the false hope of pleading.

She was too pale, the warmth of her skin drained away with the blood spilled on the floor. Alban took one of her hands from her throat with cautious delicacy, comprehending the inches-long gash there without fully allowing himself to see it. That memory would be there, seared into his memory, at any time he might want to revisit it, and, like Ausra's death, like Malik's, far too often when he did not.

She had stopped bleeding, the pool spreading with its own slow viscosity. Red clots thickened the edges of the wound, as though she had almost succeeded in holding it together. Almost succeeded in surviving.

With utmost care, Alban replaced her hand at her throat, folding her fingers as they'd been, creating a barrier over the cut. Then he rose, blood-covered, and turned back to the battle with a cold determination he'd never before known. Death, it seemed, was the fate of every woman whose path crossed his. There could be an end to it; there *would* be an end to it.

All he had to do was die.

It had to be the dragon, or possibly its vampiric partner. No one else had the strength or speed to destroy a gargoyle; the djinn and selkie were far too feeble, and Alban's rage much too great. Only the dragon could stand up to it, though the vampire had shown enormous fortitude in attacking the female gargoyle. She had escaped and huddled against a wall now, transformed to healing, protective stone.

Her life would not also be forfeit tonight. It no longer mattered how any of this had come to pass. All that mattered was that it would end, and that he would end it. He flung himself into battle with an abandon he'd never known before, free of all constraint, determined only to reach the dragon, and nothing more.

The loading-dock doors melted in a wash of flame, and the dragon met him.

It had gotten larger, somehow. Much larger, in the space between deciding his fate lay in the dragon's claws and the moment of impact. There'd been no concussive explosion of air to suggest it had transformed, and once what little intellect he had left worked its way through that thought, it was all wrong anyway. Dragons had one size, one shape to transform into and out of. That size changed over the millennia, growing ever larger, but it did not change in the space of a breath.

Then thought was gone again as they bowled over, flattening everything in their path. Alban's feet hit the floor and he drove talons into concrete, forcing all his strength into the sinuous coils to stop their roll. There was too much dragon to stop so easily, and he howled frustration, words far beyond him.

Another impact shuddered Janx's long body, a sudden flash of white stone shoving and slamming with the same vigor Alban put into the effort. Flame sprayed everywhere in a hiss of outrage, and Biali came through it unscathed, a broad smile splitting his scarred face. Alban understood in an instant: it wasn't for Margrit's sake Biali fought, or for Alban's, but simply for the joy of pitting himself against the one breed in the world who could fight a gargoyle to the ground. Without him, Alban wouldn't have stopped the tumble before Margrit's fragile body was crushed.

For all that his own purpose was to die in battle, Alban acknowledged the other gargoyle with a nod of thanks in the eternal moment before Janx slithered around and roared fury as he pounced again.

Alban went down under the dragon's crush, knocked breathless as Janx scrambled over him. Insulted, he grabbed the dragonlord's hind leg and hauled.

Janx dug his nails into the floor as he was yanked backward, the shriek of torn concrete echoed by his full-voiced rage. He strained with the effort of moving forward, utterly ignoring Alban and Biali, all his attention focused elsewhere. His enormous wings buffeted the air, sending cyclones of heat burning through it, and djinn, sent panicking from their native element, began to flee the garage. Alban had never seen them endangered by anything other than salt water and, more recently, vampire blood: the idea that they could be burned out, guttered by flame, was in equal parts fascinating and horrifying. But a handful of them lay broken beneath Janx's talons, spattered with blood and crackling with flame.

Profound wrongness twinged under Alban's skin, as bone deep and discomfiting as iron bound to flesh had been. Janx was a thousand things, a killer among them, but to so ruthlessly end the lives of his fellow Old Races was unlike him. Faint humor twisted the sense of transgression: only a handful of seconds ago that was exactly what Alban had sought from the dragonlord.

Another serpentine form slithered in front of Janx and he redoubled his efforts, flame gouting as he surged forward. Alban didn't know when all the gargoyles came to his side, but now half a dozen of them held the infuriated dragon back as he lashed at his smaller counterpart. It danced out of his way, taunting his captivity.

A black cloak settled around its shoulders, then became a woman, black-haired, dark-eyed, blood drooling down her jaw and coating the insides of her arms, as though she'd slashed her wrists. She dangled a bundle from one hand, and it took long dreadful moments for Alban to recognize it as a head, as smeared with blood as the woman was.

Much too late, *much* too late, understanding came.

Janx drew himself in, dragging gargoyles to his center, then burst upward in an explosion of power, wings flung out to clap the air. He dislodged Alban and the lanky gargoyle youth, the latter from surprise and Alban through inattention; his gaze was on the murderous twins before him.

If murderers they were. Janx launched himself forward again, this time smashing into the pair with the same strength he'd tackled Alban with. They rolled roughshod through the melted door, landing in the parking lot with an eruption of flame and fury that lit furious panic in Alban's breast. He charged after them, voice lost beneath the sounds of battle even as he screamed warnings. Nothing stopped them, not even flinging himself into their midst, grabbing desperately for muzzles and claws, anything to pull one off the other and alert them to their danger. To *all* their danger, for at the most they had a handful of seconds before humans discovered their battle, and should that happen, it was a blow from which they would never recover.

A gunshot ripped the air, a desperately human sound, and their time was up.

AIR IⓂPLⓄDED WI+H the rattle of grenades going off. Janx collapsed under the weight of half a dozen gargoyles, his muffled cursing accompanying useless heaves as he tried to push them away. Alban climbed to his feet, offering his nearest compatriot a hand without seeing him, then said, "Keep Janx down," in a low voice.

Tony Pulcella stood at the parking lot's head, his duty weapon clasped in both hands and held steady on the mass of Old Races a few dozen yards from him. Grace O'Malley was at his side, leather-clad and clinging, one hand on the detective's biceps as if to stay him from further shooting. Alban wondered where the bullet had gone, though it could easily have struck Janx without the dragonlord so much as noticing.

Torn between choices, he finally said, "Grace," in the same low voice he'd employed with the gargoyles. Behind him, Janx was still struggling and swearing, a fact that might have made Alban smile in any other circumstances. "Grace, what are you doing here? Why is he here?"

Tony barked a laugh that had more to do with covering

fear than humor. "I might ask you the same question, Korund, except then I got a whole lot of others I wanna ask first." His voice was rock steady, and he couldn't know his heartbeat betrayed him. Still, Alban admired his facade of calm.

"Sure and it didn't take a lot of cleverness to realize you were all spoiling for a fight," Grace said. Unlike Tony, she *was* calm, even derisive. "Something had to be done to stop you, and you wouldn't be listening to Grace alone, now, would you?"

Janx's voice shot out of the background, a garbled threat that ended with the sound of flesh hitting flesh: a hand being slapped over the dragonlord's mouth. Alban wanted to admonish his people not to be careless: six of them could easily hold Janx in his mortal form, but he would eventually be let free, and a grudge-holding dragon was a bad enemy.

"She told me Margrit would be here." Tony met Alban's gaze. Then he whitened, and Alban knew that his own expression had given away Tony's worst fear.

"I'm sorry, detective. Margrit Knight is dead."

"What?"

To Alban's surprise, it was neither Tony nor Grace whose voice came out gray with disbelief and horror. It was Janx, and as though his tone told his captors the fight was gone from him, he came forward unfettered by gargoyles, shock wiping away his inhuman grace. "What did you say, Alban?"

"The djinn," Kate Hopkins said with no care for the human standing in their midst. Ursula joined her, winding an arm around her sister's waist, as Kate continued, coldly, "In retaliation for Malik's death. We came to protect her, but we were too late."

"You." Janx's lip curled. "And who are you, daring to transform in my demesne? Challenging me in such a cowardly way, without even declaring yourself first? That will be met, little girl. That will be answered."

Kate gave him a look burdened in equal parts with pity and exasperation, then turned back to Alban and Tony. "Forgive us. Ursula's been following her all day, but Tariq snatched her and even my sister takes time to track a djinn."

"I want to see her." Tony finally spoke again, strain now sounding in his voice. A wave of sympathy caught Alban, nearly shattering the calm that had settled, unnoticed, over him. He reached for it again, afraid to feel Margrit's loss, then released whatever hold he'd had on it and shuddered to find blank horror in its place. Lifting a hand to gesture back toward the loading dock hurt; breathing hurt. His insides had been drilled away and filled with regret and sorrow, but beyond a senseless hope of denial, all he could think was how much more bewildered and lost the human detective must be.

Tony holstered his gun and stalked forward, his entire body radiating tension and fear and bewilderment. He had no frame to put around Margrit's death, no explanations for the things he had seen in the last minutes, and in a very human way, seemed to be thrusting the alien out of his thoughts to focus on what was comprehensible: love, life, loss. Alban had little doubt there would be time for the rest later: Tony Pulcella did not strike him as a man willing to let the inexplicable fade to the back of his mind and be dismissed under the best of circumstances, and now, with Margrit's death, he imagined very little would stop the detective from fully exploring what he had seen.

The Old Races parted before him, and Grace walked a step or two behind him, offering solidarity without quite being at his side. Janx let them pass and then, with as much stiffness and grief as Alban had ever seen in him, fell into step behind the two humans, following them through the silent gathering to visit Margrit's body. Alban brought up the rear, though he became aware that the others had followed them back into the loading dock, and that they stood vigilance against the night.

Always petite, Margrit looked smaller and more fragile than ever lying in a wide crimson pool. Her hands were still folded at her throat, hiding the wound there and making her seem an artistic rendition of death. Tony, with far more grace than Alban himself had shown, knelt in the blood and first touched her throat for a pulse, then bowed his head over her body. Long minutes passed before he spoke, voice cracking with rage and grief. "What the fuck is going on here?"

"We are the Old Races." Unexpectedly, it was Janx who spoke again, breaking a silence that of all those gathered, only Eldred might have more right to end. Might: Alban suspected the dragonlord had more years than even the gargoyle elder, but could no more imagine asking than—

Than he could imagine Janx giving answer to Tony Pulcella's question. But Janx went on, tenor voice sweet with sorrow and regret. "I'm afraid Margrit Knight told you the truth at Rockefeller Center, detective. Selkies and dragons and djinn, oh my," he said softly, and then more prosaically, "And gargoyles and vampires. We have lived among you for all of history, some of us becoming your legends and others fading into obscurity. Your Margrit became our Margrit, and though you will not believe me, I, too, mourn her passing."

Tony turned his head, showing a grief-stricken profile to the gathering. "Janx. I shot you."

Actual sympathy tempered the dragon's response. "Do you really think one tiny bullet would bother me? A .45 won't stop a grizzly or an elephant, detective, much less something like me."

"A *dragon*." Tony spat the word, clearly no more able to believe it than deny it.

"A dragon," Janx said gently.

Tony shoved to his feet, sliding in blood as he turned to face Alban. There was no fear in his scent, and only anger more powerful than despair in his face. Both were held in check by a kind of desperation; by a need, Alban thought, to understand. The rest could come later. Would come later, if the detective was allowed to leave the loading dock alive.

"A gargoyle," Alban said, before Tony asked. "You've seen my other form." He transformed as he spoke, letting one shoulder rise and fall. "The 'mask' in the Blue Room was my true form."

Tony flinched as Alban changed shape, then shot challenging glares at the rest of them. "What about you? What do you look like? C'mon," he added bitterly, as glances were exchanged. "It's not as if you're going to let me walk away. You don't keep this kind of secret by letting people who blow your cover live."

"No." Janx turned his attention to Grace thoughtfully, air heating with the weight of his regard. "We don't."

The faintest smile quirked one corner of Grace's mouth and she sauntered to Janx, stopping bare centimeters from him. She stood on her toes, tipping her face up as though she'd steal a kiss, and instead whispered, "Be my guest, dragonlord. Try it."

Interest glittered deep in Janx's eyes, but he only inclined his head in acknowledgment of the challenge before lifting his gaze beyond Grace to look at Tony again. Smiling, the vigilante stepped back, taking up a place at Tony's side as Janx asked, "Is this your final wish, detective? That you should see us in all our glory before you die?"

"My final wish would be to die of old age in my bed, if you're granting them."

"Sadly," Janx said, "the djinn have fled, and they're not of a bent to grant wishes even on their best days. I'm afraid it is this or nothing."

Like Alban, he transformed as he spoke, the last words deep and distorted as they were spoken by a throat not intended to form human words. Only the gargoyles remained rooted through the enormous force of his transformation, air banging out as mass forced it away. Tony fell back; even Margrit's body was knocked askew, flung over to face the rear wall. Selkies scattered, while Kate and Ursula knotted arms around each other to retain their feet. Contortions ran over Kate's body, as though she struggled to hold back her own transformation, and Janx whipped his head around to hiss at her.

More than hiss: he spoke in a language of whispers and sibilance and song, rising and falling hypnotically. Kate stared at him, increasingly nonplussed, until Ursula finally said, "She doesn't speak dragon," and Janx broke off with a splutter of offended surprise. He lifted one gold-taloned foot, new threat whose translation couldn't go unmistaken.

Kate, far from afraid, exploded into her dragon shape and hunched her long, slim back like a cat preparing for a fight. Clearly disgusted, Janx swatted her and she bounced, wings over tail, out the door.

Tony's harsh laughter cracked across the loading dock. "Kids, huh? Can't live with 'em, can't kill 'em."

Anything further he might have said was lost beneath a rush of movement, Janx's wings whistling through the air as the dragon pounced on him. One clawed foot pinned the detective to the ground easily, talons making a cage around him, and Janx's tail lashed, sweeping the room dangerously. "For Margrit Knight's sake, I spare your life for the crime of having learned the truth of our people." His words rode on smoke and heat, reddening Tony's face as Janx brought his muzzle close to the detective. "Be grateful."

Alban closed his eyes briefly, discovering that he, at least, *was* grateful. Condemning Margrit's onetime lover in the face of her death seemed an unusual cruelty, one he had no stomach for.

He opened his eyes again as Ursula and Kate crept back into the loading dock, coming to stand on either side of him and slip their hands into his. They felt fragile and small: very human, though he had seen clearly where the boundaries of their humanity lay, and how far apart from the strictures of the Old Races those boundaries put them. They knew the laws of their fathers' peoples, and yet devastated bodies lay around the concrete room as evidence of how little regard these two half-human children had for the edicts which ruled the Old Races. And perhaps they should have no more care than they'd shown: after all, they had lived human lives for a dozen generations, condemned by the immortal halves of their heritage. In their place, Alban thought he might well have fought for humanity, which had at least embraced them, rather than the Old Races, who had forbidden them.

In his own place, he had.

Tony, through gritted teeth, acknowledged hard-pressed gratitude, though under the crush of Janx's claw it could hardly be anything else. Alban squeezed the girls' hands and released them to approach the dragon, suddenly tired of posturing.

Janx's tail snapped into him, a lash with so much power it could only have been deliberate. Alban, taken off guard, flew through the air to smash into a wall. Other gargoyles flinched forward as he recovered, but Janx slid a golden talon to rest against Tony's throat. "Unfortunately for you, detective, I bear another grudge. You led the human raid against the House of Cards, and I have been denied my vengeance on that matter on all fronts. No longer." A dragonly smile split his face as he arched up, ribs expanding to prepare a blast of fire and wrath.

And then came a low, distorted voice, too quiet to be heard, and yet somehow Alban heard it. They all heard it, Janx arrested in midaction by Margrit's cold command: "Dragonlord, you will *not*."

TWENTY-EIGHT

MARGRIT AWAKENED WITH a pounding head and the befuddling idea that she'd heard a gun.

Instinct drove her to sit up, but her muscles were rubbery and she faltered, barely able to lift her head.

Crimson spread out in front of her, the only clear thing in her foggy vision. It was warm, though cooling rapidly, and sticky, and she thought it should mean something to her, all that red liquid so close to her. It smelled of copper, only discernible because she lay so close to it. Other smells were far more overpowering: fire, smoke, barbecue. Her stomach rumbled and she tried to clap a hand against it, but her movements were too clumsy, and all she did was smear a hand in the blood.

Hunger twisted into nausea as she realized her unthinking recognition was right and that she lay in a pool of blood.

Recollection slammed into her, a shock of adrenaline giving her the energy necessary to jerk upright. Her vision cleared as she twisted to face the room, the world sharpening into hyperdefined focus.

The first sound she made after coming back from the dead was a laugh.

No one else heard it: it was too low and raw a sound, as she took in the impossible things spread out before her. Her blood in the foreground, yes, and the air thick with smoke and flame. Bodies, some charcoaled, some flayed, some gnawed upon as though an animal had gotten to them, lay scattered around the floor, and amongst them stood gargoyles and a dragon in their elemental forms, and selkies and a vampire who looked human to an untrained eye.

And under the dragon's claw lay Anthony Pulcella, who didn't belong there at all and who was about to pay for his audacity with his life. Beyond him was Grace O'Malley, only slightly less out of place, her peaches-and-cream complexion paled to ghostly white. Janx was speaking, something Margrit hadn't known he could do in his dragon form, and then he coiled upward, clearly preparing for a final strike.

"Dragonlord," Margrit said, and her voice was a disaster, "you will *not*."

Not if she lived a hundred years would she become accustomed to the lack of movement that came over the Old Races when something surprised them. Every being in the room save Tony went deadly still, bewilderment spasming over the detective's face. Margrit thought he hadn't heard her: the ruin of her voice was so quiet she'd barely heard herself, but the Old Races had better senses than humans did.

Janx, with terrible precision, turned his long face toward her, complex double eyelids shuttering over eyes that burned emerald with challenge. His gaze was weighted, heated; all the things she had come to be accustomed to from the dragon. For the first time she felt no fear at all; could, indeed, barely remember why it was he'd frightened her. "You will not," she said again, and air imploded as Janx returned to his human form.

"An unexpected surprise, Margrit Knight." The dragonlord looked furious, hands repeatedly clenching into fists.

Relief swept Margrit as his change agreed to her demand, or at least gave her further time to negotiate. She sagged toward the floor, then ground her teeth and forced herself upward. Not just to sitting, but to her feet, a distance she wasn't at all sure she could travel. But then there was a hand at her elbow, supporting her, and Alban was at her side, his eyes round with hope and astonishment.

Margrit laughed, so breathless it would have been fragile had her throat not been ruined. As it was it scraped, a gurgle as dreadful as her last breaths had been, and she whispered, "Hi."

"I thought you were dead." Alban's hand on her arm was delicate, as though he doubted what he saw and touched. As though she might shatter under his grip, a possibility that felt alarmingly real. The nausea she'd felt before remained in place, symptomatic of light-headedness and blood loss, but she managed another broken laugh.

"I think I was. Mostly dead, at least." Sick and trembling or not, she felt filled with laughter, its music bubbling up in her as a form of relief. "Daisani saved me. I think Tariq didn't cut quite deep enough, and Daisani's blood saved me. I was so sad I wouldn't get to see you again." She swallowed and stopped speaking, every word a strain. The room was unbelievably silent, her harsh voice and Tony's labored breathing the only sounds in it.

Every one of the remaining Old Races stared at her in the same astonishment Alban did. Overwhelmed by their gazes, she turned her face against his chest and held on with all the trembling strength she had at her disposal, grateful for his cool, stony scent and solid presence. Exhaustion held her too thoroughly for joy to turn to desire, but she could feel its call deep within her, wanting life to be celebrated.

"Margrit?" Tony's voice sounded almost as hoarse as her own did. Margrit released Alban, uncertain she could keep her feet without his support, but there was no need: Tony was there, crushing her in his arms and mumbling disbelief into her hair. "You were dead, Grit. You were *dead*."

Another raw, shaking laugh broke free. "I got better. Do you remember—" Speech hurt, and she was grateful when Alban took over, words deep and tempered with sympathy.

"A gift from another of our kind, detective. One sip of a vampire's blood offers health to your people. You recall how quickly she recovered from her injuries in January."

Tony looked up at Alban, then set Margrit back a few inches, his hands on her shoulders hard with relief and concern. "So fast the doctors thought their X-rays must've been wrong. But this, Margrit, I mean—your throat…"

Margrit put her fingers against the cut, shuddering to discover it wasn't yet fully closed. "I think every time I get hurt it steps up the recovery time. I got the shit beat out of me last night." She looked beyond Tony, finding Grace, who looked strangely insubstantial amongst the Old Races. Even Tony's strong coloring helped make the tall vigilante look less real than those around her. For a moment an answer swam behind Margrit's eyes, but it slipped away again and she whispered, "I could feel myself healing, then. I think I might not be alive if it weren't for you."

Grace executed an elegant bow, flourishing with her fingers as Margrit looked back to Tony. "What are you two doing here?"

Janx grumbled a warning that Margrit silenced with a look, while Tony fell back a step and shook his head. "Wish to hell I knew. She came out of nowhere and said I had to come with her."

"When a cadre of gargoyles goes off looking for trouble, Grace knows to call in a ringer. I didn't know we'd find a mess as bad as this one, but sometimes it takes old-fashioned human ingenuity to get people's attention. I figured the copper shooting off a round or two would do it."

"You have a gun," Margrit said blankly.

Grace wrinkled her nose and slipped the weapon from the small of her back, then knocked open the chamber to shake its contents onto the floor. Nothing fell, and with a semiembarrassed shrug, she said, "No bullets, love."

Margrit stared at Grace, remembering too vividly the way she'd pressed the gun's barrel to her forehead. Her stomach lurched with the dismay of discovering old fear had been useless, but before she found words to protest with, Kate, quiet and sullen, said, "I thought we were the ringers," to Ursula.

Janx turned on them both, clearly glad to have a target for his ire. He was nearly purple with indignation, and a purposeful pair of gargoyles stepped forward to prevent him from launching himself at the girls. "Did you think

I wouldn't notice?" he demanded. "Did you think you could come into *my* city, *my* territory, and proclaim yourself without challenge? Did you—"

"How did you even know I was here?" The curiosity behind Kate's question was clearly genuine, startling Janx and sending a pang of regret through Margrit. The half-blood children of the Old Races were so thoroughly denied their heritages it was no surprise that Ausra had succumbed to madness. Kate and Ursula had fared better, but Margrit doubted either of them truly understood the world their fathers had come from.

"You announced yourself with your transformation." Janx's anger lost its grip on him, confusion rising to replace it. "How can you not know that? How can you not know our tongue? Who *are* you?"

Kate exchanged a panicked glance with her sister, but it was Alban who stood with Margrit gathered in his arms, and replied for all of them. "This is Katherine Hopkins, Janx. Sarah's daughter, and yours."

"Daughter." Janx echoed the word dully, as lacking in animation as Alban had ever seen him.

"They've been in New York for years," Alban said. "Since…"

"Nineteen sixty-two," Ursula provided. "We've lived in all five boroughs. Kate wants to go upstate next."

Janx shook himself, dragging his gaze from Kate to Ursula. "Daughter."

"Not me. Just her." Ursula slid her arm around Kate's waist, shoring her up. "My father is Eliseo Daisani."

Janx and Tony made similar sounds of dismay, the former amusing Alban and the latter drawing his attention to the detective. Grace O'Malley offered him a reassuring touch, her long fingers light and gentle over his. They made an attractive pair, almost Alban and Margrit's mirror opposites, with Grace pale and blond and Tony golden-skinned and dark-haired. The idea traced a smile on Alban's lips before he turned back to the twins. "I didn't recognize you," he said to Kate. "Not at first. I thought you were Janx. Did you know, in all these centuries, I'd never seen your other form?"

"Of course we knew." Ursula answered for Kate, who stared greedily at Janx. "Mama drilled that into us when we were still girls. Once we could transform to the degree that we wanted, we never did it again. It's harder to get caught if you don't flaunt your differences."

"To the *degree* you want?" Janx gaped at Ursula, then looked back at the auburn-haired woman who was his daughter. "You have halfway forms?"

"Of course." Kate looked nonplussed. "Don't you?"

All of Janx's cool and nonchalance slipped away. "No!"

Margrit's voice fluted as high as it could with the injuries to her throat: "These are things that can be argued about later. Where's Tariq?"

Cara, pinch-faced with pain, looked up from one of her injured podmates. "The vampire ate him."

"I did *not!*" Offense shot through Ursula's voice, mitigated an instant later by the admission, "He got away."

Margrit stepped forward, relying on Alban's support and not trying to hide it. A flare of pride burst in his chest, that he should be fortunate enough to have encountered a woman like this one, and that she could see beyond his alien nature and care for him. She was one of the most fiercely independent people he had ever known, and the tastes he'd had of her memories told him that when she chose *not* to walk beside him or rely upon him, it was to establish herself as worthy of consideration on her own terms. That she was now willing to accept his help said as much about who she was as it did about who they were. Alban fought down a smile that felt silly with delight as Margrit shuffled a step or two closer to Cara.

"Are the selkies satisfied that my death has fulfilled the wergild against Janx and Alban for their part in Malik's death?"

Cara, bemused, said, "You're not dead."

"I was." Margrit turned her head toward Alban, who felt his insides go cold again as he nodded. "The agreement didn't stipulate I had to stay that way."

Humor crowed in Alban's chest, crowding out the cold. Margrit was still shaking and far too pale from blood loss, and yet determined to drive nails into the coffin of a war still on the edge of burgeoning. Her voice cleared a little as she repeated, "Are the selkies satisfied?"

"The selkies are," Cara said bitterly. "We give up our claim on Janx's territory—"

The dragon hissed in triumph and Cara turned a hard look on him, finishing, "And cede it to the djinn with all our support."

Margrit slumped against Alban, her hand on his arm trembling with the effort of keeping herself upright. He tightened his fingers at her waist, understanding she wanted to show as much strength as possible, and didn't nestle her close again, for all that it was in his heart to do so.

Using him for steadiness, she turned toward Eldred. "We can't let war come of this. Will the gargoyles accept the djinn as masters of Janx's empire?"

"It is of no loss to us," Eldred said. "If it will keep the peace, then yes, of course."

"The *dragons*," Janx snarled, "will *not*."

Margrit glanced at Alban, her smile exhausted, then gave that same weary look to Janx. "You're not the only dragon here today." Drawing herself up, ignoring the outrage that flushed Janx's cheeks, she turned to Kate. "What say the dragons?"

Avarice as powerful as anything Alban had ever seen in Janx's eyes flashed across Kate's face. Then she shot her father a glance, and when she spoke, her words were measured, more like Ursula's than usual. "A dragon and a vampire came here today to support the Negotiator. Neither of us have a stake in Janx's territory, and we're willing to accept djinn rule here. We'll stand together to help them hold it, if necessary."

Fury contorted Janx's face. Alban stepped forward, flanking Margrit and ready to push her behind himself if danger sparked. She stayed him with a touch, perhaps still too close to death to fear it. "And you, dragonlord? Do you cede control over your empire to the djinn?"

Janx looked from one face to another, high color still burning his cheeks, and finally brought a venomous look back to Margrit. "You've given me no choice. Congratulations, Ms. Knight. It seems you've won a round."

"I've won two." Margrit curled a hand in Alban's bloody shirt, bracing herself. "Your territory ceded, and Tony's life. I'm calling in my third favor, Janx. Just to make it clear."

Janx peeled his lips back from his teeth, far less a smile than a threat. "Are you so very certain this is how you wish to use that last wish, Margrit Knight? You have many years ahead of you, and may yet need a dragon's favor. And then there is the matter of Grace O'Malley and her children, is there not? Think carefully, Negotiator. Choose wisely."

Triumph jolted her, burning up too much of what little energy she had, but a smile flashed over Margrit's face regardless. She had won already, even if Janx didn't know it yet: he had accorded her a title, and that meant she had a place amongst the Old Races. "We've already made the exchange for Grace's tunnels, Janx. Don't cloud the issue. Of course I'm sure. Maybe it's terribly human of me, but my friends are not pieces for you to push around on your chess board or knock aside as it pleases you. Tony's life is mine."

She heard the detective catch his breath and a burst of humor cut through her triumph. Being alive made it easy to laugh. She hoped that would stay: it seemed as if her laughter was too often edged with cynicism. And she knew what caused Tony to protest, even if he didn't do so aloud. She'd made a claim on his life, staking it as hers. If, heaven forbid, he had made the same statement, she would have lashed out at him with any attack in her repertoire. She was autonomous, and so, too, was he.

On the other hand, at least once, very recently, she'd had the presence of mind to keep her mouth shut over just such a claim, and she hoped Tony would, too. It was a matter of principle in a relationship or at the office. Here, now, it was literally a matter of life and death.

"Am I to walk away with nothing?" Janx demanded. "My empire lost, cast from my temporary home, the lives of all responsible safe from my retribution? Is this your way of smoothing the waters in our world, Margrit Knight?"

"You can walk away with your daughter." Margrit sounded implacable to her own ears, the roughness of her voice gone. "I'd think that was worth any price."

For an instant—*just* an instant—Janx softened as he looked toward Kate. Her lips parted, another ingenue's look of sweet hope, but this time Margrit saw raw emotion behind it, the expression no longer an act.

"It is more than a trinket," Janx conceded, but then his expression hardened again. Kate's shoulders dropped in dismay, and Ursula hugged her harder, the two making miscolored shadows of one another. "More than a trinket, but not enough. I set a third task to you weeks ago, Margrit Knight. I would see it done. Then, and only then, are we even and is the slate between us cleared. Heed my wish and I'll heed yours." He finally smiled, sharp-toothed and angry. "Do we have an accord?"

"We do." Margrit whispered the words even as she shied away from the thought. Janx *had* set her a task, and she'd thrown it in his face in much the same way he'd just tried to do with her. Had warned him that it was his last favor, and he should be well aware of how he spent it.

She had acted to spare a life. Janx was acting to end one.

Eliseo Daisani would be destroyed. Not the vampire himself, but his persona, the business mogul who'd reigned over New York for the past thirty years. If Janx was to lose his empire, then Daisani would, too, and they would move elsewhere, begin their game anew. It would be hard enough for Janx, but nearly impossible for Daisani, whose face was known all over the world. A century earlier slipping from one life to another must have been easy, but Margrit had no idea how a well-known person would even begin to do so in the modern world.

"We do," she said again, more clearly. "You're a son of a bitch, Janx, but we have a deal."

"Why, Margrit." Janx made himself the picture of injured feelings. "I thought that was what you liked about me."

"I don't think I like any of you very much right now." The adrenaline high was beginning to burn off, leaving Margrit weaker than she wanted to be. "Get out of here, Janx. Go pack your things and leave Grace's tunnels and her children. Go somewhere with Kate. Get to know your daughter. Try to be a good guy for a while. It'd help me sleep easier."

"Your wish, my dear, is my command. Katherine?" Janx, with consummate showmanship, offered Kate an elbow, then cocked the other and said, "Ursula?" in equally inviting tones.

The twins exchanged glances, first with each other, then with Margrit, who nodded and lifted her hand, fingers spread to represent a phone, toward her ear. She mouthed, "Call me," and both the women smiled brightly, Kate nodding agreement before they each took one of Janx's elbows and allowed him to escort them away from the loading dock.

"Are you certain it's wise to encourage Daisani's daughter to walk with Janx?" Alban murmured.

Margrit turned toward him, the movement making her dizzy, and put a hand on his arm to steady herself. "I'll tell Eliseo, don't worry. I thought you didn't know who their fathers were."

"I didn't," Alban said dryly, "until I saw them in action. It became obvious, Margrit."

"Oh." Light-headedness replaced what she would normally have thought of as the sensation of a blush. Nausea followed it and she clutched Alban's sleeve, teeth set together against illness.

"Margrit?"

Her name came from two directions, Tony and Alban both voicing concern. She managed a weak smile at them, amused by the way they scowled, uncertain which of them should take precedence. After a few seconds Tony stepped back. Grace, looking surprisingly satisfied, tucked her arm through the detective's as Alban asked, "Are you well, Margrit?"

"Honestly? At the very least I need about a gallon of water, and a blood transfusion probably wouldn't hurt. But I don't think I have time for that." Margrit shrugged and straightened away from Alban. "There's too much else to do."

She managed three steps before her eyes rolled back and she collapsed to the concrete in a faint.

TWENTY-NINE

DESPITE WHAT HAPPENED in films, it was rare indeed that anyone was quick enough to catch someone as she fainted. Daisani might have done it; Alban could not. He and Tony lurched simultaneously, and Grace's face wrinkled in horrified sympathy as Margrit crashed to the floor.

Alban scooped her up cautiously, concerned she might have injured herself further, then wondered how much more badly she could be hurt than having her throat cut. "She needs fluids."

"She needs a *hospital*," Tony said at the same time, then glowered at Alban.

"Hospitals will only ask complicated questions such as how she survived so much blood loss, and will want to do blood work. I don't know what they'll find."

"The same thing they found in January!"

"Perhaps. But it's been months now, and her ability to heal has adapted and increased remarkably. A doctor might discover she is no longer fully human."

"Then what the hell is she?"

Alban looked up from Margrit, who breathed shallowly but steadily, and felt sympathy draw his features long. "Unique."

Tony's expression went bitter. "She was always that."

"Yes." Alban's voice softened and he glanced at the woman he held. "For what little it's worth, I had not meant to take her from you."

"Margrit doesn't get taken anywhere. She goes where she wants." The same bitterness colored his tone. "She didn't want me anymore."

"You're taking this very well, detective. All of it."

"All of it… You mean, all of you? I told you, it almost makes sense. Margrit doesn't hide things without a good reason, and I guess you people are as good a reason to keep secrets as I've ever seen. Besides," Tony added flatly, "she needs me to."

"She needs to not wake up to you two fighting over her." Grace dipped a hand into her pocket and came out with a plastic vial that she unstoppered as she knelt beside Margrit. The scent of ammonia rose up and Margrit hacked, then sat up, her hand knotted in Alban's bloody coat again.

"What the hell was— Smelling salts? You've got smelling salts? That's the worst stuff I've ever smelled."

Grace stood again, vial safely closed as she tucked it back in her pocket. "I've smelled plenty worse, some of it right here. You're in dire straits, love. How're you planning to get home, looking like that?"

"Alban can…" Margrit faltered, turning her face against Alban's chest. "Alban can take me home, both of us covered in blood, to the housemate who hates him. Or not."

"Wait." Tony crouched, clearly stopping himself from catching Margrit's upper arm. "Cole and Cam know about this? And you didn't tell *me*?"

"Cole saw Alban bringing me home the night of Daisani's masquerade ball." Margrit kept her face against Alban's chest, sounding exhausted. "I didn't tell him. He just found out." She lifted her head, though it looked as if it took effort, and found Cara Delaney with her gaze. "Which is not carte blanche for you to hare off and flay him, okay? He'll keep your secret. God, some secret. It's starting to seem like everybody knows."

"Five humans out of a million and a half on this island," Alban murmured. "It's not quite everyone yet, Margrit."

"It's enough." Margrit pulled herself to sitting, then, grimacing, wiped her sleeve over her face. Blood smeared and she stared at it grimly. "This is disgusting. Cara."

"Yes."

Margrit's voice went cool and steady. "You let him kill me."

Guilt flashed in Cara's dark eyes and she glanced away only to find other censuring gazes surrounding her. "It was one life for many. One life, to avert war. You saw what happened in just a few minutes of fighting."

"Actually, I missed a lot of it," Margrit said icily. "What with being dead and all."

Color stained the selkie woman's cheeks, but she lifted her chin defiantly and gestured around them, indicating the selkie bodies that lay burned and torn on the floor. "We are not well suited to battle on land. Though we might best be able to afford it in numbers, we would be decimated if it came to war."

"She didn't used to sound like this," Margrit said to Alban. "She used to sound like a normal person. I think the whole debutante-selkie thing has gone to her head."

Cara's face reddened further, her hands clenching into

fists at her sides. Alban saw blood leak from a wound in her shoulder, but the girl ignored it as she challenged Margrit. "I made my choice. I would make the same one again, if I thought it would save my people."

"Ah, there we go. The power of conviction, stripped bare of pomposity. That's what I was after." Margrit shrugged, minute movement against Alban's chest that made her seem terribly fragile. "It was probably the right choice, even if I think you made it because you were pissed off at me."

"You took everything we tried to gain!"

"Bullshit." Margrit pushed away from Alban more cautiously this time, leaning heavily into the support he offered as she got to her feet. "The one thing you really wanted was legitimacy, and you got that. But as it happens, He giveth and He taketh away. Get me Kaimana, Cara. I'm going to make a deal."

It was a motley army that escorted Margrit back into Grace's tunnels. Alban carried her, despite her weak protests that she could manage the journey on her own two feet. Not even she believed it, but part of her insisted that the pretense was important. That, in the wake of being newly alive, struck her as a tactic she should reconsider. There had to be room and reason to stop fighting battles that were only for show.

Alban's clothes were damp with blood, and hers stiffened and dried in folds stuck with his. The relentless sense of humor that had haunted her since she'd awakened suggested that was romantic. Disgusting, but still somehow romantic. More likely it was the slow, steady beat of Alban's heart beneath her ear and the surety of his arms that bore romance, but amusement niggled at her anyway.

Grace walked ahead of them, a swaying black-clad form with no evident need for a light against the darkness. Margrit's gaze stayed on her for long moments, watching the way shadows accepted and released her as she led them through the gloom. Impossible answers itched at the corners of Margrit's mind, not quite ready for revelation, and darting away when she tried to follow them. She pressed her eyes shut, then opened them again to follow Tony with her gaze.

He was a step or two behind Grace, his flashlight splashing bright white circles on the walls and tunnel floors. Margrit could see tension in his shoulders and resignation in his walk, and wanted to reach out and reassure him somehow. She didn't try: first, she was too far away, and second, she was no longer a source from which he would draw comfort. Weary regret wrapped around her at that idea, and she let her eyes close, trusting Alban to carry her without her watching the way.

That, too, struck her as a new thing, born in the last minutes since her awakening. She'd once claimed she liked the lack of control over her life that running in Central Park offered her. Grace had dismissed that with a snort, and now Margrit wondered if the blond vigilante had been right. She was out of control now, but she felt safe, and it was distinctly different from late-night jogging. Then, she realized, she *had* felt in control, even if that was nothing more than an illusion.

Light footsteps echoed around them, the sound making her flinch awake, though she hadn't realized she'd slept. The gargoyles and injured selkies who walked with them all moved with eerie silence, but the tunnels themselves picked up sounds her ears couldn't and reverberated them back at her, making her inhuman escort audible.

Not really her escort; that was a self-centered, human thought. They had their own reasons to retreat under the city. Wounds to lick, if selkies did that. Probably, she thought with another tickle of humor. After all, even humans used kisses to banish minor hurts. It wasn't far at all from licking injuries, and humans had no animal form to revert to. Seal-shaped selkies very likely did use the oldest possible method of cleaning cuts.

Margrit pressed her temple against Alban's chest, trying to stop her mind from such random wanderings. Blood oozed under the pressure and she grimaced. There were too many things to deal with to succumb to weakness. Janx was furious with her, and that had to be remedied somehow. More than just by fulfilling his demand to bring Daisani down; she wanted the dragon-lord to like her again.

Of course, if she did succeed in toppling the corporate bloodsucker, it was unlikely she would have a future in which to worry about whether Janx still liked her or not. Irrationally reassured by the thought, Margrit opened her eyes and found that while she'd dozed, they'd traveled most of the distance to Grace's downtown hub.

"Why here?" After a little while of unuse, her voice croaked like she'd— Margrit winced, trying to stop the thought before it finished, but the analogy worked its inexorable way through to completion: like she'd had her throat cut. Still cringing, she said, "Won't there be a lot of kids around?"

"It's Friday night," Grace said with humor. "Tonight they're topside having fun, and this center's got more lockable doors than any of the others. It's safest for all of you and yours, and that means it's safest for me and mine. There'll be plenty of hot water for bathing in," she added to Alban. "I'll need the cisterns refilled, though, after you're done scrubbing. And I'd just burn those clothes, if I were you."

"They're too wet," Margrit said tiredly. "Too bad. I liked this shirt. I can walk." She patted Alban's arm. He shifted his hold, but didn't put her down, and after a few seconds she decided that was agreeable.

Agreeable. A little blood loss, and she became the heroine of a Jane Austen novel. Margrit tried to laugh, but exhaustion swamped her again.

The next time she awakened it was because cool stone was beneath her body, chilling her all the way through. Alban, stripped to the waist and carrying two steaming buckets of water, edged into his room as she sat up. The front of his slacks were entirely soaked in blood from the knees down, and the thighs were badly spotted with it, all the pale material discolored and stiffening as it dried. Margrit shuddered, suddenly aware of how cold she was. Cold from her center to her skin, as if her furnace had shut down.

Alban looked pained at her tremble. "Forgive the accommodations. There seemed little point in putting you on the bed while you were still…"

"Covered in gore?" Margrit picked at the buttons of her blouse as Alban poured the water into a tub she'd never seen in his room before. Fingers too thick to operate properly, she let her hands fall and watched the muscles in his back play easily, as if he picked up a piece of paper instead of gallons of water. A moment later he put the buckets aside and turned back to her, spoiling one lovely view but offering another. Margrit hunched her shoulders against the chill and managed a smile. "I could watch you do that all night."

Gentle humor crossed his expression. "Except you seem to keep falling asleep. Shall I leave you to bathe?"

"No!" Sudden panic spurted in her at the idea, its wake leaving her more exhausted than before. "I don't even think I can undress myself, much less be trusted in a bath. I'd probably drown, and I've had enough of being dead for one night." To her horror, tears scalded her eyes as she spoke.

Alban crossed and knelt by her, a solid, comforting presence as he began to undo the buttons she'd been too clumsy to manage. "I believe I've had enough of you being dead for a lifetime. When you're stronger, I think I'll take the opportunity to go to pieces on you." Teasing glinted in his eyes as she gave him a sharp look.

"Go to pieces, huh? I didn't know you knew words like that."

"I've been keeping bad company of late," Alban said solemnly. He undressed her with quiet efficiency, no eroticism in the act, for which Margrit was wearily grateful. Passion stereotypically arose in the aftermath of danger, but she had no energy left for anything beyond relief that someone was there to care for her. Alban lifted her into the bath with all the gentleness of a practiced nurse, and she sank to its bottom with a whimper.

That quickly, the hot water demolished all her defenses. She began to shiver uncontrollably, teeth chattering at a decibel that would be funny if she wasn't suddenly so frightened. She reached for Alban's hand, her own shaking so badly it looked like a caricature of cold. "Is there enough room in this thing for two?" She couldn't control the stutter and bit her tongue harder than she meant to in trying.

Concern lined Alban's face. "Not with as much water as is in it now."

Margrit's gaze skittered around the room, and all the books safely on their shelves. "The f-floor will d-dry. I n-need you t-to w-warm me up. P-p-please, Alban."

A moment later he climbed in, his own blood-sodden slacks left on the floor behind him. Water cascaded over the tub's sides as Margrit twisted herself against his chest, hands fisted as she rattled with cold. His arms encompassed her, gentle fingers stroking her temple, and she finally let go of control and fear in terrible, body-wracking sobs.

THIRTY

SHE HAD N⊕ idea when sleep had taken her, but wakefulness came easily. Margrit rolled over to search for her alarm clock and the time, and found neither in the gray concrete walls surrounding her. Confusion rattled her before memory caught up and rendered Alban's room into something that made sense. He was crouched in a corner, solid stone protector, and Tony Pulcella, reading a leatherbound book, sat in a chair across from him. "Tony?"

He clapped the book shut as he glanced up. "Hey. Welcome to the world of the li—" Regret for his choice of words spasmed across his face and Margrit found it in herself to laugh.

"Thanks." She sat up, scrubbing her face with her hands and then scratching them through her hair to send curls bouncing around her shoulders. "What time is it?"

"About two-thirty. Drink this." He got up and brought her an enormous bottle of water. Margrit wrapped both hands around it and drained it greedily, not stopping for air until more than half the water was gone. Tony's eyebrows climbed higher and higher as she drank again, and when she finally lowered the nearly empty bottle, said, "Wow. I didn't mean all at once. You're going to get water poisoning."

"You said drink it! Besides, I feel like a mummy." Her skin was dry, pinched against her bones, and her lips felt cracked and thin. "Do I look like one?"

"You look anemic. On the other hand, that's a hell of a lot better than you should look, so don't knock it."

"I won't." She finished the last few sips of water, then shook her head. "Did you say two-thirty? In the morning?" Even as she asked she knew it couldn't be: Alban was sleeping, and wouldn't be if it were still night. "Shouldn't you be at work?"

"I called in sick. Alban asked me to keep an eye on you." Tony gestured toward the statue, and for a moment they both looked at the gargoyle, words inadequate to the topic.

"And you said yes," Margrit finally ventured. "Thanks."

"What else was I gonna say?" Tony sat down on the end of the bed, a few feet away from Margrit. "Margrit, this world—"

"I know. I know I've got a lot to tell you, Tony. I don't even know where to begin."

"Grace covered most of it." The detective shrugged at Margrit's look of surprise. "We spent most of the night talking, until Alban came to ask me to watch out for you. She's not what I expected. A lot more fragile than I imagined."

"Grace?" Margrit, remembering Grace's fist connecting with her face, eyed Tony. "Tall blonde in black leather? That Grace? Fragile?"

Tony studied her a moment or two. "Doesn't matter. She filled me in on everything. Her world. Their world.

And then I watched the gargoyles when the sun came up. It's magic." He shook his head. "It's goddamned magic. I wish you'd told me, Grit."

Margrit put her head in her hands. "I couldn't. I'd promised Alban, and then when Cole discovered them, he was so angry. Like he was personally threatened by Alban, by the whole idea of the Old Races. I thought that was how most people would react. I thought it was how you'd react."

"I might have," Tony admitted. "I might've, if you hadn't come back from the dead in front of me. But, I mean, *dragons,* Grit. There are dragons out there. Like all those old maps say."

"Yeah," Margrit said absently. "I think those were actually sea serpents they were seeing…."

Tony shouted laughter and Margrit jumped, blinking at him. "Sorry," he said, still grinning. "You just said that like it was matter-of-fact. Sea serpents, not dragons. Of course. I'm still wrapping my mind around dragons."

A rueful smile crawled across Margrit's mouth. "I've had a few months to get used to it."

"Wish I had." Tony's laughter faded. "Part of me's completely freaked out. The other part…it's like it's okay if the world doesn't make sense and stupid shit goes wrong, if there are dragons. Like how the hell can we be in control of anything, if we don't even know about the dragons."

Regret rose in Margrit, a physical thing clogging her breath. She put her hand out and Tony caught it, holding on hard as they met eyes. Margrit found herself looking at the life she might have led, if she'd chosen to trust Tony with the impossible. It was more comfortable, no doubt, than her relationship with Alban would prove to be; there would have been no awkward hours, no carefully kept secrets from the world; not, at least, about each other. It would have been a human life, as ordinary and extraordinary as that, and for a moment it shone brilliantly. "I underestimated you. I'm sorry."

Tony nodded. "So'm I."

Something physical popped inside her as he spoke, the release of one dream for the pursuit of another. Margrit caught her breath, feeling its loss, and released Tony's hand. He crooked a smile that said he, too, knew their moment had passed in a more final way than emotional breakups framed. "Guess this is the part where we promise to stay friends, huh?"

"You told me not to say that," Margrit reminded him.

"You're not. I am. You're gonna need friends, Margrit. You're going to need people who get why you go off fighting dragons."

"In four years of us dating you never understood that, Tony. I mean, it's what running through the park was, pretty much. That's always been my way of fighting dragons."

"Yeah, but that was before I knew they really existed." He held up a hand, smiling wryly. "I know it doesn't make sense. Don't ask."

"It makes a kind of sense."

"Grace told me about these favors you've exchanged with Janx," Tony said abruptly. "Is that my fault?"

Margrit blinked, but shook her head. "It really isn't. You put his name in my ear, but someone else pointed me at him to talk to about the Old Races. I made my own noose there. Don't worry about it."

"I can't help worrying. I know what kind of guy he is." Exasperation flitted across Tony's face. "Except I don't."

"No, you do. Just because he's a dragon doesn't mean he's not also a criminal. It just gets complicated when you start looking at it in terms of human justice."

"No kidding." Slow realization dawned on Tony's face. "Shit, Margrit. Tell me you didn't tip him off the night we raided the House of Cards."

Margrit's game face fell into place far too late, a too-honest wince creasing her features long before she could school them into courtroom calm. Tony stared at her, then in genuine dismay, said, *"Margrit!"*

She winced again. "That sounded way too much like my mother. I'm sorry, Tony. I really am, but I just can't see him in one of our jails. It's like caging a lion for hunting."

"We shoot lions that hunt people!"

Margrit opened her mouth and shut it again on her argument. "All right, good point. Still, I just…I had to warn him. I just…"

Tony leaned back, arms folded across his chest as he glared at her. "Looks like the mighty have fallen."

"I fell and then I started digging a pit. I don't know, maybe this is one of the reasons I agreed to go work for Daisani. I always knew that most of the time I was defending bad guys, but I could live with that. It was how our legal system worked. But it's *our* legal system, and I got myself neck-deep in a whole world that doesn't quite follow our rules. It's easy to stop toeing the line, Tony. I never knew how easy it was. If I'm not at Legal Aid anymore I'm not in the position of making these decisions, of splitting these hairs. I don't have to decide if I put Janx away or let him walk."

"That's for a jury to decide, not you, Grit."

"Where are you going to find a jury of Janx's peers?"

Uncertainty crossed Tony's face before he looked away with a new frown. "He lives in our world. He should be judged by it."

"If you can really believe that," Margrit said softly, "you're doing one better than me."

He looked back at her, lips thinned. "I gotta believe it."

Margrit nodded, then sighed. "Would it do any good to ask you not to pursue him now? Because he's already chafing at having to promise not to eviscerate you. If you push it…"

"You think he'll go back on his word? I thought you trusted him."

"I think he might decide you're crunchy and good with ketchup now and be terribly, terribly sorry later." Margrit widened her eyes in her best imitation of the dragonlord's mockery of innocence. "I'd rather you didn't risk it."

"That's quite a mouthful coming from you, at this point."

"I know." Margrit got to her feet, wrapping the blanket around her as a barrier against the cool room. "So maybe you'll take that into consideration. Did Grace bring me any clothes, by any chance?"

"I went to your apartment and got you some." Tony got up to pull a duffel bag around the end of the bed. "What're you going to do, Grit?"

"First I'm going to get dressed." Margrit began rifling through the bag, pulling out a favorite T-shirt, a sports bra and well-loved jogging pants. She shot a smile of recognition and thanks at Tony, who shrugged a shoulder in acknowledgment.

"First I'm going to get dressed," she repeated, mostly to herself, then glanced at Tony again. "And then I'm going to topple an empire."

It had sounded good, she thought later, though the reality was that she slipped out of Grace's tunnels with very little battle plan in place. Cutting the legs from under Daisani's world-spanning corporation took more insider knowledge than she had access to.

Margrit crushed her hand into a fist. No: not more than she had access to, not if she utilized all the resources at her command. But far more than she wanted to use, if there was any potential way to avoid it.

She was running without knowing when she'd started, running for the first time in days, trying to outpace the only solid idea she had. She put on speed, not caring if she pushed herself too far: she needed the release, and the clarity that came with her feet striking the pavement in rhythmic slaps.

Janx and Daisani were symbiotic, always working as a pair. Both Chelsea and Tariq had said that when one failed in a location, the other soon moved on. Margrit told herself it wasn't betrayal to push Daisani toward that end, but rather helping nature take its usual course.

Disbelieving laughter tore her lungs. Even if she could make herself believe that—and while she was a good liar, she didn't think she was *that* good—even if she could, Daisani would never believe it. She already had a very black mark against her on his record. Pulling strings to cut his financial empire's throat would be setting herself a noose and offering to adjust its fit.

Ir rah shun al, whispered the back of her mind. She

sprinted ahead of it, trying to run faster than thought. It leapt ahead of her, taunting: if she failed Janx, his hands would be freed. Daisani losing everything seemed a fair trade for Tony's life. The vampire, after all, could start again. Tony wouldn't have a second chance.

Someday, she would be able to look back and pinpoint the moment at which she ceased recognizing herself. Maybe it had been when she'd gone with instinct and admitted to Alban that she trusted him. Maybe it had been later than that; maybe it had been when Ausra had died and Margrit had passed beyond normal human law into being part judge, jury and executioner herself. Maybe all of it had simply crept up, weighting her with incremental changes until she was suddenly, simply, no longer as she had been.

The woman she'd been wouldn't have seriously considered how to ruin vast financial holdings, much less found herself grimly intending to do so.

Fresh humor, more of the bitter stuff that had followed her lately rather than the previous night's joyfulness of being alive, surged through her. The truth was the woman she'd been before the Old Races could never have encountered the questions and problems that were now part and parcel of her life. In the same extraordinary circumstances, faced with what she now faced, the woman she'd been *would* make the same decisions. Had to make them, for the sake of people she loved. Daisani *could* start again, and at the end of the day, his welfare wasn't as important to her as Tony's.

Margrit wondered if that made her more human, or less, than she'd once been.

The thought cleared her mind, leaving her room to

simply run. She cut across streets against the lights, making her way uptown with the vague idea of going home, or to the park. It didn't matter, as long as she ran. For the first time in two weeks, nightmares didn't haunt her steps, and she felt as though the exercise was helping to replenish the blood she'd lost the night before. She still needed more to drink, but what Tony'd brought had given her strength.

She came to a halt, panting, outside an apartment building, and flipped her ponytail upside down, hands on her thighs as she panted for air. The dizziness felt good: normal, and she was beginning to forget what normal was like. Anything that reminded her was welcome.

"Ms. Knight?" A voice spoke from a few yards away. Margrit righted herself, hands on her hips while she continued to heave for air, and blinked at the doorman, whose expression split into a smile. "Are you here to see Mr. Daisani?"

Margrit rolled back on her heels, still breathing hard, and looked up toward the penthouse apartment Daisani lived in. She'd had no conscious intention to visit the vampire, and reversed her gaze to eye her feet accusingly, as though they'd developed a mind of their own. Then she smiled at the doorman. "Yeah, I am. It's Diego, right? Gosh, thanks. I didn't know if anybody would recognize me, with me turning up all sweaty and out of breath."

Diego grinned. "It's my job." He held the door for her and Margrit went inside, waiting till she was well past him to raise a mocking eyebrow at herself: *gosh?* It was the sort of thing the flighty, frantic persona she'd put on a few days ago in an attempt to rescue Alban would have said.

The elevator doors slid open and Margrit stepped in,

heel of one hand pressed against her eye as she tried to count back and remember how many days had passed since then. It was late Saturday afternoon now, and that had been Wednesday morning. She'd had far too little sleep in the interim, but felt astonishingly good for all of that.

An almost unnoticeable lurch warned her she'd reached the penthouse level just before the bell rang. Expecting a hallway, Margrit stepped out and then, astonished, glanced around a gorgeously lit, sunken living room. After the warm, rich Victorian colors of his office lobby, Margrit had expected Daisani's home to be similar. Instead everything glowed in whites and creams, making the room a bastion of light.

Daisani himself came out of an enormous kitchen off to the elevator's right, followed by the scent of garlic. "Miss Knight. To what do I owe the pleasure?"

Margrit, her intended topic entirely forgotten, blurted, "The elevator opens in your living room? Isn't that dangerous?"

Daisani arched an eyebrow. "Not especially. And, of course, I assure you the elevator only opens so indiscreetly when I know who's arriving. Its back doors open on the hallway, which is how most visitors are admitted. Margrit, whatever are you doing here? I understand there was quite a kerfuffle last night."

"Quite a… You could say that. I'm only alive because of you. Thanks." Her eyebrows shot up. "I thought you said I'd still have to sleep, by the way. I've been up for most of four days and I feel fine."

"Really. How extraordinary. I sleep very little, of course, but my blood doesn't impart that gift to humans. It's a more dragonly trait. Won't you come in? Have some wine?"

"Water, please." Margrit followed him into the kitchen, squinting. "Wait. Something happens if dragons give a human their blood, too?"

"I have no idea. They're not, as far as I know, in the habit of it. Especially since your alchemists and wizards used to hunt them down for the so-called magical properties in their blood. I wouldn't be inclined to share, either." Smiling, Daisani poured a crystal glass of water and offered it to her.

Margrit took it and drank automatically, then, child-like, held it out for a refill when she'd finished. Looking amused, he poured a second glass, and Margrit did the same thing again without realizing it. When he handed it back a third time, she accepted, then turned one palm up, searching for a cut that wasn't there.

But her own mind, sharpened with gargoyle clarity, showed her what she sought: a memory of Janx's bloody scale, torn from his body by Alban's strength. Margrit had pressed her hands against the deadly edge, watching her own skin part and meld again.

Melding, perhaps, with dragon blood.

"Margrit?"

She jolted, looking up from her hand, then drew a sharp breath. "Sorry. I was thinking." Water glass set aside, she pulled her ponytail out, then twisted it back into place. "You want to know why I'm here."

"Very much." Daisani's smile all but sparkled with curiosity. "After what I've heard about last night, anything that brings you here must be momentous indeed."

"It is." Margrit swallowed, then turned her hands up, as if pleading. "Here's the thing. I'm stuck between a rock and a hard place. Janx wants you destroyed, and my promise to do that is the only thing keeping Tony alive.

But for some reason it really gets under my skin to sneak around and backstab you, so I'm telling you that this is what I have to do. I have to try. I don't much want to, but I can't stop Janx any other way."

Daisani blinked, the slowest, most deliberate expression she'd ever seen from him. "That…is momentous, indeed. You are certainly full of surprises, Miss Knight. Do you throw gauntlets at all your rivals with such clear and forthright intent?"

Margrit blinked back, then twitched her eyebrows in a shrug. "Well, yeah, pretty much. This is what lawyers do. Meet in neutral territory, proclaim their intentions, bargain if it's possible, then step back to do battle in the courtroom."

"And is a bargain possible?" Daisani asked the question as if it were academic; as if he knew already what the final answer was, but was curious to hear her response.

"Let's assume for a moment that you were willing to relinquish all your holdings and walk away from the corporation. I don't think Janx would qualify that as you being destroyed, which is what he wants. He probably also wants it to be a surprise, but I can't help thinking that if I pull it off, you're going to be plenty surprised whether you've been forewarned or not. So, no, I don't think it is possible. I wish it was. I wish it could be that easy. But you're not going to make it that easy, are you?"

"What fun would that be? I do see a critical flaw in your plan, though, Margrit." He waited the fraction of a moment for Margrit to look inquisitive, then said, "What's to prevent me from killing you right now and ending the entire question?"

Margrit dragged in a breath, held it, then expelled it on a crooked smile. "What fun would that be?"

THIRTY-ONE

SHE COULD ALMOS+ hear Alban's voice, dismayed and resigned, saying, "That was a bad idea."

The phrase was so inadequate as to be laughable, but that was part of the delight in hearing him say it. She had pursued so many bad ideas in the months since the Old Races came into her life that more extravagant words fell by the wayside of that one hopelessly understated comment.

Daisani had laughed aloud and gestured her back toward the elevator. Grateful, Margrit had taken the out she was offered, heart pushing thick blood with such enthusiasm that it sent a cramp through her chest when the elevator doors closed without Daisani darting inside them. He could catch her anywhere, instantaneously, but allowing her to escape the building without reminding her of that seemed like an agreement to the game.

Now, after the fact, warning him what she intended felt supremely stupid. She stopped a few yards down the block, arms folded over her ribs as she tried to hold back stomach-churning nausea. Feeble intellect proclaimed that challenging the vampire openly had been the right thing to do, and she'd been confident enough in that rightness to walk into his lair without fear. Now that the moment was past, though, she wasn't certain she had strength left to get home, much less draw together the resources necessary to bring about his downfall.

"Mind over matter, Grit." She spoke the words softly, trying to encourage herself, then nodded a couple of times and pushed herself upright, leaning against the wall. "One step at a time. Um." Unable to think of another platitude, she managed a smile at herself and dug for the cell phone she'd pocketed when she'd put on her running gear. She'd set the autodial in motion and brought it to her ear before she fully noticed the screen was a pixelated mess. "Oh, goddammit!"

"Sorry?" A startled man—not a local, from both his response and from the T-shirt reading *Oklahoma Is OK!*—edged out of her way as she clenched the useless phone in her fist to stop herself from dashing it against the sidewalk in frustration. She'd ended up hurt and without a cell phone both times a djinn had snatched her. For one overblown moment, the loss of the phones seemed vastly more debilitating than the physical injuries. The fact that Janx wouldn't be replacing this phone only added insult.

Margrit channeled destructive tendencies into running and left weariness behind in the rush of endorphins. Even so, by the time she arrived home, she was gasping, thirsty and vividly aware that she hadn't eaten since lunch the previous day.

There were no leftovers in the fridge, more disappointing than the discovery warranted. She took out a cup of yogurt and stirred it into a bowl full of granola, then left both on the counter as she searched for a pint of ice cream from the freezer. Two bites told her she needed real food first, and she shoveled the granola yogurt into her mouth while she called for Chinese delivery. With a promise of Mongolian beef and cashew chicken in twenty minutes, she sank down in front of the phone to finish eating her snack.

A key in the front door warranted looking, but not getting up. Margrit's stomach clenched around the food, the anticipation of another confrontation with Cole too much to face, but it was Cameron who stepped in, gym bag slung over her shoulder and long legs shown off beneath a short, white tennis skirt.

"I thought you didn't play tennis."

Cam yelped, startled, and swung around to regard Margrit's position on the floor in front of the telephone table. "Normal people say hello first!"

Margrit smiled. "Hello. I thought you didn't play tennis."

Cameron pointed a toe to flex lean muscle. "I took it up so Cole'd buy me a diamond tennis bracelet. You like the look?"

"You look gorgeous," Margrit assured her. "Is it working?"

"Not unless he gets a substantial raise, but I don't really need a tennis bracelet." Cam smiled back and threw her gym bag into the room she and Cole shared before coming back to straighten up a kitchen Cole never left messy. "You left the party early last night, and you've got ice cream melting on the counter. Are you okay?"

"The ice cream didn't taste good. I needed real food first."

Cameron put out a hand and Margrit put her empty bowl into it for inspection. "So you ate cereal and yogurt?"

"I've ordered Chinese."

"Cole will never forgive you if you stink up his fridge with leftover Chinese."

"I'll eat it all. I haven't eaten since yesterday."

"That's not good." Cameron frowned down at her. "What's up with that?"

"I've been...it's been..."

"Ah. That, huh?" Cam sat down beside Margrit, looping her arms around her knees. "Is that why you bailed on the party?"

"Yeah, I had some things to do."

Cam gave her a sly look and Margrit laughed. "No. Not those kinds of things, or that kind of doing. It was sort of business."

"So..." Cameron hesitated, then sighed. "I don't know how much of this I'm going to be able to ask when Cole's around, so I'm asking now. I understand how you got involved. I even understand why you're staying involved. I just don't think I get...how deep you are. Because it's deep, isn't it? How did that happen?"

"I couldn't mind my own business." Margrit offered a faint smile, then scrambled to her feet as the doorbell rang. "Fastest delivery in the city. Oh, God, I'm hungry." She ran to pay, then returned to sit on the floor and start eating out of the cartons. Cameron stole a spring roll and waited, eyebrows lifted, for Margrit to continue.

"It was mostly that I was trying to help Alban clear himself of the murder charges. It just turned out that doing that kept digging me deeper and deeper into their world. Once I knew about all of them, I became an obvious choice to be a go-between."

"Obvious. Sure."

"Well, it was obvious to them. And I…thought I could do some good."

"Could you? Can you?"

Margrit shrugged and scooped up a ball of sticky rice. "I've affected a lot of change, anyway. Whether that's good or not, not even I'm sure anymore. But there's no going back on any of it, so I have to keep going forward."

Cam balanced the spring roll on her fingertips, blowing steam away from it. "Are you ever going to tell me more than generalized statements?"

Guilt twisted around the food Margrit had eaten. "Maybe, but maybe not, too. This is dangerous, Cam. They depend on secrets."

"Yeah, I know. That's one of the things Cole hates."

Margrit ducked her head. "Just one, huh?"

"He's genuinely freaked out." Cameron got up to pour a glass of milk and gestured with the carton to ask Margrit if she wanted some. At Margrit's nod, she brought a second glass, then returned the carton to the fridge and leaned on the broad orange door. "It's not just that you're sleeping with a gargoyle. It's that they exist at all. You won't take it wrong if I say you're about all we've been talking about the last couple days, right?"

"Heh. No. I'm not surprised. I'm sorry, Cam. It wasn't supposed to go this way."

"I know, Grit, but the more we go around about it, the less sure I am any other way would have made much difference. I don't think it'd be easier for Cole, and that means it wouldn't be easier for us."

"Us you and me or us you and him?"

"Any of us. The worst part is I can feel myself siding with him. I mean, I'm not angry like he is, but…"

"Cam, he's your fiancé. You're supposed to side with him. It's okay. You don't have to make apologies. He spelled it out last night at the party. 'I love you but I can't watch you do this,' though not in those exact words. It's okay." Margrit sighed. "The sad thing is I thought he'd be the one to understand. I mean, out of him and Tony. The men in my life."

"Wait, Tony knows? I thought he didn't."

"He found out last night. After the party. He saw…not just Alban, but a lot of them." And he'd watched Margrit herself come back from the dead, a gift which might well have tempered him toward accepting the Old Races. The juxtaposition of truths made Margrit's bones ache. She knew as well as Tony did that if it weren't for her involvement with the inhuman races, she wouldn't have been so badly injured in the first place. On the other hand, that involvement taken as rote, she'd survived through their gifts. Nothing could be taken for granted, and nothing was made easy. She looked down at her food and shook her head. "Maybe if Cole talks to him…"

"That could help a lot." Cam spoke quietly. "They're friends. If Tony's okay, maybe it'll help smooth things over." She offered a hopeful smile. "Next thing you know, they'll all be going out for beer and football."

Margrit laughed and got up to hug her housemate. "What a horrible idea."

"Isn't it? Sit back down," Cam ordered. "You've got a lot of food to get through before Cole gets home."

"I've got a lot of other things to get through before…" Before when? she wondered. Janx hadn't demanded a time frame, though clearly the dragonlord expected results sooner rather than later. For a moment the idea of putting him off indefinitely with promises of Daisani's financial ruin at any moment struck her as amusing, but the humor faded. He might allow that to go on for a little while, but he would no doubt remain in New York, threatening both Tony and Grace O'Malley's under-city charity operation until Margrit came through on her end of the deal. Time was of the essence, not for her own sake, but for the sake of the lives she'd managed to disrupt.

She shook herself and collected the food cartons from the floor, heading into the living room with them. "I'll finish eating before anything else. And then can I borrow your cell phone for a couple of days? Mine got ruined last night."

"You can have mine if you buy me a spiffy new one!"

"Your generosity overwhelms me." Margrit sat down on the couch to finish dinner, feeling at least temporarily lighthearted.

Cam did lend her the cell phone. Margrit, wanting privacy and to keep her housemates as uninvolved as she could, left the apartment well before sunset to call her mother. Rebecca Knight's voice mail picked up, sending a pang of relieved regret through Margrit. Her mother, a stockbroker, was the only contact she had who could possibly advise her on how to take down a financial empire, but the idea of asking made Margrit cold with dismay. She left a message and Cam's number, then worked her way downtown to Chelsea Huo's bookshop.

Chelsea, chatting with customers, waved Margrit toward the back room and called, "Help yourself to some tea," after her. Glad to do so, Margrit wound her way through the stacks and through the rattling bead curtain that separated Chelsea's private quarters from the rest of the store. A few minutes later, hands wrapped around a mug of tea, she curled up on one of the overstuffed sofas and waited for the second rattle that would announce Chelsea's arrival.

It took longer than she expected, long enough to finish her tea and nod drowsily against the sofa's back. Chelsea's soprano rose and fell in the front room, sometimes with laughter, sometimes with words, while other voices made deeper counterparts to her pleasantry. It seemed very normal, reassuringly far away from the Old Races, and for a little while Margrit drifted on the idea that she could perhaps someday find a role as comfortable as Chelsea's seemed to be.

Finally the beads chattered again and Margrit pushed upright, blinking sleepily. Chelsea clucked her tongue and made another pot of tea before turning her bright smile on Margrit. "So you survived the djinn negotiations. Has everyone agreed?"

Margrit eyed her. "Are you being funny?"

"Not at all." Chelsea's smile faded. "What happened?" Her expression grew increasingly grim as Margrit explained, and when she finished, Chelsea shook her head. "You have the luck of the devil, Margrit Knight. I'm not sure any other human would have survived that."

"Any other human." Margrit pressed her lips together, looking hard at the tiny bookseller. "Chelsea, do you say it that way because you're one of them?"

Chelsea tilted her head. "Do you not find yourself thinking in terms of humans and gargoyles and vampires now, Margrit? Naming your own race separately, in a way you didn't before?"

Margrit sighed and slumped in the couch. "Yeah, I do.

I thought Hispanic and African-American and all could get confusing enough. I never counted on adding gargoyle-Americans to the mix." She was silent a moment, wondering if Chelsea's response answered the question, and then let it go. "What about Vanessa Gray? She had to have had a healing sip to get the second sip, the one for long life."

"She did, as have done a handful of others. But I believe they came together, two sips at once."

"Does that make a difference?"

"Vanessa didn't survive an attack less direct and devastating than a cut throat," Chelsea pointed out. "I would say it might well make a difference. Think of it this way. You've had some three months in which your body has learned to heal itself. Time in which the smallest blemishes could be undone, from pimples to extraneous chromosomes, and whether deliberately or not, you've pushed that healing ability to its fullest. Vanessa and the others had no time for their bodies to adapt. They went from mortal to—" Chelsea broke off, drawing a breath as if to give herself time to consider her words. "Immortal," she finally said, though she didn't look pleased with it.

"Demi-mortal?" Margrit asked with a half smile. "Demigods are half human, half gods, right? So a human whose lifespan's been extended beyond the norm would be demi-mortal."

Chelsea's smile blossomed. "Demi-mortal. That will do nicely. They went from mortal to demi-mortal inside a few minutes. I would think the flaws they were born with would continue into demi-mortality, having been given no chance to be wiped away. I should think that even without a second sip of Eliseo's blood, short of traumatic accidents, you might live a very long time indeed."

Margrit stared at her, then shuddered. "Demi-mortal sounds better on somebody else, Chelsea. I'm only human."

"Yes, I think that's true. I suspect that if you underwent examination you would be nothing more than human, but you might very possibly be a perfect specimen. No errors in the template any longer."

"Wouldn't that make me sterile, or something?" The idea was so extreme it had almost no meaning as she voiced it. "I mean, isn't human development born from mutation? How can anything mutate if I don't have any flaws?"

"I think as long as you intend to reproduce sexually instead of asexually you're in no danger of flaw-free reproduction," Chelsea said dryly. "Which, fascinating topic as it is, is probably not why you came here this evening."

"No, although I'm beginning to think maybe it should have been. I never even thought about—" Margrit drew herself up, stopping the line of speculation. "I came to ask if you think it's possible to take Daisani down."

Chelsea's feathery eyebrows shot up. "You're asking me?"

"Well, I can't exactly ask *him* for pointers. You…know things," Margrit said, suddenly aware that was the phrase Grace often used. Putting that aside, too, she added, "And they listen to you. Why?" The word carried stress as she found herself up against the question of whether Chelsea was human or not a second time. "I've never seen any of them so much as mock you. They tease me all the time."

"Margrit." Amusement warmed Chelsea's voice. "It's early April. You've been part of their world for three months, and they have, in fact, all jumped at your command. I'm easily twice your age, and have known about them for a very long time. Even if you do no more than hold the place you now stand in, in twenty years you'll be treated with more reverence, too."

Margrit regarded Chelsea over the mug of tea, then blew exasperated ripples into it. "Did I sound like I wanted a logical answer? Still, they do listen to you."

"You think Eliseo Daisani will listen if I suggest he roll over?"

Margrit huffed into her tea again. "No. Just wondering if you know of any…vulnerabilities."

Chelsea's eyes darkened to the color of old tea. "How seriously do you intend to disable him, Margrit?"

"Even if I could, I'm not after his life. I won't go that far, not now, not ever. Not even for Tony." She put the tea aside to drop her face into her hands. "Good to know I've still got boundaries."

"Did you doubt it?"

Margrit looked up through her fingers. "More and more every day."

"As long as it's a matter for concern, you're probably safe." Chelsea studied her for long moments. "I have a piece of information that will help you, but it carries a tremendous price. You have undone the strictures that have held the Old Races in place for millennia. If you're obliged—or willing—to use this, I cannot be sure what Eliseo Daisani will do in retaliation. It could very easily cost you your life."

"Chelsea." Margrit ducked her head again, fingers laced behind her neck, then craned it to look at the bookshop proprietor. "There's part of me that's kidding myself, okay? Part of me that says if I pull this off for

Janx, it's all going to be all right and I'm going to walk away with a happily-ever-after. I need that part to keep going. I need that part because it's what's letting me face this at all. I need it because without it, Tony's going to die, and I can't live with that. But the truth is, I'm not going to live through this. I'll manage to orchestrate Eliseo's fall or I won't, but if I fail, Janx is going to have to go through me to get to Tony, and I have no doubt he will. If I succeed, Daisani's not going to let me see another sunrise." She gave a sharp laugh. "I wanted to change the world. I'm doing it. But I don't see me being around to admire what the future looks like."

"I haven't heard you be that fatalistic before."

"If I'm wrong, you can tease me for my melodrama. If I'm right, I'd like my tombstone to read, *She changed the world. A lot.* Either way, I have got to save Tony, and I'll do whatever it takes. If you can help at all, Chelsea, please."

Chelsea sat back, silent and contemplative once again before she nodded. "Very well. When the moment comes, Margrit Knight, ask Eliseo Daisani where the bodies are buried."

THIRTY-TWO

"THE BODIES? WHAT bodies? Come on, Chelsea! You can't send me after Daisani with just the question! I have to know!"

"I would advise having Alban with you when you ask," had been Chelsea's implacable response. She'd invited Margrit to finish her tea, then dismissed her with steely pleasantry that was impossible to stand against. Margrit found herself on the street with an accelerated heartbeat and no answers to her questions.

Wherever the bodies were, *what*ever they were, asking Daisani a question like that seemed tantamount to suicide. Margrit shot a final glare at the bookstore and stomped away, uncertain of where she was going, but determined to leave Chelsea's cryptic advice far behind.

Barely a few steps beyond the entryway, Cam's phone rang, its ringtone so unfamiliar it took Margrit a moment to realize it was her own pocket. She picked up with, "Mom?" and heard Rebecca Knight's mystified "I'm on the train into the city. What on earth is so important, Margrit? Are you all right?"

"I need financial advice." The explanation, identical to what she'd left on voice mail earlier, still sounded pathetic. "I'll explain at your office, okay?"

"Margrit, unless you've won the jackpot, I can't imagine—"

"You really can't, Mom. You really can't. I'll see you in what, about an hour?"

"Forty minutes," Rebecca said with asperity. "I want a full explanation, Margrit Elizabeth."

"I know." Margrit hung up, all too aware she hadn't promised that explanation. The cell phone told her it was a quarter to seven, and for a moment she considered rushing home to change clothes, as though a smarter outfit would make her mother take her more seriously. Being late, though, would be worse than being untidy, and Margrit sighed, breaking into a ground-eating jog toward the financial district.

She arrived well before Rebecca and paced in front of the office building until a security guard gave her a hard look. Margrit made her hands into fists and found a place to sit, watching the street for her mother's approach.

Forty minutes from their phone conversation, Rebecca appeared down the street, looking fresh and put-together in a linen pantsuit that made her slim form more imposing. Margrit slumped, wishing anew she'd taken time to go home and change, then reluctantly got to her feet to wave a greeting.

Rebecca paused, purse-lipped, to consider Margrit's running gear, then with a silence far more condemning than commentary, nodded a greeting to the security guard and key-carded herself into the building, gesturing for Margrit to follow. Feeling considerably more intimidated than she had by the Old Races in the past few days, Margrit shuffled along meekly.

Neither spoke as they took the elevator up to Rebecca's pale, beautifully appointed office, but once ensconced within its walls, Rebecca turned to her with an arched eyebrow of inquiry that brooked no nonsense and very little leeway for whatever had brought her there, even if it was her own daughter.

Margrit pulled her ponytail out and let unruly curls cascade everywhere as she tried to find a place to begin. A moment's silence led to blurting, "What I really need to know is if you can provide me with any financial vulnerabilities in Daisani's empire, and some advice on how to exploit them." Voiced aloud, the proposition sounded even worse than it had in her imagination. Margrit clenched her teeth, trying to smile, and knew it was a wince.

Rebecca's brief stare ended in a disbelieving laugh. "Margrit, have you lost your mind?"

"I'm beginning to think that's possible. Mom…" Margrit trailed off, the absurdity of her request vividly clear to her, and helpless to find another course. "It's Tony. I—"

"Tony needs information on Eliseo Daisani's financial weaknesses? I've told you before that Eliseo's not the kind of man you put in jail. I understand Tony's ambitious, but any pursuit of Eliseo or his corporation is going to end up an embarrassment at best and a dead end to his career at worst. You need to—"

"If I don't find a way to cut Daisani's purse strings Tony's going to die." Margrit's voice sounded harsh and loud over her mother's impassioned tirade. Rebecca went quiet, staring again, and Margrit closed her eyes against the weight of her mother's regard. "Mom, you do not want to know the details. I'm not saying that because I think you shouldn't know."

She forced her eyes open again, meeting Rebecca's gaze with no little challenge in her own. "I'm saying it because I've watched you with Eliseo. Because I've *watched* you shut away what you're seeing, not because you don't believe it, but because you don't want to know. And you know what? That's fine. I don't get it, but I don't have to. But I can promise you that I've got to find a way to do this, that you're my best chance, and that you do not want to know the details."

"Margrit." Rebecca found nothing to say after the name, mother and daughter looking at one another across a distance that seemed impossibly vast to Margrit. Finally, full minutes later, Rebecca spoke again. "GBI handles a dozen of Eliseo's largest accounts. You're right that I could help you, but how could you have ever imagined that I would?" She lifted a hand sharply, cutting off anything Margrit might say. "I understand that you believe Tony's life is at stake, but I very much doubt Eliseo is the sort to—"

"First, he is, but more important, he's not the one gunning for Tony. It's Janx, the guy who used to run the House of Cards up in Harlem. Tony took the House down and Janx is looking for retaliation. If he didn't owe me a favor, Tony would be dead already. Unfortunately, I owe him one, too, and this is what he's asking for."

"What on earth could someone like Janx have against Eliseo?"

Margrit ground her teeth together, then repeated, carefully, "You do not want to know."

A difficult expression—regret, distress, perhaps mixed with chagrin—crossed Rebecca's face and faded, leaving it neutral with acceptance. "If you say so, Margrit. But if Tony is being threatened by a criminal, that's something for the police to deal with, not—"

"Mom!" Exasperated almost to the point of amusement, Margrit tied her hair back up with quick ferocious movements before she trusted herself to speak again. "Mom, if there was any other way to deal with this, I would. There isn't. So it's pretty simple, really. Are you going to help me?"

Regret and its closer cousin sorrow left marks in Rebecca's face this time. "I'm sorry, sweetheart, but you know the answer to that. You know I can't."

Margrit turned away, finding one of the soft leather sofas to sit down on hard. Conflicting emotions rattled her: relief and dismay in equal parts, neither of them certain what to do with themselves. She had known on every reasonable level that Rebecca couldn't possibly agree. It was too black an area, too obviously illegal, and the fact that she herself had been willing to follow it said more than she wanted to consider about the path she'd taken since meeting the Old Races. At the same time, her mother had been the only real inside chance she'd had. "Yeah." She heard her own voice distantly. "Yeah, I knew that. I shouldn't have asked."

"No," Rebecca said, surprisingly cheerful. "You shouldn't have. And you could have saved us time and trouble by asking on the phone, Margrit, really."

"There was always the chance you'd say yes. I wanted you here where you could act before you came to your senses."

"Margrit." Rebecca's voice gentled. "There was never any chance I'd say yes."

Thick pain settled around Margrit's heart, squeezing. Without that help, legal or not, she was out of options as to how to take Daisani down. Out of options she wanted to consider: Chelsea's cryptic advice lingered at the back of her mind, nerve-wracking and tantalizing. "I know. But I hoped I was wrong. It wasn't a bad plan, except for it being illegal. I even had a buyer for the stock."

"Call your stockholders," murmured a voice behind Margrit. Familiar voice, touched with the hint of desert sands, and as Rebecca's face whitened, Margrit realized the pressure around her heart wasn't just exhausted emotion. Not with the soft, faint threat in Tariq's words: "Prepare Daisani's fall, Rebecca Knight, or watch your daughter die."

An offended part of Margrit's mind protested, silently, that she'd been dead once lately and facing the sentence twice in a day seemed unfair. As though he heard her thoughts, Tariq leaned in close, body warmth no more than a mist by Margrit's cheek. "Your life was forfeit, Margrit Knight. Imagine my surprise to see you at Eliseo Daisani's apartment today."

Margrit caught her breath, or tried: it hitched, as did her heartbeat. "What were you doing there?" Her voice sounded like Rebecca's had when she'd stood in this same position, Tariq's fist around her heart: weak, fluttery, pained.

"Ensuring the glassmaker's empire was ours. Your offer was generous, but merely cemented a deal already in the making. We had never, since we left our deserts, intended on sharing it."

Sudden clarity blazed through Margrit, making the

pain in her chest seem worse. Clear as gargoyle memory, the moment of exchange between Daisani and Tariq after the trial played vividly for her mind's eye. "You double-dealing bastard." A note of admiration wheezed through the words. "You're playing both sides against the middle. That's why Daisani wouldn't agree to let Malik's death go, even though Janx asked him to. He promised you."

"So he did, and we cannot allow a lack of retribution. Your life would have sufficed, had Daisani's gift not made it so hard to take."

"So now what?" Speaking made Margrit dizzy, but stopping seemed like giving up. "Now you're going to take him down, too, for backstabbing you whether he meant to or not?"

"In essence." Tariq sounded smug. "Why settle for one empire when we might command two?"

"You'll command nothing if you don't release my daughter." Rebecca finally broke in, voice strong and confident after Tariq's murmurs and Margrit's breathless attempts to keep talking. A surge of pride and panic rose in Margrit: she had hoped to distract the djinn from Rebecca's presence, though to what end she didn't know. In case of sunset and a psychic link warning Alban she was in need of rescue, perhaps. Even with a hand fisted around her heart, the idea amused her.

Tariq lifted his gaze to Rebecca, misty presence shimmering in the edge of Margrit's vision. "You're in no position to issue commands."

Rebecca's eyebrows rose. "Do you have access to the accounts that could bankrupt Eliseo Daisani? No," she said after a judiciously brief pause. "I didn't think so. I see a few choices here, Mr.—?"

"Tariq," Margrit whispered when Tariq didn't speak. "His name is Tariq."

"Tariq," Rebecca repeated. "You can kill Margrit, or me, or both of us, none of which will achieve your goals, or you can release her, earn my goodwill and accomplish what you're attempting. It seems like a simple decision to me."

Tariq made a soft, derisive sound. "And what prevents me from killing you when I have what I want?"

"Your word on it," Rebecca said calmly. She sounded as though she was brokering a business deal, not bargaining for her daughter's life. Margrit, mixed with admiration and terror, wondered if she sounded like that when bartering with the Old Races. "Your word that you won't harm Margrit or myself, or any of our family, not now and not ever," Rebecca concluded.

No, Margrit decided, she didn't sound that confident, and she didn't think she was ever that thorough. Tariq laughed, murderous sharp sound. "And you'd trust my word?"

"Yes." Rebecca spoke with no caveats, no doubts, nothing but serene confidence, and then offered a soft, pointed smile that had put the fear of God, or at least Rebecca Knight, into Margrit for her entire childhood. Something like a laugh tried to break free of her constricted chest as Rebecca explained, almost gently, "I would trust your word because, if for no other reason, you owe Margrit your freedom."

Tariq's hand spasmed around her heart, as much show of shock as Margrit had ever seen a djinn indulge in. She was certain his astonishment was echoed in her own face, a suspicion that was confirmed by Rebecca's brief acknowledging nod.

"Not wanting to know doesn't mean I don't watch, Margrit. I understand that sometimes you need a weapon at hand even if you don't want to use it. Am I right?" She turned her gaze on Tariq, an eyebrow lifted.

For a moment the events of the past hung over them all as though they replayed on a screen, clear and precise. Margrit had faced down Daisani over Tariq's freedom when the djinn had been captured in a binding circle of vampire's blood. Daisani had been more than willing— eager, even—to enslave Tariq as punishment for damages done to Rebecca, and Margrit had threatened the vampire with everything she could in order to gain Tariq's release. It had been a gesture of passion, borne in the moment, and Tariq and Daisani had both thought her a fool. Margrit had had no idea her mother had paused to watch the exchange, and now wondered if the honor that seemed to hold so much sway within the Old Races—even amongst those who denied its power—would be visited upon mortals.

The djinn made a bitter sound and the pressure around Margrit's heart lessened, then disappeared entirely, leaving an ache of pain in its place. She coughed and doubled over, arms folded against her chest and tears flooding her eyes as she heard him say, "I am no glass-maker to play at this game on levels and levels. This is your one moment of grace, human. I will not be denied a second time or offer another chance."

Rebecca waited until Margrit looked up with a tight nod that said she was all right, then dipped her head in acknowledgment. "I think we understand each other, then." She stepped around her desk, switching her computer on with a brisk motion, then glanced around her office.

A pang that had nothing to do with her heart being crushed spasmed through Margrit's chest. She'd come to ask for what Rebecca was about to do, but she'd known the price was too high and that her mother would refuse. Watching her now take in the office for what was very likely the last time hurt worse than she'd anticipated. "Mom..."

"Eliseo's major holdings will go on the open market when the bells ring Monday morning," Rebecca said steadily. "I can't guarantee it'll destroy him, but it will certainly be extremely costly." She sat down at her computer. "You said you had a buyer, Margrit. I suggest you contact him immediately and have him liquidate any holdings he can in order to have cash on hand to purchase with."

"But what about you?" Recriminations pounded at the inside of Margrit's skin, trying to break free. If she hadn't been foolish enough to ask Rebecca to help in the first place, her mother wouldn't be about to ruin her career. If she'd refused Janx—

Then Tony would be dead. Margrit's hands knotted into fists. Ruining Daisani's career was a price she was willing to pay for the detective's life. Rebecca herself had decided Margrit's life, and by extension, Tony's, were worth her own career. There had to be a limit, though, a point at which the needs of the many overrode the good of the one. Two lives was a high price to pay for one. More would become untenable. "It ends here," Margrit whispered.

Rebecca looked up with a smile. "That will be good enough for me, Margrit. Now go, and take your unpleasant companion with you. I have work to do."

THIRTY-THREE

SUNSET'S RELEASE BROUGHT wakefulness with a burgeoning sense of responsibility, wholly different from the small tasks Alban had set himself over the decades. The gargoyles had held themselves apart for millennia. To put themselves forward as they'd done so precipitously the previous evening heralded an involvement with the world they'd never before had. For all that it had seemed right and necessary in the moment, it was only now that the enormity of his decision—and the fact that the others had indeed followed him—began to sink in.

And yet nothing would convince him that he had chosen badly. Margrit's horrifying experience aside, had the gargoyles not arrived when they did, many more of the Old Races might have died. For a people who regarded themselves as observers and recorders, they also had clear strengths as enforcers.

The idea sent a shock of bemusement through Alban. To move so quickly from passive to active participants— especially in a world as changed as theirs was now—well, that was what Margrit Knight had made of him, perhaps.

It was what she would make of all the Old Races, given the chance. He wondered if that thought might cause her sleepless nights, and then humor caught him: the Old Races themselves gave her enough sleepless nights. Any changes she wrought, and their consequences, would have to haunt her daytime hours.

She was gone, her scent faded enough to say it had been some hours since she'd slept in his rarely used cot. Regret slipped through him and fell away again: it was enough to let dawn and stone take him with Margrit at his side. She could and did live in a daylight world; to hope she would be there when he woke was too much. He, after all, would never be there when she woke.

A rap sounded at the door. Alban unfolded from his crouch, wings stretching, then disappearing as he changed to human form before saying, "Come in."

For some reason it surprised him when Grace entered. Aside from Margrit, she was the most likely, but Alban had half-consciously expected Tony Pulcella.

"Janx isn't understanding Margrit's orders to leave this place to me now," Grace said without preamble. "And I'm talented, love, but I can't shoo a dragon from my doorstep. Maybe a word in his ear?"

Doubt made Alban lift an eyebrow. "Didn't I watch you face that dragon down only last night?"

"You've mistaken me for Margrit," Grace said blithely. "Maybe a bit of her spark carried over, that's all. And for all my boldness I'm no good pushing him around, much less two of them and that vampire lass. Gives me the creeps, she does."

"Ursula? I always thought she was the calmer of the two."

"Aye, and it's always the quiet ones to watch out for, now, isn't it? You saw what she did." Grace shuddered. "Thought you'd have taught them better, Stoneheart. Thought you'd have taught them the laws that bind you all."

"I would not have imagined them to be so careless with our lives," Alban murmured. "But they've lived apart from the Old Races since they were born. How constrained by our laws would you feel if you were they?"

"Not at all, but then, laws and Grace, we've never been on speaking terms. What will they do to them?"

"I have no idea," Alban admitted, "but change has run rough over our world. We'll find room and a way to make it work. After all, it's hard to exile a pair who've never belonged, and I doubt their fathers will allow them to feel unwelcome."

Wicked interest glittered in Grace's eyes. "Fathers, indeed, and how does that work? Which of them was being cuckolded, and which was the cock, do you suppose? Or did they share a woman gracefully, mmm? Don't tell me their fair lady had them fooled. None of you have a weak nose for scent, and not even the nobility scrubbed clean often in that day and age."

Alban rumbled, "I would never dream of asking," and Grace laughed aloud, clapping her hands like a pleased child.

"No, and of course you wouldn't, solid, stolid, stone thing that you are. Well, and maybe I'll have a chance to ask myself, someday. But go on, Stoneheart." Grace sobered. "Rid me of the dragon, will you? He's only stalling anyway. Your Margrit laid it out for him clear enough, and I've never seen one such as he tuck tail and turn that readily. What was the task?" she asked, curiosity and caution turning her voice sharp. "What'd he set Margrit to do?"

"I don't know. It seemed Margrit did, but I wasn't privy to whatever favor he asked."

"Ah." Curiosity lit Grace's eyes before she waved him down the hall. "Well, go on, then. Go find out, and then send him packing. The sooner these tunnels are my own again, the happier I'll be."

Amusement washed through him. "Where do you come by your command, Grace? Even I find myself inclined to leap before realizing I've been given an order."

"Born to it, love, and you're not meant to notice. Gargoyles," she said with a sniff. "You pay too much attention. I'll be glad to have the lot of you gone from my territory, so I will, and yes, that means you, too, Alban Korund. I've had enough trouble from the Old Races. My kids and I need our peace."

"So you haven't set your cap for Eldred?" Alban asked, still amused, and Grace mimed adjusting one.

"Not at all. There's a fine man out there for Gráinne Ui Mháille, and I'll capture his heart when the time comes. Now go on, Alban," she said again. "Protect me and mine. That's what you're here for."

Tariq had shown an iota more subtlety than Margrit had expected, and had waited until he'd left Rebecca's office on foot before dissipating. Margrit had stared at where he'd been, wondering why discretion mattered now, when he'd materialized in front of Rebecca, but had restrained from casting the question into the apparently empty hallway. He'd spared her life and given his word against further attempts, but where she would have trusted

Janx or even Daisani on that promise, she was reluctant to test the djinn.

When she was certain he was gone, she'd turned back to her mother's office, about to enter and offer…solace, or penance. In the end, both had seemed somehow arrogant, and she'd walked away, then begun to run once she'd left the building.

Within minutes she'd brought herself to one of the handful of entrances to Grace's under-city haunts that she'd finally learned in the past few days. That, at least, was one good thing that had come of the exhausting week, though that it qualified as "one good thing" filled her with rue.

She was more confident of finding her way to the central hub where the trial had been held than Janx's off-the-path lair, but she risked trying to pick her way through the tunnels to the latter. Wisdom dictated otherwise, but Grace had an uncanny knack for finding her when she was lost, and Margrit trusted that even more than she trusted Janx's or Daisani's word. She breathed, "Oh, what a tangled web we weave," as she worked her way deeper into the underground system, and was oddly unsurprised when, minutes later, Grace's voice echoed the second half of the couplet back at her.

"When first we practice to deceive. Where do you think you're going, Margrit?" Grace came out of the shadows, ethereal as always. More than usual, even, as slightly detached from the world as she'd been when Margrit had first awakened in the docking garage.

Margrit stopped, not quite looking at her and half ex-pecting that she'd fade away, nothing more than an illusion. "To Janx's place. Or I hoped I was. It's funny." Her voice sounded hollow and light to her own ears.

"Getting lost finding the dragonlord's chambers is funny?"

"Do you think I was dead?" The question felt like a non sequitur even to Margrit, thoughts and speech not quite in tandem with one another.

Grace, at the corner of Margrit's vision, looked startled. "Near enough to it, love. Why?"

"Because you've looked different since I came back." Margrit risked a full-on glance at the blonde, then shuttered her gaze away again, watching Grace all but shimmer in her peripheral vision. "Because I keep thinking, only not really thinking, because when I think, it gets cloudy. I just have this idea down in the back of my brain. About how you always turn up places faster than you should be able to. About how sometimes in that fight I was sure I'd hit you but it kind of shivered off. About how you got Alban out of those chains, and how you got through my locked front door."

Margrit blinked hard and turned her full attention to Grace. "And about why a modern-day folk hero would name herself after a centuries-old pirate and brigand. You're human, aren't you. But you're not…alive. And the only reason I can see it is because I died myself."

"It's been a long time since anyone's seen Grace so clearly." The tall vigilante disappeared from sight as she spoke, not in the coalescing manner that djinn did, but simply gone, blinking out and leaving her voice to linger. It came again from behind Margrit, light and amused and traced with approval. "Grace has her secrets. Grace has her ways."

Margrit spun around, heartbeat high with excitement and confusion. "What are— Are you a ghost? How—?"

Grace spread long fingers in a move both dismissive and accepting. "Cursed, love. Making up for old sins, I told you that once and again. Grace O'Malley spilled a fair lot of blood in her day, and some of it should have stayed in the veins it fell from. What will you do, now that you have the truth of me?"

Feeling stupid with astonishment, Margrit blurted, "Can I help?"

Surprise filtered over Grace's expression, and her white-blond hair and pale skin lit with a glow, as though a veil had been taken down from Margrit's vision. A stronger feeling of foolishness rose in her, tightening her chest: it seemed impossible that the inhuman woman before her ever could have been mistaken for someone ordinary. "Not unless you can give me the kiss of angels, Margrit Knight. I've searched for it for four centuries and found nothing yet, and I think you'll take it right if I say I don't think it'll be from your lips. The thought is kind, though, and more than I might have expected. What will you do?"

"Grace has her secrets," Margrit echoed. "None of them know?"

"There's a reason I won't cross the likes of Janx or Daisani. They know I've been around a long time, but I might've drunk of a vampire's blood, or I might be born of some illicit union like the one that fathered those two girls. It's better not to ask, sometimes. It's better not to know. And I stay in the shadows most often, doing my work and staying out of their way."

"But you haven't. You've been helping and interfering all over the place the last few months."

Grace flashed a smile. "It's not often that a gargoyle

and a lawyer walk into my tunnels, love." She rolled her eyes to the ceiling, said, "That ought to start a joke," then looked back at Margrit, smile fading to something gentle and wry. "And I suppose that for all the years, I'm still only human at heart. Curiosity gets the best of us every time."

"Who cursed you? What happens if you find the kiss of angels? What *is* the kiss of angels?"

"A witch, Margrit, and don't say what I see in your eyes. There are gargoyles and ghosts and dragons, my girl, so don't say there are no witches. I don't know," she said easily, for once offering a straight answer. "If I knew, maybe I'd have found it long ago. And perhaps if I do find it, I leave this world behind. I've haunted it long enough that I wouldn't mind. What," she asked for the third time, "will you do?"

"The gargoyles are going to want to know how you freed Alban, but until they come asking, I'll…" Margrit turned her palms up, and with the gesture finally understood the reticence that had stayed Alban's tongue, had stayed all the Old Races when she'd asked them about their peoples or others. Alban had said more than once that some stories weren't his to tell, and for the first time, sympathy and comprehension settled in Margrit's bones. "I'll keep your secret, Grace, and send them to you for the answers."

Grace bowed her head, the gesture of thanks taking some of the glow away, so that when she looked up again, her brown eyes were little more than ordinary. Margrit could still see a subtle aura of wrongness around Grace, but it was something her eyes could forgive as a trick of the light, if she let them.

A great deal of the world she'd been thrust into was a

matter of letting, and being, and accepting, all in ways that rubbed uncomfortably against her skin. But the art of compromise was one lawyers were supposed to be good at, and, watching Grace almost fading into the shadows again, the letting it be seemed one Margrit could live with. "Can you show me the way to Janx's room before you go?"

"Pah," Grace said, suddenly cheerful. "I'll have to, won't I, or I'll be listening to you crash around in the dark all night. This way, lawyer. Let's go." She tilted her head and struck off down a tunnel, leaving Margrit to catch up.

Familiar voices warned her that they'd found their way, but as she drew breath to thank Grace, the vigilante shrugged and disappeared. Margrit's jaw flapped before she pulled it up into a smile and shook her head at the theatrics she was becoming accustomed to.

Janx, somewhere in the near distance, was speaking with his usual insufferable self-satisfaction. Margrit's smile turned to a grin as she recognized his tale of the tapestries that softened the walls of his chamber. She wondered what stories had taken father and daughter and sister through the remaining night and all of the day, if he was only just now telling them of the tapestries and the windows that had been made in their likeness.

"The last of the arachne made the tapestries," he was saying. "The youngest, as it happened. There were only ever three, and fate turned its hand against crone and mother."

"There couldn't possibly be only three," Kate said tartly. "They must've had parents."

Janx made a sound remarkably like a snorting dragon,

though from the depth and clarity of his voice it was clear he was in his human form. "If you know so much, you tell the tale."

Kate's muttered, "Ow" suggested an elbow in the ribs, and Margrit's grin broadened.

Janx, satisfied, continued, "As it happens, you're presumably correct, and in retrospect, I wonder if they weren't chimeras, as well. I've no idea what race mothered them, if that's the case, but perhaps the crone's age was honestly come by."

"Harpies," Ursula said distantly. "I think if the sisters of fate were born of man and the Old Races, that their mothers must have been harpies. We should ask Alban."

"I'm beginning to doubt the gargoyle histories are as complete as we've all believed," Janx said. "It seems a number of important details have been left out. You, for example."

"But you made sure we wouldn't be forgotten," Kate pointed out. "Alban kept your secret about our mother, but he knew we existed. If he'd died, the memories would've gone back into the histories. We'd have never been forgotten the way the selkies let themselves be. Or maybe the way the arachne chose to be."

Silence swept out of the room, tickling Margrit with its depth. Janx and Daisani had perhaps known of Sarah's pregnancy, but not her survival; the secret Alban had kept, as far as they'd known, was that they'd loved a mortal woman, and told her about the Old Races, an exiling offense in and of itself. The half-blood children— *chimeras,* Janx had just called them—were a more complex confidence than that.

But the dragonlord let it go, as Margrit imagined he

might. "Perhaps. But I was trying to tell you about the tapestries," he said petulantly.

Kate put on a patient child's tone: "Yes, Father."

Margrit could all but hear Janx twitch. "I'm not sure I can become accustomed to that name. It sets firesnaps against my skin each time you say it."

"Fatherfatherfatherfatherfather," Kate chanted, and Janx laughed over the sound of Ursula's impatient sigh.

"What about the windows? Who made the windows?"

Janx, with all the nonchalance in the world, said, "The newspapers say they're Tiffany originals."

"This is where you get it from," Ursula muttered, and Kate's laughter broke, an alto echo of Janx's tenor. "You wouldn't have brought them up if they were Tiffany windows," Ursula went on accusingly.

Margrit's eyebrows lifted in surprise as Janx made a smug confession: "I made them.

"Oh, well, all right," he said half a moment later. "Not by myself. Tariq and I, actually." And his voice darkened as he mentioned the djinn. "Over a century past, now. Desert sand to liquid glass, shaped by wind and dragon-fire. Things were different, then."

"We remember," Ursula said dryly.

Margrit could imagine Janx refocusing on her, surprise coming into his voice. "I suppose you would, although you'd remember different things than I."

"So would we all." Alban's voice broke in, coming from the other direction, beyond the curve Margrit stood behind. She startled, not expecting him, then smiled and leaned against the wall to listen a moment longer. She'd never had a chance to listen to the Old Races talk appar-ently unobserved, and had gained one insight already:

Janx was far more willing to tell secrets to his chimera daughter than to the fully human Margrit. It was a soft disappointment, one she could expect and accept, but it reminded her again that she wasn't truly part of their world. That there might yet be time to escape, if she wished.

"Janx," Alban went on in a rumble. "I've been sent to ask why you're not packing your bags."

"Because Margrit wouldn't expect me to leave these hallowed halls until she has accomplished the task I've set her," Janx said easily, then lifted his voice: "Would you, my dear?"

Guilt spasmed Margrit's skin and ended in a sheepish laugh as she crept around the corner to peer into Janx's chambers. The dragonlord was draped across his chaise lounge, indolent and clearly terribly pleased with himself. The twins were curled up in armchairs, both of them peeking back at Margrit as if they were children rather than hundreds of years her elders. Alban stood just within the doorway, wry humor curving his mouth. "I'm afraid you're less sneaky than you thought."

"I wasn't trying to be," Margrit protested. "I just stopped to listen. I forgot you could smell me."

"And hear your breathing," Kate offered.

"And your heartbeat," Ursula finished.

Margrit put a hand over her face. "Remind me of my inadequacies, why don't you."

"Hardly." Janx unwound from his couch and came to stand before her at his full height, a gambit that would have been more imposing had Alban, slightly taller and considerably broader, not been a few feet away. Margrit crooked a smile at the dragonlord, whose expression was mixed with challenge and curiosity. "Have you set the wheels in motion already, my dear? I would so dearly love to admire your alacrity."

"I'm not here to talk about that."

Janx's lips thinned and he turned to Alban. "She's gotten very bold, hasn't she. I don't think we frighten her anymore."

"I've been dead," Margrit muttered. "You can't trump that."

"An excellent point." Good humor restored, Janx fluttered an extravagant bow and gestured Margrit toward seating. Alban, looking dour at not having been invited himself, followed, then shot Margrit a sly wink as he took over the lounge Janx had abandoned. Grinning, she settled down against him and deliberately pulled his arm over her shoulder to snuggle comfortably before looking up to see Janx's mercurial features gone duck-lipped with exasperation.

"Forgive me," Alban said with enormous innocence. "The other chairs are less well suited to my build."

"I am losing all control." Janx pulled another chair up to the chess table and flung himself in it with the abandon of a tantrum-throwing two-year-old.

Margrit, unable to stop herself, applauded in the same lazy fashion she'd seen him do in the past. Janx, knowing himself outplayed, laughed and spread his hands in defeat. "Very well. What are you here to discuss, Margrit Knight, if not my oldest rival's downfall?"

Alban shifted behind Margrit, the tiny motion somehow conveying dismay. Janx's smile lit up. "Oh, you didn't know. Really, Alban, you might have guessed. I could hardly let Detective Pulcella go for anything less."

By the end of his speech, his smile had fallen away, leaving reptilian coolness in his jade eyes.

"I might have," Alban murmured, "and yet I hadn't. Must it go like this, Janx?"

"It always has." An unexpected flash of injury darkened his gaze. "And Eliseo, this time, has taken it upon himself to stand on honor, and not let certain unfortunate events be forgotten."

"That's not his fault." Margrit was surprised to hear her own voice, as though Alban and Janx had been carrying on a conversation and she, like the twins, had been left to listen in silence a long time. "Or— Oh, well, it doesn't matter. You're going to be furious either way. Might as well leave it alone." She set her teeth together deliberately, trying to stop talking.

Janx, eyebrows elevated as high as they could reach, said, "You can't possibly expect me to let that go now, Margrit."

Exasperated with herself, Margrit sighed. "No, I can't. The djinn made a deal with Daisani, Janx. I don't know when. After the quorum. It had to be after the quorum, maybe when Malik died. That gave them something in common," she concluded aloud. "They both wanted answers so they could exact revenge."

"Your point, my dear. I'm sure you have one."

Margrit shook off her musings. "The point is they were never going to settle for sharing your territory with the selkies. Daisani agreed to support them. That's the deal that makes him unable to back down over Malik's death." Though Tariq's part in helping Daisani's financial empire crumble would probably provide the vampire with the excuse he needed to renege on that matter.

Margrit bit her tongue, not wanting to complicate matters any more than she already had.

Hurt so astonished it hadn't yet become rage filled Janx's voice. "Eliseo made a deal with *Tariq* to gut my empire? *Why?*"

Margrit shook her head. "You'd have to—"

"Because it means he wins," Ursula interrupted thoughtfully. "Neither of you are kidding yourselves, right? You know you're going to have to leave New York soon anyway, because the modern world will notice you sooner rather than later, after this much time. So if you've both got to go, then what greater win could my father have than to set up your replacement? To fill the vacuum your absence inevitably creates? That's game, set and match to him, and it leaves you floundering like a fool."

Palpable anger rippled Janx's skin, contorting his features. "There is only so much ignominy I will take gracefully, Margrit Knight. There is only so much humiliation I will stand. I have lost my territory to conniving djinn and cowardly selkies. I am sent from my new quarters at the whim of a human. I will not watch Eliseo Daisani gather the spoils and mock me with them before he exits this mortal scene. Tell me you have a plan, Margrit. Tell me you will fulfill my favor."

"I can do better than that." Margrit took a deep breath, thinking of her mother working alone in an office building. "I've set it up so you can hand the keys to his kingdom to the selkies."

THIRTY-FOUR

TWO DISTINCT THINGS happened: glee lit Janx's eyes again, and Ursula went uncomfortably still. Margrit's stomach clenched at the latter, a warning that she ought to have not spoken in front of the vampire's daughter. It was Ursula who said, into a silence that suddenly seemed very loud and long, "So what legacy do I inherit?"

"The same one I do," Kate said, full of irritation. "You get to meet Daisani. You get to know your father. It's not as if I've waltzed into a treasury full of gold here. But that was never the point, was it?"

Ursula clamped her jaw shut, staring at her sister. Then she looked away, lip thrust out in defeat. Kate got up and crawled over the back of Ursula's chair, squirming and squashing down until they nearly shared the same space. Ursula twitched as though she'd try to escape, but in truth gave Kate a few more inches to fit into. Kate looped her arms around her sister and put her chin on her shoulder, whispering into her hair. After long moments Ursula sniffed, then harrumphed and squished back, peace evidently restored. Margrit, certain she was the only one in the room who hadn't heard Kate's whispers, felt a brief flash of envy for their sorority.

"My mother works for a company that holds a dozen of Eliseo's accounts," she heard herself saying quietly. Janx's attention came back to her, bright with greed. "She's working to destabilize his holdings. Kaimana's the only one I know with the resources to take advantage of that kind of weakness. Will that do, dragonlord?"

Some of the pleasure faded from Janx's gaze as she spoke. "Your mother. That delightful woman will go to jail for this, Margrit. While I'm not typically averse to incarcerating humans, I find it difficult to believe you asked her to do such a thing. Or that she agreed."

"Tariq made her an offer that was hard to refuse." Margrit bit the words off, too aware that *she* had asked for something that could send her mother to jail. That Rebecca had refused took away none of the guilt at having asked. "Either way, I've got to talk to Kaimana—"

"I'm surprised," Janx interrupted, "that you're willing to offer the selkies anything, given how they've betrayed you."

"I'm beginning to think anger over betrayal is something I can't afford. There's no reason not to put Daisani's holdings on the open market and let humans take him apart in a free-for-all, but I thought you'd appreciate the irony of handing his empire to the selkies, if he's handed yours to the djinn."

"Oh, I do, I do. I'd rather take it myself, but—" Janx gave a sharp look around the room as all three women and Alban inhaled to speak. "*But,* as you've taken pains to remind me several times, our days in this city are limited. Too many people know my face, and have for too many years."

"No one knows ours," Ursula murmured.

Janx tipped his head forward until red hair slid into his eyes. "True, but I trust you understand why I'm reluctant to offer such reins to Eliseo's daughter." His eyebrows elevated and he transferred his gaze to Kate. "Or to my own, for that matter. One leaves my old rival with too much potential influence, and the other, I fear, leaves me with too much potential loss. I have only just found you, child," he said softly, as Kate's eyebrows drew down. "Do not make me face the possibility of losing you so soon."

Kate's mouth twisted, an expression just shy of offense. "Child? We're nearly four hundred years old."

"And I have no intention of telling you how old I am," Janx said easily. "You may be assured, however, that at four centuries you're barely more than broken free of the shell. Besides," he added impudently, "you're my daughter. I can call you child if I want to, regardless of your age or my own."

"Was Mother ever this annoying?"

That whisper, Margrit heard, and grinned broadly. "I think Janx has cornered the market on irritating. You get used to it."

"No," Alban rumbled, "you don't. He does, though, seem to have some modicum of charm which women are susceptible to, and I believe that prevents him from meeting an untimely expiration."

"That," Janx said cheerfully, "and dragons are hard to kill."

Margrit snorted. "You're all hard to kill."

Kate, far too forthright, said, "Selkies aren't," and Ursula, a breath behind her, said, "Neither are djinn, if you know how."

"There are going to be repercussions for that," Alban

said above Margrit's head, clearly speaking to Janx and no one else.

Janx opened a hand and let it fall closed again. "We seem to be living in an era of repercussions. Our world has changed, and changed mightily. I have little fear that some accord will be reached on my daughter's and niece's murderous behavior."

"Niece?"

"Niece," Janx said firmly. "I shudder to think of how we might wrestle over terminology, and choose to streamline it as best I can. After all, I'm only a simple dragon, untutored in how to manage family affairs."

Alban ducked his head next to Margrit's and breathed, "The world has indeed changed if Janx is proclaiming his simplicity. Margrit, when will these changes you've wrought in Eliseo's empire begin to spread?"

"Monday morning." Margrit pressed back against Alban's solidity, gaining warmth and comfort from his presence. "I've got to talk to Kaimana before that, but I think we're looking at a lull in the action. We have thirty-six hours to just be together before anything else goes to hell."

Even Janx paused, waiting, like everyone else, for Margrit's comment to trigger disaster. When it didn't— no chamber cave-ins, no Grace appearing with a dire warning, no cell phones ringing to bear bad news—she laughed and put a hand over her mouth before speaking through her fingers. "I honestly expected something terrible to happen."

"Human superstition," Janx said dismissively.

Margrit picked up a chess pawn and threatened to throw it at him before replacing it on the board. "You froze up, too, dragonlord." She sighed and snuggled back against Alban, then deliberately got to her feet as briskly as she could. "So when shall we five meet again? Janx, I take it you're not going to clear out of here until Daisani's in ruins."

Janx slid his head to the side, smooth snakelike action, and considered her. "I am not. I shall, however, leave Grace and her motley crew alone for the duration of my incarceration here. For your mother's sake," he said as Margrit felt astonishment cross her face. "For the sacrifice you, and she, are making, I shall make one in return." His lips curled back from his teeth, brief angry expression. "I do not like to be beholden, and you've made it quite clear you're willing to use your advantages when you hold them."

"I've learned from the best."

Janx bowed his head and came to his feet, as much honor as dismissal. Margrit turned to Alban and offered her hands, tugging him to standing when he accepted them. Joy fluttered within her and she stepped into the gargoyle's arms for a fierce hug before turning back to Janx. "I'll call or come down when I've talked to Kaimana. I assume you'll want to be there, or at least know, when the rug starts to come out from under Eliseo's feet." Her pleasure faded before she finished speaking, but Janx's flared.

"That would be superb. I look forward to hearing from you."

"Yes," murmured Eliseo Daisani. "I imagine you do."

The only saving grace about Margrit's startled yelp was that everyone around her looked as surprised as she felt. Given the company in which she stood, that seemed like a triumph: even the Old Races could be taken off guard by a vampire.

Alban recovered first: of the others, Janx looked too irritated to recoup gracefully, and Ursula held Kate's arm until white flushed around her grip. The gargoyle stepped forward, putting himself between Margrit and Daisani. "Eliseo."

"Alban. Do you think hiding Margrit behind you will protect her from me if I choose to hunt her?"

"I think even a vampire must consider whether he wants to risk battle with a gargoyle."

"Have you a wooden stake?" Daisani teased, then, as Margrit peered around Alban's width, made a light welcoming gesture. "I am not, at the moment, here to exact any kind of vengeance. In fact, I have something of a conundrum, and our dear Miss Knight is, as usual, at its heart."

"As usual?" Margrit protested. "You've known each other for centuries, and I've earned an *as usual* already?"

"You must admit, you've gone to extraordinary lengths to become an *as usual,*" Janx said lightly. "Do come in, Eliseo. Do sit down and tell us all your troubles. Oh, and might I introduce you to Sarah's daughters? Katherine, called Kate, and Ursula." He offered a sweeping bow, falling back a step in order to better present the twins.

For once, despite being in a safe area, Daisani chose not to show off, and approached the twins at a merely human pace. He stopped a few feet away, gaze hungry as he studied the twins, and as they studied him in return. Ursula's grip had moved to her sister's hand, both of them bloodless with it.

"You have the look of your mother about you," Daisani finally said. Even Margrit could hear the restraint in his soft words; as much restraint as it must have taken to walk at a man's speed, the better to not challenge either woman, and perhaps be found wanting.

Wanting, or worse, alone.

Ursula nodded. "That's what she always said. She didn't think we took anything from you."

"Me," Daisani whispered, and Kate flapped her free hand toward both him and Janx, and said, "You. Both of you. Either of you. Except what we did, of course."

A look of perfect befuddlement washed over Daisani's face as he glanced toward Janx, the expression by far the most human thing Margrit had ever seen grace his features. "Ursula is your daughter," she said, taking sudden pity on the vampire. "Kate is Janx's. There's no doubt of it once you see them in action."

"Ours?" Daisani asked in astonishment. "Ours both?" He looked back at the twins. Ursula lifted a shoulder and let it fall.

"Chimera, Janx called us. Children of two races, but not three. I'm all vampire. Kate's all dragon. I think if we were anything less, we wouldn't be able to do what we do." She kept staring at Daisani, eating him with her gaze, though neither of them moved any closer to the other.

"The selkies said half-blood children are full heirs to their Old Races gifts," Margrit recalled. "What would happen if a dragon and a vampire had a child?"

Daisani turned a dangerous look on her, so quelling that goose bumps rose on her arms. Bewildered, she gaped at him, and some of the warning in his gaze faded. He looked back toward Ursula, leaving Margrit to wonder what bit of precious knowledge she'd come so close to treading on. A quick glance at Alban garnered no evident answers: the gargoyle lifted his eyebrows in as much question as she had, then dropped a wink that promised they would explore the question later, together.

"I would like to know you." Daisani spoke so quietly it almost went unheard under Margrit's silent conversation with Alban. She glanced back toward the father and daughter, and discovered she recognized the control with which Daisani held himself. He had stood similarly when Rebecca Knight had been in his arms; he had stood so when he had ordered Margrit to find the man who had murdered Vanessa Gray. He had even, she thought, perhaps stood that way when he'd invited her to dance in a ballroom filled with six sentient races, and it shot an agony of sympathy through Margrit's heart. Immortality, she had realized only recently, was a lonely business, and to read the vampire's emotions and vulnerabilities so clearly took her breath away. Inhuman, yes; they were all inhuman, but not at all incomprehensible.

"I'd like that, too," Ursula finally said. "Mother told us what she could about you, but it's not the same."

Something unbent within Daisani, his next breath more easily taken. "No, it's not. I am honored for the opportunity."

"Yeah." Kate tossed her hair and gave the vampire a defiant look. "You should be."

"Kate," Alban murmured, and she looked a little abashed.

Janx draped himself over the abandoned chaise lounge and folded his arms behind his head in a soft blur of thin blue smoke. "Lovely as this all is, I'm sure it's not why you came sneaking to my lair, Eliseo. Why are you here?"

"Ah." Daisani turned away from the twins with one last glance at Ursula. "My conundrum, yes. I received a phone call a little while ago, Margrit. A call from, if you'll excuse the colloquialism, the last person on earth I might expect to receive such a thing from."

A cold fist wrapped around Margrit's stomach and clenched. She felt her expression turn stricken as guesswork ran ahead of Daisani's words. "Mother?"

"Indeed. She laid out a conundrum of her own, one dealing with dragons and djinn and daughters—"

"Oh my," all three of the daughters in the room murmured, and Janx's tenor ran below them with the same phrase. Margrit wrinkled her face as Janx waved a finger at Alban in admonishment. "Really, Stoneheart, you couldn't possibly have failed to see that coming. Won't you at least play along?"

"Not until I learn what trouble Rebecca Knight has had that she turns to Eliseo to solve it." Alban folded his arms over his chest, making his breadth that much more impressive.

Daisani's lighthearted telling sobered, not because of Alban's unvoiced threat, but because his focus narrowed on Margrit, a hint of anger coming through. "It wasn't a bad idea, Miss Knight. Calling on your mother to help lay my empire low. Not that she would agree, which even I could have told you. Even to save her daughter's life, she wouldn't act on a promise like that, perhaps especially one made to the djinn who'd threatened her, as well. So she called on me, and on the weight of the secret she has held for me for thirty years, I found myself reluctant to deny her what she asked. And now I find myself with a promise of protecting you on the one hand, and a promise to permit your execution on the other. Tell me, Margrit, what shall I do?"

"I've been dead once. Isn't that enough?" Margrit passed her own question off with a wave she recognized as having been adopted from the Old Races; from Janx, specifically, she thought. "You could call the playing field even," she said more quietly and more seriously. "You're in a position to do that."

Janx tipped his head, small motion that still managed to be a warning. Margrit fought off a grimace, briefly exasperated with the ancient battle of one-upmanship the two elders had. "I wish you would," she went on. "Walk away from New York. Let this lifetime go. You've got plenty more ahead of you."

"You're not answering the question, Miss Knight."

Margrit made her hands into fists. "Tariq's happy to backstab you now over a decision you made months ago, a decision that doesn't have anything to do with him or his people or any deal you made with them. He's playing my survival off as being a betrayal of your agreeing to my death, and he's…" She trailed off, finally fully realizing what Daisani had said. "My *mother* double-crossed a djinn?"

"Really, Margrit, how many times have I told you that your mother is a remarkable woman? I'm sure she doesn't think of it as double-crossing. I'm sure she considers it to be…survival of the fittest. If she could lie bold-faced to one of the Old Races, then turn around and ask another of us for help, I would say she's most certainly fit to survive."

Pride rose up in Margrit as a blush, heating her cheeks and bringing a foolish smile to her face. "Go, Mom. Wow. The best I've done is mislead you."

"Which is fairly remarkable in itself," Daisani said dryly. "Once more, you've failed to answer the question."

Still riding on a wave of pride, Margrit let the truth out unvarnished. "You should break the deal with the djinn and let me live. At least I was up front about trying to take you down. I'm an honest enemy, if I've got to be one."

"An honest enemy. One who will report to work Monday morning as expected?"

"Keep your friends close?" Margrit asked with a wince. "I'd like to. I'd actually like to, and part of me is saying if I go to work for you, I have a chance at getting my hands on the right kinds of material to bring you down. I can't just try like I did tonight and walk away. I have to succeed, because Janx isn't going to let Tony go on a good try from the home team."

"Janx?" Daisani wheeled to face the indolent dragon, who looked up with mocking apology.

"I'm afraid she's right. If she'd like to go to work for you, I'm happy to take the cost out of Detective Pulcella's hide. Entirely up to you, Margrit, of course."

"Of course." Margrit pressed her lips together, arms folded across her chest defensively. "You know, I actually came down here to ask you something, Janx. Something I didn't think Eliseo would answer."

"Really." Janx kicked his legs off the lounge and sat up, fingers laced and interest brightening his eyes. "Whatever could that be?"

"I came to ask about one of his vulnerabilities." Margrit watched the vampire as she spoke, unconcerned for Janx or his reaction. "I came to ask if you knew what it would mean if I asked him where the bodies are buried."

Sound erupted around her, a cat's shriek melded with

a whale's song and all of it accompanied by an explosion of movement vastly unlike anything Margrit had seen from the Old Races before. Daisani seemed to fly apart, a black viscous splash of oil and night, and then came back together again so quickly she doubted she'd even seen the change.

He was in Margrit's face, and somehow stopped from tearing her apart: Ursula was there, between them, moving as fast as he did. Then Alban, crushing Daisani's biceps in an unforgiving grip. Janx was on his feet, flexing with eagerness, and Kate crowded in beside Ursula, helping make a barrier.

Margrit had seen none of them move. Her heartbeat was sickeningly fast, making her light-headed with the panic of being in the midst of a reckoning that she had no control over. Chelsea's warning, to have Alban with her when she asked that question, seemed pitifully inadequate now: without the entire quartet who held Daisani off, she was certain she would already be dead. That she would have died so quickly that she would never have seen it coming.

Daisani craned his head toward her, neck elongating to an impossible degree. Ursula snaked into his path, half blocking Margrit's view, clearly protecting her. "Me first, Father."

Hesitation flickered in Daisani's black eyes. His jaw opened too far, starting to unhinge, and then he snapped it shut again and withdrew into himself, suddenly the same contained businessman Margrit had met him as. He shook off Alban's hands, and to Margrit's horror, the gargoyle let him.

"You will come to regret asking that question, Margrit

Knight. You will come to regret it, and so, too, will the one who guided you toward asking.

"Catch me," the vampire whispered. "Catch me if you can."

THIRTY-FIVE

DAISANI'S WORDS LINGERED far longer than he did, sounds left on a whisk of wind as he sped away. Ursula, unexpectedly, squealed with glee and disappeared after him. Even Kate look startled at her sister's departure, taking a few abortive steps to follow before stopping. Alban flexed his hands, regretting that he'd released the vampire, but uncertain Daisani couldn't have slipped free regardless.

"Chelsea," Margrit whispered. "He's going after Chelsea. Can Ursula stop him?"

Kate shook her head. "Ursula's not trying to stop him. She just wants to race. She's never had anyone as fast as she was to go up against."

Janx snorted beneath Kate's denial. "One does not go after Chelsea Huo. Not even Eliseo is that rash."

Margrit stared at him and Alban put himself between the two of them, catching Margrit's hand in his own. "Would you go after the serpent at the heart of the world, Margrit?"

The petite human transferred her stare to him, becoming incredulous. "How could you?"

"No more than you can go after Chelsea. Don't worry."

Margrit dropped her chin to her chest, forehead pinched with the force of her frown. "So her referring to humans wasn't just because she's gotten in the habit of thinking of all the races by their specific names." She lifted her gaze, lips thin, and pulled her hand from Alban's to fold her arms. "What is she?"

Alban fought off the temptation to follow her and simply shook his head. "Some secrets aren't ours to tell."

A beat of silence, then two, filled the room before Alban, half apologetically, said, "Some secrets aren't ours to tell."

Margrit threw her head back, scowling at the chamber ceiling. "Of course not." She set her teeth together, then, jaw still held tense, visibly tried to let it go. Tried, and almost succeeded: Alban barely heard her threat of, "One of these days I'll get inside your memories and find out."

"Not now that you've warned me," he said with more apology.

Margrit glared at him. "All right. All right, fine, whatever. Never mind what she is. Some secrets have to be kept." She sighed suddenly and pulled her hair loose to scrub her fingers through it. "How about the secret of where the bodies are? Do either of you know what that means?" Worry washed away her frustration and she hugged herself. "I don't care how safe you think she is. I want to make sure."

"My dear—"

Margrit spun to face Janx, exasperation filling her voice to the edge of lividity, mercurial human emotion a wonder, as always, to Alban. "I heard you. What if you're wrong? She's the one who told me to ask the question that just sent Eliseo Daisani running out of here like a bat out of hell, Janx. How often does Eliseo run from anything?"

Janx looked toward Alban, who opened a hand in answer to the question. "There was Moscow. But then, you left rather precipitously, too, didn't you? With your tail between your legs, if the stories have it right."

. The dragon's nostrils flared, and Margrit looked from one Old Race to another with an expression that demanded explanation. Alban flashed a smile and shook his head. "That's all anyone knows about it. But aside from that, I don't remember the last time Eliseo ran from anything, and a gargoyle should."

"You've been out of the memories a long time, Stone-heart. There was Van Helsing." A hint of smugness slithered over Janx's face as Alban lifted his eyebrows. "You wouldn't know about that. It was what sent him—and me, in the end—to the Americas. Van Helsing is why there've been no vampires but Daisani these past hundred and fifty years."

"Van Helsing is a story," Margrit protested.

Momentary silence filled the chamber before the dragonlord smiled. "You can stand here, in this company, and say that with such authority? You asked once what happened to those humans who executed the Old Races. Your own facetious answer was immortality, but you're not so far off, my dear. Human fiction disguises worlds of truth."

Margrit shot a look from Janx to Alban and back again, then cast a wary glance toward Kate, as though checking to see if the other woman could tell if the Old Races were having her on. Kate made a tiny motion of denial and Margrit's gaze came back to the dragon and gargoyle. "Are you telling me Abraham Van Helsing existed and hunted vampires? That he came to help some woman who was bitten— But it doesn't work that way. You can't turn a human into a vampire."

"Ah, but what if you flip the story around? What if Lucy lies dying of consumption, and her doting suitor discovers a sip of vampire blood will cure all her ills? What if he begs help from a doctor friend and they pursue the panacea at all costs, but are refused and the beloved wife dies? The lover might retire, his heart broken, but the doctor might be unable to let the idea of a universal cure go. He might make of himself a hunter, perhaps the best in all the world."

Margrit lifted her hands to her temples, massaging.

A burst of sympathy filled Alban and he stepped forward to touch her shoulder.

She dropped her hands and stared at the ceiling before exhaling heavily. "Yeah, okay, I guess he might just. I mean, all the other stories are turned on their ears. So what happened?"

Janx shrugged. "Eliseo determined retreat was the better part of valor, and fled. Shortly thereafter he met Vanessa, and you know the rest."

Margrit laughed, short, sharp sound, and turned a despairing look on Alban. "That's so far from the truth I don't even know where to begin."

"Why are we still here?" Kate demanded with what struck Alban as very human impatience. "Even if Daisani can't do anything to this Chelsea person, shouldn't we still be going after him? What if you're wrong?"

Janx sniffed. "I'm rarely wrong, Katherine. And there's no haste, because it's not possible to catch up with him. Your sister might have, but as for the rest of us, we may as well wait for him to come to a stop."

"Wherever that may be," Kate said sourly.

"Most of us do have somewhere we call home." Janx gave Margrit a telling look. "Unless it's been stripped of us, of course. Either way, I have very little fear for our friendly neighborhood bookseller."

Margrit glowered at the dragon. "Chelsea told me to ask about the bodies when I asked if Eliseo had any vulnerabilities. I'd think you'd be just a little bit interested in what the answer was. If you're not, that's fine. I won't pursue it, but you'll release me from this promise, no holds barred. I leave Daisani alone, he retains his empire, and you don't go after Tony. I'm going to check on Chelsea. Come or don't, but make your choice, dragonlord. I'm sick of this."

Janx said, "I liked it better when she was afraid of us," to Alban, then bowed melodramatically to Margrit. "Very well. I'll chase your wild goose."

Kate and Janx walked ahead, red-haired vanguards of a tiny army. Margrit itched to turn to Alban and plead for him to take her and take wing. They'd left the tunnels as close to Chelsea's bookstore as any of them knew how, but the intervening blocks could have been swept away under a few beats of Alban's wings. The idea of a few minutes of time alone in the sky with him was as appealing as making certain of Chelsea's safety that much more quickly. But neither Janx nor Kate could transform as discreetly as Alban, and with Janx's grudging agreement to join them, Margrit was reluctant to now leave him behind.

"Did I do this?" Her voice sounded wrong to her own ears, too soft and high. Alban looked down, concern creasing his forehead, and she fluttered a hand at the pair in front of them; at the world. "Did I make your world this place where we're all running around trying to stab each other in the back before someone else gets a chance?"

"You had help," Alban said with a ghost of humor.

Margrit twisted a smile. "I feel so much better, then."

"Even my people have come to believe this is necessary, Margrit. Even I have. Not the politics and machinations, but a forcible entry into the modern age. Perhaps the one doesn't come without the other. Everything has a price."

"I hope it's worth it." Margrit's phone rang and she clapped a hand against her hip, then pulled the phone from her pocket to say, "Hello?"

Kaimana Kaaiai's easygoing voice came across the line, sounding, as usual, as though he had a smile in place. "Margrit Knight. Cara asked me to contact you. She seems to think you have another trick up your sleeve."

Margrit stopped walking and scowled at the sky, lips thinned as she considered what to say. After a moment she shrugged and chose the truth. "I had one. It fell out."

Some of the geniality fell out of the selkie lord's voice. "Really. I was given to understand this trick would compensate us for a significant loss. I'm disappointed to hear it won't be coming through. What, if I may ask, was it?"

"Does it matter?" The brusque question was just better than the ill-advised suggestion to *suck it up* that Margrit was tempted to give. "I'm sorry to have bothered you, especially if you're back in Hawaii. It must be about four in the morning."

"On the contrary, it's seven in the evening. Nothing to worry about," Kaimana assured her. "Will you be providing another form of recompense?"

Margrit pulled the phone away from her ear and stared

at it. It was a moment before she trusted herself enough to say, "I'm afraid not," politely. "It was a gamble. You lost. It happens."

"It was your gamble, Ms. Knight."

"'Ms.' You people always pull out the honorifics when you're annoyed with me. You know what, Kaimana? If you really want to destroy your own people and the rest of the Old Races by taking it to the mat with the djinn, be my guest. Go be offended that you're not getting your big fat paycheck and take it out on whomever you want. I have done my goddamned best, and if that's the game you want to play, I wash my hands of it." She hung up the phone and spun around, arm lifted to fling it against the nearest wall. Only the fact that it belonged to Cameron stopped her, and after a few seconds, she lowered her hand with a curse.

Alban's quiet presence appeared behind her, more felt than heard. Margrit turned her profile to him, shoulders sagging. "Well, that was mature."

"Perhaps it was necessary." His warm hands enveloped her shoulders, sending a wave of comfort through her. She relaxed a little, leaning against him, and felt him lower his head over hers. "You've been thrust into a world about which you knew nothing, and have stood fast for what you've believed to be right, even at a personal cost. Perhaps, having shaken us up, it is as necessary to let us condemn or save ourselves of our own accord. I do not believe Kaimana Kaaiai will guide his people into open warfare with another of the Old Races. But if he does…we reap what we sow. Isn't that the phrase you use?"

"Me personally or humans in general?" Margrit turned in Alban's arms to bury her face against his chest and let go an exhausted sigh. "I feel as if there's no way out of this alive, Alban. Janx is playing it like a cat with a mouse. It's all fun and games, all light and mocking, but if I don't manage to completely ruin Eliseo somehow, he's going to kill Tony."

A last vestige of hope was smothered with Alban's nod. Dismay soured her laugh. "You were supposed to tell me that he wouldn't really."

"But he will," Alban said steadily. "Human lives mean little to Janx, and Detective Pulcella has humiliated him. Had Janx not been injured so badly at the House of Cards, I doubt Tony would have survived the night. He's been fortunate."

"I'm not sure anybody involved with me is fortunate, right now. Russell's dead, Tony's under a death sentence, Daisani's threatened to eat Cam more than once, my mother nearly had her heart pulled out... Jesus. If I thought leaving town would work, I'd do it."

Alban, carefully, said, "Sarah did."

Margrit shook her head. "Her situation was different, and you know it. I have to see this through. I'm not going to let Tony pay for my involvement with the Old Races."

"You're a worthy adversary, Margrit Knight." Alban tipped her chin up, his pale eyes serious as he studied her. "Regardless of how lacking in control you may feel, I assure you that no one amongst the Old Races thinks you are anything but worthy. As much trust as you put in Janx's integrity, if you hadn't earned his respect, he wouldn't have honored the favors you've played against each other."

"Which is why I've got to hold up my end of the bargain. My own honor's as much at stake as his is."

Margrit took a deep breath and released Alban, her whole body aching as the comfort of his presence withdrew. "I said humans were good at leveling the playing field. I have to keep trying to do that. This'll end soon," she added more softly. "Either I'll succeed and this horrible mess will be over, or I'll fail and I'll be—"

"You will not." Alban's voice dropped to a dangerous growl.

"Janx'll take Tony's life over my dead body."

"Then we shall make very certain he has no reason."

"We?" A new spark of hope lit in Margrit, so unexpected it tightened her throat. "What's this *we,* white man?"

Alban blinked at her, nonplussed, and the flicker of hope turned into a shaking laugh. "Haven't you ever heard—it's a Lone Ranger joke. Haven't you— Never mind. Never mind," she repeated, and Alban chuckled, then cupped her jaw.

"We, Margrit. I have no intention of allowing you to fall at Janx's whim, and regardless of Chelsea's dramatic questions, we can't deal Eliseo such a crippling blow that he'll never rise from it. His life is too long and his resources too great. We," he said again, gently. "Your allies may be few, but they do exist. I am here."

"That makes me feel better." The words scratched out through a still-tight throat. Margrit stepped into Alban's arms for another fierce hug, then let him go again with fresh determination. "To hell with the selkies and the djinn and all of them. We'll deal with Daisani and go from there."

"A wise plan. Now, come." Alban offered his hand. "Kate and Janx have outpaced us. We should catch up."

Margrit glanced hopefully at the sky, and the gargoyle

chuckled. "I was thinking of something more prosaic. You are, after all, wearing your running shoes."

"Oh." Margrit looked at her feet, then shot Alban an impish smile, the first time she'd really felt like smiling in what seemed like hours. "Race you."

She won, crashing against Janx to slow herself down as Alban came up from behind to plow past the dragons like a battering ram, too much weight to be denied. Janx staggered and clutched his kidney. Hot embarrassment flooded Margrit and she babbled an apology that went on until she saw a wicked glint in the dragonlord's green eyes. "Yoooouuu…!"

Janx smiled beatifically. "Aren't I, though? The transformations help set things to right. I think I told you that. And I've had more cause and opportunity to change form these last few days than I have in…"

"Decades?" Margrit ventured.

"At least. There was Chicago, but—" Janx broke off as Chelsea's bookstore came into sight. His nostrils flared and he glanced at Alban, whose eyebrows drew down as he took in the dragon's expression, then grew darker as he, too, inhaled. Without speaking, they both broke into a run, leaving Margrit and Kate to double-take at one another, then follow.

Janx, the lither of the two, reached the door first, and burst through with literal accuracy, glass shattering and erupting as he crashed into it. Margrit skidded in a step behind him, with Alban and Kate a few steps farther away.

The always-crowded store was in a shambles, once-tall stacks of books knocked across it, their spines broken and torn. Shelving had been knocked over, dominoing up to the walls with their fallen volumes filling the spaces between them. Even Margrit recognized the too-familiar scent of blood.

"Oh, God. Chelsea? Chelsea!" Easily the lightest of the four of them, Margrit crawled across broken-down shelves, scrambling for the bead curtain at the back of the shop. Alban, behind her, called her name as she lost her balance and reached to catch herself on the curtain.

Beads raked through her hands, clattering to the floor and bouncing across it to stick in the crimson blood that spread out around Chelsea Huo's lifeless body.

THIRTY-SIX

"IMPOSSIBLE." JANX WAS at Margrit's side somehow, his transition from the foyer to Chelsea's apartment
gone unnoticed. "This is impossible."

Margrit backed away, rattling what was left of the
curtain, and fell over toppled bookshelves on its other
side. Tears she hadn't noticed beginning to fall scalded her
cheeks and blurred her vision as she climbed to her feet
again. "Looks pretty fucking possible to me." She didn't
recognize her own voice, strained with disbelief and pain.
Swiping a hand across her eyes, she crawled back over the
bookcases. "Get out of there, Janx. Don't touch anything."

His shadow against the beads said he wasn't listening,
that he'd knelt by Chelsea's body. Margrit could still hear
his murmurs of denial, though unlike her, he seemed to
have no rage, only bewilderment.

Alban caught her as she stumbled over the last of the
bookshelves. She made a fist and pounded it against his
chest, silent, useless expression of misery, then ground her
teeth against tears and took her cell phone from her pocket.

"Who—?"

Margrit lifted a finger, silencing the gargoyle, and whispered a tortured, "Cam," when her housemate picked up the phone. "This is Margrit. Is Cole home?"

"Yeah? Grit, are you okay? You sound—"

"I need you to do something for me." Margrit's heart pounded hard enough to make her body sick. Tremors shot over her skin and her stomach twisted, heaves making her dizzy. Her vision had filmed again. She tried to blink tears away unsuccessfully: new ones rose to replace those that fell. "I need you to go get on a train to my parents' house right now. If it's too late for a train, take a taxi. I'll pay you back. I just need you to do it right now, with no questions."

"What the hell—?"

"Somebody's dead who shouldn't be, Cam, and I want to make sure you stay safe." Margrit closed her eyes, tears burning her face. Cole would never get beyond this, never find a way to trust or accept the Old Races, not with a phone call like this in the middle of the night. "It's the only way I can know you're safe. Please, Cameron. This is really important."

Cam was silent a few long seconds. "How long are we staying?"

"Until I call you again. Until tomorrow, at least. Do either of you work tomorrow?"

"No. We were going to go birthday shopping for you."

"The best present you can possibly give me is to do this." Margrit swallowed against nausea, then nearly laughed in relief as Cameron said, "All right. Okay, Grit. Are you going to tell us what's going on later?"

"Yes. It's just more important to get you to Mom and Dad's right now. I'll call as soon as I can." She hung up and found both Alban and Kate watching her with uncertainty.

"Daisani is not going to go after my mother," she said softly. "No matter what else happens, he's not going after her. He cares about her too much. He won't go after her and I seriously doubt he'll go after anybody under her roof."

"Perhaps we should all take refuge there." Janx, voice filled with cold fury, came across the fallen bookshelves as silently and gracefully as he'd done once before. He stalked past the trio in the ruined foyer and out the door, all rage and beauty as he disappeared down the street.

Kate stared after him, then turned back to Margrit and Alban with an expression of uncertainty.

"Go," Alban said after a moment. "Family is—"

A too-familiar eruption shook the windows, the impact of air displacing as Janx transformed. Car alarms went off, and even Alban flinched before scooping Margrit into his arms and running for the door.

"Put me down! Put me *down!*" Margrit pounded on his shoulder as he sped toward the closest alley. Kate sprinted past as Alban slowed, and launched herself into the air barely a few feet into the safety of the alley's darkness. Air exploded more softly, her form vastly smaller than her father's, and moments later a second sinuous dragon beat its way past rooftops and into the city sky.

Alban rumbled in obvious frustration, then, to Margrit's astonishment, cursed quietly and flung himself after Kate, transforming with a comparatively inaudible *bamf* as he strove for the rooftops.

"Alban! I have to call the cops, I have to—"

"You have a cell phone," Alban said implacably. "Nothing is preventing you from calling."

They broke above the roofs to the sound of shouts from below, people swearing about car alarms and the shotlike explosions of air. Margrit twisted to see if anyone was looking up and nearly fell from Alban's arms, his grip not intended to hold someone writhing around. They both shouted with panic, Alban tucking his wings in preparation to dive after her if necessary. The beat of falling instead of striving upward brought them dangerously close to the rooftops again. Margrit knotted her arms around Alban's neck and bit back a scream as he swore a second time and glided over a break between buildings, catching the updraft to work his way higher into the air.

Not until they were well above the skyline did he unclench his jaw enough to say, "Are you well?"

"No." Margrit muffled her answer against his shoulder, willing her heartbeat to slow from its panicked rush. "I've never heard you swear before. I didn't know you could."

"Given sufficient cause, yes. There they are."

Margrit, clinging to him, turned to catch a glimpse of Kate's slim serpentine form hundreds of yards ahead of them, and losing ground to Janx's much larger shape. It took only a glance to know where they were going. Margrit buried her face against Alban's shoulder again and whispered, "Daisani's penthouse. Don't let me fall."

"Never."

The promise, which had in the past been sensual, was now simply grim. Margrit had never heard the gargoyle sound so severe, and remembered abruptly that the only reason she knew Chelsea Huo was that Alban had sent her to the bookseller as a place of safety and refuge for them to meet at. A burst of apology for asking him to stop, to not pursue Kate and Janx and the more distant Daisani, filled her. She hugged him hard, whispering, "Sorry," into the lashing whiteness of his hair, then brought her phone back to her ear to call Tony.

He picked up with a groggy, bewildered, "Cameron?"

"No, sorry, this is Margrit. I'm borrowing Cam's phone. Did I wake you up?"

"Grit." Tony cleared his throat, and she could all but envision him rubbing his eyes, sitting up, kicking his legs over the side of the bed to plant his feet on the floor and putting an elbow on his knees so he could lean into his hand as he woke up. She'd seen him do it often enough in the years they'd been together. "It's the middle of the night. What's going on? Where are you? Sounds like a wind tunnel."

"I'm…flying. Tony, Chelsea Huo is dead. Somebody needs to get over to her bookstore right away."

"Che— The one who owns Huo's On First?" The detective woke up fast. "Are you there?"

"I was."

"And now you're…?"

"On my way to Daisani's apartment."

"Why? Did he—?"

"I don't know. I hope not. Can you get somebody to go to Chelsea's bookstore? I'm sorry to call like this."

"Margrit, you…" Whatever he wanted to say was eaten by professionalism as he sighed. "Yeah. Yeah, I'll take care of it. Is there any point in telling you to be careful?"

Margrit glanced toward the rapidly approaching apartment building. Daisani's helicopter was knocked on its side and in flames, as though Janx had regarded it as a rival and dispatched it before entering the building. The fire showed that the rooftop access door hadn't just been ripped off its hinges: the entire framework for it had been shattered, concrete blocks and steel lying in a shambles.

Kate reached the roof as Margrit watched, flying too fast to come in for a graceful landing. She rolled nose over tail, tumbling in a long, wing-tucked line, and came out of it as a human woman running at full tilt. She disappeared through the ruined door, and Alban put on a burst of speed, wings straining to race through the night and catch up with the unfolding drama.

"No," Margrit said. "No, there really isn't. I'll call you later, Tony. Thanks."

Alban backwinged a moment later, crashing down to the rooftop hard enough to jar Margrit. She squirmed free of his arms as he transformed, the rush of air temporarily overwhelming heat from the helicopter fire, which blazed with enthusiasm. The smell of aviation fuel corroded the air and she ran for the rooftop door, uncertain if the flame had already reached the fuel and not wanting to be on hand if it hadn't. Alban was her pale shadow, though he overtook her inside the building by dint of simply springing over the railings as she took the stairs.

A flare of frustrated amusement hit her and she yelled, "Cheater!" after him as she swung around the turn of stairs, jumping down them with the railing as her own guide.

Seconds later, as Alban burst into the chaos of Daisani's apartment in front of her, she thought it was just as well that he'd cheated. Even with his broad body protecting her, the heat in the flat was appalling. For the first time she wished she had an elemental form to change into, something that would protect her from inhuman extremes. As if hearing her thoughts, Alban flashed to his gargoyle shape, stony body blocking more of the heat and allowing her to gain some sense of what went on before her.

Daisani's apartment, which had been lush and full of brightness earlier, was black and red with fire. The power no longer functioned, only the city glow and Janx's flame lighting the room.

Dragon and vampire rolled together in a mass of kinetic energy, Janx's tail and wings flicking out and smashing tall windows as their body weight flattened furniture and sent walls to shuddering. It was nearly impossible to see Daisani: he was a sliver of darkness in the dragon's gold-tipped claws, so formless Margrit's eyes slid off him as she tried to find edges upon which to focus.

Ursula, looking impossibly small and fragile against the roiling bodies, leapt on Janx's shoulders and pounded on his neck with both fists, like a toddler throwing a fit. Her usual tidiness was disheveled, clothes torn, hair flying askew as Janx rolled again, letting go of Daisani with one foot to claw at the younger vampire riding him.

Daisani slipped free, a fluid wash of blackness. For a fraction of a second Margrit saw puncture wounds, but then he was moving, his presence nothing more than a blur of rage in the room. He ousted Ursula from her bronco ride, taking her place, and Janx contracted like a cat and flung himself upward. The ceiling fell in a rain of plaster and sparks, but Daisani leapt free with casual arrogance.

"Stop them!" Margrit's scream was nearly inaudible even to her own ears, making her realize the sheer cacophony in the ruined apartment. Alban shot her a bewildered look, as if asking how, and she grabbed his arm to pull him around and make him look at her. An explosion erupted behind him and he collapsed over her, protective, as fire fell from above.

"*Stop* them?" Even Alban's bellow against her skin was all but impossible to hear. *"How?"*

Impatience surged in her, sheerly human response. She wanted to shake the gargoyle, rattle sense and the obvious into him. "Attack them! Use your telepathy! Find out what the *hell* he's hiding that's worth all of this!"

The idea was appalling.

Margrit had suggested such a thing before, as astonishing then as it was now. Changes, changes everywhere, but to turn his people's gift against another of the Old Races still ran deeply contrary to anything he'd ever considered. And yet, watching the two ancient rivals battle, Alban was unable to see another way to stop them. He could throw himself into the fray, but he would only add another dimension to the battle, give them a third target, rather than have any hope of calming them. Not with the rage that had driven Janx; not with whatever fear of discovery had forced Daisani's hand. In the thousands of years that they had played their game, they had never, to his knowledge, taken the fight directly to one another.

But now Janx had nothing left to lose, and Daisani, it seemed, still did. Whether it was his empire or his secret, it was worth fighting for. Worth killing for, though Alban's mind balked at the idea that Chelsea Huo was dead. Balked at the idea Eliseo could have taken her life. That *anyone* could have, but that Daisani would even try was almost beyond comprehension.

The vampire screamed as Alban stood frozen with indecision. His speed was phenomenal, but Janx had the knack of fighting such a rival. It wasn't a matter of catching him, but anticipating him. Daisani's blurred form had rushed one way; Janx had turned another, not as swiftly, but quickly enough, and the vampire had impaled himself on gold-tipped claws. Blood now ran from those talons. Janx roared fire, melting blood and gold alike as Daisani, weakened, thrust himself back and darted away.

Ursula, similarly, raced back into the fight, but this time Kate was in the way, tackling her sister. Her greater weight pinned Ursula, and incomprehensible arguments broke through the flame and ruin. That was something: a small something. The twins, at least, would probably not lose their lives in Janx and Daisani's battle.

Clarity, like metal striking stone, rang through Alban at that thought. Short of extraordinary measures, the two combatants would kill each other, and for all their sins, the idea of a world without them was infinitely worse than the world with them in it.

Alban breathed, "Forgive me," without knowing from whom he begged absolution, and for the first time in his life—for the first time in the history of his people—reached to create an uninvited bridge between minds and memories.

The world split in two.

THIRTY-SEVEN

MARGRIT CRASHED TO the floor, clutching her head in her hands as Alban's presence became larger than he was. Gullies opened up around her, deep stony rents in the earth that she feared plummeting through, and from them mountains shot up, heaving and writhing, as though the gargoyle memories were under attack. Static washed through her mind, blaring white noise louder than her own thoughts, louder than anything she'd ever experienced, even the endless ruin of the House of Cards, even the shattering destruction of Daisani's apartment.

She forced her eyes open, trying to see in the world she knew still existed around her. It wavered through the concepts of the gargoyle overmind, but Janx had stopped fighting. The dragonlord looked as stricken as she felt, taloned feet clawing at his own head, as though he might scrape away the double-world that surrounded him. The twins, too, writhed in pain, all of them experiencing the same blasted reality she saw.

Of all of them, Daisani remained on his feet, countenance angry as he faced Alban. *Challenged* Alban: the slight vampire leaned into the chaotic world as though he might edge his way forward, put himself in the gargoyle's space and fight for whatever last vestiges of control might be his.

Wrong; it was wrong. That undercurrent came through clearly, Alban's agony and worry over how the world had changed. There was certainty in him, certainty that forcing his way into Daisani's mind had opened a channel that wasn't meant to be. Certainty that Margrit's presence exacerbated the wrongness, her bewildering talent for connecting nongargoyle minds to the gestalt hissing to deadly life. None of the Old Races in the apartment could escape it. Margrit felt Alban's fear that none of the Old Races in the city, perhaps the world, could escape it; that he had gone much too far in a pursuit of dubious justice, or in a misguided attempt to save Old Races lives.

With that conclusion, she felt him begin to draw back, trying to break the forcible link he'd created. Dismay tore at her throat and she shoved to her feet, finding strength to stand against the relentless noise in her head. She pushed by Alban, determined to meet Eliseo Daisani in the battleground of memory herself, if the gargoyle could not.

The ground under her feet steadied as she approached Daisani, though whether that was through his willpower or her own, she had no idea. She felt Alban's protest at the back of her mind and ignored it; felt Janx's curiosity driving her on, and took strength from it. Daisani only smirked at her, faint expression of superiority, as though he considered himself untouchable.

It was oddly satisfying to reach out and slap the expression from his face.

Fury followed shock, and the vampire blurred, disappearing from visible sight. Margrit whipped to follow him, and when he struck against her, slammed a hand up to catch his blow.

Astonishment wiped every other emotion from Daisani's eyes. Margrit's answering smile felt ugly with smug delight and she leaned toward Daisani, still holding his wrist. "You're only faster than me in the real world."

He yanked away and fled again, impossible speed across rough terrain. Margrit, gleefully, gave chase. In the human world, constrained by her human body, she could never hope to catch the vampire, but in her mind, oh, in her mind, she was *fast*.

The thought tasted of Alban, as though he'd given up trying to pull back and was now urging her on. Urging her to finish the race, urging her to end the game and release them all from the harsh, static connection she created within the overmind, amongst the Old Races. Remembering her own deadly headache, Margrit overcame regret at being unable to play cat and mouse with Daisani, and put on a surge of speed that turned the world to Doppler effects, stretched light and sound whisking by her.

She caught Daisani in a floodplain that seemed a thousand years away from the gargoyle mountains. His territory, she thought, though it was as easily hers, tall wild grass and open land looking like a birthplace of humanity.

They came together with a monumental crash, Margrit flinging herself off the ground to tackle the slender vampire. She had no particular strength, but then, neither did he: any preternatural power came from speed, and she thought she had the slight weight advantage. Dust and earth kicked up around them as they crashed to the savannah floor, and Margrit gathered Daisani's lapels in her hands to haul him up, nose to nose.

"Where are the bodies buried, Eliseo?"

Daisani hissed, a sound of pure fury and insult that lost any vestige of humanity. His face, his body, his whole form melted away, becoming oil-slick and hellacious. His jaw unhinged into a maw of black teeth, and his eyes disappeared into nearly invisible slits. Segmented, insectoid wings sprang from his back and slammed toward her, razor claws along their edges slashing at her face and hands. Margrit screamed, kicking away, and he pounced after her, a lashing, barbed tail whipping toward her feet. He was altogether more alien than any of the others, every trace of earthly presence turned into a slick, violent predator too fast to stop.

Panic rose in her, then unexpectedly broke, leaving a calm tide behind. Daisani's pounce landed, sending them tumbling again, and rather than try to escape this time, Margrit surged forward and embraced the vampire, shuddering at the way his oil slid over her skin.

Surprise froze him in place for just an instant, and into that stillness she whispered, "If I'm going to die, I'm sure as hell going to find out what I'm dying for. Alban, *please!*"

For the second time in as many minutes, the world fell apart.

It re-formed much more solidly, a structure imposed that had not been there before. Daisani screamed as though the sound was being ripped from his soul, then writhed back into the dapper human form Margrit was so accustomed to. Panting rage in his eyes said it was not his choice to be so shaped, and his skittering glance at the echoing building in which they stood told Margrit he knew where they were.

Alban's presence surrounded them, his will a thing of stone, indomitable. More and more walls built up around Margrit and Daisani, each of them borne from a snarl or a whimper from the vampire. Tangled in Alban's mind and Daisani's memories, Margrit recognized that the gargoyle was literally stripping hidden knowledge from the vampire and re-creating it openly. His own reluctance to do so was buried beneath a determination to save her; he had failed her more than once, and the price of doing so again was far too dear.

For the first time Margrit's own will faltered, but it was too late: the church was built, and a familiar voice was speaking. "They must be bound by iron, staked with wood, buried in earth and water."

"Yes," said another voice irritably, "very dramatic, but how do I *catch* them?"

The angle reeled, Daisani turning to face the man with whom he spoke. A big man, his regular features lined with intense determination, he was dressed in clothes of a wholly different era, clothes that marked him, to Margrit's eye, as out of place and time, though she knew it was she who was out of time. But recognition worked its way through the minds linked to Daisani's memories: *vampire hunter,* Janx whispered. *The most successful of them all.* Margrit was afraid to even think the name, afraid she would be wrong, afraid looking into history-made-fiction might somehow unravel time. She knotted her hands against her mouth, stopping all sound, and held her breath to listen to Daisani's murmur.

"Ah. You caught me. Can you not manage it again?"

Fresh shock coursed through the link, Margrit's added

to it all. Daisani's rage, beneath the power of memory, was muted, so muted she couldn't tell if it was fury from decades ago, or newly born at being made to relive and share remembrances.

The big man made a disdainful sound. "You are no more captured than the wind might be. You've walked into this trap, and I want to know why."

"My kind and I are half sick of shadows," Daisani said lightly. "Half sick of jumping at them, at fearing some idiot human will embody the very persona of fortune and slaughter us in our sleep. I have therefore come to make you a bargain."

Tension sizzled through the link, Margrit's breath catching as profoundly as the hunter's did. "What sort of bargain?"

"One you'll agree to or die here," Daisani admitted, then shrugged. "But I think it'll be to your tastes. I will deliver you my brethren, and in exchange, you will forget I exist, and let me make my way in the world."

Ursula's cry of outrage broke through memory and brought with it the scent of fire, reminding Margrit of the world outside history. The apartment was enveloping in flame, and while the Old Races might survive, she had very little time.

"Why would *you* do that?"

"Because in a very few years humanity will overrun this planet, and my people are too poor in impulse control to survive unnoticed. Because you are on the brink of revolution that will change the face of your existence, and it will inevitably change ours, if we do not find a way to wait it out." Another thought whispered beneath Daisani's spoken words: *And because I am the master of my kind, and I will survive at any cost, but you, mortal, need not know such things.*

"They'll come?" The hunter's voice was rough. "They'll come to your call?"

"Those in Europe will. The rest of the world, well. Perhaps you and I shall do some traveling together."

Memory drew back, showing the shape of the world. Subtle flashes highlighted pinpoints across the globe: southern Europe, Australia's outback, a riverside in China, Central America. Others faded too quickly to be seen, and when the image faded back to the scene, even that had changed. Daisani stood outside the Vatican, the broad-shouldered vampire hunter at his side. "Buried in earth and water," the hunter said. "Holy water?"

Daisani smiled, humor warping his memories. He said, "Holy water," aloud, but his thoughts made mockery of the idea. Holy or not, salt or fresh, it made no difference. Submersion held his people in stasis, just as earth comforted their bones as they rested. Wood thrust through the heart stopped their bodies and their thoughts, and iron held them against any chance of tearing free should stakes disintegrate without being replaced. The holy men of any faith would keep their secret charges, thinking all the while that the vampires were vanquished, dead to the world and all time. No one, no one at all, knew the vampires were the only true immortals.

The modern world crashed back into existence around Margrit, Ursula's furious shrieks splitting the air in time to the crackling of fire. Janx, with utter disgust, slapped Daisani aside and imploded back to his human form to stand over the damaged vampire. Scorn laced his beautiful voice. "I had thought better of you, old friend. I had thought you were a survivor, not a traitor. Your own people, all but murdered, for the sake of walking alone yourself."

"For walking *safe* myself." Daisani spoke without a hint of repentance, but his voice was shockingly weak. "Tell me you would do no less, should your people waken from their slumbers." He coughed and slumped, an arm wrapped around his middle.

Margrit strained to see through smoke and fire, remembering that the dragon had skewered the vampire more than once. Even Janx hadn't easily walked away from lesser injuries, and for all that Daisani's memories claimed immortality for his people, she thought she could hear his labored breathing over the sounds of the fire.

Alban answered her unspoken question: "Immortal, perhaps, but not undamageable. I wonder if he might yet die." There was sorrow and censure in the words, as though he regretted the loss of a friend, but thought the loss might be greater in living than in death.

Janx turned away from Daisani with all the grace at his command, very much the picture of a sovereign leaving an unworthy subject to suffer whatever indignities might befall him. Daisani, clearly drawing on all the strength he had left, came to his feet and watched the dragonlord go, a mixture of anger and injury written across his features.

"You are free of your favor to me." Janx paused by Margrit, his gaze fixed ahead. "You have more than brought my rival low, and none amongst the Old Races would dispute that he is unworthy to walk among us. Tony Pulcella's life is yours. Goodbye, Margrit Knight." He stalked past her gracefully, then stopped at the doorway, looking back toward Kate Hopkins.

She cast a desperate glance at him, then at Ursula, who stared at Eliseo Daisani as though he had betrayed her personally. After a few seconds, as if sensing her sister's gaze, Ursula looked up and offered Kate a brief, sad smile.

Kate bolted across the room to hug her, then darted after Janx, stopping just long enough to shoot a quick smile of her own toward Margrit. Then the pair of them left together, leaving burning memories behind.

Daisani collapsed. For all her anger, Ursula let go a low cry and jolted forward, then stopped herself, expression going hard. Alban touched Margrit's shoulder, inviting her away, and she looked from the vampire to the gargoyle and back again.

"Do you really think it's so awful?" To her surprise, she could hear herself over the flames. "He betrayed them and left himself to walk free, but isn't that better than nobody being left to know where they were? Nobody being left to know how to free them? And he was right, the world was changing." She was walking through the fire without a conscious decision to do so, kneeling at the vampire's side in the midst of an inferno. "What if they couldn't restrain themselves? What if he was right, and he was the only one who could make a choice that hard?"

"Margrit." Alban's voice held warning and despair.

She looked up with a helpless smile. "Since when have I played favorites, Alban? You've all needed help in one way or another. I've given it, if I could. Daisani's saved my life, and I've repaid him with this." She gestured to the burning apartment and realized for the first time that the smoke didn't seem to be clogging her lungs. Another gift from the vampire, or maybe the dragon if his blood had, in fact, mingled with hers. Margrit pushed the thought away, only distantly curious about it, and spoke to Alban again. "Maybe he won't die, but he's sure as hell not healthy, and it's not like we can leave him here for the police or fire department to find. Go on. Get out of here before the cops *do* get here. I'll be right behind you."

"I am not leaving you."

"You'd better." Tony Pulcella's hoarse voice came from the doorway. He stepped inside, holding a hand up against the heat, the other covering his mouth as he coughed. "All of you. It's going to be a hell of a lot easier to explain a building fire if there aren't a handful of people standing around like potential arsonists. And you can't afford to be in custody when the sun comes up," he reminded Alban sharply.

Margrit, as much as the gargoyle, stared at the police detective without comprehension. "What are you doing here?"

"You said you were on your way here. I didn't know you'd be busy destroying the place, but I thought I'd better come over even before I saw the fire. *Go,*" he said more urgently, gesturing to Alban. "Margrit's right. You can't be here."

Alban closed his hands into fists. "Margrit…"

Memory flashed through her again, Hajnal's near death on a rainy Paris night, and Alban's reluctant agreement to abandon her to dawn and stone. "I know, Alban. I know. I'll be right behind you, I promise. Get Tony out of here, too. He can't see what's about to happen."

No one saw a vampire's natural form and lived to tell of it. The warning haunted her, but before any more arguments could be made, she bent her head over Daisani's shuddering form, and offered him her throat.

* * *

An image stood out in her mind. The last image, she imagined, that she would ever see. It was dramatic: a slim, dapper man standing before a wall of fire, looking down at her. Despite the fire, she was freezing, as though all the warmth had been drained from her body. Even her heartbeat seemed sluggish, as though there were nothing left to push. She'd felt that way once before, very recently, when her blood had spilled out on a concrete floor, taking her life with it.

Clarity brightened everything for an instant, letting her understand that the same thing had happened again. Nearly the same thing: this time she had chosen to buy one life with her own. Daisani crouched at her side, murmuring under the crackle of flame. "I will not see you again, Margrit Knight. You had best pray for all your days, however long they may be, that I will not see you again. Eliseo Daisani is dead, thanks to you, and the only reason you do not follow him to the grave is this act of grace you have offered. Live with that, if you can survive the fire."

Margrit nodded, a flimsy motion that stole what strength she had left. Her eyes drifted closed, Daisani's image dancing behind her eyelids for a little while before it faded.

Liquid brushed across her lips, so sticky she tried to wipe it off. She couldn't: as before, her muscles were watery. Licking it away was a compulsive reaction, her body working without command from her mind. Iron's tang was drowned by sugar, so sweet she gagged before involuntary swallowing overrode the weak attempt to spit up.

For a brief eternity there was nothing.

Then life came roaring back in, a surge that rolled her onto her hands and knees, coughing and spitting against too much smoke inhalation. Heat said the fire was behind her. Margrit crawled away, trembling with effort, and collapsed outside Daisani's apartment door. Cool air rushed to fill her lungs and she heaved for it, trying to clear her mind.

"Margrit." Tony put a hand on her shoulder, then pushed her back to sit on her heels, keeping her upright with his own strength. He was blackened with soot, sweat making lines through it. "Grit, I couldn't get back in there to go after you—"

"Alban was supposed to get you out of here." Her voice wasn't as bad as it had been after her throat had been cut. Margrit took it as a small favor, focusing on that instead of on the bewildered fear that pounded through her. "Where…?"

"Here." The gargoyle, in his stone form, crouched at Tony's side. Margrit blinked at him, further bewildered until she realized she'd taken his broad white form to be part of the wall. She relaxed, fear draining away as she became more aware of the heat behind her. Alban offered a faint smile. "You couldn't imagine we'd leave you. Not after all of this."

"You should have. I told you I'd be right behind you."

"You weren't," Alban said with the same tiny smile, though it fell away. "I've left you too many times already, Margrit Knight. Never again."

"He wouldn't let me past him," Tony growled.

Margrit folded her hand over Tony's at her shoulder, testing her own strength and finding it wanting. Memory flashed behind her eyes: Daisani's fluid, oily form a nightmare of blood-stench and fear that made her shudder. "Good. Daisani…"

"Is dead." Tony took away the explanation she'd intended to make, speaking with unexpected firmness. "Which we're all going to be if we don't get out of here. This place is an inferno, Margrit. I've got to get downstairs."

Margrit nodded, feeling sweat slide down her spine. She set her jaw and shoved to her feet, refusing either Tony or Alban's help for a few seconds. Just long enough to determine she *could* stand unaided if she had to. Satisfied, wobbling, she put out a hand, and both men reached for it. Margrit caught a glimpse of their exchanged expressions, and almost found a laugh to tease them with. Tony, after an instant, dropped his hand, and Margrit's laughter turned to a weak smile as she leaned on Alban. Her thoughts were clearing, as were her lungs. She still felt drained, exhausted from blood loss, but one idea came into focus: "The elevators will be locked down, and you can't run down forty flights of stairs. Come up to the roof. Let Alban bring you down."

"Uh—" Tony shot a look between the two of them, and Alban shifted, causing a rumble of amusement under Margrit's ear.

"She's right. It would be quicker, if you're willing to trust me."

"Trust you?" Flame exploded from the apartment. Alban scooped Margrit into his arms and fell into step behind Tony, protecting the humans as they ran for the stairs. Tony's bellow echoed over the noise. "I trust you a hell of a lot more than I trust that fire!"

They burst onto the rooftop, Tony sliding to a stop as his voice broke in dismay. "You set the roof on fire, too?"

Margrit patted Alban's arm, half reassurance and half a request to be set on her feet as she looked over the burning helicopter and flame-eaten expanse of blacktop. "I forgot about that. News helicopters—"

"Are already on their way." Alban flashed into his human form, still holding her, and nodded skyward, where lights were converging on the building. "Let's hope their cameras are washed out by the fire. Detective, if we're to exit discreetly, we had best do it now. Margrit, I think you'd better come with us. I won't be able to return without drawing attention."

"Can you fly with both of us?"

Alban gave her a foreshortened, nonplussed look that finally brought out her laughter. "I guess that's a yes. All right. How—"

The question was cut off as Alban, with an apologetic twist to his mouth but no more ceremony than that, jerked his head toward the darker edge of the building and dropped Margrit from the bride's carry he held her in, wrapping a single arm around her waist instead. He offered the other arm to Tony, eyebrows lifted as he said, "Detective, if you would…?"

"You can't carry us that far!" Tony fit himself into the offered space awkwardly even as he protested, and let out a baritone yell under Margrit's shriek of laughter as Alban did, in fact, lift them both easily, and ran across the rooftop to leap into freefall.

Alban transformed, the charge of bursting air earning another bellow from Tony. Their plummet broke as Alban's wings snapped open, and he turned on a wingtip, updrafts pulling tears from Margrit's eyes. "I'm afraid this will be a rougher flight than usual," Alban murmured. "I don't dare circle the building for fear the news cameras will catch a glimpse of us."

"That's fine." Tony's voice was strained. "Just get us on the ground." His face was pale. A death grip locked around Alban's neck. Margrit grinned wildly at him, then shouted in panicked delight as Alban folded his wings and cut toward the ground at dramatic speed.

They landed harder than they ever had, her hold around the gargoyle's neck slipping and reminding her that weakness hadn't yet passed. Alban set Tony on his feet and transformed into his human shape.

Tony staggered away, staring toward the distant rooftop and then at Alban. "Jesus. I thought we were dead."

"Not at my hand, detective."

"Good goddamned thing. Grit…?"

"I'm fine." Margrit slid out of Alban's arm, still leaning on him for support, and found her cell phone. "Tony, if the docks aren't a hundred-percent quieter by tomorrow night, you're going to have to—" She broke off, suddenly wishing her clarity of thought would fade a little. "This is going to sound insane."

Tony shot a finger toward the sky. "*Now* you're worried about insane, after jumping off a forty-story building?"

Margrit glanced upward, then shrugged in acknowledgment. "If the docks haven't quieted down, you're going to need to go in with FDNY trucks of salt water and hose all your malcontents down. A lot of them are djinn, and that'll keep them from misting. If you can find Ursula Hopkins, ask for a pint of her blood and line your handcuffs with them. You're not going to be able to hold the djinn for long, but it'd at least shake them up."

Tony pulled a hand over his mouth. "Salt water. And blood."

"Not just any blood. Vampire blood." Margrit winced

at Tony's expression, but he turned his hand palm out, refusing any further commentary she might have.

"Salt water and vampire blood. Anything else, Grit?"

"No, except…" Margrit turned away, searching for the call-back feature on Cameron's phone, and dialed the number that came up.

Voice mail answered, another small gift she was grateful for. "Kaimana. This is Margrit Knight." For an instant the world rushed up around her as it had when Alban had leapt off the building, all too overwhelming. As if he sensed her wave of exhaustion, Alban tucked himself behind her. She leaned back, shoulders dropping a little. "You get your bag of tricks after all, Kaimana. Eliseo Daisani is dead. Be prepared to hit the market hard Monday morning." She hung up, fisting her hand around the phone, then put it away to the sound of Alban's low chuckle.

"Not ten minutes ago you were nearly dead, Margrit Knight, and now you stand in the wreckage of Eliseo's life and make deals. No wonder they've named you the Negotiator."

"You've got to get out of here, both of you." Tony drew Margrit's attention from the warmth and comfort that Alban's arms offered. "Cops'll be here any minute. I can hear the sirens."

"If you wish to depart with us, detective…"

"No—I called it in. They're going to expect me to be here. Go on, get going."

Margrit marshaled failing strength and put a hand out toward Tony. He caught it and held on a moment, then released her. "Go, before I have to explain who and what the hell you are. And don't worry," he added, resigned, "I never saw any of you."

Margrit whispered, "Thank you, Tony." And then she was in Alban's arms and they were running, leaping, soaring into the space between buildings, leaving the life she'd known behind them, and a future of indefinite years and infinite possibilities ahead.

Trenton

THE BRIDE WORE a fitted bodice that showed off her strong shoulders and arms, and a meringue of a skirt, all frothy and light, that was at odds with her athleticism, but which made the most of her height and slim form. Margrit, standing for her at the altar, a bunch of daisies clutched in her hands, felt tears of idiotic joy well up as Cameron came down the aisle on her father's arm. She snuffled into the flowers, then swallowed a sneeze that sent tears spilling after all, and caught Cole's quick laugh as he tore his eyes from Cameron to check on her. Margrit jerked her head back toward Cam, and Cole's gaze returned to her more than willingly, his smile turning dazzled.

Cameron's smile was as wide and foolish as Margrit's own; as wide and foolish as anyone's at the wedding. People were packed into the Dugans' backyard, the ultimate in intimate affairs, but Margrit could think of nothing better suited to her friends.

Tony stood opposite her as Cole's best man, more

gorgeous than usual in a tuxedo that had to be far too hot under the late-afternoon sun, though neither he nor Cole looked inclined to complain. Margrit sought out Tony's date in the crowd, still astonished to see her in public, much less clad in something other than black leather. Grace O'Malley cleaned up well, wearing a crisp pantsuit that was both formal enough for the ceremony and somehow flawlessly herself, as well. She arched an eyebrow when Margrit caught her eye, then did much as Margrit herself had just done: gestured with her chin, telling Margrit to pay attention to what was important.

Beaming, Margrit did so, taking Cam's bouquet when it was handed to her; watching Tony fumble for the rings and Cole's expression of alarm; laughing, after the vows were exchanged, when Cameron's bouquet, flung into the air, landed squarely at Grace's feet, the vigilante woman staring at it as though it was a pit viper.

And when the afternoon turned to evening, then slipped toward night, Margrit found her way to the newlyweds and exchanged fierce hugs, then slipped away from the party, skirts gathered like Cinderella so she might find her lover when daylight's spell was broken.

Manhattan

The police-locked door opened easily enough, though she didn't technically have a key. Most of the mess had been cleared up, shelves put to rights and books replaced on them. The stock hadn't been sold off; instead, someone had bought the establishment wholesale, intending to keep it as a bookstore. The back room was no longer curtained off by a fall of beads, and furniture had been removed so more shelves could be brought in. It made the front of the store roomier, in fact, much less precarious to navigate. Still, it lacked a certain hominess with all that extra room.

But it was no longer her concern. The one item she wanted was still there, tucked into a corner where it had somehow gone unnoticed as the new owner made changes. Well, not somehow: no doubt it had been obvious that a touch of greenery made the place cozier, and no one liked to throw out a perfectly healthy plant. Especially one with a rich, comforting scent. It was no surprise that it remained.

Chelsea Huo collected her tea tree and slipped out of the bookstore again, not bothering to lock the door behind her.

Krakatoa

Jewels sweated, gleaming in waves of heat. This was the deepest room, closest to the heart of the earth, where only the sturdiest of treasures could be kept. More fragile winnings—Fabergé eggs, worked metals, mummies, scrolls liberated from Alexandria—stayed in safer climes, caves with natural temperature control, or even in modern secured vaults, though nothing of real importance, of course, was kept in such places. Janx wound his way through treasures to dip his talons in a pool of molten gold, sighing with satisfaction as the gleam worn down by too many battles returned to its former beauty.

Kate's heartbeat was that of a hummingbird's, so rapid even his ears couldn't tell one beat from another with any clarity. Amused, he finished dipping his claws and waved them dry before turning to see her wide-eyed expression. One dragon shouldn't look so impressed at another's hoard, but then, in her brief life she'd never seen one at all. He moved to the side, inclining his head in invitation, and Kate's eyes widened further before she roiled forward to dip her claws, too.

Metal cooling, she curled up around the base of the molten pool to admire her nails. Janx, with a hiss of smoke and amusement, left her to preen. It would be days, by his reckoning, before she lost interest in the glimmer of her own adorned talons, and there were vast rooms of beloved prizes he had not visited in far too long.

Rome

It was too easy, really. Done in the middle of the night at speeds only her kind could achieve, it was easy. Damp earth was slung aside, iron chains stricken, wooden stakes thrown into the ground. She wasn't strong, but they were desiccated, barely more than bones in skin sacks. The task took barely three hours, even with moving them to safety.

Finding enough blood to revive them, that was harder.

Tokyo

A slim man, short by Western standards, not particularly handsome, but animated enough to hide it, lifted his eyes in the midst of a business meeting. He looked on a city half a world away, gaze blank with it; blank with the awakening of his brethren and all it portended. Then someone spoke his name and he brought himself back to his duty, a small job in a small company. His apology was made in fluid, flawless Japanese, and his transgression was forgiven, which, all things told, was just as well.

Brooklyn

An older woman—no, an elderly one—came out of her house to tidy snapdragons and tiger lilies in the evening sunlight as she talked on the phone. She crouched in the dirt more easily than a woman of her age might be expected to, pulling and digging at roots and plants with thoughtless practice as she nodded at the voice on the other end of the line. Then she snorted and straightened, and the years fell away until she was no more than *older,* silver-haired, suddenly still beautiful, and with a raw note of London's slaughter fields in her voice when she didn't bother to train it away. "Don't be ridiculous. I'll move on when you two have found somewhere new to settle. Be careful, darling, and give your sister my love."

Manhattan

It is the highest point in the city easily accessible to a human, especially at night. He's wiser than to have remained there during the day, but in the first minutes after the sunset releases him, he wings his way there and waits well above the observation deck, observing from his own unique vantage.

And as promised, not too terribly long after the sun has fallen over the horizon, she appears on the observation deck below, a broad smile shaping her face as she turns to search the building's upper reaches for him.

She's dressed in a copper gown that fits her curves and makes the warm tones of her skin rich even in the artificial light of a city night. She waves when she sees him, and her smile lights even more, until it reflects the joy within his own heart.

With an incautious glance around, he plummets from his waiting place, landing in a solid crouch at her side. She slides her fingers into his hair, then laughs as he stands and takes her with him. Like any two ordinary lovers, he spins her around in a circle, reveling in the sound of her delight. Reveling in holding her in his arms, and most of all, most incredibly of all, reveling in wonder as Margrit Knight touches her lips to his ear and whispers, "I love you."

* * * * *

We'll leave the Old Races for a while as
C.E. Murphy returns to Seattle
with the next installment of
THE WALKER PAPERS,